Within the Solstice Cages

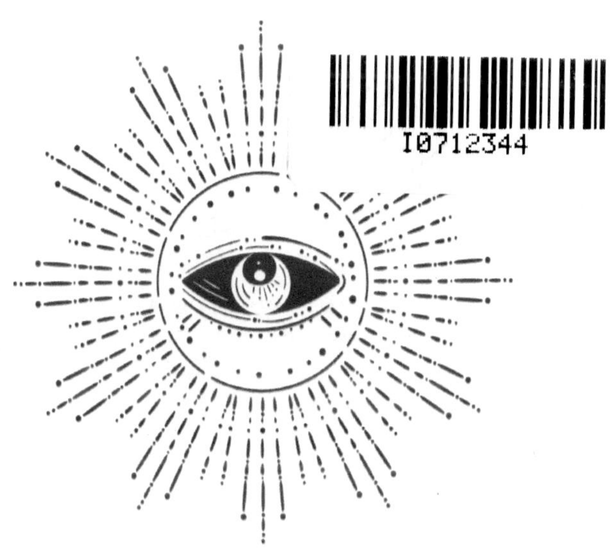

Sadie Hewitt

Copyright © 2024 Sadie Hewitt

All rights reserved. This is a work of fiction. Names, characters, places, and incidents are products of the author's imagination or are used fictitiously and are not to be construed as real. Any resemblance to actual events, locales, organizations, or persons, living or dead, is entirely coincidental.

No part of this book may be reproduced or used in any manner without the prior written permission of the copyright owner, except for the use of brief quotations in articles or reviews.

Editing by Mozelle Jordan
Cover art by Rebecca Frank

Paperback ISBN: 979-8-9876432-5-9
E-book ISBN: 979-8-9876432-4-2

To all of those grieving the loss of friendships and lovers through time, separation, or death...

Let's rip of the band-aid together, shall we?

Within the Solstice Cages is a paranormal/urban fantasy set in three realms where all things wicked, dark, and dangerous collide.

This story includes elements of battle, hand-to-hand combat, anxiety-inducing situations, blood, slavery, kidnapping, graphic violence, death of all kinds, including a drug overdose, graphic language, exploration of grief after the death of a loved one, on-page consensual sex, and mention of off-page non-consensual sex.

Readers who may be sensitive to these, please continue with caution.

Welcome to Samsara.

VERITAS
Dead Man's Brush
Meridian of Wrath
Jung Burhi
Meridian of Gluttony
Abandoned Pastures
Nakki Marsh
Meridian of Indolence
NAKKI VILLAGE
The Wastes
Meridi
MAP OF
SAMSARA

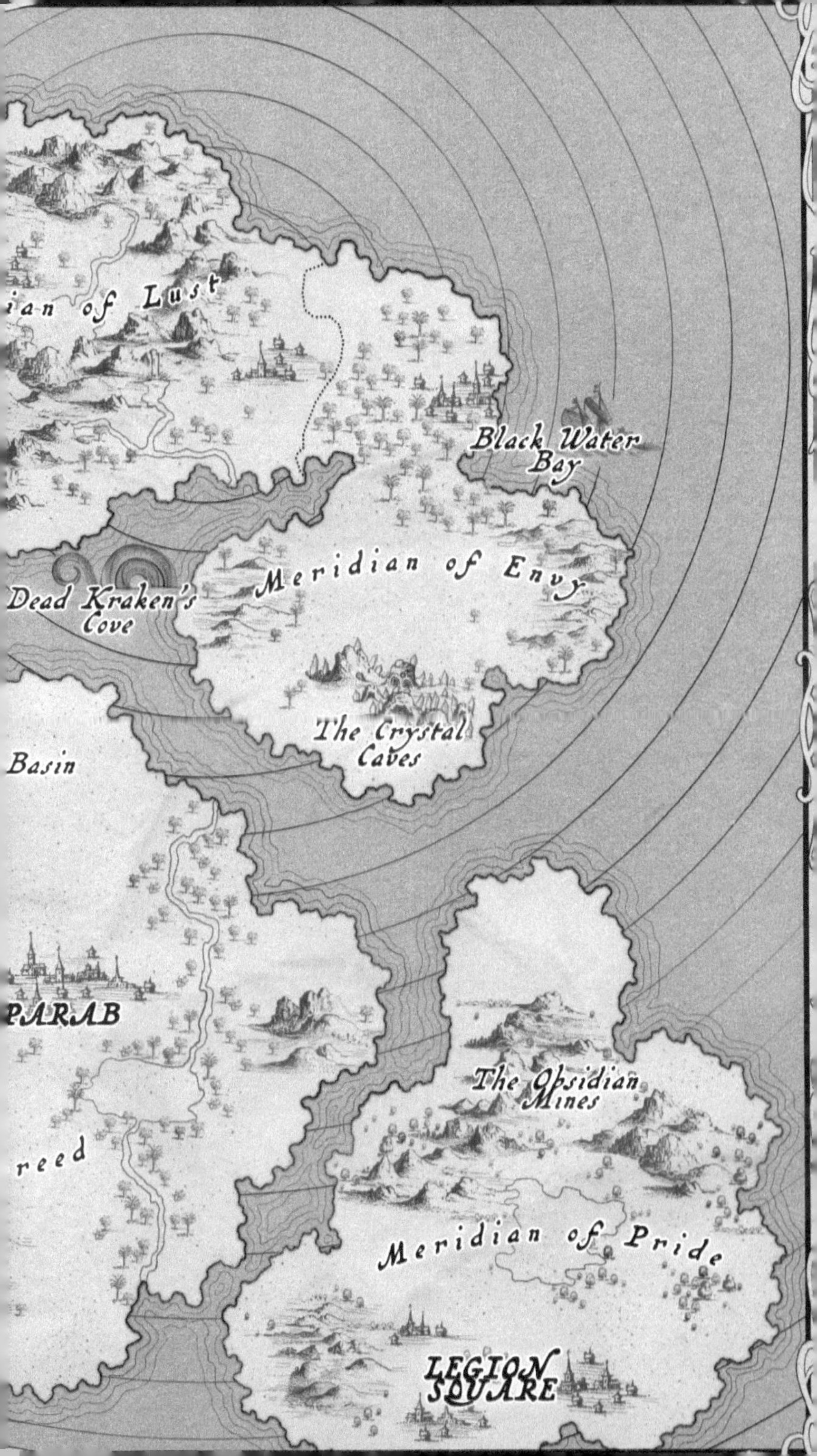
ian of Lust
Black Water
Bay
Meridian of Envy
Dead Kraken's
Cove
The Crystal
Caves
Basin
PARAB
The Opsidian
Mines
reed
Meridian of Pride
LEGION
SQUARE

PROLOGUE

AGNES

Year 1656

Gripping a heavy bucket of water, Agnes had forgotten how goddamn cold the Kingdom of Bohemia was during the winter. How frigid the air was when it passed through her lungs. How the icy rain stuck to her hair and froze, leaving her constantly damp. No matter how many layers she put on, the wind still bit through the wool.

So. Goddammed. Cold.

Agnes had treated more than her fair share of human villagers for frostbite the last month, many of whom would have lost fingers and toes without her intervention. Most of them were willing to look past the tinctures, rubs, and potions she handed out just to get a taste of the healing warmth only she could provide.

Of course, not one of them was screaming witch...yet. Not in this weather. However, the chances of that possibility would rise when the storm cleared and the temperature rose.

Agnes approached the familiar house she had built before the freezing rains. It was so different from the timber-framed farmhouses in the village, mainly because the style of the single-room cottage was one she still preferred after all these years. The hearth with an open flame, her dried herbs hanging from the rafters, her bed shoved into the corner. It reminded her of her youth when she and her mother would sit by the fire in the dead of winter, looking over the grimoire that only Agnes could read.

Growing up, their cottage was in the middle of a glen, muddy and typically awash with rainwater. Agnes would practice spellwork, and her mother would sew thick spools of wool into skirts, shawls, and full-length shirts so they could prepare for the upcoming seasons. Periodically, they would look up at one another and smile over the crackling flames, Agnes wondering how life could get much better than this.

Over five hundred years later, the cottage she lived in was backed to the river, a wide-mouthed one fed by the mountain streams in the distance. It still left her with plenty of room to plant her garden when the summer months allowed.

Not now, though. Now it was too goddamn cold.

As she reached the front of her cabin, Agnes's fingers clasped the iron knob, and she shoved her shoulder into the wooden door, a flurry of snow and wind following her over the threshold.

"I thought I was going to find your frozen body on the bank of the river."

Agnes' eyes darted up at the voice to see a man standing near the small table she had set for lunch before leaving earlier in the day. She took in his handsome face, high cheekbones, and raven black hair and rolled her eyes.

"Next time, I'm sending you out there," she retorted, lowering the hood of her green cloak before tugging the strings at her collarbones.

The man put down the knife he was holding. He had taken over chopping the dried herbs Agnes had started before venturing into the storm for a fresh bucket of river water. Standing up from the table, he sauntered over to her and grasped the wet cloak to pull it from her shoulders before hanging it on a peg near the hearth. The icy droplets were already beginning to thaw, steadily dripping from the hem.

"I distinctly remember telling you that I would go."

Agnes threw him a withering look, setting down the water-filled bucket near the front door. Afterward, she paused near the hearth to hold her hands to the fire. The flames licked at the frozen tips of her fingers, sending waves of relief thrumming through her body. She sucked in a deep breath through her nose, taking in the scent of burnt, smoky wood and dried rosemary. The logs under her cauldron crackled merrily, sending sparks tumbling onto the stone floor.

The man returned to the table, picking up the knife once again. "The father of that werewolf pup returned this afternoon while you were gone."

"Oh?" Agnes asked, glancing over her shoulder. She admired his black curtain of hair as it cascaded over his chest while he remained focused on the herbs. It was a quarter-inch cut—just as she liked it. "And did he pick up the potion as I told him to?"

He chuckled. "Not without grumbling how in his day he didn't have fancy potions to lessen the pain of the first transition."

Agnes scoffed. "One would think you wouldn't want your children in pain, especially needlessly terrible pain you've experienced yourself." Her heart stuttered as she thought back to her daughter, Beatrice, now long gone centuries ago.

Agnes barely had enough time with Beatrice, certainly not long enough for her daughter to remember her. It seemed silly to ponder, really, considering Agnes had purposefully gotten pregnant by the local farmer's son as a means to an end.

"The line needs continuing," her mother proudly told her when Agnes was eighteen years old. "I did it for you, and my mother did it for me. We have a duty, my love, to provide for this world."

By the end of the month, it only took her and the farmer's son four half-hearted romps in a hay field. Well, half-hearted on Agnes's part. He held up his end of the bargain by providing her with Beatrice.

And Beatrice was perfect. She had large, hazel eyes, wavy locks of brown hair, and freckles adorning her nose and upper cheeks. Agnes could have been content for eternity just loving her, but near Beatrice's eighth birthday, she became the Mage and never saw her again. She had been careful to steer clear in case the Paladin Society came sniffing.

The man set down the knife again and looked over to her, assessing the sudden shift in her tone. Agnes swallowed as she shook her head, adding, "At least he picked it up." She promptly turned back to the fire, suddenly missing Thailand and Cambodia's humid rains and warm sun.

She hadn't been back to this side of the world in nearly twenty-five years, opting to move around so the daemons would have equal opportunity to access her magic. Agnes had to remind herself that she missed these wild winters while she was stuck traveling through India during monsoon season. The grass was, indeed, not greener on the other side.

As the man watched Agnes attempt to thaw herself before the fire, the same thought seemed to cross his mind. He bent at the waist and leaned his elbows against the table, absent-mindedly saying, "I seem to remember a summer. Mmm...ten years ago, perhaps? Where you complained every single day about the sweltering heat of Dai Viet."

Agnes looked over her shoulder at him once again and clicked her tongue. She rose to standing, taking a moment to adjust her skirts and woolen hair covering. "I don't seem to remember asking," she said pointedly, watching his eyes darken, glinting like the heated flames behind her.

Their eyes connected, and Agnes felt her core clench.

"You know," he began, not removing his eyes from hers as he straightened and stood, weaving around the side of the table. "We've been together centuries now, and I think I love you more today than I did then." He approached her slowly, placed his hands on her chilled cheeks, and leaned down to kiss her softly.

"I hope so," Agnes replied with a smile. "It would be a shame if you needed to trade me in for a younger Mage."

He nipped at her nose playfully as she ran her hands up the front of his linen shirt. "Maybe not for a younger Mage, but certainly a goat or two."

Agnes laughed as she stood on her tip-toes to plant her lips on his again. His hands glided to the back of her head, falling to her waist, then drew her in closer as he deepened the kiss.

"You're still freezing," he murmured against her lips. "I may have a secret to warm you up."

"Is that so?" She asked, sliding her thumbs into the waistband of his trousers. "I may be open to you showing me."

The man smiled again as his hand cupped her breast. Agnes was getting into the rhythm of her tongue exploring his when a knock sounded on the front door. It was less of a knock and more of a pound. The man let go of her and quickly made his way to her bed, pulling the dagger he had gifted to her from under the mattress where she kept it hidden.

The three gemstones embedded in the hilt shone against the fire-light.

"Agnes! Agnes. Let me in, will ya? It's cold enough to freeze the teats off a frog!"

The man groaned, his fist relaxing around the dagger's hilt before walking back toward Agnes and resting his forehead on hers as he took her hand. "How did he find you so quickly?" He asked, letting go of her hand to lean against the wooden table.

"Cian makes quick work of anything he sets his mind to."

Agnes walked toward the front door and tugged it open, seeing the familiar vampyre on the other side of the threshold.

"Fuckin' hell," Cian said in his thick Irish brogue, pushing past her while rubbing his arms. He didn't hesitate to peel his coat off and steer toward the fire where she was just a moment ago. "Three months of walkin' to get here. Thank our Lord the fire is hot. Do you know how many villages I had to pass through? Jonas is still in the forest. Probably left a trail of bodies from--" He turned to warm his backside, spotting the man at the table for the first time. "Who are you?"

The man arched a brow at the vampyre, whose eyes had dropped to the dagger still in his hand. The man snorted, tossing the blade onto the quilt. "I'm leaving," he announced, taking his own cloak off the second peg by the hearth and wrapping it around his shoulders.

"So soon?" Agnes asked, her heart dipping in disappointment.

"I'll be back in a while," he replied with a wink. Fastening the cloak's button, he pulled open the door, sending in a third flurry of white. The flames in the hearth flickered with the cold breeze, the snow and sparks dancing together in a swirl of ice and fire.

He stepped over the threshold before spinning back to face Agnes, seeing Cian turn around to plant his hands near the fire again. The man released his feathered wings, large and brilliantly black against the white winter landscape behind him, before pushing off the ground and shooting into the air. Once he cleared the door frame, he flapped his wings, making snow billow from the slanted roof, joining the flakes blown around by the storm.

Then, he was gone.

Once he was out of eyesight, Agnes shut the door, latching the lock with a stiff pull.

"Who was that?" Cian asked, reaching up toward the ceiling to pull down a bundle of tomatoes.

He popped one off the vine and tossed it into his mouth.

Agnes sighed. "A...friend," she said, hesitating. She had been sworn to secrecy about his identity; honestly, their connection wasn't something she was willing to share. "A very, very old friend."

PAIGE

She was nothing, and she was everything. Cradled in a bed of darkness, not a single shimmer of light to orient her to where she was.

But there was time, and she was suspended in it. At peace and warm, no longer in pain and no longer afraid, she was whole, but she wasn't. It was both familiar and unfamiliar, like returning home after a long day, except she had a suspicion in the back of her mind that she had forgotten something. It started as a gentle prod, followed by a tickle, before culminating in a mind-numbing shake that woke her from slumber.

A rushing wind clawed at her. It felt different than the gust coming off of a briny sea or a gentle breeze in a meadow, rustling the long grass. This was *alive*. It pierced her very existence, inspecting every piece of her, questioning her presence.

She opened her eyes, surprised to see another set of cerulean ones staring back at her.

Then, she fell.

ONE

Odette

The log cabin seated in the clearing was a familiar sight that Odette hadn't seen in nearly ten years. The trees at the forest's edge had grown taller in that time, and the leaves that brushed the bright blue sky had already begun to tint yellow in anticipation of the change in the season. Even with the breeze that blew through the brush, her sensitive hearing could still pick up the rustling of mice against the pine needles and undergrowth.

Sweet cedar and wild mint danced in the air, wafting through the herb and vegetable garden that Nerea had planted at the front of the house. *That* certainly hadn't changed. Despite the lingering summer sun, the meticulously kept vegetable patch was still growing in their wooden boxes. The last of the sun-ripened vines of tomatoes crawled up the metal cages, and the eggplants' skin had begun to thin, indicating they were close to ripeness. Given the fresh dirt and empty spaces, it was clear that Nerea had already started to pull the old plants from the soil, tossing them into a pile at the base of the wooden boxes. Her garden tools had been discarded atop the weeds.

"I certainly wasn't expecting to see you here."

Odette glanced over her shoulder, spotting Nerea from around the corner where Odette knew the entrance to the root cellar was. Gloves tucked in the front pocket of her dirt-stained apron, Nerea was busy wiping her sweaty palms on the end of the cloth.

"I certainly wasn't expecting you to look so dirty. Your nails are disgusting," Odette shot back.

A shit-eating grin split Nerea's bronzed face. As she approached, Odette saw her comment stand true for more than just her nails as she could spot the smears of mud on her cheek and the fly-aways of her salt and pepper hair escaping the two braids she always wore.

Odette studied the woman for a long minute.

While Nerea was older than Odette by nearly seventy-five years, her human side had started to show through since her husband's death. It seemed as if she had aged nearly thirty years in the short time he had been gone.

"Come, get some tea," Nerea said, pivoting toward the cabin. From this angle, the sun's afternoon rays shone against her hair, reflecting off the raven black strands and exhibiting the layers of dark that ran through them.

Odette's swallow was thick as her eyes looked closer to the ground, watching Nerea's subtle left-sided limp. That was certainly new, too. "I...can't stay long, Nerea," she said, hedging forward to follow her friend up the porch stairs. "I'm getting ready to leave town. I just wanted to say goodbye."

The hinges of the screen door squeaked as Nerea pulled it open. "You only come to visit when you say goodbye, Odette. I knew why you were here when I heard your shoes on the driveway." She held the door nonetheless. "Come inside. I know your wings are tired."

That was true. It had been some time since Odette had traveled a long distance using her wings, and the corded muscle holding them to her back had begun to ache. Grumbling, she clomped up the stairs and brushed by Nerea to enter the cabin, who then disappeared into the kitchen.

Odette glanced around and saw the interior looked the same as it had ten years ago: mismatched rugs scattered on the wooden floor, paintings Nerea had completed over the years, beaded ceramic vases on the coffee table, and dried herbs hanging above the small kitchen window that shifted in the breeze.

Even if Odette's life was falling apart, she knew she could come back to Nerea and this cabin—a strong, centered, loving Nerea with a home that never changed.

Nerea bustled back into the living room, clutching two glasses of iced tea. Droplets of condensation dripped down the sides, soaking the tips of her fingers. Her eyes swept over Odette. "What happened?"

"What do you mean, *what happened*?" Odette asked, feigning ignorance. She reached forward, took a glass from Nerea, and sipped the sweet tea, tasting notes of honey and lemon. It was cool against her dry throat. She took a second sip as Nerea raised her brows.

"Something happened. I can see it in your eyes." Nerea's gaze slid down, surveying Odette from her head to her sneakers. Odette shifted uncomfortably under her scrutiny. "This isn't you just moving on. You're running again."

Odette scoffed. "It's nothing. Just a few dozen devils, the death of a human, and that damn djinn showing up."

Nerea sank into a cushioned seat, the wooden frame groaning under her weight, as Odette remained standing. "Eligos? He found you again?"

"He did, but I don't have to worry about him anymore," Odette responded, shifting from one foot to another. "The new Mage appeared and finished him off."

Nerea leaned back in her seat, tapping her pinky finger on the glass. "Greer? I like her. I think she'll be good for the daemons."

"You thought that about Agnes, too," Odette admonished, taking another sip of the tea. "And look where that landed me."

Nerea's smile was faint on her lips as she turned her dark eyes up toward Odette. "Agnes didn't land you anywhere, Odette."

Odette bristled. "I didn't come for a history lesson. I asked Agnes for help, and she said no. End of story."

"And you stopped fighting after that."

"What choice did I have?" Odette's eyes narrowed against the late afternoon sun streaming through the window. "I didn't have anyone."

"You had me."

It took a deep breath and a moment of pause to keep Odette from rolling her eyes. "You're not an army." She tipped her head back, finishing off the tea. The ice clambered forward, clinking against the glass. "And besides, my position here has been given up. Adair could come and track me down any moment. The *only* reason I felt comfortable coming to visit was because Eligos is dead."

Nerea pursed her lips just as a wave of warm air fluttered the curtains bracketing the window. "Speaking of, you mentioned a dead human."

Odette glanced down, suddenly interested in the shapes of the ice cubes as they melted in the glass from the heat of her hand. "Her name was Paige. Good friend of the Mage from what I gather. Jumped in front of a dagger for her wife." Her pause was longer this time, harkening back to the male who had done the same for her. Except his head had been removed from his body with a single sweep of a sword. "Anyways, I burned down the warehouse where the devils attacked and helped cover up the human's death."

Nerea's brows rose. "The human?"

"Yes. Paige. The human."

"Since when are you so callous?"

Odette dropped to the chair opposite Nerea, running a hand through her auburn hair. "What do you expect from me? It's time for me to–"

"Move on, I know. You said that already," Nerea interjected, fingering the ends of her right braid. "Before you disappear into the wind again, I have something to ask of you."

Odette said nothing as she waited for Nerea to continue.

"It's been six months since I've heard from my father."

Odette stilled, flicking the tips of her wings in irritation. "He must be busy. Being the Lord of the Court of Mist and Tide is a heavy title."

Nerea reached from her seat to set her glass on the end table, a dull thud echoing across the room. "He hasn't missed a correspondence in nearly nine hundred years. You know he sends one every solstice and equinox."

Odette tracked a fly buzzing through the doorway leading to the kitchen. It landed on the countertop, wings twitching, before it shot into the air and bounced against a closed window. "Let's say something is wrong." Her eyes followed the fly until it found an open window and zoomed away. "I'm not sure how you would expect me to find out. I haven't been back to any court in centuries."

Nerea fingers danced along the armrests, tracing the wood grain patterns of the chair. "I need you to go."

Laughter bubbled up Odette's throat, an instinctual response to a ludicrous request. When Odette cleared the mirthful tears from the corners of her eyes, she looked up to find Nerea staring at her with a blank expression.

Odette's brow furrowed. "No. No, I'm not going back. I'm never going back."

"I'm worried about him. I received the last letter six months ago, and it was concerning. He mentioned dissent amongst his people, within the court."

Trying to buy some time, Odette took another sip of the tea in her hand before remembering it was already gone. She desperately glanced around the room as though some of the paintings or woven baskets would come to her aid. "Why don't you go back? Check for yourself?"

"I'm old," Nerea responded with a tsk. She leaned back in her seat, crossing one knee over the other.

Odette rolled her eyes. "You're barely older than me."

No, I mean, I'm *old*," Nerea punctuated, eyes boring into her counterpart's with impatience.

Odette felt her chest constrict with the realization. "No— no, that's not possible. You're still young in comparison. You're—"

"I spent centuries alone," Nerea cut in. "Centuries looking no older than twenty-five. Centuries being a secret from my father's court, watching my friends die, watching my mother die. Then I met Tommy and–" She trailed off, and Odette knew what she meant. Nerea watched Tommy die, too. "I gave up my immortality when Tommy began to age. I don't know how much time I have left, and I would like to know my father is safe before I go."

Odette was silent, struggling to form a coherent sentence from the bomb that exploded in her mind. She and Nerea had been a team since Nerea's father assisted in smuggling Odette from the Fae realms following Adair's betrayal. He trusted Odette with his biggest secret: the half-fae daughter sitting opposite Odette now.

Fae were not forbidden to mate with humans, but it was a taboo of the highest order. Best case scenario, half-blood children were looked down on and ostracized from the courts. Worst case, they were killed before reaching adulthood to keep the bloodlines pure and clean.

Nerea was certainly the oldest half-fae Odette had ever met. And for the Lord of Mist and Tide to have fathered a child by a human woman he fell in love with...a child who would have become an heir to his throne—that was a secret he was willing to take to the grave. Odette was sure of it.

What made her even more sure of this was that he entered into a political marriage with a woman who bore him a son. Odette had met him a few times while she was still heir to her throne.

And, Princes of Samsara, Odette *hated* the boy. Sniveling, arrogant, and whining when he was a child and downright dangerous once he learned to wield a sword.

"Nerea, I'm sorry, I just can't—" Odette began.

"If you won't go of your own volition, I'm afraid I'll have to insist." Nerea took a deep breath, and when she went on, her voice was devoid of emotion. "I will invoke the Fae Accord of Equal Exchange."

Odette's face shed any expression of pity or sympathy, and her eyes steeled over as she held Nerea's gaze. "Are you willing to lose nearly three hundred years of friendship to do that, Nerea? You weren't born into the realms. You don't know what invoking that accord would mean."

"I'm willing to do what I need to make sure my father is safe." She tilted her head, braid sliding off her shoulder. "I would much rather you agree to help me from your own free will, though."

Odette's fingers tapped against the armrest as she studied Nerea. Her eyes, while stern, were still kind, and her lips were pulled into the signature small smile Odette was accustomed to seeing. "If I get caught—"

"You won't," Nerea responded simply.

"Or killed."

"You won't."

Nerea stood from her chair, the wood groaning again, and padded to the front closet nearest the screen door. She tugged it open and stood on her tip-toes to reach toward the top shelf. After her hand rummaged for a beat or two, Nerea grasped onto something before pulling it from the hiding place where she had stuck it. Her palm swept over the lid of a wooden box, cleaning off a layer of dust that had settled on top of it before she unlatched the copper lock and lifted the lid.

Odette watched Nerea with diminished interest as the half-fae poked through the box with her thumb and pointer finger. Nerea withdrew her fingers and walked toward Odette before extending her hand, who took what was clasped tightly within it.

Breath hitching in her chest, Odette stared at a worn metal emblem. Two wings spread on either side of a shield, complete in the front with two crossed swords. The four courts were represented with four symbols in the shape of a diamond: Wind and Storm at the top with a cloud and lightning bolt, Cedar and Sand to the right with a tree, Flame and Ember at the bottom with a flame, and Mist and Tide to the left with a wave.

Odette's mouth went dry as she looked down at it, her thumb running over the cool metal. It was her father's emblem, the old king's insignia.

"How did you find this?" She finally asked in a cracked voice. She looked up to Nerea, eyes wide and searching. "He's been gone for centuries. Adair had everything destroyed."

"Not everything," Nerea responded softly, the wooden box still tucked tightly to her stomach. "And not everyone." She paused and resumed her position in her seat. "My father knew the risks of sneaking you from the realm, and he did it anyway. I took you in, a broken down and beaten heir to the throne, knowing that one day it might expose me to those who want me dead, and I did it anyway. I've never asked you anything, Odette. But I need this from you now."

Odette's hand trembled, and, for a short moment, she considered throwing the badge through the nearest window out of anger. Instead, she took a deep, calming breath, filling her lungs with air that still smelled softly of mint and deeply of newly churned earth. She listened to the crickets chirping and owls swooping through the tree branches.

Fingers closing around the crest, the metal digging into the skin of her palm, Odette lifted her gaze to Nerea.

"Okay," she said with a slight nod, "but you must do one thing for me in return."

TWO

GREER

G reer Myers was sure of three things.

One: there was a grief so deep within her, so filled with rage that she knew she would never recover.

When she closed her eyes, she saw Paige lying on the concrete, blood still seeping from a wound that cut to her spine. She saw Delia, her gaze blank and unseeing, as she stared down at the unmoving body of her fiancée. She saw Odette, covered in thick, black goo, and her chest heaving with forced breaths. Finally, Greer saw Cian, his features filled with pain and regret. She wanted to rip that look off his face. She wanted to stomp on it and scream at the top of her lungs, making him feel even a sliver of how she now felt.

Two: Greer knew Paige's death was no one's fault except hers.

She had performed that summoning; she had forgotten to seal the salt and invited Eligos into her life. She had ignored every warning of how powerful a djinn was, how she was no match for the likes of Eligos.

Greer had been swept away by two primordials, and she hadn't even had the chance to tell Delia that. She didn't even get the chance to say goodbye.

That brought Greer to the third thing she knew with certainty.

She desperately needed to get away from this winged, overly-leathered pigeon.

Greer had tried to conjure any brush of magic she could scrape out of her tattered soul, but the man, Samael, had quickly snuffed out any spark she could wrangle forward. She had, then, attempted to throw herself out of his arms, but he tightened his grip and held her close to his chest.

His bronze buckles pressed against her shoulder. Greer's eyes stung with tears of pain and frustration as he continued through the golden-rimmed portal.

She wasn't proud of it and would never admit to taking the cheap shot if anyone asked, but Greer finally resorted to leaning her head back and clamping her teeth around the muscled posterior of his arm. She tasted the salt on his skin as he tried to yank his arm away, but she only bit down harder.

Samael let out a hiss of shock before swearing under his breath. In mid-flight, Greer felt his strong fingers pinch at the corner of her jaw until she was forced to release her bite. Her body was, next, reworked until she faced away from Samael, his arms gripping her around the waist.

"Do not bite me again," he seethed into her ear as they sped through the opening.

The wind blew past Greer's ears, making her eyes water. The rush of air was loud and buzzing as if someone had increased the volume of a static television. She struggled to catch her breath, the air so quick and pressured that she couldn't gulp it down fast enough.

Then, she was falling. Her stomach swooped in her belly with the sudden shift, and as she attempted to scream, it was swallowed by the black void they were racing through.

By the time they exited through a second, golden-rimmed portal, Greer's lungs were burning in her chest. "Then...let...me...go," she managed to say between heavy pants. His dagger, sheathed against his hip, dug into her lower back.

"Don't tempt me," was all he responded.

Greer wiped the water from her eyes, a bone-chilling cold passing over her as they flew on. Azazel, her father, had been soaring ahead of them since leaving the warehouse, and his white wings beat against the strong headwinds. She shivered as she glanced down, sweeping her gaze through the misty, frigid clouds and the terrain opening below.

Four mountains, each covered in snowy white, stood jagged and tall below them. Rivulets of water trickled down the mountainside, carving through the rock. The streams merged, growing in size until they formed a raging river. The water was dumped into a large lake, and sediment mixed at the mouth and lapped at the frozen bank. Waves crested over the blocks of ice pushed onto the pebbled beach. The cliffs were rocky and iced, dotted with green, spined trees.

Each was bent against the weight of the ice, their branches sinking into the depths of the snow.

Samael dipped below the clouds, and Greer saw the city for the first time.

Stone houses lined the switchbacks climbing the mountains, each precariously balanced on the rocks as though held in place by a breath and a prayer. Greer spotted small figures weaving in and out from the buildings before realizing, as they flapped closer, that some of the figures bore a pair of feathered wings. More figures crossed the stone bridges spanning the river roaring through the valley of the cliffs.

Greer glanced over a group of three younger women, each wearing heavy parkas and giggling at each other as they walked, pointing up to Samael from their places on the stone bridge. One had a book tucked in the crook of her elbow.

The sun, just beginning to rise beyond the mountain passes, splattered the navy sky with pink and orange splotches. The stars, still speckling the blanket above them, winked out one by one as each ray peeked over the snow caps.

A sharp breath whistled through her nose, and Greer was sure Samael had heard it. The view was beautiful—the city teeming with life despite the cold.

Samael dipped lower still, banking his giant wings to the left as he approached the city's apex. Nestled there, in a deep mountain hollow, stood a looming stone palace.

Stone turrets and steepled towers overlooked the city below, each spiraling upward toward the peaks. She could see that one of the towers had a large, circular window complete with stained glass and encased in black metal on the front. A lone bridge, flanked on each side by an iron and stone railing, spanned the gap between the two sides of the palace. The bridge was decorated with ceramic planted pots and gargoyle-like statues perched on the edge of the balustrade.

A balcony jutted from the cliffside, creating a grand entrance to the palace before them. Six monstrous and winged marble statues, four men and two women, were erected on the edge of the terrace. Shadows from the rising sun accentuated each angelic creature's chiseled jaws and cheekbones. All had an arm extended into the ether, and their palms turned upward with a sphere nestled into the cupped groove.

When Samael banked a second time, swooping by one of the middle statues where Azazel had landed, Greer noticed the familiar shape of the South American continent etched into the side of the sphere.

She had just opened her mouth to ask about them when Samael dumped her onto the terrace, her knees colliding painfully against the stone. Greer spun to glare at him, but he had already tucked in his wings and swept by her without a second look.

"Welcome to Veritas," Azazel said as Greer clambered to her feet, swiping her dirty palms against the fabric of her pants. "The capital of Samsara."

She approached the edge of the balcony, no barrier or parapet shielding the drop, and glanced down. They were hundreds of feet above the valley floor, where Greer could see houses nestled against the craggy cliffs. From the corner of her eye, she saw Samael adjust his stance as if he were readying for her to leap over the edge.

"Don't tempt me," Greer shot at him, her tone mocking his own, and she turned toward the palace.

Samael said nothing as he narrowed his eyes at her, but his shoulders relaxed nonetheless. His hand rested against the dagger's hilt, the three emerald stones glinting against the sun's rays now shining over the lowest turret. As Greer directed her attention to Azazel, he remained stoic and silent behind her.

"Where did you bring me? What is this place? I want to go home. Take me home. *Now*," Greer said, her tone quick and demanding. She didn't give either man the chance to reply.

"No." Azazel was the epitome of nonchalance as he leaned against the nearest marble column, his arms crossed over the buckled leather armor covering his chest. Behind him were spindled trees with orange leaves planted in large, blue pots, their leaves rustling in the breeze—a breeze that, due to her anger, Greer realized no longer chilled her.

Greer took a deep breath as she flexed her fingers. It was a sore attempt to calm the flaming itch growing in her palms, one of magic and power begging to be released. "That wasn't a request."

Azazel tilted his head, golden hair shifting onto his shoulder. "This isn't a negotiation."

Greer whipped her hand toward him, power webbing from her outstretched palm. It would have been a catastrophic hit to anyone else, but Azazel merely brushed it away with ease as he continued to lean against the column.

Greer was panting from the effort, her chest still tight from the portal.

Rage found her again, but this time, Greer sent her power in a formless blast toward one of the blue pots near the base of the grand staircase. It exploded, shards of clay and dirt ricocheting across the marble and spraying against the set of tall double doors at the top of the stairs. The spindled tree cascaded to the floor, and the branches groaned, threatening to snap under its weight.

Azazel waved his hand, and Greer watched as the broken pot reversed course and came back together once again. The tree straightened as dirt packed tightly around its roots.

Greer threw her magic at a second pot, which shattered just the same. Azazel said nothing as he waved his hand and put it back together.

"I could keep going," Greer warned, though she felt her stores of power waning. "I could destroy this entire place."

Azazel smirked. "You can't." He pushed off the column and took three steps toward her. "You work under the assumption that I haven't been preparing for teenage primordial tantrums since the day you were conceived."

Greer bristled. "I'm twenty-seven years old, not a teenager—"

Azazel's eyes shifted dramatically to the first repaired planter and then the other. "Could have fooled me, then. Arista." He made the call over his shoulder, lifting his chin toward the staircase.

A young woman appeared, her cream-colored wings peeking out from her back and mousy hair pulled tightly into a thin braid. She was shaking, each feather seemingly quivering as she approached the three. She kept her eyes fixed on her feet when she moved, and her cotton dress pulled at her shoulders when she bent into a deep curtsy that had her wings grazing the marble tile.

"Yes, Your Grace," Arista answered when she lifted.

"Arista, this is Greer, my daughter. Greer, this is Arista. She is your handmaiden."

Greer's brows rose as Arista dipped into a second curtsy directed at her. "No. No— please stand up." Arista stilled, her hands trembling as she slowly rose. Greer turned back to Azazel. "I— I can't stay here. I have a job. I have friends. I have a home—"

"And now you're here. Aren't you lucky?" His eyes glimmered with satisfaction as he watched her. "Arista, would you be so kind as to show Greer to her bed-chambers? I'm sure she would appreciate getting cleaned up."

Arista flicked her brown eyes from Greer to Azazel, her features fracturing into a bundle of nerves. "S—sir?"

Greer clenched her jaw. "I'm not staying here—"

"Samael?" Azazel tossed lazily over Greer's shoulder, and the Primordial took a threatening step forward, arm outstretched to grab Greer once again.

Greer lurched away from him, gaze steeled and hard. "Show the way, *Arista*." She spat the name out as if it were venom in her mouth. She said nothing else as she followed the handmaiden, the sun warming each staircase step.

The two doors split open upon their approach, revealing a brightly lit stone interior with a domed ceiling so tall that Greer had a hard time making out the figures painted across it. The white marble continued into the palace entrance and toward the back of the hall, where one main staircase with a thick, ruby carpet curved upward to the balcony overlooking the entrance.

Behind the staircase stood five floor-to-ceiling windows with unobstructed views of the mountain passes and subsequent bodies of water in the valley beyond. A massive crystal chandelier hung above the curving staircase and caught the morning sun, sending dancing refractions of light across the floor. They crossed the hall, and Greer's gaze swung around, noticing the golden trim surrounding the windows and the green flora curling up the columns on the second floor.

Greer lifted her head to survey the two white statues erected near the base of the stairs, not noticing that Arista had already peeled to the left. The handmaiden held a wooden door open, patiently waiting for Greer to finish gawking.

Greer walked through the doorway and stepped subtly to the side, letting Arista retake the lead. The side door led to a long hallway that ended at a narrow, winding staircase, and Greer noticed that, even though Arista had her wings tucked tightly into her back, the feathers nearest the edges still tickled the stones as they passed. Reaching the end of the hallway, they began to climb up and up and up until Greer was slick with sweat and her breath sawed from her throat. Arista, on the other hand, didn't seem to be affected.

They exited the staircase into a hallway dimly lit by sconces bolted to the walls. The passage was cold from the stone despite the flickering flames, and Greer felt her sweat chill almost instantly. Greer spotted the stone handrail of a balcony to her right and stopped dead in her tracks to see what the view revealed.

The balcony overlooked a hall nearly as large as the entrance. Instead of statues and endless marble, this chamber was filled from floor to ceiling with wooden bookcases. The marble flooring had been replaced by textured sandstone tiles, and a bronze chandelier, layered and asymmetrical, hung from the domed glass ceiling.

Books zoomed one way or the other, crisscrossing in their paths as they exited or entered their designated spots in the bookcases. Some people were on tall, wooden ladders, studying the spines with marked concentration. Others seemed to be Primordials like Arista and Azazel, their wings beating to stay afloat. One woman, clad in olive green robes and a bronze chain surrounding her waist, was laden with a stack of books. The stack was steady in her arms, despite the rise and fall of her body, as she put them back on the bookshelf, one by one.

Greer felt Arista approach her, laying gentle hands on the railing beside hers.

"This is the library, open to the public for all to use," Arista said. "You would also have unfettered access, Your Highness."

Greer's gaze continued to move from person to person. She noticed the pointed ears of the Fae, some people with curling horns protruding from the tops of their heads, and leathery wings on their backs. Some patrons had slitted eyes akin to a snake and viper-like teeth sticking out between closed lips. A group of children formed a line as they entered the chamber, flanked on either side by women dressed in the same olive green robes as the lady putting the books away. The children giggled and hushed one another as they moved through the stacks.

"Don't call me that," Greer retorted with a slight delay as she turned her back to the library and continued down the hallway.

Arista followed in silence, her linen gown sweeping at her feet. After a moment, she said, "Here," pointing in the direction Greer needed to take as she remained in front of her.

The two women climbed another set of stairs before exiting to a cozy, circular landing. Greer recognized the shape and the view from the circular window as one of the steepled towers set high against the mountain. Arista crept past her, opening a wooden door to the left, and she stood to the side as Greer entered. The bedroom was large enough that Greer knew the entirety of her rented house could have fit easily inside of it. Most walls were gray stone, but one was accented with a plum-colored damask wall covering made from thin silk fibers. Another bronze chandelier was centered in the room, lit with a myriad of pillar candles.

The four-poster bed was rimmed with bronze and featured curtains in deep plum that matched the accent wall. On the other side of the room stood doors that led to a bathroom, the end of a claw-foot bathtub peeking from the crack in the door, giving it away.

Greer knew this bedroom was supposed to give off a luxurious, modern vibe, and someone had kept the room immaculately clean for her arrival. But, to Greer, the room's darkness felt repressive and isolating compared to her small rental home's wicker furniture and white walls. That thought made her stomach clench, and she swallowed the lump growing in her throat.

"I brought some tea and breakfast to the room for you, your High— princess," Arista said from the doorway.

Greer made her way over to the window, where a wooden table held plates filled with piles of biscuits, sausages, and eggs that seemed to have cooled since they had been set out. A silver teapot was placed in the middle of a matching tray and the small amount of steam still curling from the spout fogged the glass pane.

"It's just Greer," was her only response to Arista as she absentmindedly picked up a biscuit. "You can go now."

Arista curtseyed one last time before backing from the room and closing the door behind her with a slight click.

The thought of eating made Greer feel sick, further validated by the taste of ash in her mouth after biting into a soft biscuit. She set down the pastry with a sniffle, allowing a single tear to drip onto her cheek. She swiped it away with a rough pass of her palm. She turned toward the tea next, a regular weekend occurrence with Delia, but the memory made her chest tighten to the point of pain. Her eyes brimmed with more tears, but Greer blinked them back this time. She had no right to cry. She had no right to grieve. It was her fault that she was here and that Paige was gone.

Turning away from the unwelcome breakfast, Greer spotted a decanter filled with an amber liquid on a side table. She grasped the glass topper, pulling it off before lifting the bottle to her nose.

The contents smelled strong, with a complex scent of earth and smoke that usually turned her away. Instead, Greer retraced her steps back to the table filled with breakfast foods and collapsed into the chair before it. She lifted the decanter to her lips and took a strong pull, feeling the alcohol burn the lump in her throat. She finished the decanter in record time, hoping upon all hopes that the alcohol would make her drift away.

THREE

GREER

"I brought you some dinner, Your High—Greer," Arisa said as she placed the silver tray on the table.

The wafting smell of warm stew and freshly baked bread met Greer's nose. After three days of not eating, she expected to be near starving. However, the thought of eating was equally nauseating and required more energy than Greer currently had in her stores. Her stomach clenched painfully as saliva pooled in the back of her throat.

"I don't want it, Arista," Greer replied from her seat on the floor, her knees pulled to her chest and her arms wrapped tightly around the fronts of her legs. She rested her cheek against the top of her knee, staring out the circular window to the city below.

Windows flickered as candles were lit, awaiting the setting sun over the mountains on the opposite side of the lake. Greer watched as figures crossed the stone bridges and others swooped through the air.

"You should eat something, Greer," Arista said gently, following a moment of silence. "It's been days now and-"

"I do not want it, Arista," Greer repeated, dramatically punctuating each word. She heard the whisper of slippers against stone as Arista shifted her weight from one foot to another.

"I'll try again tomorrow then."

Greer said nothing as a tinkle of glass against wood sounded and stayed facing the window until she heard the door click shut behind the handmaiden. Greer unfolded her legs and pushed herself from the ground, turning to walk toward the side table where Arista had refilled the decanter with the amber-colored liquor.

Greer grabbed it from the table and pulled the topper off, taking a swig from the bottle. It was clear to her that Arista had little, if any, experience with harmful coping mechanisms in humans following a trauma. If she had, Greer wondered if she would have bothered to refill the decanter for the third time in so many days without even commenting on it. She also briefly considered that Arista may not have the choice.

Greer approached the door, weaving around the table and crossing the room. Wrapping her hand around the knob, she yanked it open with a quick tug, the decanter dangling at her side. She strolled into the circular landing room, swiping a forefinger over the framed artwork that hung from the walls. She took in the texture and felt the strokes of paint that made up each piece— all the while taking swigs of alcohol from the container clutched tightly in her hand.

Greer wanted to forget, and, for that night, she was well on her way.

Her footsteps echoed against the narrow staircase that led to the hallway overlooking the library. There was an armchair tucked in the corner of the balcony, and that had become Greer's favorite place to sit once night came, as it was almost a guarantee that she would be left undisturbed. She would be there for hours, staring into the dark abyss of the library below. The moon's glow cast long shadows between the bookcases, and she didn't feel quite so alone in the silence, surrounded by the thousands of stories begging to be read.

But tonight, instead of immediately sitting in the armchair as she had done the nights before, Greer approached the railing and rested her forearms on the cool surface. She tapped the decanter quietly against the stone, listening to the rhythmic echo across the stacks and staring through the glass dome of the ceiling to watch the stars wink into place.

"Thought you might be here again."

Greer didn't even flinch as Samael approached; her senses were already dulled, and her cheeks were already numb from the swigs of alcohol. She took another as he leaned onto the railing beside her, his cerulean eyes flicking between her face and the bottle in her hand.

"Arista said you didn't eat again."

Greer snorted. "Did she ask you to come and convince me to?" *Tap. Tap. Tap.*

"She's worried your father will transform her into something extremely unpleasant if you don't turn yourself around soon. She's responsible for you, so if you fall into a deeper depression, she's going to think that she's failing."

Another swig from the decanter. "Do you think she'll still come nosing around if she's turned into something unpleasant?" She saw Samael's lips tighten from the corner of her eye as he struggled against a ghost of a smile.

"I think she's worried about you and doesn't know how to help."

"I don't need help." Another swig.

"That is clear enough."

Greer felt her shoulders stiffen as her heart pounded in her chest. Her singular attempt to stifle the rage racing through her extremities was unsuccessful. She pushed off the railing, took the final gulp from the decanter, and threw it as hard as she could into the depths of the library below. It arced through the air— falling, falling, falling— before cracking against the side of a bookcase and shattering onto the stone floor.

"That seemed unnecessary," Samael merely said as he assessed her, his forearms still casually resting in front of him.

Greer pinned him with a chilled and disinterested stare but remained utterly silent. He ran a hand over his brown hair, pulled into a tight bun near the top of his head, and scrubbed it down the shadow of his beard. She knew he was taking in her tangled curls, the dark circles under her puffy eyes, red-rimmed from on-and-off tears, and the sallow tint to her skin from non-existent sleep.

Samael sighed through his nose. "You need to ask us for help, Greer. We need to know what we can do for you."

Greer let out a sharp, humorless laugh that seemingly caught Samael off-guard. "I asked you for help. I asked you to save Paige, and you said no."

Samael swallowed, but his eyes hardened as stared down at her. "I didn't kill your friend. I just helped her move on. She was already dead."

The words shot through Greer like an arrow, gripping her by the heart and dragging her deeper into the pool of misery she was barely holding herself afloat in. She spun on her heels and marched away, wholly ignoring the calls of her name coming from behind her as she climbed the stairs again.

Greer dreamed of Paige again. She had seen her best friend, whole and uninjured, standing in front of her on the pavement near the garage. Greer glanced down at her hands, palms turned toward the sky, to see them covered in thick, red blood. Her vision warbled like she was looking at her hands through murky water. The blood dripped from her fingertips, staining the toes of her white sneakers. She looked back up at Paige, who had turned pale against her smattering of light freckles. Her friend clutched the hilt of the dagger now embedded into her chest and ripped it from inside of her, where it clattered noiselessly to the space between them. Red stained Paige's shirt, growing larger and larger until she fell to her knees.

Then, Paige was whisked away by a dark shadow, and Greer struggled for breath as it surrounded them. As it choked them, drowned them.

Still asleep, Greer screamed, tearing her from her dream and sending her jolting upright. She clutched at her chest, breath sawing her dry throat.

The bright sunlight shone through the circular window, beaming against the silver teapot filled with a steaming, aromatic liquid. Arista had been here, replacing last night's stew with a small fruit and yogurt plate. Still panting, Greer glanced at the sun's position, estimating the time to be nearly nine in the morning. She closed her eyes to inhale one deep breath and then a second and a third, willing her heart to calm its rapid beating.

"Must have been quite a terrible dream."

Greer launched herself out of bed, wild eyes turning toward the corner of the room where she spotted Azazel lounging in one of the patterned, plum armchairs. His elbows rested against the arms of the seat, fingers steepled in front of him. He looked at her with a tilted head, his golden hair brushing the tops of his shoulders with the motion.

"Were you watching me sleep?" Greer demanded, her eyes darting to the clothes she still wore from the night before. She hadn't bothered changing before passing out, drunk, on top of the comforter.

"Was I watching you sleep? No." He pushed himself to stand, his white wings adjusting into place at his back. "Was I watching you flail like a fish on the bank of a river? Yes." He walked forward, passing by the console table. Azazel smirked as he caught her looking at the empty decanter stand. "I assured Arista that you will no longer require a daily bottle of our finest."

Greer flared with irritation.

Azazel arrived at the small breakfast table and pulled out a chair. He sat down, his wings draping over the low back. He leaned forward to pour tea into two porcelain cups before setting the teapot back onto the silver tray. Picking up the sugar spoon, he dumped one cube into each cup before gesturing toward the empty seat in front of him. Greer only crossed her arms, glaring at him with hardened eyes.

"Very well." Azazel paused momentarily to adjust in the seat, his leather armor creaking as he moved. "Arista says you haven't been eating."

"Does Arista tell everyone I haven't been eating?"

"Only those that matter."

Greer cocked her head and narrowed her eyes. "What makes you think that you matter to me?"

Azazel pondered her for a beat. "When I thought of how our first meeting would go, it wasn't you kneeling over the dead body of your friend following a devil attack, I assure you."

She desperately wanted everyone to stop bringing Paige up. Instead of telling him this, though, Greer retorted, " When I thought of how our first meeting would go, it wasn't me as a twenty-seven-year-old. It was me at the age of five, after wondering why my father wasn't there to eat a bagel with me on my first day of kindergarten." She paused for good measure. "That I assure you."

"Do you want to eat bagels together, Greer?" Azazel steepled his fingers once again, the cups of tea in front of him still steaming, sitting on the table, utterly forgotten.

"A little late, don't you think?"

Azazel sighed as he ran a finger over his bottom lip in thought. "What do you want from me? An apology? An explanation? You won't be getting either."

"I want to go home," Greer said, "and I want you to leave me alone."

At the last word spoken, an inadvertent shell of power blasted from her, leveling every ceramic vase, porcelain mug, and glass pitcher into dust. Greer spun on her heels and turned away from Azazel, fear curling in her stomach and horror crinkling the carefully painted mask of indifference she had glued over her features. It was the first time in days that her magic had come out. She had been so careful to ensure it stayed contained.

Azazel was quiet for a long minute, her back still to him. "Your magic can't hurt me," he finally said. Greer heard the chair groan as he lifted himself from the seat. She said nothing as she tightened her arms around her chest. "I added you to the bank accounts connected to the city. You can use them if you want to get out of this room."

"You're trying to buy my love?" Greer shot at him, glancing over her shoulder to glare at him. In her peripheral, she noticed he had fixed everything she had broken.

"Enough," Azazel said, and his power was hair-raisingly sufficient to get Greer to clamp her lips together. He must have sensed her trepidation because he added, "I'll send Arista in. You should eat something. It looks like she brought a tray in earlier."

Less than two minutes passed before Arista swept her, her eyes trained on the plush carpet. She held a freshly laundered pair of pants and a cotton tunic. Arista finally looked up at Greer as she held the clothes out in a gesture.

Keeping her eyes tightly fixed on the handmaiden, Greer made a scene of picking up her fork, stabbing a piece of fruit with it, and taking an overly large bite. She spit the seeds onto the silver trays. "Now you can report back that I ate something."

Arista lifted her chin. "I'm trying to help you—"

"No, you're trying to stick every one of those god-damned feathers into my business."

Greer watched as Arista's bottom lip wobbled before she replied in a quiet hiss, "I don't even want to be here with you. I thought we could at least be friends since neither of us has a choice in this."

"I don't care what you thought we could be," Greer snapped back as she took an angry gulp of hot tea to wash down the fibers of fruit that stuck to her dry tongue. "What I do want is more liquor."

Arista went straight as a rod, each limb stiffening. "His Majesty said no."

"You don't work for his majesty. You work for me."

"He is the king, and he has explicitly told me no."

It had always been a talent of Greer's to sense what made others tick—what made them lose any semblance of self-esteem, what made their hearts swell with self-importance. She tilted her head as she surveyed Arista further, zeroing in on the frock, the color of her wings, and the way she held herself. The corner of Greer's lips curled into a cruel smirk.

"You're weak. That's why you're with me, isn't it? Don't you think you would be treated better, treated with respect, if you had even a little power? Don't you think you would be more than just a hand-maiden if you had something to offer Samsara besides bringing me tea and biscuits? You're nothing to these Primordials, Arista."

Greer knew she hit the mark when Arista's eyes brimmed with tears, and she drew in a long, shuddering breath.

"You're horrible," Arista finally responded.

Pain bit at Greer's throat, feeling that lump she had been swallowing back for the last few days. As Arista tossed the pile of clothing onto the bed, shame washed over Greer. She knew, in that moment, that Paige would have been filled with anger and embarrassment if she had seen how cruel Greer had been. Without the alcohol, Greer would have to be sober as she lived with this knowledge.

FOUR

DELIA

The sun was bright and beautiful in the Italian sky. The wispy clouds that moved across the landscape were quickly whisked away by the autumn wind that rolled off the mountains to the north. In a sick twist of irony, Delia knew she would always come here— she just thought it would be with Paige. They had talked extensively about what to do on their honeymoon and always returned to Italy. After Delia had proposed to Paige, she would daydream in her corner office about laying in the sun, spending endless amounts of time in bed, and eating an unhealthy supply of handmade pasta. Frolic through the Italian Alps, laze on a catamaran off the Amalfi coast...

On the way to Italy, Delia grieved her lost dream the entire flight, wireless headphones firmly pushed into her ear canals so she could pretend she was with someone else...anyone else. God, literally anyone else.

"Cian," Delia hissed as she stood outside the family restroom door. She pounded on the wooden door before grasping the handle. It's been thirty minutes. Our luggage is at baggage claim. I want to get out of this airport." She shook the handle again, this time rattling the entire door in the frame.

The door cracked open, and Cian's right eye peered out from the restroom. "We can't leave until the sun is down," he said. "I will burn up." With that, the door snapped shut.

"One could only hope," Delia retorted, pounding her fist against the door again. The noise had attracted the attention of an older couple departing from the gate across the vast, tiled hall. She smiled sweetly and waved, but they merely returned looks of disgust. Delia dropped the smile and turned back to the door. "I'm going to leave you here then. I'm not waiting in this airport for–" She checked her fitness watch. "Another ten hours."

Cian cracked the door again, a smug smile on his face. "How do you plan on getting the hotel room? It's in my name."

Delia crossed her arms over her chest and shifted her weight to one leg. "I would rather drag a suitcase filled with flaming, hot dog shit around the city than wait here with you."

The one visible eye narrowed. "You wouldn't dare."

Delia spun on her heel, stomping away from the restroom, and began to follow the signs for baggage claim. Behind her, the door swung open with a squeak, and pounding footsteps charged after her.

"Are you really going to leave me here?" Cian asked in disbelief as if floored she would opt to spend the day out in the city rather than be stuck in the airport terminal with him.

"You see me walking, don't you?" Delia asked, flicking her thick hair over her shoulder.

The flight with Cian had been terrible enough, and she wasn't about to do him any favors. Being within six feet of him made her want to vomit. She had to board the plane before she could talk herself out of it, try as she did. She wanted nothing more than to be at home, curling into the warmth of the bed she once shared with Paige and forgetting all this had happened. Deep down, though, she knew doing this would yield the same results as always: receiving an unmanageable pile of casseroles, memories of dead monsters, and the vision of her wife lying face-up on that pavement, her unseeing eyes staring at the darkened sky. It was worth taking sleeping pills these days to suppress the dreams; otherwise, she would never shut her eyes again.

Cian reached out to her with a gentle hand on her forearm, preventing them from going any further. A group of people had to split to accommodate their sudden stop. "Come on, Delia. You can't leave me here all alone." She looked up at him, and he flashed her a half-smile, which she assumed worked to pull females into whatever scheme he wanted them to be part of. "What will I do all day?"

Delia scowled. "Read a book. The fuck do I care?" She shook off his grip and continued her walk down the long corridor, shouldering past travelers hurrying toward their gates.

"I liked you better when your wife was still alive," he grumbled, jogging to catch up with her.

The words were like a shot to the heart, but Delia suppressed the urge to kick him in the shin. "And I never liked you, yet here I am." She stepped onto the escalator, dragging her carry-on suitcase with her. "The only, I repeat, the only reason I am here is to find a way to save Greer from this society. If it were you they were after, I would send them a postcard with your personal address on it."

"Ouch," Cian said, placing a hand over his chest. "You wound me, Delia."

Delia didn't bother responding as she stepped off the escalator and turned the corner toward the baggage claim. Two suitcases remained, slowly snaking their way around the conveyor belt. She grasped her suitcase's handle, tugging it off the belt and letting it drop to the floor. The second suitcase promptly returned to the backside of the terminal and disappeared through the plastic flaps hanging over the carousel's opening.

Cian looked at her blankly. "Seriously?" he asked, gesturing toward the empty conveyor belt. "You couldn't have grabbed mine?" Delia merely blinked. "I should have eaten you," he added when she remained silent.

"And it sounds like you'll have plenty of time for it to return." Delia inhaled through her nose, taking in the smell of old rubber and stale cleaning products that stained the stagnant air. She pulled the suitcase handle upwards, where it clicked into place. "Listen, while you're stuck here, why don't you make use of your time? You know, contemplate the meaning of life, or whatever." Pulling her sunglasses from the top of her head to the bridge of her nose, Delia marched toward the exit.

"You're a fucking bitch, you know that?" Cian called after her, garnering stares from a crowd who had just entered the terminal.

Delia waved over her shoulder as she approached the automatic glass doors, which split on her approach. She was suddenly bathed in that Italian sunlight she had been dreaming about.

After giving the driver the hotel address she decided to book, Delia closed her eyes as soon as she sat in the taxi cab and leaned her head against the seat back. She realized it was probably a mistake to make the trip. She should have just headed to Florence instead. She had already taken an extended leave of absence due to Paige's death, so she may as well make the most of her time. The cab zipped through the ancient streets toward the address Delia had given the driver, though her eyes remained closed despite the sharp turns and uneven pavement.

In a second twist of irony, Italy was one reason she and Greer connected in college when they first met. Delia wanted to lie on a beach in her bikini, and Greer wanted to pick through every piece of art she could feasibly get her hands on. Nonetheless, the two had talked about visiting for years before Delia met Paige. Not only did Paige love Italy, but she also laughed when hearing the story of how Delia and Greer became friends in the first place. They had been assigned different roommates for their freshman-year dormitory, living down the hall from one another at the time. Delia had walked into the bathroom to find Greer crying at the sink over an argument with her mom, Celeste. Being the over-sharer she was, Greer had dumped her life story onto Delia in a three-minute word vomit.

The over-sharing was foreign to Delia, and she wasn't one to cry either. Before Paige's death, the last time she had was at her mother's funeral at the age of eleven. She didn't cry when she and her two brothers were kicked out of their step-father's home, nor did she cry when her brothers found a nice family that wanted nothing to do with her. By then, she was getting ready to enter high school and moving on to bigger and better things.

Even though the two would be unlikely friends, given the emotional start, they became inseparable. The decision to move from her hometown in southern Texas to the moody, rainy environment of Oregon was indeed a gamble, but it was one she never regretted...until now. What had Greer gotten herself into?

Gotten both of them into?

The taxi screeched to a stop outside of the four-star hotel Delia had booked for herself on the way to the taxi stand at the airport. She smirked as she opened the car door, looking up to see St. Peter's Basilica perched at Vatican Hill. Her smirk turned into a genuine smile when she thought of the rat-infested hovel Cian had surely booked for them. She retrieved her luggage from the trunk before tipping and thanking her driver, watching as she quickly pulled away from the curb in search of another passenger. Time is money, after all.

She turned back toward the hotel and started making her way inside. The glass doors opened to a large lobby, revealing crisscrossed orange, gray, and white marble patterns covering the floors. Burnt orange drapes hung on the large bay windows that faced the basilica, and gray couches furnished the sitting area, where magazines and travel guides littered the coffee tables. Seated on one of the cushions was a teenage girl, her hands in her lap as she surveyed the crowd. Her brows rose in surprise when Delia briefly made eye contact with her.

Delia wove her way toward the check-in counter, passing large square columns decorated with white wainscoting. She smiled as she reached the desk. "Checking in for Delia Savas, please?"

The streets of Rome were teeming with late-season tourists. Children darted between the shops, and locals sat on the terraces of various restaurants; some were chatting, some smoking, and others were watching the tourists with sharp eyes. Delia pushed onward, a sweat building up in her lower back as the late September heat barreled down on her.

The main view of the basilica and the subsequent square stood at the top of the street, the impressive structure towering over Rome. Delia paused to look at it, her heart pounding from the steady climb. The wide, cobblestone path opened to the square, lined with tall columns in two staggering rows that stretched to the left and right.

Black chandeliers hung from the roof that covered the column rows and, planted directly in the middle of the square, was an Egyptian obelisk flanked by two streaming fountains. Delia couldn't help but gaze up at the architecture in wonder. The beauty of the terracotta-colored buildings and stone walkways was matched only by the majestic styling of the square itself.

Delia reached into the crossbody purse she had stuffed into her carry-on to take out one of the printed guides she had taken from the hotel's front desk. She dragged her eyes over the map, noting the placement of every building in correspondence to its location in the square. Nothing particularly stood out to her as she studied each section. Nothing that screamed *secret society predicated on hunting monsters* anyway.

On the map, Delia found a building labeled *chapel* and made the quick decision to check out that area first. When she lifted her head toward the left side of the square, however, she eyed the long lines of red-faced and sweaty tourists waiting to enter and thought better of it. Her gaze slid toward a tour group led by a guide carrying a stick with a plastic number taped to the top. The group stopped as they exited the church, and each tourist thanked the guide as they passed, handing over various amounts of euros as tips.

Delia waited for the crowd to clear before waving her hand high in the air and approaching him. "Excuse me, I was wondering how to avoid that." She paused to gesture to the line now wrapping around the square. "I saw you just finished up. Do you have any more tours planned for today?"

The man looked down at her through darkened shades and smiled, warm and friendly. He was young, more than likely eighteen or nineteen years old. His dark hair was curled against his bronzed face, and his nose was slightly larger than average, widening the distance be-tween his eyes.

"You are American, yes?" he asked in a thick accent.

"Yes," Delia replied with a smile to match his. "It was a spur-of-the-moment trip, and I didn't do much planning." She did her best to sound like any other tourist, but truthfully, she didn't count watching the zip drive Cian had gotten of Greer's mother, Celeste, that contained the vast amounts of documents they were working through as planning.

"Unfortunately, that was my last tour today," he replied, removing his drawstring bag from his back to shove his hand inside. "I do have a tour starting early tomorrow." He withdrew his arm to pull out a business card with a website link on the front. "Twice a day. You will find no one better." The sun glinted off the front of his sunglasses enough that she could see the wink he sent her. "You can book here. We meet in the square fifteen minutes before the tour begins."

"You are a lifesaver!" Delia said in a voice that wasn't quite her own, too high-pitched and cheerful, though she did tuck the business card into her bag.

He looked at her for a beat, tilting his head as he studied her. "My father works in the excavation office at the basilica. I help him run tours of the necropolis below the church." He rubbed his chin with his long, thin fingers. "If you want, I could add you to the tour for tomorrow afternoon."

Delia's heart leaped in her chest. That was precisely what she needed and what was sold out during her internet searches. "The necropolis?" she asked, feigning a lack of knowledge as she looked down at the map still in her hand. "Is that the burial chamber below ground?"

The man nodded. "Yes, that is where Saint Peter himself is buried. Tours usually sell out very far in advance, but we had a cancellation for tomorrow."

"I'll take it," Delia replied eagerly.

"I'm Lorenzo," he said, grinning back and twirling the numbered sign in his hand. "I look forward to seeing you tomorrow."

FIVE

DELIA

Delia woke the following day to the sun streaming in through the window of her hotel room. Surrounded by plump pillows and soft sheets, she stretched her arms over her head and groaned. It had been weeks since she had slept that hard, though the flashes of devils and pools of blood still ripped through her dreams. And it was when Paige's face popped into her mind, she decided it was time to wake up.

She reached over and opened her phone's home screen with a swipe. Sixteen missed calls and twenty-five text messages from Cian. She shut the screen off without replying and rolled out of the bed, padding to the bathroom.

The night before, Delia had spent the evening sipping wine under the dimly lit street lamps of Rome while reading through a guidebook on the history of the Vatican. She took notes in the margins and marked different locations that may best serve to hide documents or a headquarters. When she had thoroughly read the same passage four different times, she scrolled through the website of the tour Lorenzo had booked for her earlier in the day.

She secretly hoped it wasn't a scam, though the website and subsequent links had seemed legitimate enough.

Delia got dressed and headed out of her room for the day. The morning was already warm; the sun had barely risen over the buildings to burn away the lingering humidity. The walk to the basilica had become more familiar to her, having done it multiple times the day before. Delia finished the coffee and pastry she picked up from a café just as she entered St. Peter's Square, spotting the tour guide leaning against one of the stone pillars on the side of the courtyard. He waved at her when their eyes connected, and she adjusted the strap on her crossbody purse as she walked toward him. The crowd for the tour had already begun to form, visitors laden with cameras and using pamphlets to fan their faces, forming a semi-circle around him.

"I was hoping that was you," Lorenzo greeted her with an easy smile as he brushed the curls away from his face. "I added you to the necropolis tour for this afternoon. You're still interested, yes?"

Delia vigorously nodded. "Very much, yes."

She had already ripped through every internet blog post she could find looking for pictures, and she was not surprised to learn that cameras were not allowed. She almost felt guilty when she stopped at the nearest electronic store, purchasing a small camera she could stick in her pocket where it fed to a file on her cell phone and stay unnoticed. She felt like a spy, but she had briefly wondered if she would go to hell for desecrating a holy site. If they couldn't get her out, at least she would spend eternity with Greer.

A few more people sidled up to the group, and the tour guide was scanning their tickets with an app on his phone. He clapped his hands a few minutes later, whistling to get their attention. "Welcome to

Vatican City and St. Peter's Basilica, everyone!" A soft, early-morning cheer rang through the crowd. "My name is Lorenzo, and I will be your guide. Before we go inside, I need to go over the tour rules. I'm happy to see you all saw the rules for the dress code. Thank you for that."

He paused to gesture toward the front of the church. "We will enter toward the right, first seeing Michaelangelo's Pieta, St. Peter's statue, the baldachin, and St. Peter's cathedra. From there, we will move on to the dome, the museums, and the Sistine Chapel. It will take us about three hours to complete, yes?"

The cheering commenced again, and he waved an arm, motioning toward the entrance. Delia fell into step behind him, listening intently to his spiel regarding the church's history, why it is so famous, and the architecture used to create it. Delia's chest tightened when a thought crossed her mind; this was right up Greer and Paige's alley. The art, the monuments, the history. This was something they could have done together. Delia shook her head, zoning back into the lecture.

The group walked past the growing queue, stopping near the metal detector and the security station standing guard at the front door. Delia emptied her pockets and placed her bag on the conveyor belt, holding her breath as she walked through the metal detector. The man who sold the camera assured her that it would not be picked up, and this was the practice test. She was waved through with no alarm, and she let out a breath, picking up her bag and pocket contents after they passed through the X-ray.

Delia's lips parted as she glanced around at the basilica. Statues erected on pedestals surrounded the circular room, set into alcoves high on the wall. Paintings covered the ceiling, the upper walls, behind the statues, and between the windows. Her sandals were slick against the dark marble floor, and she almost ran into a thick maroon rope separating the entrance from the exit as she stared up at the center of the dome.

"In this part of the tour, please take all the photos you like. Over here," Lorenzo said after he made it through security, tucking his guide tour badge back into his pocket. "You will see Michaelangelo's Pieta…"

Delia glanced at the white statue encased behind a wall of thick glass. It was a breathtaking statue, but that wasn't what she was here for.

She dropped back in the throng of people, allowing tourists the room to take pictures. She scanned the chamber, pretending to take in the art covering the walls. Corridors split from the main room, leading to smaller chapels and tombs, but nothing unusual. She grabbed her cell phone and opened the camera, taking dozens of pictures of the surrounding hallways. She would analyze them later. Looking over her shoulder, she saw Lorenzo waving them onward, and she quickly followed.

Next was St. Peter's Statue, then the Balachin. Delia raised his brows at the imposing canopied statue. Four bronze pillars shot toward the center of the dome, each twisting in a spiral that made them appear to spin in the sunlight. The cloth making up the canopy was tasseled and scalloped with golden thread. Delia approached a plaque in the corner, which stated that the Balachin marked the location of St. Peter's tomb. She took more pictures as she moved forward with the group.

What the fuck, Delia? A text message from Cian popped through as she closed the camera. *This isn't funny.*

"Yes…yes, it is," Delia chuckled as she swiped the message away.

On and on they went, winding their way through the cathedral and into the museums. Delia had taken dozens of pictures by this point, each as inconspicuous as the next. Nothing out of the ordinary, though she realized that may be the point. And Cian had sent her dozens of additional text messages, each she easily ignored. She was getting antsy about moving on to the next tour, but the beautiful view from the top of the dome dampened her anxiety. The climb had been awkward, especially as it wound through the narrowed passageways of the staircase, but the view of the courtyard and extending into Rome was worth the heart-pounding ascent.

Delia typically wasn't one for art, especially religious art, but the Sistine Chapel was something to behold. The detail of the painting on the famous ceiling, with colors that popped against the marble walls, was incredible. However, as she raked her eyes across the mural and spotted the winged creatures and the depictions of God, men, and angels, she briefly wondered how factual it was. How much did Michaelangelo know? Or did he know anything at all?

"What did you think?" Lorenzo asked as the first tour ended precisely three hours later. "It's a beautiful example of architecture, isn't it?"

Delia had to agree. "I'm not usually one for tours, but that one surprisingly held my interest."

Lorenzo quickly thanked the man who pressed a handful of euros into his hand before turning back to Delia. "What brings you to Rome and the Vatican anyway? A solo trip? Finding yourself?" His smile widened, his teeth sparkling against the bright Italian sun.

Her heart stuttered in her chest, and momentarily, she allowed herself to think about Paige next to her. She would have laughed about the pomp and circumstance of it all and would have definitely found something quicker to say. "Helping a...friend...with research." Her stomach twisted at the thought of calling Cian a friend.

And, as though he had heard her, Delia's phone buzzed again.

Lorenzo must have sensed her sudden shift because his swallow was thick, and he looked awkwardly toward the basilica. "I'm happy to give your friend some research if you need a hand. I've done plenty myself in the last few years."

Delia thanked him quietly, her grieving thoughts suddenly bogged down with Paige's death, before pressing a few euros into Lorenzo's hand as a tip for the first tour and making her way toward the end of the square. She entered the first restaurant and ordered a handmade pizza with a glass of wine. It was an upscale place, and although she wasn't usually one to go to expensive places to eat, the time constraint was pressing on her. As she ate, she transferred the photographs from her phone to her cloud storage to access them more easily on her computer when she returned to the hotel.

Before she knew it, she was heading back toward the square for the second time that day. A much smaller group was gathered, and Delia remembered the notes on this particular tour: only two hundred fifty people were allowed per day, twelve per group. It was easier to map out the attendees with such a small group, five other women and six men, and she hoped that would lend itself to the location.

On the other hand, Lorenzo was standing next to an older man with a similar oval face shape, presumably his father. The guide smiled as Delia approached, and she sent him a small, apologetic wave. Lorenzo dipped his chin in response.

At the top of the hour, the group followed Lorenzo's father to the other end of the courtyard, just to the left of the main entrance for the basilica. The doorway was built within the colonnade, where a separate security posting of guards had been stationed. Delia was the first to pass through the screening process, holding her breath once again as she put the camera pen with the contents of her pockets.

She hoped there wasn't a glitch the first time around.

Her breath loosened as she was waved through. As everyone else approached the Swiss Guard, she casually reached for her pile of things and grasped the pen. She flicked the power switch on the end of the pen twice until the camera adjusted to video. It buzzed against her palm, notifying her that it had successfully activated.

Delia waited near the door to the office, and when everyone had passed through the security checkpoint, they were herded into the Scavi area for the tour. Delia felt down to the core of her bones that she had hit on something important by coming here. She could barely focus as Lorenzo's father described the history of the excavation process that dated back to the thirties and forties. Instead, she kept her focus on why she was there in the first place, making sure to slowly turn as if she were merely taking in the area so that the camera could capture everything.

The group shuffled down through the basement level, between rows and rows of tombs containing the bodies of popes and other important religious figures. They turned a corner and followed a long hall, culminating in a narrow staircase. The tunnel was dark, and despite Lorenzo's reassurances, Delia couldn't help but feel her stomach clenching with nerves at the sight.

She had never been good with tight, enclosed spaces.

As the small group descended in a single-file line, old, exposed brick lined the wall, crumbling under Delia's feather-light touch as her fingers scraped against the side. Her walk was slow to match the older woman in front of her, a pronounced limp stiffening the woman's knee with every downward step. The air became increasingly hotter and more humid the closer they reached the bottom. The staleness of the space, thick with dust, coated her tongue like a thin sheet. Delia reached up to twist her hair in a bun, the back of her neck sticky with sweat.

The staircase leveled to an ancient floor, a cracked stone pathway covered in a thick layer of dirt at their feet. It seemed as though someone had attempted to sweep but only managed to gather the dirt in clumps that crowded each fissure. Looking around, Delia saw mosaic stones on the ceiling and floors. It was broken but still visible between the larger slabs of marble anchored to the walls.

Even with the fractured and smudged tiles, Delia could tell the mosaic was made up of images that included warriors with swords on horses, women gathering in courtyards, and busts of younger men with strong jaws and crooked noses. The walls surrounding the pictured tiles were once painted vibrant shades of yellow and orange but faded over time.

The group headed deeper down the excavated passageway, one taller man needing to duck to avoid scraping his head against the top of the tunnel. Lorenzo and his father pointed out the tombs and mausoleums dating back to the second century BC. Inscriptions were carved into slabs of stone centered at the foot of each burial slot, detailing the date and the name of the person interred in expertly carved letters.

With limited tourists and workers, the space remained isolated enough to go mostly undisturbed. There was nothing unusual at first glance, but she hoped to spot something when she went through the footage later that evening. Even with the eerie location, it was hard for her to imagine anything hidden in these dusty, old tombs. Still, Delia knew the Paladin Society was as ancient as the mosaic tiles she stood on—if not even older than that.

If she knew Celeste as much as Greer did, which wasn't very well, she also knew that Celeste would have kept meticulously accurate records of her time with the Paladin Society. The documents told her she was in the right place—she just needed to trust herself that she could work it out in time for her and Cian to find the entrance to Samsara.

The elevator dinged when it reached Delia's floor. She stepped onto the plush carpet, immediately maneuvering away from the cart of cleaning supplies parked on the opposite side of the hallway. A heavy scent of citrus soap was in the air as she walked toward her room, murmuring voices speaking Italian threaded from under the doors she passed. She fumbled with the room key before placing it against the lock on the door, which opened with a sharp click. Delia pushed the door open with her hip, her hands busy uploading more pictures and videos from her phone to the cloud storage connected to her computer.

The sound of a throat clearing reverberated through the room, and Delia's eyes lifted, landing on the familiar vampyre perched on the edge of the vinyl couch. His brown hair was tousled as though he had recently gotten out of the shower, and he had placed his forearms on his knees, bouncing the heel of his foot against the floor in agitation.

"Hello, Cian," Delia said casually, swinging her bag from her shoulder and tossing it onto the bed. "You look unwell." She leaned down to pull her computer from her carry-on suitcase and placed it on the desk, tapping it to wake it from sleep mode.

Cian's eyes flashed with simmering anger. "And here I thought you ran away to France."

"I thought about it," she replied, sitting down and clicking through the laptop's contents until she found the cloud storage app. It opened with another click, and she slumped against the back of the desk chair as the images downloaded onto her drive.

"It took me twenty-four hours to track you down."

"You must not be very good. I booked the room in my name."

"I had to use the sewers to get through the city just to stay out of the sunlight."

Delia's gaze flicked over the still images as the long video from the necropolis downloaded. "Oh, no. How terrible for you," she responded in a flat, bored tone.

Cian shot up from the couch and was on her with preternatural speed. He spun the chair she sat in and clamped his hands around the armrests before bending over to snarl in her face. "I'm not here to play games," he said, lip curling in disgust. "If you aren't going to help me, then go the fuck home. Chasing you around the city is a waste of my time."

His hot breath on her face made her want to reach forward and two-handedly shove him away. But Delia said nothing as she glanced over her shoulder to see the laptop screen—the video loaded and ready to play.

Cian's gaze followed, sliding over as his eyebrows knitted together. "What is that?"

Reaching over, she pressed the spacebar on the keyboard, and the video immediately began to play. It was shaky from her steps, and her pocket was visible in the corner of the frame, but the image was clear enough.

"I went to St. Peter's today and did a tour of both the basilica and the necropolis underneath." She pointed at the screen with her thumb. "I think the necropolis will be the best place for the Paladin Society to hide a secret headquarters, depending on how they accessed it. It was excavated in the thirties, with very low amounts of foot traffic and heavy security. I also took close to five hundred pictures documenting guard locations and checkpoints."

Cian stood, straightening his spine, and Delia felt a surge of victory explode from her chest.

"You are truly a hero among men," she said, breaking the silence. "And it is impossible to underestimate you." She crossed an ankle over a knee, her foot bobbing in the air. "By the way, that little act you pulled was so laughable. If you intended to scare me, you'll have to try harder than that."

He stared back at her, his features unreadable, but Delia still saw the tick of his jaw as it clenched. She didn't bother attempting to hide her grin of satisfaction.

"I'm going back tomorrow to see when the guards change shifts and how long it takes them to circle the square. Please do whatever you want while I'm gone. The sewers do call to you these days. But if you aren't going to be helpful, then go the fuck home."

If looks could kill, Delia would be dead on the floor, but her heart soared a final time when Cian looked away from her, shifting his weight from one foot to the other.

Delia: one. Cian: zero.

SIX

ODETTE

Odette was pissed.

Hot, exhausted, and pissed.

Reaching Iguazu Falls, the set of waterfalls between Brazil and Argentina, was no easy feat. It took her nearly a week of border hopping to get there. Getting to the waterfalls *was* the easy part. The hard part was still coming; it hung over her head like an executioner's rope.

If she could make it to the Court of Mist and Tide before the equinox was done, and that was a big if, she would be stuck in the Fae realm for three months waiting for the portal to open again. And there was a high chance that would be a very long three months.

Odette's glamour held well against the jungle background, and her aching wings beat with the wind sweeping over the canopy as she attempted to spot the best place to land. The jungle enveloped the trailheads, though the national park's signs and metal boardwalks made it fairly easy to navigate.

She hadn't been to this watershed in nearly two hundred years. She sought refuge at this portal when she first escaped the clutches of Adair, wrapping around from the Fae portal in Scotland, and had been here a few other times in her younger years while still leading her father's armies.

Otherwise, Odette hadn't returned since it turned into a tourist destination. She landed on a thick branch amongst the canopy of lush, gleaming leaves and peered toward the main road. Tourists filed out of buses, flanked by guides with microphones and numbers taped haphazardly to yardsticks. Eyes squinting against the late afternoon sun, she listened for the exotic bird calls and monkeys shrieking in the trees around her.

The air was thick with the scent of plant growth and the overly sweet smell of rotting fruit. Odette adjusted the straps of the pack she harnessed between her wings, the loose blades of the swords, and two daggers clanking together with the sudden movement. She took off again, and the humid breeze was a relief as it blew against the dripping sweat on her skin.

Managing to find a hole in the tree line, Odette banked through it and dipped around the vine-wrapped branches until she landed ten feet under the metal boardwalk that cut through the jungle. Her shoes sunk into the soft mud, but despite the water soaking into her socks, she held still to hide from the tourists who had heard her entrance and swung around, hoping to locate a stray animal bustling through the foliage.

Their faces downturned with disappointment, and Odette was relieved when they finally turned back toward their tour group. The brush against a thorned bush on her descent left a burning scratch and a trickle of blood leaking down her elbow. She swept her hand across the cut to get a better look at it but smeared the sweat and blood into an intermingling of metallic salt instead. She would wash it later.

Odette tucked against the tree line, shoes squelching in the puddled mud, before prodding at her glamour to ensure it was still in place. Success.

The constant roar of the waterfall breaking over the rocks was interrupted only by the squawks of toucans and the chittering of monkeys swinging through the trees above. She trampled through the jungle for some time, pausing within the foliage every so often to avoid drawing the attention of a stray tourist gazing toward the jungle floor.

Odette crept along the brown-hued river, passing swarms of ants devouring fallen fruit and snakes looping around the branches, sliding over tree roots. Downed moss-covered logs had become home to colorfully patterned insects. At one point, she was sure she caught the shadow of a stalking jaguar in the branches above, but the cat was gone by the time she darted her eyes upward to confirm.

The Court of Mist and Tide was one of the more heavily protected portals set up by Nerea's father himself. The only way to access it without prior authorization was by navigating a series of waterfalls before swimming into a sunken pool on the second tier of the cliffside. It was dangerous and exhausting.

Which was why Odette was pissed.

Finally standing at the precipice of the flowing water tumbling into the rushing river near her feet, she grumbled under her breath as she stared pointedly at the sun setting over the top tier of the waterfall. The waterfall's spray against her skin was cool and refreshing, but it did nothing for the beading sweat that trailed between her wings.

Odette took a few steps forward, struggling to pull her shoes from the thick mud, her red braid catching the mist blowing from the edge of one of the waterfalls. She approached a large boulder, thrust into the side of the cliff face, and brushed aside the thicket of moss growing atop it. There, carved into the rock, was the ancient sigil of the Court of Mist and Tide: two waving lines bracketed by two symmetrical orbs, signifying the sun and the moon dancing along the ocean's horizon.

If there was any lingering doubt that she would remember the portal's location, it was gone.

The ancient sigils demonstrated the beginning of the defense system in place by the Court of Mist and Tide. Her ability to fly would be nullified as soon as she passed through the invisible barrier. Not that she would have had the strength to fly regardless, but she knew that this was only the beginning and the perils of reaching the portal were far from over.

Odette cursed Nerea again.

Watching from her perch astride the river, the sun disappeared beyond the thundering waterfall, and the moon began its march across the sky. The chittering of monkeys had been replaced by the hum of insects buzzing through the winding, thick vegetation. In an instant, just as the cool moonlight illuminated the sigil carved into the rock, Odette felt the familiar pulse of the portal opening, as if energy had been released into the air and thrummed away from a center. The equinox was upon them, and the fabric rip between realms was opened. The countdown in Odette's mind began to tick, and she knew exactly how many minutes she required before it closed.

Without the use of her wings, it was going to be tight.

Odette crept along the basalt wall. Ivy and moss wove up the wet rock, and the jagged edges of the canyon scraped her arms as she walked the path behind the first waterfall. Her shoes slid against the muddy rock, and her foot slipped into the river as the water from above battered down onto her shoulders. Pulling her foot from the murky water and grumbling under her breath at her newly sodden sock, she slowly slunk through the other side. She stood sandwiched between two of the falls.

Pausing to get her bearings, Odette released her grip on the wall with one hand to wipe the water from her eyes and find a better hold on the slippery basalt stone. There were four more waterfalls to go. She stealthily snaked through the second, water battering down on her once again as she went.

After she made it through, she readjusted her bags and handholds to prepare for the next one. Slithering through the third, this one much bigger, the mighty rush of water on her wings forced Odette's footing from the rock. She fell, her fingers wildly scraping and scrambling to gain any grip on the stone. Her previous cut split open once more, forcing a hiss of pain to escape through her lips, but she managed to regain her placement.

Odette clambered through waterfall number four with little difficulty before pausing beside number five, the mightiest of all five waterfalls that made up the path to the Court of Mist and Tide. The frothy cascade of water against the plunge pool sprayed the backs of her legs, and the lichen clinging to the rock underfoot. Drawing in a breath that smelled heavily of algae, Odette squinted upward to see the hazy, mist view of the second tier opening above her. Checking her footing and digging her nails into the rock, she began her entrance into the final waterfall.

The water pounded her wings, pulling her backward and throwing her off balance. Her fingertips and underneath her nails were raw and bleeding with the force it took for her to hold on. *One step, slide. Second step, slide.*

Odette let her mind wander to when she and her father had been invited to the Court of Mist and Tide nearly six hundred years ago. The Lord, Nerea's father, had formatted a staircase out of water to allow them access to the rift. Princes of Samsara, she wished that was the case now.

Nearing the end of the fifth fall, she side-lunged out, collapsing onto the flat stone near the riverbed. Chest heaving in an effort to catch her breath, Odette glanced up toward the sky to track the moon's position against the stars. Her heart dropped when she realized it had taken her longer than anticipated to navigate the path. She no longer had time to take the much-needed break.

Pushing herself up to a standing position, Odette wiped the last of the water from her eyes and shook the droplets from her leathered wings. Her hand brushed the canyon wall until she found what she sought— the rocky overhangs that made up the ladder scaling the wall. Her bloodied and beaten hands gripped the weathered overhang as she shoved her shoe into the foothold near the foundation of the gorge.

Odette let out a strangled breath as she found the second foothold and thrust herself upward, catching the third overhand. The waterfalls and the fifty-foot climb weren't even the worst part...it would be the swim. Getting to the Court of Mist and Tide was hell. Nerea's father made it nearly impossible for anyone to stumble upon them, preferring their solitary existence away from wandering humans and prying members of the fae.

Tiny rivers of water trickled down against the stone, making the wall slick and wet. Thousands of years of erosion had polished the footholds and overhangs. Odette's arms burned as she scaled the cliff, and all she could do was keep her focus on making one movement at a time. Her lungs were tight and heavy in her chest as she continued. Even with her heavy wings tucked tightly into her back, they threatened to send her pitching backward as she climbed, where she was now high enough that her head would certainly shatter against the basin below.

The moon rose higher into the night sky, pebbled by stars peeking through the low clouds hovering over the jungle canopy. Finally, with one last pull, Odette managed to clear the edge of the second tier, rolling over the side of the rock. She lay on her back, wings pinched against the stone. Heavy pants and sore shoulders met her as she rose to her knees, raking her gaze over the view from the second tier of the falls.

Just across the river was Gargata del Diablo, the Devil's Throat. The sight sent a shiver up Odette's spine, the sheer beauty and power of the water plunging into nothingness. With effort, she stood, pressing her hands against her hips as the humid air sawed against her dry throat. A second boardwalk extended over the pool near the middle of the pools, and for a brief moment, she wondered if the humans would have built the boardwalk there if they had known what lurked just under the surface.

Odette shifted the straps on her shoulders again, the canvas now heavy and waterlogged. The fringe of her red hair was pinned to her forehead, and she scraped it back as she surveyed the terrain before her. Tilting her head, she studied the faint glow in the pool near the end of the empty boardwalk.

She shucked off her mud-riddled shoes and waded into the water, the level quickly rising to waist height. Odette held the bag above the water to protect what little dryness it had left, but she knew that was wishful thinking for what came next. Pausing at the edge of a deep shaft, her toes curled around the edge that had been curated by Nerea's father to hide the portal further.

Odette kept her eyes trained on the shimmering rift fifteen feet below the surface. The portal seemed to dance under the water, a seam in space and time. She drew a deep breath and dipped below the gentle, lapping waves.

The water bit at her chest, throat, and brow. She kicked into the shaft, struggling to ignore the temperature of the water, and followed the wall down, down, down toward the rift near the bottom. Hooking the bag straps around her elbow, she spread her arms and propelled herself forward. The movement was slow from her wings and the canvas bag, but she needed to hurry. Her chest was already burning, and she wasn't even halfway down yet.

Odette flurry-kicked her feet and descended deeper, the darkness enveloping her as she kept squinted eyes on the seam. It had begun to shrink. She was running out of time.

For the Court of Mist and Tide faeries, whose magic included the ability to manipulate water, it was merely a matter of dividing the water in two and using the sides of the cavern to clamber in or out. But for everyone else, you swam to the bottom successfully...or you didn't.

She was nearing the portal, but Odette's gaze began blackening. Mind turning fuzzy and dizziness taking over, Odette inhaled in confusion, flooding her lungs with the jungle water. Her eyes shot open when she realized what she had done. The burn in her chest had shifted into a raging forest fire as she thrashed under the surface, clutching her fist to her chest.

The moonlight above her began to fade, and Odette's lips parted as she stilled, feeling her body become one with the water surrounding her. This wasn't so bad. She was cradled and warm, her hair floating around her as the last air from her lungs left through a trail of bubbles.

In the next instant, Odette's hand brushed against the portal, and she was sucked through the rift. The feeling of falling was still familiar after all these centuries, and her stomach swooped as the wind rushed over her ears. She could faintly hear the roaring of the falls as she tumbled through the vast void of nothingness.

Odette was released from the rift and spilled onto a beach, rough waves breaking over her wings as she lay there. She managed to roll to the side to vomit, water spewing from her chest as she heaved a wet cough. She again collapsed onto her front, laying her cheek against the wet sand.

The briny smell of the sea surrounded her as she let out a soft chuckle. She had made it; she couldn't believe she had. Her light laughter stopped abruptly as a gleaming and sharp sword was placed against the column of her throat. Odette stilled as she assessed the situation, but the male behind her spoke first.

"Hello, General. You do have quite the price on your head."

SEVEN

GREER

Greer soaked in the bath for a long time, toeing at the faucet handle. She turned it on and off until the tub overflowed and water spilled onto the floor, flooding the area around each claw foot. Greer stared into the dark corners of the bathroom, sinking beneath the rim of the tub and sending more water crashing onto the tile until her breath burned in her lungs and her brain forced her to surface. She took in gasping breaths and wished she could trade places with Paige.

She repeated this until the lavender oil she had added to the water had dissipated, her fingers had pruned, and the feeling of a towel on her sensitive fingertips sent shivers up her spine.

Pulling herself from the tub, Greer dried off and changed into the clothes Arista had thrown onto the bed. The pants were loose, and the tunic hung limply around her shoulders and waist, physical evidence of her refusal to eat. She braided her wet hair, the ends sticking together in one clump, before dropping onto the edge of the bed.

The afternoon sun was morphing the sky into a blended mix of pink and indigo, misty clouds curling around the peaks of the mountains and basking them in a light fog. She had yet to go into the city and was curious about it. More importantly, there was potential for her to be able to find at least a shot or two of alcohol.

That last thought made up her mind.

Greer pulled on her sneakers, guilt tugging at her when she realized that Arista had cleaned them at some point, and headed into the circular landing. It was the first time Greer had been near the library while the keepers flit around, so she passed by in the shadows of the long hallway, just in case someone on the floor below had glimpsed her leave her room. She jogged down the stone staircase, concentrating heavily on each step as she went down. She was quicker than she had been in the days before when she followed Arista up the same staircase, and a moment later, Greer slipped onto the marble terrace that overlooked the city.

The chilled mountain air was cool on her face, and she felt the skin of her upper arms tighten against the breeze. Greer hadn't thought to grab a jacket since she had spent the last few days inside and immediately regretted her forgetfulness.

She paused in the shade of one of the winged statues, pondering whether she should go back to get one. Shaking her head, Greer remembered the walk to the top of the steepled tower and immediately pressed on instead. She found a staircase to the left of the statues, lined with the same spindled plants, and trotted toward the city to keep herself warm.

The marble stairs ended at a gravel path that began one of the switchbacks down the mountainside. Trees peppered the trail, rugged roots growing in twists around rocks and boulders cemented to the cliff face. The view of the city square grew larger with each step, and Greer took a deep breath, reveling in the fresh, floral-scented air.

When Greer neared the first plateau, she reached the initial set of homes, smaller than the palace but more prominent than the ones built on the banks of the lake. Servants swarmed like bees on a pollinated flower, rushing around to prepare dinner. They carried platters of fruits, meats, and cheeses as their employers sat on cushioned seats in the parlor overlooking the city, sipping on glasses filled with red wine.

Greer went further down the mountain, by-passing upscale, busy restaurants, art studios, and jewelry stores filled with well-dressed patrons.

When she reached the valley of the mountains, coming upon a square near the banks of the freezing lake, she stopped to get her bearings. The cobblestone road was flanked on both sides by wooden buildings, dimly lit by candles on the windowsills. Weeds and mud filled the spaces between each brick. Vendors selling street food, handmade clothing and accessories, and various knickknacks had set up shop in the square, each protected from the wind and rain by a brightly colored tent. Banners of patterned pennants were strung from the rooftops, the thick ropes that held them aloft criss-crossing above the alleyways. When Greer glanced up, she noticed that the palace sat like a dollhouse on the mountain.

People of all species, vampyres, fae, and shifters, littered the square. Groups bounced from tavern to tavern, traversing the stone bridges connecting each side of the river, laughing and chatting as they walked. Greer watched as a woman admired a pair of earrings perched in a brightly lit shop window. Her friends cooed at her, begging her to buy them, and she finally relented, the bell dinging as she opened the door to the shop. Greer felt a pull of jealousy at the simplicity of the interaction.

Greer navigated her way across the square, the crowds keeping her tucked safely away from the biting chill of the wind, and entered the first tavern she came across. A wooden placard named *The Bronze Serpent* hung on iron posts above the entrance, and Greer had to shove her shoulder into the heavy wooden door to open it. She stumbled over the threshold, her sneaker catching on the corner of the door jam.

The tavern was packed, teeming with life from every angle. A band of a lute, a fiddle, and a crumhorn played a jaunty tune from the corner stage, their feet tapping to the beat. Three barmaids, each wearing a stained apron, carried tankards from the bar to various tables filled with post-work patrons. Every table was filled, and every staff on hand was needed.

Seeing there wasn't any room for her, Greer was readying to leave when the crowd split just enough to reveal a single stool open at the bar. She cut through the crowds, passing a group of snake-eyed females who giggled at her appearance before hiking herself onto the seat. She sat there for a moment or two, contemplating her foolishness for coming to a place that only reminded her further of Paige and wondering how she would pay when the bartender finally wandered over.

"What'll you have?" He asked gruffly, his hands spread on the wooden surface as he leaned forward to hear over the noise. Greer glanced up to take in his balding head and large mustache.

"I– I don't know what you have," she replied.

The bartender said nothing as he reached below the countertop and pulled a pewter tankard from one of the lower shelves. He slammed it down in front of her before turning to grasp a long-necked bottle from one of the upper shelves behind him. He popped the cork with a flick of his thumb, draining the bottle's contents into the tankard. He pushed the tankard toward her when it was nearly filled to the brim.

"Mead. You'll have mead. How will you pay?"

Greer leaned forward to grasp the tankard with both hands, pulling it the rest of the way. "Erm, bill it to Azazel?"

The bartender stilled as he stared at her, his thick eyebrows rising on his forehead. "Okay," he said as he turned to jot her order down on a piece of paper near the register. "What's your name for the coin request?"

"Greer. You— you don't want proof? A card? A...photo ID?" Greer asked as she lifted the tankard to her lips and sipped the semi-sweet liquid. It coated her tongue, a smooth alcohol with a distinct taste of honey and raspberries. It was even better than the liquor Azazel had cut her off from.

The bartender pursed his lips and shook his head. "Either you have permission for me to send a coin request to His Majesty's city account, or you have a death wish." He paused to wipe the counter with the rag he pulled from his back pocket. "And whichever one it is doesn't matter to me. I'll get paid either way."

Greer took another deep gulp of the mead, a warming shiver making its way up her spine. "Keep them coming then," she said, tilting her head back to polish off the stein, the last of the mead sliding down her throat.

The bartender shrugged as he turned to refill her stein from a newly opened bottle of mead. And keeping them coming, he did.

Greer slammed tankard after tankard of alcohol, becoming increasingly more agitated that it didn't seem to affect her. She was ready to order another—perhaps this one would win a pronounced widow's peak on his forehead. She felt someone slither up to the bar beside her, placing their forearms against the rounded, wooden edge.

Greer glanced over, surprise taking over her features, when she saw a male with copper skin and raven-black hair staring at her. His eyes were a layered brown, much like wet river rocks, and his ears were shaped into points. She recognized the features similar to Odette's, and her heart tugged painfully against her chest.

He smirked at her, tilting his head slightly to the side. "You're new here." He leaned forward to sniff her, and Greer shifted away, her jaw clenched with reserved restraint. "I certainly haven't come across you before. The name is Sindri."

"What do you want, Sindri?" Greer asked, taking another sip of the newly filled tankard.

Sindri chuckled, mouth opening to reveal white teeth. "To get to know you." He moved again, attempting to close the gap she had created. "My mates in the corner don't think I can get you to come home with me if I'm being frank. None of us have ever had a human before."

Greer glanced over her shoulder to see a group of males, each with pointed ears, drinking from tankards near the corner stage. All four looked in different directions when her eyes planted on them, pretending they hadn't been watching,. She looked back at Sindri to study him.

He was good-looking enough, with high cheekbones and oval eyes. His black hair was shoulder length and shaggy, culminating on his forehead in a pronounced widow's peak. His nose was long and narrow, and his body had the same lithe build as Odette's, but...

Cian was the last person she had slept with, and she could still remember the feeling of his hands in her hair, his lips on her inner thighs, and his fingers trailing down to stroke her sex. She could imagine his smell, and suddenly, she needed it gone. She needed it, and him, out of her memory.

"Let's go then," she said, sending a sultry and challenging stare toward Sindri.

His lips parted in bewilderment before curling in the corner to the smirk he had been sporting, a dimple appearing on his cheek. "You jest."

Greer took another sip of her mead, keeping her eyes fixed on his. "Are you going to take me home with you, or are just you going to stare at me with that dumb fucking look on your face?"

The speed at which Sindri slapped a handful of coins against the counter would have been amusing during any other period of Greer's life. He held out his hand, and she took it, noting the softness of his palm. It directly contradicted how Cian felt, and she had already begun to doubt whether she should go through with it. But then Greer pictured Cian's green eyes, his infuriating condescension, and steeled herself as she hopped off the barstool. The stein, still over half full, was left on the countertop.

Dusk had fallen as they entered a second alleyway off the square, and Sindri spun her, gripping her jaw and forcing her to look up at him. "What's your name?" He asked, and Greer said nothing. Instead, he ran the edge of her palm down the front of his pants. His cock twitched beneath her hand, and she heard a garbled moan rumble deep in his chest.

Sindri's lips crashed onto hers, his fingers still gripping her jaw. Yes. She wanted to bruise, she wanted it rough, and she wanted it to hurt. His tongue darted out, running along her lower lip. She tasted him, the bitter, citrus beer and cigar smoke, as she ran her palm down the front of his length once more.

"You must have had quite the reckoning for you to crawl from the river and still act like this," Sindri said as he pulled away from her. "Do you want me to fuck you?"

"I want you to stop talking and take me back to your place."

Sindri led her deeper into the alley, stopping at a door furthest away from the square. Greer gripped his forearms, pulled at the waistband of his pants, and kissed the crook of his neck as he jangled a set of keys in his hand. He unlocked the door, her teeth nibbling his earlobe, and tugged her inside.

His home was a townhouse with wooden stairs leading up to the second floor, but she barely had time to take in the living space, seemingly shared between a handful of other roommates. The coffee table contained two ashtrays and a few beer steins and smelled just the same, but Greer was whisked upstairs before she could study it further.

Sindri pulled her over the threshold of his bedroom, the second door after the landing, and his lips were on her again before the door snapped shut behind him. One hand thrust in her hair and the other sinking under the waistband of her pants, Sindri walked her backward until her hamstrings hit the edge of his bed. He swiped at her folds, a single warning before he dipped two fingers into her.

Greer moaned as she fell onto the mattress, realizing, for the first time, that candles lit the room from each corner. She looked up at him, seeing the layers of brown reflecting against the closest flame, and he released her long enough to drag her pants over her hips with one resolving jerk.

She felt the chilled air from a drafty window waft against her, pebbling her skin, as Sindri straightened to stare down at her. A predator's gaze. He licked his lips when he reached down to unbuckle his pants, stroking himself once as he watched her. He released his hold on his cock long enough to crawl toward her and settle himself between her thighs, cradled awkwardly and incompatibly in the dip of her hips. Greer opened her mouth to tell him to taste her with his tongue when she felt him nudging at her entrance, his head widening her.

Whatever. That'll do.

Sindri thrust his hips forward, sliding into her with one clunky jerk. Greer moaned in pleasure edged with pain as he withdrew before sheathing himself again. His face contorted into that of concentration, his fists bracketing her head as he began to piston in and out of her.

Greer struggled to keep up, agitation boiling under the surface of her skin. She had come here to forget, be touched, and be pleasured. Not...this. Not irritatingly lousy sex. She wrapped her legs around his waist, flipping him onto his back. He stopped moving, shock flicking over his features, as she braced herself with her hands on his chest.

"I'm tired of you men pretending to know what to do," Greer said through gritted teeth. "If you don't know how to please a woman, I'll do it myself."

Her fingernails dug into his chest, where crescent-shaped carvings appeared on his skin. Sindri let out a gasp, his eyes widening, as she lined herself up with his cock and sank onto it. She circled her hips, rubbing the apex of her thighs against the steel of his shaft.

It wasn't enough.

Straightening her spine, she lowered her fingers and began to coax at her clit, feeling herself moisten under her direction. The build started in her lower belly, cresting as Sindri gripped her hips and pumped into her, matching every stroke.

"Yes, just like that," Sindri murmured, meticulously studying the spot where their bodies met. His lips had parted, his brow furrowed in concentration, as his gaze locked to her sex. "That's it."

Greer drew up and slammed down again and again. Sindri knocked her hand aside, his fingers replacing hers, and they stroked her with every thrust of his hips. She threw her head back, feeling her locks of hair brushing against her shoulders, and she moaned in response.

At least Sindri was receptive to learning.

She felt the heat continue to build in the base of her spine, and Sindri pressed hard against the meeting of her thighs. Her body fractured, speeding her into an orgasm that she could no longer control. She felt him thicken inside of her, and, in the next moment, he found his release as well.

Sindri sat back, gripping her hair and forcing her head back. He planted his teeth at the column of her throat, and she felt those elongated canines dig into her skin. They continued their assault on each other until their bodies relaxed into a state of euphoria. Covered in a sheen of sweat, she swiped the loose locks of hair from her forehead.

"That— that was—" Sindri looked at her like he had found god.

Greer thought she could have done a better job by herself.

Sindri was asleep less than three minutes later, his body curled around her and his hand resting tightly against her hip. A tear slipped from her eye, dripping onto her cheek. His soft snoring echoed in her ear, reminding her that she was emptier and more lonely than an hour before.

EIGHT

SAMAEL

"She spent the night in the city," Azazel said the following day as he ran a finger over the rim of his water goblet. He picked it up and tapped the glass twice against the wooden table in thought before finishing off the rest. "I half-expected her to come back, but..." He trailed off.

Samael said nothing as he rested his forearms on his thighs. The sword on his back shifted between his wings.

He certainly understood Azazel's worry, but the woman, Greer, was in more pain than Azazel could imagine. No amount of concern from him, who was a stranger to her, would change that. On the other hand, Samael only knew from being able to sense it himself.

"I need you to go find her, Samael. A tavern in the square sent a coin request. Start there. Find her and bring her back here."

Samael looked up, his cerulean eyes sweeping over to Azazel. "Is that an order?"

Azazel clicked his tongue. "We both know it is not." He paused to refill his water goblet from the water carafe at the table. "I think she'll be more receptive to you than me, though."

Samael snorted. "I think she'd be more receptive to a venomous snake." He didn't dare echo his empathy for the woman out loud. And certainly not to Azazel.

Azazel shot him a withering look, and Samael held up his hands in surrender. He stood from his seat, the legs of the chair scraping against the stone floor, and said nothing as he left. He felt Azazel's eyes on his back, watching his leather armor move as he walked away.

Samael had once been the leader of kings, ruler of all. But now... Now, he was chasing a drunk through the city and couldn't stop the resentment inside him from building. Resentment for being relegated to babysitting duty, resentment that he couldn't access his never-ending pool of power, which lay just out of grasp, resentment that he was stuck following the orders of a Primordial when he was so much more.

Although, at the very least, being chained to Samsara and Azazel was better than the alternative, the others still bowed when he passed, looked at him with fear and trepidation, and fled when they felt his presence approaching a room.

Samael opened his wings when his boots touched the marble terrace overlooking the valley. Clouds covered the sky, painting the day in a gray hue that only worsened his mood. He splayed the feathers, enjoying the breeze through each attachment as he shook the kinks from the muscles banding his back and shoulders.

Then, he pushed off, rocketing into the sky.

Samael banked to the right, following the curve of the mountain and the trail below into the city. The morning was still early, evident by the fresh smell of thawing frost and the brisk chill of the pending winter. People had just begun to leave their homes, heading to their taverns and shops to start the day.

All souls here, daemon or human, had crawled from the river. Their souls had taken the journey through Samsara to face their choices, a second chance at eternal life gifted to them if they succeeded. And the souls that didn't make it were sequestered as creatures of misery for the rest of their existence.

Some of those devils actually managed to escape Samsara, and that happened occasionally. A horde of them was killed when they attacked Greer less than a week ago, led to her hometown by Eligos, the djinn.

Eligos wasn't the most powerful djinn he had encountered, but he certainly had the ego of one. Samael chuckled when he thought about the djinn being torn apart by a beginner, one not even in control of her magic.

Samael's leather boots touched down in Veritas Square just outside the tavern, which was desolate and dirty compared to night. Trash blew across the cobblestones in the morning wind, coming to a halt against the exterior of the buildings. He could hear the water lapping at the shore, ice creaking as each danced in the waves. The vendor owners, at least, had begun opening their shops. The scent of baking pastries and brewing tea wafted on the cool breeze.

It figured that Greer would make her way here. Samael wished he was surprised.

Letting what power he could access tendril outward like spokes on a wheel, he probed the surrounding area to see if he could sense her further. She was close. He could feel her grief, her sadness.

He cut down an alleyway, and a red-eyed daemon skittered away at his approach.

Samael came upon the wooden door of a townhome in the corner of the alley. The front door faced a pair of garbage bins, where a shifter was curled in wolf form between them. He tempered the urge to sigh but threw the wolf a glare of disgust instead. They merely slept on, matted fur ruffling in the wind.

Samael tried the knob and found the front door was unlocked, as most in the city were, and he tucked in his wings as he entered the apartment. It was outdated, and the fresh scent of the lake was the smell of stale beer, pipe smoke, and females quickly replaced the fresh scent of the lake—multiple females.

Yes, Greer was here.

He ascended the stairs to the second floor, following the path of her power to a bedroom hidden behind another door. His muscles stiffened, and his thoughts were brought to a grinding halt when he sensed her release...mixed with his.

Samael shook the vision away and kicked the door open. It splintered in the frame and fell to the worn carpet, landing on a pile of clothes. He saw Greer jolt from the mattress, wrapping the stained sheet she had been tangled in around her breasts as she scrambled from the bed.

The male, a fae, didn't move quickly enough, so Samael reached forward and yanked the man from the bed. The fae male let out a yell of surprise as he tumbled to the floor with a loud crash, scrambling to cover his lower half with an old, flat pillow.

Samael grasped the man by his long hair and pulled, forcing the male to bear the column of his throat—a position of submission. Samael pricked the skin with the dagger usually sheathed at his hip. He didn't draw blood. He had more restraint than that.

The dramatic entrance was for nothing but his own entertainment. Samael felt an odd sense of pleasure at the fae's sudden shift from lazy morning lust to spine-tinging terror. The male fell from Samael's grasp and landed on his knees, his head bowing at the sight of Samael in his bedroom.

"Are you insane?" Greer cried out, keeping the sheet knotted in a ball at her breastbone. "What are you doing here?"

Samael casually glanced at her, taking the time to scan her tangled curls, flushed cheeks, and swollen lips. "I thought this male had taken advantage of your honor." He wasn't sure, but he had the distinct feeling that the grin and wink he added at the end contributed to the red-faced anger she had woken into.

Greer sucked in a breath, and Samael was sure that fire would explode from her nostrils when she released it. "He didn't take my honor, you pigeon. That's my new friend, Simon."

"It's Sindri, actually," the man said, a pillow still covering his front as he knelt on the ground.

Both ignored him.

Samael narrowed his eyes. "As a demi-primordial–"

"Demi-primordial?" Sindri sputtered out, his eyes darting between Samael and Greer.

"—You are bound to a certain level of reputation, formality, and decorum."

"Formality this," Greer spat back, flashing him a lewd gesture with her left hand.

Sindri's jaw dropped as if he couldn't believe anyone would talk to Samael that way. In Sindri's defense, this was the first time anyone had spoken to Samael that way. No one had the nerve. Samael found that he liked it.

"Classy," Samael replied as he turned back to Sindri. "This is the only daughter of Azazel, Primordial of the Underworld and King of Samsara. It would be in your best interest if you stuck your cock in someone else next time. Azazel isn't known to be the forgiving type."

Greer's eyes widened as Sindri's complexion turned ashen, and in that moment, Samael knew he had crossed a line—perhaps more than one line—between the mention of sex and the threat of Azazel. He wasn't one to walk on eggshells, though, so he committed to firmly stepping over it. His gaze did a lazy sweep back to Greer.

"You are better than mediocre sex to cover up your sadness and shame."

This time, Greer did explode.

Samael put a shield around himself and Sindri just in time to protect themselves from the blast of power coming from Greer. It cracked the walls, shattered the mirror, and flipped the mattress, sending the rest of the covers sprawling to the floor. Her chest heaved with anger as she glared at him, jaw clenched tightly together.

Samael withdrew the shield and reached out to grab Greer's hand. "Now that we have that out of the way, come on. Your father wants you home."

Greer sidestepped his outstretched arm, dragging the sheet with her, and wove around his large wings to storm from the bedroom. Samael bent over to pick up her pile of clothes, briskly following her into the hallway. He spotted her halfway down the stairs, the sheet streaming like a billowing robe behind her. Much to his surprise, the damage from her outburst extended past the bedroom. He found splinters in the ceiling, paintings decorating the walls torn in two, and posts from the stair's handrail hanging precariously from the railing.

"Greer—"

She yanked the front door open, the knob bashing against the wall behind it with an ear-splitting crash.

"You don't have any damn clothes on—"

He grabbed her upper arm, the skin pebbled and cool beneath his touch. She whipped around to grasp his hand to peel away his fingers, but he had already torn it free of her. Glancing down at his fingertips, he saw the pads black and charred.

Seeing he removed his grasp, Greer was already on the move again, her curls rustling in the breeze as she marched away.

Mouth agape, Samael stared after her. No one, not a single creature, had ever burned him before.

Samael spread his wings, the tips tickling each building, flanking the alleyway, and shot into the sky. It was a short flight, only a few hundred feet before he landed in front of her. She halted in her path, the sheet still firmly knotted at her front. Samael grinned down at her, holding the pile of clothing in the space between them.

Greer snatched the pile from his arms with a glower and brushed past him once more. His skin prickled at her touch.

"Do you want a hand back to the palace to change?"

Greer continued her march into the square, which was now beginning to bustle in the glowing morning light. A few vendors had already opened their shops, selling tea and pastries to those heading into work or stumbling to their own beds—those like Greer, for instance. And, as if by divine intervention, a barmaid cracked the door to a tavern called *The Cornerside*, flipped the wooden sign to open, and closed the door again.

Samael snarled in warning as Greer tossed him a victorious smirk over her shoulder before quickly turning to her left and stomping off, her bare feet slapping against the stone as she went. He followed, splaying his hand against the rough wood to hold the door open when she tried to slam it shut behind her.

Greer made a beeline for the bathroom, attracting the bartender's attention, who was wiping a stein with a dirty, wet rag. His eyes followed her, brows high on his forehead, before catching Samael's glare.

The bartender dropped his stare, his hand working quickly against the inside of the stein.

Samael crossed his arms over his chest and spread his legs wide in a defensive stance. He wholly ignored the curvy barmaid who was watching him through thick lashes. His eyes were fixed on the bathroom door, waiting.

Two minutes went by, then five, and finally ten. Samael huffed with agitation, the dark markings surrounding his biceps flashing in the morning light streaming through the front windows. The tips of his wings flicked when he moved, and the bartender sent him a sidelong gaze, now putting away the clean tankards left out to dry from the night before.

Samael couldn't remember the last time he had been in Veritas Square— he certainly didn't go on purpose. The smell of old mead and the stickiness of the floor under his boots only steeled his resolution.

Samael pushed out his power, feeling the magic lash from him, probing and interrogating. He sent that power through the wall, knowing that Greer would have something to say about it when she noticed its examination and felt not even a whisper of her.

He treated it like the cat-and-mouse game that it was: Walk twenty paces, blast of power. Walk another twenty paces, an explosion of power. He had fallen for the oldest trick in the book and was across the tavern, kicking open the bathroom door with his boot. The window had been shoved open, the small curtains rippling in the chilled breeze. On the floor, he spotted the thin sheet she had used wadded into a ball. Anger rippled through him as he spun on the balls of his feet and stalked from the tavern.

Samael sent his power out in a withering blast, trying to locate her amongst a sea of melding magic and auras. He barely felt her, and her quick movements ensured he couldn't hold her location.

He let an agitated sigh whistle through his nose, and treated it like the cat and mouse game that it was. Walk twenty paces, blast of power. Walk another twenty paces, blast of power. He had fallen for the oldest trick in the book, did not even realize that she would dare to try it on him.

It took him nearly an hour of hunting through the city to establish her general presence and another twenty minutes for her to stop walking long enough for him to hone in on her. His jaw clenched when he realized she was in the same tavern she left him in, seemingly circling back around when she thought she lost him.

The Cornerside was busier than it had been, and the barmaid was darting between tables, delivering fresh pots of tea and steaming plates filled with eggs and bacon. Samael spotted Greer at the bar, her hand wrapped around one of the tankards the bartender had been putting away. She wasn't even attempting to hide.

He eddied up next to her, leaning his forearms against the rounded edge of the surface. She took a sip from the tankard, mead by the smell of it, and glanced nonchalantly at the window overlooking the square.

"That took you longer than I expected. The sun is fully risen now."

He felt his jaw tick again, and at that moment, he wished he could toss Greer into the lake without any consequences. "I have limits to my power."

"Is that what you tell all the girls?"

Samael felt a zing of satisfaction at her blanched expression when he sat on the barstool next to her and ordered two breakfast plates. Greer recovered, scoffing and rolling her eyes as she took another drink of mead. He leaned over to pluck the tankard from her hand.

"Hey–" she started, but her face slackened into disbelief as he raised her tankard to his lips and drained it. "You owe me a new one." She raised a hand to flag down the bartender.

Samael pushed the tankard away from him and waited patiently for the bartender to place a second glass in front of Greer. Not a moment after the pewter bottom touched the wood, Samael reached over and took it, downing the mead in three deep gulps.

Greer stared at him.

"You're joking." She turned away to flag down the bartender again, but Samael was already intervening.

"She doesn't require anymore," he said as the bartender approached, the wet rag draped over his shoulder.

The bartender's gaze shifted between Greer's incensed expression and Samael's smug one just as the barmaid placed the two breakfast plates in front of them. Samael watched Greer look down briefly at it and then back up to the bartender. She pushed the plate out of her reach.

That zing of satisfaction Samael had felt mutated into one of disdain.

"You should eat something," he said, shooing the bartender away with a quick flick of his wrist. Greer lifted her hand to call him back, but Samael pushed her hand to the bar. "You don't need any more mead."

"You don't know what I need," she barked back, her stool legs scraping against the wooden floor as she stood.

From the corner of his eye, Samael noticed the tavern patrons studying the scene through sly, subtle glances. Their gazes averted when they connected with his own, returning to their breakfasts with a wolfish vigor that they seemed to have instantly developed.

"Where are you going?"

"Out," Greer replied as she stomped toward the front door, now bolstered open by a large, jagged rock. The breeze blew her lackluster curls, and her eyes squinted against the deluge of sunlight, even from behind the canopy of clouds.

Samael sighed. "To Azazel," he ordered the bartender, who only gave him a curt nod, before following Greer into the square. "Your father wants you back at the palace," he went on as he caught up to her.

Greer paused in front of a storefront, taking in the display of silver jewelry through the glass casing. A moment later, she shoved open the door, the bell above tinkling to signify their arrival. Samael barely managed to hold in the sigh of aggravation caught in his throat. He followed her over the threshold, tucking in his wings.

The shop was relatively small, sized just enough that he knew he would be able to touch wall to wall if his wings were outstretched. On the opposite side of the store were wooden shelves, bolted one on top of the other, each clad with gemstones of amethyst, opal, amber, and turquoise. They ranged in size and price, each harvested from the Crystal Caves in the Meridian of Lust.

On the wall to his right, Samael took in stacked boxes of incense and their melding scents of sage, frankincense, patchouli, and lavender. Each had been powdered and dried by hand. Two sticks were lit, the smoke curling toward the ceiling in a plume of warm sandalwood. The glass casings containing the jewelry were to his left and directly beside the front door. The gemstones inset into the silver prongs glimmered under the light streaming through the front window.

And that is where Greer stood, her hands delicately resting on the casing before her.

The shopkeeper, a younger woman, dark-skinned with long hair tied behind her with a red scarf, appeared from the backroom.

"What can I help you with?" the woman asked, her smile faltering when she caught Samael still hovering near the front door.

"What is the most expensive piece of jewelry you have?" Greer asked, her head tilting to the side as she studied the display counter under her hands.

The shopkeeper chuckled, adjusting the large, oval glasses perched on the bridge of her nose. "The most expensive thing in this shop isn't something you can afford."

Greer's smile turned sickly sweet, and Samael felt his stomach twist at the sight. "I assure you, it is. You can charge it to Azazel."

The shopkeeper paled, her mouth slackening as she stepped away from Greer. "Y–you're the demi-primordial. I heard you were home, but I didn't think–yes, princess. Anything you want." She dipped into a low curtsy, her glasses slipping down her nose.

Samael snorted. "Now you're the princess?"

Greer sent him a scathing look over her shoulder, her dulled eyes lighting with fire for the first time since they had met. His lips curled into a knowing smirk as she turned away from him. He was pleased to see a slight flush had reddened her otherwise sallow cheeks.

"Your Highness, what I have for you today is a teardrop pendant composed of one large saltwater pearl and surrounded by sixty-two perfectly cut diamonds inlaid in the silver setting."

Samael lifted his chin to see further over the top of Greer's head, his brows rising as the shopkeeper removed the velvet pillow from the glass casing and carefully set it on the surface.

"I'll never wear that," Greer admitted, running a hand through her hair. Her fingers tangled at the ends of her strands and she yanked them through with relative ease. "How much?"

The woman swallowed before continuing, and Samael recognized the resulting bob in her throat as nerves. "...Thirty million coins, your highness."

Greer's back straightened, and Samael growled, "Don't you dare."

She didn't bother with another withering look before saying, "I'll take it."

NINE

GREER

Greer took the pendant and immediately threw it into the lake. It sailed through the air, hit a piece of ice floating in the waves, and slid into the depths of the water. A smug smile quirked her mouth as she dramatically clapped her hands together, as if wiping off a layer of dirt, and turned back toward the square.

"Are you happy with yourself?" Samael asked, his tone flat and unamused.

"A little bit, yes." Greer swept her eyes around the square, taking in each shop and tavern, all open and busy. "Are you going to follow me around, or are you going to report back to Azazel?"

Samael's jaw clenched. "I was ordered to stay with you until I can convince you to return."

Greer made a noise of interest from the back of her throat. "Should we go shopping, then? I see a nice little cart over there with leather-made bags."

"Are you going to throw everything in the lake?"

Greer chuckled under her breath as they crossed the square. Daemons and people, each venturing into the early afternoon markets for fresh vegetables and meat, eyed Samael and his sword with tentative stares. She wished he would, at the very least, walk ten paces away from her to limit the attention on herself. She knew it wasn't worth requesting— she had already burned that bridge by shimming out of the bathroom window mere hours ago.

"I'm not a monster," Greer replied, sweeping her hair into a messy bun near the top of her head. "I'm not going to do that to anything handmade."

Samael laughed, and the sound rumbled unexpectedly in Greer's chest. "Makeba is one of the better jewelry makers in the city," he pointed out as he casually strode across the bricked street at her side as though it were something they did every day. "I'm sure she wouldn't appreciate knowing you tossed her prized piece in the water."

Greer tripped over an upturned brick, and her head twisted upward to gape at him. "You're joking. She— she made that?"

He laughed again, his eyes sparkling with mocking amusement. "I have no idea. I've never met her before."

Greer blinked before her pained expression shifted into a snarl. "That wasn't funny."

Samael pressed his lips together in a poor attempt to hide his laugh. "I thought it was."

Scoffing, she turned back toward the cart, watching as the canvas covers flapped in the breeze. The wind picked up the scent of freshly dyed leather, the smoky hide mixing with traces of tobacco. She reached upward, brushing her fingers against the soft suede. The buckles on the bag were copper, and Greer found herself staring at them long enough to attract the attention of the owner.

He emerged from the other side of the cart, his shirt sleeves rolled to his elbows, exposing his tanned, muscular forearms. The black, leather smock he wore was stained with dyes. "How may I help you?"

"This bag is expertly made." The man dipped his chin in thanks as Greer dropped her hand from the thin strap she had been playing with. "How much?"

"One hundred and ten coins."

"I'll take it."

The man reached up to remove the bag from a hook before wrapping it in a linen cloth he retrieved from a storage compartment under the cart. "Coin?"

"Coin request. Under Azazel."

The man's fingers stopped moving, still threaded in the cloth. His shoulders stiffened as he glanced at her sidelong. "We were notified of your removal from the request account less than two minutes ago."

Greer blinked again; this time, her face upturned with a bemused smile. A giggle escaped her lips, followed by a snort of a chuckle. Then, she turned away and doubled over, clutching her sides. She howled with laughter for a long moment, finally straightening when Samael wound around the cart, an air of forced indifference surrounding him. He leaned to the side, resting an elbow on the lip of the cart.

Greer wiped the tears from her cheeks, feeling the rosy flush filling her face. "He did quick work of that, didn't he?" She gestured toward the bag, still wrapped in linen under the vendor's hands. "I'm sure I'll be back."

The vendor cleared his throat. "Do you want me to stow it for you, princess?"

Greer bristled, her voice turning cold. "I'm not a princess."

"You were an hour ago," Samael goaded her. "What changed?"

Greer felt a roiling heat grow in her belly, utter contempt overtaking her mood in one big wave. Her fingers curled at her sides as she turned away from him. Her lips pinched together in an attempt to bite back the ugly pigeon-filled insult threatening to bubble up her throat.

The clouds parted above her just long enough for the sun to coat her face in a sudden warmth, and the waning chill sent a shiver up the back of her neck. Spinning on the balls of her feet, Greer marched toward the path that carved its way back up the mountain.

If Azazel wanted her back in the palace so badly, that is precisely what he would get.

Samael entered into step next to her, and Greer, not bothering to look at him, could hear the sheath of his sword creak against the fighting leathers he wore. The crowd, thickening as the day approached the lunch hour, split as they walked, eyes darting toward them, looking them up and back down again before averting their gaze entirely.

"I could fly us to the top of the mountain," Samael said. The path turned upward, and the beginning of the grade change burned the back of Greer's legs. "Save us the trouble."

"I think I'll walk, thank you," Greer replied, ignoring the sweat dripping down her lower back and her chest tightening with each breath. It had been much easier to make her way down the mountain the night before.

Samael said nothing, but Greer could feel his smirk brushing over her.

They entered the neighborhood of the stately mansions, gardeners flitting over the flowers like a colony of bumblebees. Trimmers snipped at hedges, dirty gloves pulled at weeds, the smell of freshly tilled earth filling Greer's nostrils as they made their way up the switchbacks. Greer wanted to sit down. No, she wanted to collapse on the dirt path until her heart stopped rattling her ribcage. Sweat was dripping in rivulets down her temples now, stray hairs sticking to the side of her face. She couldn't believe she had ever been cold and scraped the hair away with a trembling hand. Her swallow was heavy and dry as she glanced at Samael.

He was infuriatingly calm, his breath even and unchanged. The feathers of his gray wings seemed to ripple under the sun's thin bands of light streaming through the clouds.

If she had even an inkling less stubbornness, she would have conceded and allowed him to fly her up the mountain. Alas, she didn't, so she wouldn't. She kept walking, one foot in front of the other.

Greer's eyes lifted toward the palace, still small and too far away for her liking. She turned her focus inward, trying to ignore the blister forming on the back of her heel and the seizing muscles in her thighs with every step. When she finally reached the marble terrace of the palace, she let herself crumple on the landing. Ignoring Samael's snort of reprove, she sighed with relief when she laid her heaving chest against the cool stone.

"Thirty million coins is quite impressive for your first outing to the city," a voice above Greer said.

Greer smiled as she glanced up, spotting Azazel a few feet from her, his arms crossed tightly over his chest. "I could have done more damage." She paused to settle her cheek against the stone. "But you were quicker than I thought you would be."

Azazel's boots were silent against the marble as he closed the gap between them. He dropped into a squat beside her, and before Greer knew it, his hand had threaded into the locks of her bun, and her head was yanked back in a show of force. Her overconfident smirk melted as her hand shot upwards, her fingernails scraping at the back of his hand.

"You will return whatever you bought immediately." His tone was low and threatening, and Greer felt her scalp biting with pain as he kept a tight hold on her hair. "And you will apologize for your behavior."

Greer managed to rip herself from his grasp, leaving a sizable amount of stray hairs between his clamped fingers. Rubbing at the sore spot on her head, she pushed herself to stand and directed a burning glare toward Azazel. "It's at the bottom of the lake," she seethed. "And I won't be apologizing to anyone." Much to her dismay, her voice trembled, but she compelled it to steady as she continued.

"You brought me here. You *made* me come here. And I'm going to make your life absolute–"

Azazel flicked his wrist, vast boredom covering his features.

"—fucking hell." Greer was back in the deep plum bedroom as she finished her sentence.

It looked just as she had left it, save for the perfectly made bed and the water cleaned up from the bathroom floor. She let out a cathartic scream of anger, turning toward the wooden door to track down Azazel and finish their argument when it cracked open.

Arista stepped inside, a tray of food tucked against her forearm. Her body jolted as she stuttered to a stop at the sight of Greer, her eyes wide as her mouth popped open. "I– I didn't realize you were here," she began, hastily dropping into a curtsy. "I brought lunch in case, but–"

Greer wasn't listening or paying the slightest bit of attention to the handmaiden who had stepped over the threshold. Her eyes were fixed on the food tray, where a bowl of tomato soup had spilled with Arista's curtsy. The red liquid dripped from the side of the tray, tracking in thick, grotesque lines down the front of Arista's linen dress.

Greer thought the oxygen had been removed from the room. Her heartbeat became irregular and jarring, and her breath sawed out in a series of short bursts. A heat washed over her, followed by a douse of cold so immense that her body broke out in a sheen of sweat. Her stomach churned as her insides quivered, and she felt a sharp pang of discomfort at being inside despite the vast openness of the bedroom.

"Your– Greer?" Arista started.

Greer was hyperventilating, choking on the air that refused to expand her lungs. The simmer of power that brewed just under her skin rose to a boil, and even though she told herself that the red stains were soup, she quickly realized she couldn't contain the imminent burst of magic. Opening her mouth to tell Arista to run, Greer was too late. Magic erupted from her like a shooting star, colliding with everything in its path. Glass shattered, the stone walls cracked with a deafening boom, and Arista let out a marked gasp as the power hit just below her heart.

Arista crumpled to the ground, the tray slipping from her grasp and hitting the floor with a tinkling clatter of porcelain against stone. The bowl of soup flipped upside down as it fell, messily coating Arista's front. It mixed with the blood pouring from the shredded injury on her chest, various shades of red now staining the powder blue dress.

"Arista— *Arista*!" Greer cried out as she stumbled forward, landing painfully on her knees, as she collapsed next to the wounded handmaiden. Greer's fingers trembled as she placed her palms on the gushing laceration, pink tissue puckering under the ripped flesh. Blood pooled between her fingers, leaking into the divots of her knuckles. "Help. *Help*!" The words cracked in her throat.

It only took a moment for heavy steps to echo into the landing of the hallway, leaving Greer to wonder if the librarian had heard the commotion before Greer's shout for assistance. The female, seemingly not much older than Greer with black wings and sharp, brown eyes, lifted her robes to kneel at Arista's side, jingling the links around her waist.

Arista's face was pale, her eyes still wide with shock.

Greer scrambled backward as she glanced down at her hands to find them caked with Arista's drying blood. Her back hit the wall behind her as she curled her arms over herself and tucked her head between her knees. Wracking sobs pulled from the depths of her soul as she lifted her head long enough to watch the librarian struggle to fix the damage she had done.

Azazel and Samael surged into the room a heartbeat later. Azazel knelt next to Arista and immediately administered his controlled power to heal the gaping wound Greer had left.

On the other hand, Samael's attention was wholly on Greer as he took quick strides toward her from across the room.

His hands, calloused and rough against her cheeks, were still gentle as he assessed her. Fingers scraped against her brow with each attempt to pull Greer's arms from the locked position above her head. But Greer rocked on her tailbone, trying to ignore the painful cries from Arista. Cries that only reminded her of the last gurgling breaths Paige had taken.

It was Greer's fault. It was all her fault. She did this. She couldn't help herself. She couldn't help any of them.

"Greer. *Greer.*" Samael's defiant tugs became stronger, but his voice sounded muffled as if she were underwater.

The roaring wind rushed past her ears, fading any noise into the background. And Samael was ready when that second wave of power crested over and blasted through.

He covered them in a shield of his own magic, and Greer's power ricocheted off his. When their powers intertwined, a flash of brilliant, white light emitted before fading into the ether again.

"Greer," Samael was still saying, a hand planted firmly between her shoulder blades. "Greer, Arista is fine. She's fine. She's already awake."

But Greer didn't look up. Still rocking and still sobbing, she let the feeling of shame pull her down deeper into herself until all she knew was darkness and the knowledge that she was a danger to everyone around her.

TEN

ODETTE

The voice was cold and sharp as its owner pressed the edge of the blade into Odette's throat. "Up," it said, digging the sword's point further.

Odette lifted her chin and slowly rose from the ground, the front of her shirt and both cheeks sticky with mud. "Turn." Odette obeyed, her stare catching the man's cold, rage-filled eyes. "Don't think about it," he warned as her eyes glided toward the soaked bag at her feet. "I can run you through before you reach the strap."

Odette's gaze snapped back to her captor's just as a wave crested over the tops of her shoes, dumping water into her soggy socks and sinking her deeper into the wet sand.

"The Lord will be very pleased to see you, I'm sure," the male said with a wicked grin. He reached to his side with his free hand and pulled a pair of clanking metal handcuffs from the belt around his waist. He clasped them onto Odette's wrists, and she felt the immediate dullness of her magic as if someone were stifling a fire within her.

Obsidian. Intruders were not welcome in the fae realms, and while she was unhappy with the less-than-warm greeting, she understood. The handcuffs were temporary until she reached the palace and could plead her case to Nerea's father.

Odette was marched up the sandy beach, her wet shoes sliding against the loose dunes and waving seagrass lining the shore. She glanced over her shoulder, taking in the closing rift for the last time. It zipped shut, sealing her in. Blowing out a small breath to temper the anxiety growing inside her, she squared herself toward the jungle that mimicked the one she had just left. She peered up at the male faerie, his eyes as golden as a hawk and just as fierce, and his nose was dented as if someone had broken it long ago.

While Odette knew he appeared young, at the most in his mid-thirties, she also knew that he had to be an experienced and well-respected guard to land the duty of protecting the rift. His pace quickened as he stepped in front of her, tugging on the chains at her wrists. She glanced over his back as he led her past the washed-up driftwood and scattering of seashells strewn along the sand. His build was tall and slender, clad in a green tunic with polished wooden buttons. Darker green slacks and boots covered his lower half, held up by the black leather belt with a sheath and loop for the handcuffs now around her wrists.

The sheath was empty, and the sword usually encased in it was held tightly in his right hand. His other hand held her duffel bag, still water-logged and filled with her sword and daggers.

The male led her onto a muddy path that split the jungle, and if she had not been in this position, it would have been a peaceful hike. Ferns, fallen trees covered in thick moss, and short plants with large, vibrantly colored, blossomed flowers covered the jungle floor like a blanket. Towering trees with leaves the size of her wingspan made up the canopy, protecting against the piercing sun rising where the sky met the sea. Chirping birds and chattering monkeys filled the space surrounding her, while the leaping of larger cats from one branch to the next made the wood creak dangerously.

The humid air carried a heavy scent of fresh water, and a thundering river came into view a few moments later. They crossed a wooden bridge that spanned a waterfall crashing over the craggy rocks below, foam floating on the turbulent surface. Rainbows danced on the misty haze that sprayed upward.

As Odette continued through the jungle, the forest floor opened to clearings made up into small villages. The huts, set high into the trees with ladders braided from vines that swayed in the breeze, were bustling with bronze-skinned fae. Females hung tunics and sewn dresses over the sides of the wooden railings that wrapped the balconies. Children swung to and fro on the vines dangling from the canopy, their legs wrapped around the spindly plants as they let out shrills of laughter. Males seated in a half-circle on the forest floor watched the children, broad smiles on their faces.

One fae child, a teenage girl, was settled on the bank of a fast-moving stream. Her feet were plunked into the cool water, and her hands were lifted into the air, playing with water droplets she had suspended around her. They floated like bubbles, colliding with one another before popping and sending the water raining back into the stream.

They passed village after village, and the homes were built closer and closer to the ground as they approached the edge of the jungle. Odette's hair, loose from her braid, clung to the back of her neck from the humidity. And, though they had been walking for hours, her clothes were still damp and heavy.

Finally, just as the sun arced to its apex on its trek across the sky, the pathway turned from dirt to the same basalt stone that made up the canyon walls of Iguazu Falls. Odette lifted her gaze for the first time in a while, her neck sore from craning to look for uplifted roots and skittering lizards on the trail.

A decadent palace stood before her, surrounded by a tall, basalt stone wall connected on both sides by a black, wrought iron gate, with three soldiers standing guard on each side. Odette felt her heart sink in her chest at the unfamiliar sight as she was led up the path, her legs shaking from exhaustion and adrenaline. This stone wall had not been built the last time she visited, nor did she think Nerea's father would allow it.

He always preferred to have open access to the villagers under his rule.

The two soldiers closest to the gate broke formation in unison, each grasping a handle and tugging the doors apart. The doors split, revealing the continued path toward the palace. She darted her gaze around the familiar grounds as they crossed the threshold of the wall. Waterfalls, the water reversed and flowing upward toward the sky, were spread along the interior of the border wall. Large flora with orange, pink, and yellow flowers bloomed along the path, and lone canopy trees dotted the expertly trimmed front lawns.

The deep breath Odette took was tanged with the smell of cut grass. It was a fresh scent starkly different from that of the Court of Storm and Wind, her homeland. In her mind, there was no wonder the families in the villages were spending time outdoors— she certainly would too if she grew up here. The Court of Storm and Wind, where her father had sat as king, was rocky, cloudy, and cold on a good day. Unlike everyone else she grew up with, Odette still spent most of her time outside, preferring the grassy knolls and stone outcrops to the crackling fires lining the halls. Her mother would have to drag her inside when her fingertips had shriveled, and her lips were tinged blue.

Odette was tugged to the steps leading up to the palace, yanking her from her thoughts. She took them slowly, her gaze still sweeping across the open-air courtyard that fronted the Lord of Mist and Tide's home.

Four pools of water, each marble basin carved into a square, were set into the ground and sported a differently shaped fountain installed in the center. Waterways had been dug to connect the four pools, each funneling water from one to the next like a circular river. Marble bridges devoid of handrails spanned the artificial streams, creating walkways connecting one side of the garden.

A breeze flowed through the courtyard, ruffling the leaves of the ferns planted at the foot of each statue. And, for the first time, Odette realized the statues had been replaced. At one time, each statue represented one of the four courts of the fae, but now, there were four statues of the same male. Her heart sank further when she recognized the face carved into the marble.

"This way," her male soldier said as he whisked her up the stairs to the first set of large, wooden doors. The gold framing the edge glinted in the sunlight, and Odette had to squint against the overwhelming shine.

Two more soldiers were posted on each side of the double doors, and they, too, turned in unison to tug the doors open as they set foot on the landing. The formality of the palace was new to Odette, as the Court of Mist and Tide was long considered the most relaxed of the four.

Nonetheless, Odette was ushered into the throne room— the basalt stone of the garden ending where a deep green marble flooring began.

Floor-to-ceiling pillars constructed from the same deep green were rimmed with gold at their bases. Wooden sconces lit with a soft flame had been affixed to each pillar, emanating a calming glow through the silent hall. The cut-outs on the wall for windows contained no glass barrier, allowing the breeze to flutter the flames, sending the shadows to dance across the floor. The same green marble crept up the stairs leading to the dais on the other end of the long hall, where a throne made of gold was erected.

"My Lord," the soldier said as he approached, bowing to the faerie seated on the throne. The Lord's legs were crossed, each arm settled on a green-cushioned armrest. "We had an unexpected guest come through the rift early this morning. I believe you will recognize the general to the former Fae King, Odette Milne."

Odette lifted her eyes to the Lord of Mist and Tide, her breath stuttering as she focused on the male. This was...not Nerea's father. This was his son and Nerea's younger half-brother, Kaique. Nearly as old as Odette with half the experience, Kaique trailed behind Adair like a puppy to a child when he visited her father's court on royal business.

This was bad. This was very, very bad.

Kaique stood from his throne, descending the stairs with purposeful steps. "Renan, my friend, she is a guest," he admonished with a smile, the familiar dimple forming on his left cheek. He assessed Odette in a way that made her want to squirm. She held her stance. "Please remove the handcuffs from the general. This isn't how we greet our visitors."

The guard, Renan, immediately stepped forward and unlocked the cuffs with the key tucked next to his sheathed sword. He managed to grab the iron chains before they crashed to the marble floor. Odette massaged her wrists just as Kaique waved his hand. The droplets of water that had kept her clothes damp were ripped from the fabric, leaving her warm and dry.

"That's better, isn't it?" Kaique replied, and Odette politely smiled in return.

Upon his approach, a deliberate decision to stand on the bottom step to stay a head above her, Odette could take a better look at him in the light from the sconces. His skin was the same bronzed complexion as Renan and the families in the villages, and his hair and eyes were dark brown. His ears were pointed, the only thing between subspecies of fae that remained similar. His tunic was also colored the same green as Renan's, though his was hemmed with threads of gold to mark his status.

"Thank you...my Lord," Odette returned with a curtsy, the motion unnatural when directed at him.

Kaique turned his back to her, climbing the stairs of the dais once again. "I'm surprised to see you here. The Court of Mist and Tide is difficult to travel to, especially unexpectedly."

Odette drew in a breath, her mind scrambling to procure an explanation that didn't involve Nerea. "Yes, you are correct. It was a long journey." She paused to lock eyes with him as he settled back onto his throne. "I am here to inquire about your allyship with the Fae King and whether you would consider realigning your vision with my own." From the corner of her eye, she saw Renan, who had remained beside her, still, the knuckles of his fists whitening as they tightened around the manacles.

Kaique's brows rose as he steepled his fingers in front of him. "Interesting. With your felt absence from the fae realm for two hundred years, I must ask. Why now?"

Odette allowed a long heartbeat to pass before answering. "The Mage has reappeared," she started slowly. Kaique's smile slid from his lips. "The Fae King has been caught working with the Paladin Society and Eligos to overturn the human realm. I'm asking you and your court's assistance to stop him from furthering his plans."

Kaique was quiet for a moment, the only sound echoing through the hall being the fountain's streaming water from the garden. He studied her, eyes narrowed. "Have you met her? This Mage?"

"Yes. I worked closely with her for the last few weeks—that is, until she killed Eligos."

A shiver of satisfaction shot up Odette's spine as Kaique's composure slipped, his hands falling into his lap. "Killed Eligos? Is that— that cannot be possible."

"I assure you, it was. I witnessed it."

Kaique crossed his legs once again, bobbing his foot in the air. "You have intimate knowledge of how one obtains a throne, whether it be Lord or King." His smile grew as he watched for her reaction. However, Odette didn't allow a flicker of hurt or surprise to thread her expression. "I was shocked to hear of Adair's betrayal against your father, how he slit your father's throat and watched as the blood soaked into the linens he slept in. Then he took your mother as his own before removing her wings and discarding her over the edge of the nearest cliff." He paused to let the weight of his words sink into Odette, goading her into a response. When she gave him none, he finished with, "It was said that you could hear the crack of her skull against the rock echo across the valley."

Odette trembled with rage, her fingers curling into fists behind her back. Kaique had always been callous and cold-blooded, preferring to watch the torturing of others instead of learning the ways of his people. Odette wasn't sure how he had descended from the same kind man who helped create Nerea.

"As you can see," Kaique went on as he gestured to himself and the throne he sat upon. "I took inspiration from Adair." In place of his ever-growing smirk, his jaw clenched so tightly that Odette heard his teeth grind together. "I went to him, requesting his alliance in the ongoing battle for the fae realms. And he rejected my offer." A cold chuckle escaped his lips, the sound rumbling over Odette's prickled skin. "He doesn't trust those who kill their superiors, ironically enough, and he couldn't align with someone who showed the ambition to do so."

"I'm not sure what you're asking, my Lord," Odette said through gritted teeth, keeping her voice as light and unencumbered as possible.

"I haven't been privy to the goings-on of the other courts," Kaique said, his voice dropping and turning into a pout that made Odette look up at him in disgust. He didn't seem to notice. But you were raised in it, submerged in it from the earliest of ages. You are going to teach me."

Odette's lips parted in surprise, and her fingers unfurled as they slacked behind her. Her initial and immediate reaction was to say no, though she read his underlying warning. She would teach him, or he would use her to secure that alliance. One way or another, she was still stuck in the fae realm for the next three months, and she knew she needed to protect herself from him.

She lifted her chin, her braid shifting between her iridescent wings. "Sounds as though I don't have a choice."

"Turning you into Adair does nothing to help me gain the trust of the other Lords who no longer support the Fae King. The Courts of Flame and Ember or Cedar and Sand have seceded from the realm. Both do not recognize my claim to the throne. With your assistance, they will. Renan, please assist our guest to her chambers. I'm sure she'll find them accommodating."

With that said, Kaique dismissed Odette with a wave of his hand.

ELEVEN

GREER

Following Arista's injury, Greer spent the night curled in the corner of her bedroom, tucked between the four-poster bed and the stone wall. It was the only place she felt safe enough to be.

Safe for both herself and the others stuck in the palace with her.

She had fallen asleep but awoke quickly at the rap against the wooden door. Her neck was tight and cricked from dozing off against the stone, but she ignored her aching muscles as she straightened to peer over the top of the mattress.

Arista bustled in, pausing at the threshold to sweep her gaze around the room. She sighed when her eyes connected with Greer's. "Did you sleep there all night?"

Greer sank below the level of the plush mattress, her eyes once again in line with the wooden frame of the bed. "You shouldn't be in here," she managed to reply in a rasping, dry voice. "You almost–"

"I'm not afraid of you," Arista retorted. Greer might have believed her if it wasn't for the waiver in the final word.

Greer settled against the wall, stretching her legs forward until her feet were tucked under the bed. "You should be."

Arista's shoes tapped against the stone as she approached, depositing a pile of freshly laundered towels on the bed and a pot of tea, steaming from the spout, onto the table. "I'm fine. Your father healed me."

"He's not–" Greer sighed, keeping her head below the level of the mattress. "I'm sorry." She quickly cleared the lump that had grown in the base of her throat. "For everything." Absent-mindedly, she began to pick at the loose thread hanging from the hem of the down feather bedding.

Arista stilled, and Greer saw her feet shuffle in discomfort. "You don't need to apologize, your grace. I'm here to–"

"No, I do need to apologize." Greer paused to pull herself to her knees, resting her chin on the edge of the mattress. She looked over at Arista, half expecting her dress to be stained with blood as it had been the night before. Instead, Arista stood tall, her hair pulled into a smooth bun at the back of her head. "I've been really awful to you and–" She cleared her throat again, blinking away tears gathering in the corners of her eyes. "You've been nothing but nice to me. And I almost killed you."

Arista stifled a sigh, glancing down to watch her entwined fingers. "You wouldn't have killed me. It would have been a slow recovery, but I would have survived whether your father interfered or not."

Greer lifted her chin to inspect Arista. "Did you, I mean, what are you?"

"What do you mean?"

Greer straightened to standing, crossing her arms over her chest. "When did you die?" She smelled the light aroma of brewing mint tea with her deep, calming breath.

Arista's face opened in realization, her wings shifting as she clasped her hands in front of her. "I'm not— I've never— I'm a Primordial, like your father." She laughed to herself, shaking her head. "No, not like your father. I'm not a legion general. I'm a Lesser Primordial. The Primordial of Fertility and Beauty, to be exact."

Greer's lips parted in surprise. "You're a Primordial? And you're—" She stopped herself from saying what had bubbled to the surface.

Arista must have understood, for she responded, "Michael and your father split the Lesser Primordials into two. Some stayed in Elysia, and some came to Samsara. I was picked to come here. My magic doesn't translate in a land fueled by the most powerful Primordial in the universe, so here I am."

"When you were in Elysia, did it? Translate, I mean."

Arista nodded. "I've been bound, similar to the other Primordials in Samsara." She lifted her wrist, where a dark, rune-like mark was cast just on the inside of it. She tugged her sleeve back into place, covering it. "Samael's markings are bigger. His power is harder to contain."

"Samael? Azazel's right-hand man?"

Arista bit her lip, trying to quash the smile tugging at her mouth. "Don't let him hear you say that. He's much more than any of us."

"What is he?"

Arista surveyed her before letting her gaze fall to the towels she had set on the bed. "That's his story to tell."

"Did you— did you want to come here?"

"Does anyone want to be forced from their homeland?" Realizing her snapped reply, Arista's neck splotched into flushed red. "His Majesty was hoping you would join him for breakfast."

The change in conversation was abrupt, and Greer felt her stomach churn icy and cold as she looked away, staring unseeingly out of the circular window overlooking the city. "I don't want to go to breakfast."

Arista rubbed the back of her neck in discomfort. "He thought you might say that, so he wanted me to tell you that if you denied his request..." She trailed off for a moment before rushing out the next statement. "That he would send Samael up here to retrieve you himself."

Greer's gaze swept from the window and fell to the linen clothes she still wore. Arista's dried blood was blotted across the front of the shirt. The pants, well-worn and stained with spilled mead, were crinkled from lying on the floor of Sindri's bedroom.

Arista, seemingly reading her mind, said, "You have time to bathe. That's why I brought the fresh towels."

Greer felt like she was walking to her execution as she followed Arista down the hallway that overlooked the library. Out of habit, she stuck to the shadows of the large marble columns to keep away from the prying eyes of the people down below.

The rustling of pages, wings flapping, and feet echoing on the stone floor reminded her of the library she once sought refuge back when she was working in Oregon. A pair of winged creatures, fae by the looks of their pointed ears, were chatting to each other as they perused the stacks nearest the massive double doors.

Greer stepped deeper into the shadows as every face swept upward to glance at Arista. Her chin lifted a tick as Greer followed her into the spiral staircase. They descended to the familiar hallway, two-storied and bedecked in marble, but Arista made a sharp left at the landing and crossed the threshold of a door hidden in the shadows of the mezzanine.

The wooden door, shaped to match the wooden arches set against the walls, had no handle. It blended so well, in fact, that Greer wouldn't have known it was a door if Arista hadn't pushed against it. The door opened to a hallway similar to the stairwell— stone and devoid of any decor save for the lit sconces. Her footsteps echoed against the walls and floors, slapping loudly compared to Arista's gentle ones.

Greer continued to follow Arista down the long hallway, growing colder with every step away from the heated areas of the palace. After a few more minutes of walking, Greer stayed at least ten feet behind Arista at all times. The narrow hall opened to a chamber where a sweeping staircase clad in ruby red carpet stood erect. Unlike the spiraling staircases Greer had seen, this one was flush against the stone wall. Each corner landing was sharply square, directly opposing the elegant others.

Arista lifted the hem of her linen dress with a delicate pinch between her fingers, revealing slippered feet. She began the ascent, briefly glancing over her shoulder at Greer.

Seeing her quite a few feet back, her smile was soft. She said, "We're almost there. It's his personal dining area."

Greer lurched forward with a sigh, clomping one foot onto the first step. The sound was a dull thud that barely echoed off the thick carpet.

"Would you walk all this way if it wasn't for me?" Greer asked as she approached the first landing. A slit of a window had been cut in the stone, and a chilled breeze wafted in through the tight passage, whistling as it went through.

Arista seemed surprised by the question, so she slowed down to answer. "No, we would fly. Each region of the palace has a platform for arrival or exiting." She paused for a moment. "I don't mind the walk, though."

"I'm starting to believe you don't mind much of anything."

Arista giggled, a tinkling laugh that made Greer's stomach clench in shame. "High threshold, I guess."

Greer was quiet for a long minute as they walked up the stairs, her heart pumping erratically in her chest. Her lower belly was still tight and twisted, shame worming behind her navel at the thought of Paige's reaction to Greer's recent behavior. "I'm sorry...for how I treated you when I got here," she felt compelled to say for the second time that morning.

Now holding the door at the top of the staircase, Arista sent her a small smile. "I was stolen from my homeland many millennia ago, and I, too, harbored anger for it. Thank you for the apology, but it was an unnecessary one."

Greer skirted by Arista, crossing the doorway into a cavernous corridor. The hall extended nearly the length of the university football stadium back in Oregon, the stone of the walls and floors a smooth gray. Hanging from the high, arched ceiling were three massive, circular chandeliers, each two-tiered and covered in lit pillar candles the color of ivory. They emitted a soft glow through the hall, shadows from the flames dancing high on the stone above their heads.

Four alcoves carved into the stone, evenly spaced from one another on each side of the hall, contained statues of winged figures holding spheres and scrolls. Their faces were blank and inexpressive, and their gazes turned down toward the floor.

"The Higher Primordials who led the battle against Elysia," Arista said, catching Greer staring at each one as they passed. "Each leads a Meridian and, in turn, the legions of Lesser Primordials that reside there."

"Will I meet them?" Greer asked as she paused to look up at a woman's face, her feminine features hardened for battle.

Arista nodded. "They come to sit for court every so often. They mostly stick to themselves now, awaiting Azazel's plans to overthrow Elysia once again."

Greer's head snapped over to Arista. "Again?"

"Yes. The war ended in a treaty." Arista looked upward toward a statue nearest the end of the hall. The man had deep grooves carved into his unnaturally beautiful face and scars made from years of war. A dagger was clutched tightly in his outstretched hand, the fingers wrapped around the gemstone-encrusted hilt. "Michael and Azazel are fated to battle one final time, though the exact wording of the prophecy is kept from those outside of your father's inner circle."

Greer said nothing as she continued to stare up at the statue of the female Primordial before her. A handful of minutes had passed before she realized that Arista was standing at the end of the hall, her hand propping the door open as she patiently waited for Greer to be finished.

Hesitantly, Greer pulled away from the statues and exited through a second arched wooden door. The corridor opened to a throne room, large enough that the entirety of the palace library could have fit comfortably inside. Sconces had been fixed to each towering column, and the torches set inside were extinguished. The sweeping ceilings were bedecked with nearly another dozen of the same two-tiered chandeliers, and the lit pillar candles cast a ghostly glow across the empty hall. And it was there, flush to the wall and tucked under a circular window containing panes of stained glass, a stone dais had been built.

Spanning the width of the hall, the dais sat atop three long steps and held eight thrones spaced evenly along the platform. Each empty throne was equal to the next and made of the same smooth, black stone the columns flanking the hall had been. The only difference from one to the other was a single gemstone embedded into the headrest of each seat.

Citrine, ruby, amethyst, moonstone, topaz, pyrite, amazonite, and jasper.

"When court is in session, and the Higher Primordials are here, this is where they oversee Samsara." Arista's voice echoed through the empty hall, flitting over the stone. "But that isn't often." She cleared her throat as she approached a third door just to the left of the dais. "Come, the formal dining is just off the throne hall."

"I thought we were going to Azazel's private dining area?" Greer asked, crossing in front of the dais.

Arista's face was half hidden in shadow as she pushed open the final door, exposing a sliver of a long wooden table just beyond the threshold. "We are," she said swiftly, "His Majesty uses the formal dining for his private residence when the court is out of session."

Greer noted the subtle shift of Arista's tone. The warm voice once straddling the line of friendly had hardened to one shared between royal and handmaiden. And when Greer peeked into the dining room, she knew why.

At the head of the long, wooden table sat Azazel, his brilliantly white wings splayed over the low-backed chair, illuminated against the roaring fireplace. His fingers tapped on the dark grain surface as he studied Greer with sharp, gray eyes.

"Sit." Was all he said, tilting his chin in a gesture toward the empty chair at his left.

Greer stepped forward, making it a show to appear overly casual, and sent him a hollow stare that she usually reserved for men she wanted to look down her nose at. He seemed to bristle in irritation as she sank into the cushioned seat, and she couldn't help the smug pull at the corner of her mouth, which only agitated him further.

"I want to talk about your insistence on stretching my generosity," Azazel started as Greer heard the door click behind her. Glancing over her shoulder, Greer realized Arista had evacuated the room just as quickly as she had entered it, leaving Greer alone in the room with her father. Trapped, more like.

"You didn't set any sort of limit," Greer replied as nonchalantly as possible. "I thought I could help myself."

"Spending tens of millions of my coin on a bender was to send a message. Not to help yourself."

"So you caught on then, did you?" Greer spat back before snapping her mouth shut. She drew in a breath to calm herself. "I want to go home."

"You are home."

"This isn't— I'm not—" Greer went quiet again as Azazel cocked his head in amusement. The gesture made a shot of rage rise beneath her skin, tingling her fingertips. She felt a gentle rush of power smother her, tightening against her arms and pricking the base of her spine.

"I'm not in the mood to clean up your mess." Azazel leaned forward to drop a spoonful of eggs on her plate and pour hot tea into the mug to her right. "Eat before it gets cold." He picked up his own fork and knife, cutting into an omelette that had appeared on his gold-brushed plate.

"I'm not hungry," Greer gritted through clenched teeth, crossing her arms over her chest as her stomach flipped in protest. It was a clear lie, one that they both could see through.

Azazel placed a bite of food in his mouth. He chewed slowly, considering her, and Greer briefly wondered if he wished she were the thing between his teeth. A flimsy piece of nothing for him to devour and spit back out. He swallowed, and Greer watched his throat bob, heightening the anxiety coursing through her.

She hadn't ever felt like prey in his presence before, not until that moment. Not until his calm anger prodded at her inner thoughts, flaying her nerves and exposing her without saying a word. Her thoughts trekked back to her first and only conversation with her grandfather, James Whittley. He had told her about her father, detailing that calculating anger that prodded him into covering his house in wards. Greer realized now that his fear was valid and how much of a fool she had been for provoking it.

"That piece of jewelry you purchased," Azazel said, slowly cutting another piece of omelet. He punctured it with the fork, lifted it to his lips, and chewed again. "You'll return it, of course."

This was a game to him, watching her break under his power. Greer bit the inside of her cheek to stop herself from saying what she wanted— that she couldn't see what Holly ever found in him. Instead, she said, "Only if you fish it from the bottom of the lake."

"I could make you fish it from the bottom of the lake." Another bite and more chewing. "The lake is terribly cold this time of year. The ice wouldn't be a friend to you."

Greer's heart skipped a beat. "You wouldn't," she responded quietly. "I don't think Holly would want that, do you? Her only daughter forced to dive into freezing water?"

Azazel stilled at his mate's name, his fingers pausing on the fork hovering above his plate. "Pick up your fork and eat." He never lifted his gaze to look at her and Greer knew from the edge of his tone that this was not the time to press him.

She reached forward and clasped the fork in her hand. She dipped the prongs into the eggs and lifted them into her mouth, chewing slowly. It was the first solid thing she had eaten since coming to Samsara, and her stomach clenched painfully at the soft, decadent taste. Her hunger broke open, and Greer shoveled piles of eggs into her mouth at record speed, barely swallowing before the next forkful was lifting.

"Arista will be pleased you've eaten," Azazel said, and Greer flicked her eyes over to see him staring at her with a bemused expression. "She's been concerned that your clothes are hanging too loosely."

Greer swallowed heavily, following it with a gulp of scalding hot tea, but remained silent.

Azazel placed his fork neatly on the table, aside from his plate. "I want to make you a deal, Greer."

It was Greer's turn to stiffen. She let her hand, extending forward to grab a warm, flaky biscuit from the golden tray in the middle of the table, withdraw back into her lap. Her eyes narrowed with wariness. "What kind of deal?"

"Samael is one of the best teachers in Samsara regarding raw power and weapon wielding. You agree to work with him, get your magic under control, learn how to protect yourself, and I will open a portal to Earth and allow you passage to return...home."

Greer dropped her gaze to her hands. The fire behind Azazel crackled as a log snapped, sending sparks skirting along the patterned rug under their feet. "No," she said, barely above a whisper, as she picked at the edge of her fingernails.

"No?" Azazel quirked a brow, not bothering to hide the look of surprise etched on his face.

Greer looked up, locking eyes with him. They were so similar to her own, from the shape to the color, and she felt like she was talking to a mirror. She cleared her throat. "I'm done making deals. I won't train. I won't use my magic. And I will not wield a weapon."

Azazel's fingers tapped against the wood surface as he had been doing when she entered the dining hall. "Then you won't be returning to the Gaian realm. Do you understand?"

Greer leaned forward, reaching for a biscuit once again. It was warm in her grasp and split with a simple twist of her wrist. Steam poured from the middle like it had just come from the oven, and she popped a piece into her mouth. Buttery and soft, it melted against her tongue. "I guess we'll see about that," she said with a simple shrug, and she could have sworn a brief twinkle of approval flashed in his gray eyes.

TWELVE

ODETTE

Odette was led by Renan to the royal apartment afforded to her by Kaique, and when he opened the door, the large greeting room was revealed. The wooden floors were covered with thick, green rugs, and the banana wood furniture, delicately made, was set in the middle of the room. Two pine doors flanked the room, one on the right and the other on the left. She spotted the bed frame and green curtains of the bedroom to one side, but she was most pleased to see a marble tub built into the floor of the bathroom.

If there was one thing the fae did right, it was luxury.

Renan took the bag of her daggers and swords and plopped them onto the table, the metal clanking together as they shifted inside. "You'll be expected for dinner. One of the servants will collect you." He raked his gaze down her front, still caked in dried mud and sand. "I would change, if I were you. I hope you brought extra clothes."

Odette sent a withering look at his back as he shut the door with a click, and then she was set to pacing. Every court protected the rifts during the equinox or solstice, and Odette knew she would find herself meeting a guard when she crossed. Additionally, she knew that she would be forcibly taken to the Lord of Mist and Tide, as guests always had to be presented immediately. She didn't expect Kaique to be seated on the throne instead of Nerea's father. *Where was he?* And his insistence on her help with the politics of the courts.

Pausing at the table, she grabbed the bottom of the bag and up-ended the contents onto the wooden surface. The blades tumbled out, clattering together before settling in a pile of leather and exposed silver. As she thought, Odette ran her hand over the leather sheath of her favorite sword.

Kaique's father was Lord of Mist and Tide for centuries before she was born and had remained Lord, at least until the last time she visited two hundred years ago. While Nerea had been receiving correspondence from him up until months before, it was hard to say whether or not those letters came from Kaique or their father.

And her first order of business was finding that out.

If Kaique knew about Nerea and her true claim to the throne, that made him dangerous, especially since she had given up her immortality...

Odette's swallow was thick. The rifts had closed, and that gave Odette at least until the next equinox to sort through everything. The only blessing, certainly still in disguise, was that the Court of Mist and Tide was very much out of the Fae King's graces. When they were younger and still in training, Kaique would have licked horse shit off of Adair's shoes if he was asked. His desperation gave her leeway to manipulate him as she pleased, as long as she threaded the needle just right.

She just needed to keep her composure together until then. Though, she knew that was going to be easier said than done. Her jittery anxiety and paranoia had already begun to return, the need to bolt skittering along her bones.

This was for Nerea, though, she had to remind herself. It was all for Nerea.

A knock on the door pulled Odette from her thoughts, and she crossed the room to open it. A female faerie, bronzed skin with a pretty face and dressed in a beige tunic tucked into a long, green skirt, curtseyed at Odette. She held a package in her arms, tightly wrapped in brown paper.

"Ma'am," she said softly, keeping her gaze to the ground. "My Lord thought you might prefer to wear something of the court to keep you cool in this humidity." She held her arms out toward Odette. "I brought you a dress he picked from our stores."

Odette grabbed the package from the servant.

"I was also asked to relay a message. Dinner will be served in one hour. I will come to collect you and you will be presented to the Lord as his honored guest." The servant dipped into another curtsy before scampering from the doorway.

Odette's mouth watered at the thought of dinner, and she knew, with Kaique's inclination toward all things extravagant, that it would not disappoint. She shut the door and turned to get ready.

The bath was completed in record time, despite the warm water soothing the sore muscles of her back and legs, and Odette used her elemental magic of manipulating air to dry her hair, thankful her magic returned once she entered the realms. The loose locks hung down her back, still frizzy from the thick humidity that blanketed the jungle. She tugged the ribbon that wrapped around the package, the brown paper falling open in the next breath.

Odette sighed with disgust as she glared down at the dress enclosed inside. The dress was, to be certain, a mockery of her expulsion from the fae realm. While other ladies and ranking female officials would have been given high-quality tunics and skirts, Kaique had provided her with a dress for a courtesan.

Even so, the dress was a brilliant shade of white, opulent and rare in the Court of Mist and Tide. The top half bore two thin pieces of fabric that would act as straps over her shoulders. However, they did less than the tight bodice chest piece would. Each breast pad was adorned with dried ferns and flowers, hooked to the delicate fabric with gold pins. The white fabric was split at the midriff, a sheer piece of fabric that was surely more see-through than anything Odette had ever worn, connecting the bottom and top like a bridge.

The bottom half of the dress was just as revealing, and at a quick glance, Odette knew the hem would sit just above mid-thigh. A band of dried ferns and flowers belted the waist, matching the breast pads of the top half. Two long, sage-colored pieces of chiffon were sewn just under the band of ferns, hanging between her legs in a way that didn't afford her any more privacy than if they were removed.

Odette knew it would be considered a deep insult if she refused the dress, but she also knew what the members of his court would think if she arrived at dinner wearing it. With her predicament in mind and realizing that she needed to walk a thinly veiled line to stay out of Adair's clutches, she donned the dress without a second thought.

The private dining room of the Court of Mist and Tide had always been Odette's favorite. The room was circular, as was the table in the center, and the blue-hued windows gave the rippling appearance as if they were under water.

Seven of the eight seats surrounding the table were already filled with high-ranking male officers. While she recognized a fair few of their tanned faces, she was less enthused that each one took more than enough time to look her over from her red locks to her bare feet, save for Renan, who kept his eyes firmly planted on the empty plate before him. Kaique's smirk behind his wine glass was only seen by Odette, the dimpled cheek peeking out from the side of the rim.

"Welcome, Odette," Kaique said, setting down his goblet and standing from his chair. The other males followed suit, the sound of wood scraping against the patterned tile echoing through the chamber. "I'm glad you could wear the dress we found for you."

A smattering of snorts reverberated through the guests, a choked laugh as though they could not believe Kaique would dare.

Odette only lifted her chin, looking down her nose at each and every male. "I'm glad you left it for me. The Court of Mist and Tide is certainly more humid than I'm used to." She swept past the males, sitting at the far side of the dining room.

Kaique lifted his goblet, tipping it toward her before taking a large gulp. Red wine dripped from his chin, droplets staining his green tunic like blood. He wiped his lips with the back of his hand as he dropped the goblet onto the table, and in the next breath, he snapped his fingers toward the servant standing ready near the kitchen door.

In a flurry of activity, plates of okra, shrimp, crispy fritters stuffed with black-eyed peas, and fluffy, baked cheese rolls appeared. The nearest servant, an older gentleman with thinning white hair and trembling hands, spooned a heap of pork and black bean stew into the wooden bowl in front of her before moving on to the next guest. But when Odette slid her gaze toward the man to send him a small smile in thanks, she noticed something strange about him.

His ears were the rounded shape of a human's.

Eyes narrowed, Odette darted her pointed stare toward Kaique, who was watching her with malicious amusement. Her stomach turned, threatening to spill what little it contained onto the slowly filling plate.

Her father had directly outlawed the capture and enslavement of humans, something that had been in place for hundreds of years, and Nerea's father followed the law just as tightly. But now...Odette picked up her spoon and swallowed a mouthful of the stew, the spicy pepper taste heating her tongue. Kaique knew she was vehemently opposed to slavery, and he was looking for a reaction. She refused to give him one.

"Odette, you remember our good friend, Caio?" Kaique asked, placing emphasis on the word that connected them together. "He's the guards' leader overseeing our newest servants now. Some of them have needed...breaking. He's had many ideas to–" Kaique was interrupted by the trembling gentleman dropping a silver platter of smoked fish onto the floor, clattering noisily against the tile.

The room went silent, only the ringing of the platter resounding in the spaces between all of them.

"You *fool*," Caio spat, his thick hands slamming against the table with such force that the tableware bounced against the wooden surface as he pushed himself to stand. Odette barely had time to react before Caio reached for the whip belted to his left hip.

In a flash of screaming agony, Caio reeled back his arm before bringing the whip down with devastating effect. The slim leather strips cracked against the slave's back, splitting his tunic and sending him tumbling to his knees, his head whacking against the stone as he fell. Caio reeled back again and again and again until the man's back was nothing but a bloodied mess of ribboned flesh. His screams transitioned into whimpers before he fell silent entirely, his limp body jerking with each blow.

Odette flinched with every snap of the whip and swept her gaze along the males at the table, surprised to see Renan squeeze his eyes tightly shut. Her lips parted as she made to stand, ready to end the showing, but Kaique had raised his hand. Caio stepped back immediately, his chest heaving at the exertion.

"I'm sure he won't be making that mistake again," Kaique said with a simpering chuckle, which the officials surrounding him returned.

He snapped his fingers, and two more slaves appeared in the shadows of the dining room. The man and the woman, their eyes cast away from Caio, shuffled forward. They bent at the waist, each linking an arm underneath the unconscious man still leaking blood onto the floor, and dragged him from the chamber. The blood that had pooled underneath his body smeared against the tile, his toes snaking a macabre pattern of red.

Odette couldn't be sure the man was still alive.

"Luckily for our guest," Kaique began again as Caio took his seat. "We have a special servant set aside for Odette. Renan." The soldier's head snapped upward, a blank expression expertly covering his features. "Please see to it that Luisa is brought to the throne room after we have finished our meal. She will be given as a daytime gift." Kaique turned, staring expectantly at Odette.

She felt bile claw up her throat at the words but managed to swallow it back with another mouthful of pork stew. "Thank you, my Lord, I am grateful."

Kaique waved a hand, the rings bedecking his fingers and glinting against the rays of sun that shone through the blue windows. "Of course, it is no trouble." He returned to his dinner, taking a gulp from the goblet that had been refilled.

The blood was left to dry.

Nearly an hour later, Odette followed Kaique to the throne room, his royal robes sweeping behind him as he walked. He was talking at Odette about something that had to do with the quality of the meal, but she wasn't listening. Her mind was racing with the thought of the whipped man, wondering if he was still alive, and a sharp prong of guilt that she hadn't stopped it sooner.

They entered the throne room from a side door, the dais appearing as soon as they crossed the threshold. Kaique climbed the stairs and settled himself importantly on the throne, one knee nestled over the other. Odette glanced around the hall and saw Renan stationed at the foot of the stairs. Next to him was one of the most stunning human women Odette had ever seen.

She must have been only nearing her early thirties, though creases had begun to form in the space between her brows from a constant look of worry. Her thick, black hair was knotted into a tight bun at the base of her skull, and it didn't take Odette long to notice that her clothing was vastly different from the loose tunics and pants of the other slaves.

Her skirt was split up the side, hemmed back together dangerously close to the apex of her well-shaped thigh. Her tunic had been shorn to show her midriff and shoulders, clavicles and ribs poking out from beneath her flesh. It was clear to Odette that she had once been curvy, but that extra weight had been lost over the course of her time in the Court of Mist and Tide.

She presented herself differently than the other slaves as well. While most were demure and shrunken, she held herself tall with her chin raised as though she were perpetually looking down her nose at those around her. Her brown eyes, deeply layered, bore into Odette's, and she found herself nervous from the intensity of the stare.

"Luisa," Kaique called from the dais, and the woman tore her gaze away from Odette.

"Yes, *my Lord*," Luisa retorted with a disinterested drawl, her voice heavily accented.

Kaique narrowed his eyes at Luisa, but he pressed on. "Luisa, this is Odette." He paused to sweep a hand in gesture over to Odette. "You will be her companion for her time in the Court of Mist and Tide."

"Goodie," Luisa replied, screwing up her eyes in a sore attempt to suppress them from rolling. Odette stifled a laugh but watched Renan's eyes widen in horror.

With preternatural speed, Kaique flew off the dais and screeched to a stop in front of Luisa. In a swift motion, Kaique backhanded Luisa, sending her sprawling to the floor. Her skirt lifted as she fell, revealing the rest of her leg and the base of her backside. Kaique's eyes darkened at the sight, but he tempered it back. He bent down and hauled Luisa to her feet before grasping her chin.

"You will be respectful in my presence." He shook her face and Odette saw there was already a bruise forming near her cheekbone. If looks could kill, Luisa would have murdered Kaique on the spot. "And you will be respectful to our guest." Luisa said nothing in return but jerked her chin from Kaique's fingers, her lips pursed into a tight line. "Luisa, here, has been with us for two years." He reached up to stroke her hair, the tips of his fingers grazing her collarbones near the edge of her tunic. Odette watched as Luisa shuddered under his touch. "We have been working to tame her. Maybe you will have some luck."

Kaique turned and waltzed back up the steps. Odette noticed Renan murmur something low in Luisa's ear, and this time, she rolled her eyes.

"General, please feel free to take Luisa to your chambers," Kaique said as he settled onto the throne.

Luisa's eyes darted up, snapping between Kaique and Odette. "What?" she asked, brow knitting together.

A malicious grin split Kaique's lips. "Did I fail to mention that Odette was the general to the former Fae King's armies?" He leaned forward, placing his forearms on his thighs. "Caio certainly learned from the best, didn't he?"

Odette had assisted in training Caio and had even gone toe-to-toe with him in the battle rings. Kaique had also failed to mention that Odette had personally expelled Caio from the legion. She didn't dare correct him, though, knowing that would only fuel Caio and Kaique further.

A burst of terror lit Luisa's features before her gaze returned to that bored, unbothered expression. "Yes, *my Lord*," she spat, but Kaique had undoubtedly noticed the fear still lurking behind her eyes, his smirk a tell as he reveled in it.

He dismissed them with a flick of his hand, and Luisa curtseyed before stomping toward the back of the hall.

Odette didn't dare exchange an accidental look with Renan, though she felt his eyes on her wings as she followed Luisa from the hall. Luisa was waiting for her in the courtyard, her arms crossed tightly over her chest. Her exposed skin pebbled in the cool breeze.

"Where to then?" Luisa asked, accentuating each word.

"You don't need to come with me—" Odette started, but Luisa cut in.

"Yes, I do," she responded forcefully.

Odette shifted in discomfort, the floral scent of sweet flowers rolling with the wind. "I'm not here to harm you. Maybe we should go somewhere more private to talk."

Luisa snorted. "You prefer to play with your food before you eat it, too? I know what *you fae* mean by *somewhere private*."

"Kaique does more than hit you, doesn't he?" Odette asked quietly.

Luisa seemed momentarily taken aback, her hand lifting to the deep purple blemish darkening her cheek. She dropped both hands to her side. "What does it matter to you?" she asked fiercely, which was enough of an answer for Odette.

"I'm not here to cause trouble."

Luisa scoffed, clicking her tongue against the roof of her mouth. "You cannot cause more trouble than there already is; it isn't possible. We are stuck here...with him." It was said with such venom that Odette was shocked a hole hadn't burnt through her tongue. "So let us go back to your room. You can get whatever you need from me, and then I can leave." She peeled away, stalking toward the wing of the guest apartments.

As she followed, Odette could have sworn she saw Renan watching from the shadows.

THIRTEEN

Odette

O dette lay on her side that night, her wings sprawled on the mattress behind her. The thrum of nocturnal bugs and the distant rush of water wafted through the pane-less window. The stars visible through the rolling clouds were bright against the dark sky.

The lack of electricity in the fae realm made for spectacular cosmic shows, and if Odette had to be here, she planned on taking full advantage. Her mother had taught her to read the stars and alignment of planets when she was a child. It had been centuries since Odette had tried, the memory of her mother too painful to linger on for long.

Sighing, Odette threw the thin sheet from her body and wandered to the large cutout overlooking the gardens. Moonlight bathed the waterfalls and brightly colored flowers in a soft glow that made it almost peaceful, along with the sounds surrounding her.

A creaking door beneath her pulled Odette from her thoughts, and she glanced down, surprised to see the familiar black-haired beauty sticking her head from the doorway below. She watched with interest as she saw Luisa turn her head to the right, then the left, before sneaking over the threshold. She then planted her hand firmly on the door to close it as quietly as possible, her bare feet almost silent against the stone as she cleared the ferns lining the pathway.

Odette was curious, something she couldn't help. Grasping the sides of the cutout, she hauled herself onto the window ledge and, in the next moment, jumped into the air and glided toward the direction Luisa had run. She was careful not to flap her wings, afraid the thwap of the leathery flesh would announce her. Instead, she used the breeze drifting over the jungle canopy to fuel her forward.

Touching down in the manicured front lawn that extended to the basalt wall surrounding the palace, Odette halted, knees almost buckling from the force it took to stop herself. She thought it best to land there and continue following Luisa on foot.

When she gained her bearings, she was stunned to find humans of all ages tending the gardens, heavy chains shackling their ankles.

The man nearest glanced up at her, sadness etching deep lines into his face, and he quickly looked away from her, continuing to prune the fern near the stone walkway. A woman was half-submerged in the pool's cool water as she used the brush in her hand to scrub algae away from the marble. When it gathered underwater, she then scooped it up with her hand, plopping it into a pile that had begun to grow on the edge. Another man was on his hands and knees, vigorously scrubbing the bridge arcing over the funneled streams. From the moonlight piercing through the leaves of the canopy tree above her, Odette could see the scars crisscrossing the man's back through the slits in his torn shirt.

Odette tempered the magic threatening to build, a mixture of anger, disgust, and sorrow sitting like a hot brick in her gut. A gust of air inadvertently shot from her fingertips, petals plucking from the nearby flowers and rolling across the stone to land in the pool near the woman's waist.

The woman spotted the petals, floating like lily pads on the surface, and shot Odette a withering look. As the woman collected the loose petals in the palm of her hand, Odette realized that, for the first time in her long existence, these people looked at her as though she were the enemy.

Spinning on her toes, Odette steered away from the garden and stalked deeper into the palace grounds.

Luisa had bypassed the area teeming with slaves by cutting through a stone arch surrounded by thick bushes, the maze-like structure seemingly walled off by the hedges. Odette furrowed her brow. This was certainly new since the last time she had visited, and judging by the red stains and ripped clothing on the thorns of each branch, she wasn't certain she wanted to know how new.

Cautiously, Odette slipped through the hedges, the thorns clawing at her exposed skin and wings, and it was a fair few minutes before she saw anything else. An amphitheater appeared from between the branches of the shrubbery, and she realized that she was on the ground floor of a miniature colosseum built on the side of a rolling jungle hill. Stone benches were set in rows high above the fence that hid the steps leading up to a wooden platform situated in the pit's direct center. A throne, similar to the throne in the marbled hall, was positioned in a box higher on the sides of the stage for better viewing.

Odette wracked her brain, trying to imagine what gardens had stood here the last time she was in the Court of Mist and Tide. Taking a moment to orient herself, and from the position of her room compared to where she had flown, she approximated that Kaique had cleared out the east gardens to make way for his new playground.

By the stains on the wood and the additional platforms erected on the stage, this set-up was not used for theater. Her eyes raked over the hangman's noose, and the square stone chunks cleaved from the center where an ax or sword had hit again and again.

It seemed that the only choice some of these slaves would ever get was the kind of death they preferred. Odette's stomach turned over, remembering back to her time in the dungeons of the castle she had grown up in.

Movement caught her eye, and Odette ducked deeper into the hedge that hid her. Luisa was running across the colosseum, dirt kicking up behind her in small clouds, toward a group of three humans huddled at the base of the fence.

"Sorry," Luisa said as she reached the group. Odette had to prick her ears forward to hear over the clearing. "Kai– that *thing*, he wanted to…" She trailed off, seemingly unable to voice anymore.

"You don't need to explain," a man with a sheared head and deep wrinkles at the corners of his eyes said comfortingly, though he never reached out to touch her. "Are you okay? How was the newcomer?"

Odette tilted her head, leaves catching in her hair. The news did travel fast, it seemed.

"She's one of them, Tomas. What do you expect?"

The man she called Tomas lifted a hand to rub his fingers along the short bristles on his cheeks. Thunder began to rumble in the distance. "They can't all be like Kaique. Some of them have been–"

"How is Gian?" Luisa interjected. "Has anyone been to visit him?" The tone of the other three shifted. Lightning forked across the dark storm clouds, marching over the tops of the jungle canopy, illuminating the bleakness that had settled over them. "What? How is he?"

"Gian, he–" a woman began, her full lips pressed tightly together in a grim twist. She adjusted the hem of her faded tunic, tugging it back down into place. "He passed away not long after the incident in the dining room."

Odette paled as Luisa's face fell, hopefulness disappearing into stunned grief as a shaky hand covered her mouth. "I don't understand," she said, her voice audibly cracking. "We've all seen worse beatings. I've *taken care of* worse beatings. How did he—?"

"He was old, meu amor," Tomas replied gently. "He's been here eight years. He's encountered too much." This time, he reached out to grasp Luisa's forearm, but she jerked away from him, taking a small step back. "Aldonza, she— she believes that Gian suffered a head injury when he fell. She tended to him immediately, but his injuries were too severe."

"He would have wanted you to have this," a second woman said, shorter and stockier than the rest, stepping forward and handing Luisa an item that Odette couldn't see with the clouds now covering the moon.

"When is the funeral?" Luisa asked with a sniff, glancing down at the item lying in her palm. Her fingers closed, and she placed the item in a makeshift pocket she had sewn into the side of her skirt.

"He was already taken to sea. Kaique ordered the boat after dinner. Said that he didn't deserve a proper send-off."

Luisa took in a deep, shuddering breath. "We'll toast in his honor tomorrow night then." The first woman made a noise of agreement from the back of her throat. "What do we have tonight, Tomas? More clothing?"

Fat droplets of rain began to plunk against the dirt of the colosseum, pricking against the leaves of the bushes Odette was still tucked into. She glanced up toward the sky, thunder rattling the stone benches. The storm was moving in fast.

"Well," Tomas started as he pulled a dagger from underneath his tunic. "One of the guards had a little too much wine at dinner in the barracks last night and left this on the table. I stole it whilst cleaning."

"Tomas! You could have been killed!" The first woman exclaimed but leaned forward to study the dagger between his hands.

Odette could tell the blade was dull by the way it shone in the moonlight. It would need to be sharpened before any damage against the fae could be inflicted.

"We need weapons, Anaise," Tomas replied as Luisa took the dagger by the hilt to examine it further. "If we want to leave by the summer solstice, we need to start stockpiling weapons, not just clothes."

Anaise opened her mouth as if she wanted to argue, but Luisa interrupted with a renewed sharpness to her voice. "He's right. We can't make it past these walls without weapons." She paused to gesture to Tomas, who went to hand her the leather sheath. "I'll keep it in my room, underneath the mattress. No one goes in there. *His* orders."

Tomas nodded his head, but before he could hand it over, Anaise said, "And what happens if you're caught with it? There is no reason for you to have a guard's dagger. You don't go near the guards long enough to take it. They'll see right through you."

Luisa took the sheath from Tomas' half-outstretched hand anyway and slid the dagger in it, hiking up her skirt to strap it gingerly to her inner thigh. Odette noticed the bruises littering her calves and circling her upper legs, each in a different stage of healing. "They can't do anything to me that they haven't already done."

"You're still alive, Luisa," the second woman piped up quietly, crossing her arms over her chest as she looked at her. "You must remember that."

"Maybe physically," Luisa replied with disinterest. "I haven't been alive inside in a very long time."

Odette stepped back, the rustling of the thorny bushes covered up by the pelting rain and cracking thunder. Her red hair was plastered to the side of her face by the time she reached the garden once again, the slaves still working amongst the tall trees despite the storm.

She knew that turning in Luisa and her gang would earn her points with Kaique, but she couldn't bring herself to do it. She wouldn't reward him for breaking their fathers' treaty. She was here to find out what happened to Nerea's father. Nothing else. And, if she were lucky, she would manage to get out of the Court of Mist and Tide alive.

FOURTEEN

DELIA

Delia took the familiar path from the hotel to St. Peter's Square for the next few days. It had become a habit of sorts to her, something to keep her mind firmly off the grief that threatened to take over her mind and soul every morning.

Instead, she focused on Vatican City and learned the guard's schedules and tourist routines.

She sipped her coffee in the morning sun, sunglasses perched on the bridge of her nose as she lounged next to the left fountain. From here, she could see the excavation office and the Swiss Guard that stood as a security checkpoint to enter. She learned that one took a break near eleven-thirty in the morning while the other went closer to one in the afternoon. The necropolis accepted two groups of tourists during the weekday and three on the weekend. The guards worked one shift— eight in the morning until five in the evening when the final guided tour exited the site for the day.

When the afternoon became too warm, and Delia felt her skin tightening from the sun, she moved to the shaded colonnade area. From here, she could observe the long lines leading into the basilica and the ongoing guided tours from open to close. Security was still present, with the x-ray machine and metal detectors built near the entrance, but those guards moved quicker than the ones at the excavation office.

The long line of people required it.

Delia settled near the right fountain by dusk and watched as the guards closed the security checkpoints and the excavation workers locked the doors leading into the building. If she was lucky and the crowds in the square were thin, she could hear mass from an open chapel window weaving through the courtyard as she watched the area around her. Though she wasn't one for religious discourse, she appreciated the break from the low hum of casual chatter.

On the other hand, Cian had developed a massive map on the back of the dresser in her hotel room. She used the term her hotel room lightly because Cian had decided the pigpen he booked for himself was no longer up to his standards, and he moved in with her on night three, sleeping on the vinyl-wrapped couch tucked on the other side of the room.

The map, hand-drawn on four pieces of white paper taped together, was a to-scale interpretation of the basilica and necropolis. He had marked the tombs of interest with stars, nixing those crumbled or too near the entrance to house anything important.

During the day, when Delia was out scouting the square and generally avoiding being in the same room as him, Cian was busy rifling through the images, taking screenshots of different locations in the excavation area via the video, and creating a timetable of security checkpoints and guard changes. At least, that's what Delia assumed he was doing. Progress was always made when she wandered back to the hotel after sunset.

It was day eight of Delia's routine when anything close to interesting happened. A fight had broken out between two women, one accusing the other of skipping the security line. A tangle of shoving and hair-pulling ensued before the Swiss Guard hurried over, stepping in to rip the women apart from one another.

Delia leaned back against one of the columns, sighing loudly. There wasn't too much left for her to observe, and she had counted how many pigeons flew into the courtyard, separating them by color and rating them by how sharp of a coo they possessed. All in all, Delia was bored as hell and couldn't think of why she would bother coming back the next morning.

She glanced down at her wrist to check her fitness watch. It was seven in the evening. At the thought of dinner, her stomach rumbled, and she felt the sudden swoop of lightheadedness that resulted from skipping lunch. She shut her notebook, where she had doodled a bad drawing of a woman across the square dressed in eighteenth-century clothing, and stood.

It took Delia less than a minute to cross to the center of the square and another two to navigate the growing crowd. The sky was already stained a deep orange that cast a golden glow over the courtyard, and everyone around was waiting to watch the autumn sun set over Rome. She scrolled over her phone as she walked down the hill, engrossed in the social media posts from her friends back home. She was so engrossed, in fact, that she didn't realize she was being trailed.

Delia exited the square and sent the screen to black as she began to pass the restaurants, checking the interior through the sharply lit windows to assess the activity level inside. Most were busy, though the scent of freshly cooked pasta and dried herbs was nearly enough to force her to stand in line anyway. Before she could decide if the wait would be worth it, a hand wrapped around her forearm just as she paused outside of a cafe, yanking her into the nearest alleyway.

A second hand shot over her mouth, covering it roughly to contain the scream that escaped from her lips. Delia's eyes widened as panic clawed through her chest, her thoughts returning to the night Eligos had entered her apartment and knocked her unconscious.

She had fought back then, too.

"Does the word Paladin mean anything to you?" the female and husky voice demanded in her ear as she spun Delia around with impossible speed, restraining her against the wall of the nearest building. Her head bounced painfully against the stone. Her thoughts began to swim, muddled and heavy.

There were a few heartbeats before Delia's vision came back into focus, and confusion clouded her mind. Like a rubberband had been released, she suddenly snapped back into reality. "What?" Delia asked through the tight fingers still clamped over her mouth. The sound was muffled against a soft palm that smelled lightly floral, a destabilizing contrast to the situation she was in.

"Paladin. Does the word Paladin mean anything to you?"

Delia attempted to reply, but the hand had tightened and suppressed any discernible words.

The woman who had pinned her against the wall went still. "If I let you go, are you going to scream?" Delia shook her head quickly, her eyes still wide. The woman slowly let off the pressure, and in an instant, Delia sucked in a deep breath. The woman clamped her hand over Delia's mouth once again, sending her an annoyed glare.

Delia was pulled deeper into the alleyway. Though the road had narrowed against the terracotta buildings, a handful of vespas were still parked between the wrought iron gates of each residence. Greenery snaked up the side of a door, growing from between the cracked cobblestone. Small trees in large pots were set outside to soak in the last of the setting sun, and they cast long shadows against the cobblestone alleyway.

They were far enough removed from the main road leading to the square that Delia was sure no one would hear her if she cried out again. She shook the woman off, who hesitantly let her go.

"Pal-a-din," she repeated to Delia as if saying it slower would make her answer the question quicker. "What do you know about it?"

Delia turned to look at her captor with a quirked eyebrow. The woman was in her early thirties, tall and slim. Her honey-blonde hair was thin but long and tied into a high ponytail that skirted the tops of her shoulders. A pink bow was tied into her hair, matching the flowers on her sundress. She sent Delia a questioning gaze, her cheeks flushed and lips parted as she waited.

Delia looked into the woman's hazel eyes and shrugged. "I'm not sure what you mean."

With a speed that rivaled Cian's, the woman reached out and snatched Delia's bag from her shoulder. She plunged her hand in to pull out the notebook, the map from the hotel front desk that Delia had marked up, and a scrap of paper that contained different spellings of the word Paladin when Delia had grown bored of sitting in the square.

The woman pinched the scrap in her hand, holding it up for Delia to see. "Yeah, I think you do." Delia noticed a light accent compared to her American one, though it was hard for her to place.

"Oops," Delia replied with a shrug, leaning forward to rip the purse from the woman's hands, but missing as the woman pulled it out of her grasp. "Not sure how it's any of your business anyways."

"I want to know everything about the inside of that church."

Delia tipped her head back toward the sky and let out a laugh. "Go inside yourself," she finally said, extending an open hand toward the intruder. "And give me my stuff back." Ignoring her, the woman opened the notebook, scanning the scribbles and drawings as she paced in front of Delia, who had begun to impatiently tap her foot against the cobblestone. "Who are you anyway?"

The woman stopped pacing, flicking her gaze up to Delia. "Kazzy," she said, snapping the notebook shut and holding it in the air to shake it. "I can't read this."

"I know. Why do you think I haven't tried harder to get it back?" Delia crossed her arms over her chest. "I created the shorthand myself."

Kazzy seemed to sag, and her eyes closed, as though she were on the brink of melting down. "You do know about Paladin, then?"

Delia shifted. "I didn't say that."

"You just implied it. Otherwise, you would have asked what it was." Kazzy appeared momentarily pleased as she reached forward to slide the notebook back into Delia's purse.

Delia bristled. "Okay, I have your name. What are you then?" There was an intuition, a tug at her gut that recoiled under Kazzy's stare. That sense left her feeling as though Kazzy was something...unnatural.

Kazzy stiffened, her eyes narrowing in suspicion. "That's an odd question."

Despite her wildly beating heart and sweating palms, Delia's unflinching stare bore into Kazzy's. "Let me rephrase to make it a little easier for you to understand. Are you human?" When Kazzy said nothing, and Delia saw a flustered blush creep up her neck, a zing of satisfaction bolted up Delia's spine. "I'll take that as a no."

"If you know that I'm not," Kazzy replied through gritted teeth. "Then you also know that I can't get into any of the churches around here."

Delia actually didn't know that. She just assumed Cian couldn't get in due to the sunlight in the square during the time the basilica was open, but also because he was the spawn of Satan. "Why can't you?" she asked after a moment of silence.

Kazzy glanced around, the cool breeze ruffling the knee-length hem of her dress. "It's not safe here," she said back in a soft whisper that Delia had to lean in to hear. "We should talk somewhere else."

"What makes you think I want to talk at all? It seems as though I have all of the information, and you have nothing," Delia said.

The cat-and-mouse game was becoming mildly irritating, but Delia couldn't help her emboldened curiosity. That curiosity was running thin, though, much like her patience.

Kazzy contemplated Delia for a long moment. Her lips pressed into a thin line. She inhaled sharply through her nose before speaking. "I need to learn about the Paladin Society. I've seen you around here the last week, watching the area and taking notes. You're different from a normal tourist, I could tell. I've been trying to infiltrate St. Peter's Basilica for three years now." She took the end of her ponytail in her hand, curling the thin strands around two fingers. "There are runes within one hundred feet of every entrance. They bar any supernatural entity from getting too close."

Delia said nothing as she held up her pointer finger to stop the woman from speaking further, digging into her over-turned purse to pull out her cell phone. The dial tone rang twice before Cian picked up the other end.

"Yes?" He drawled as a greeting. Delia could hear his two-fingered typing in the background, and she envisioned him going through Celeste's video for the fifteenth time that week.

"Are the shadows long enough for you to come to the square?" Delia replied, not bothering to acknowledge him. She picked at her nails in an attempt to appear as coolly casual as she could. Kazzy was watching with peaked interest.

There was a pause on the other end of the line. "Why?"

Delia sighed and rolled her eyes. "We have a—" She looked over to Kazzy, her eyes scanning the pink bow down to the white canvas shoes. "I don't want to say a problem, but you should make your way here."

She heard a squeak from a squeak of a chair and assumed Cian must have sat up from his usual reclined position where he propped his feet on the desk. "What kind of problem?"

"Will you just get here?" Delia snapped in response, agitation finally edging into her voice. "We're in the third alleyway on the right side of the square."

There was a *clack* of the laptop closing, and a shuffle sounded as Cian pushed himself off the chair. "I'll be there in less than a minute."

Delia didn't respond; she merely removed the phone from her ear and pressed the end call button with her thumb. Her fingernails tapped the backside of the hard case as she turned her attention back to Kazzy. "He's on his way."

"Who is *he*?" Kazzy asked though she seemed to hesitate before asking the next question. "And why can he only walk in the shadows?"

"My associate is allergic to the sun," Delia retorted, leaning a shoulder against the terracotta wall closest to her.

"Allergic to the sun?" Kazzy replied incredulously. "Are you messing with me?"

Delia activated the front screen on her cell phone once again, scrolling mindlessly through her social media account as she waited. "Nope," she said, popping the 'p' at the end of the response. "That's what I said."

"If your associate were truly allergic to the sun, he would—" Kazzy stopped mid-sentence, her gaze becoming fixed and unseeing. She turned to glance over her shoulder, her movements jolting and stiff as she spun to face the mouth of the alleyway.

Delia raised her eyes from the screen, spotting Cian standing just as still and inert as Kazzy. His eyes were sharp and focused, staring at Kazzy as if she were something worth killing. Delia pushed off the wall, her intuition suddenly screaming at her to intervene, but she was too late.

Kazzy and Cian launched themselves at each other, colliding in the middle of the alleyway with a crack so violent the noise echoed off the cobblestone corridor.

FIFTEEN

GREER

Greer's return to eating was slow and steady. She ate a plate of breakfast here and a bowl of soup there. Half the time, she was able to keep it down, but the other half, it turned sour the moment it hit her tongue, and she had difficulty swallowing it back. Her anxiety and shame were another thing. They seemed to creep up when she least expected them, leaving her reeling and broken when she thought she had taken a step toward healing.

In the days following her conversation with Azazel, it was clear that he was not done propositioning her. Arista started to sneak in questions in the morning, clearly gauging her temperament toward the subject of her magic. And it was when Greer finally snapped from the questioning while she was getting dressed behind the bathroom door with Arista peppering her from the other side and the porcelain, clawfoot tub cleaving in two under a burst of power that Arista gave it up.

Greer sat on the edge of the terrace overlooking the city, the fresh breeze pushing her hair behind her. With every swirl of wind around the marble statues, loose strands tickled the back of her neck. She watched the city below her, full of life despite the chilled air whistling through the passes of the mountain peaks.

It was probably mid-October back in Oregon. She didn't know if the calendar translated over in Samsara or not. If she were right, the university campus would be decorated with corn stalks and bales of hay. A buzz of excitement in the throngs of students as they picked out their Halloween costumes and impatiently awaited the short autumn break that followed.

The leaves would be a vast range of gold and red, steadily covering the sidewalk leading to the library's front doors. Roger, the security guard stationed there, had a tradition of dressing as a different researcher every day through the month of October, name tag and all. It was all in light fun of the season. She remembered the first time Roger had dressed as her, and they had laughed for hours afterward.

Greer already missed the crunch of the leaves under her feet, how she would carve pumpkins with Delia and Paige the weekend before Halloween. They would have planned to hit the bars with the handful of friends coming into town to see them. She always expected that tradition to end as they got older, but not like this.

"May I?"

A low voice pulled Greer from her thoughts, and she glanced up in time to see Samael sitting next to her, not waiting for an answer, and dangling his legs over the side of the terrace just the same way she had. He leaned forward to allow his wings to splay onto the marble floor, resting his elbows on his knees and extending his hand toward her.

"Et tu, Brutus?" Greer asked, but she took the object bundled in a napkin from him anyway.

Samael chuckled. "Those biscuits are the only thing you consistently eat. They weren't made for breakfast, but I thought I would bring you one."

"Thank you," Greer replied. And she meant it. "It's— it's the only thing that tastes like home." Her fingers, numb from the cold, deftly unwrapped the napkin. The biscuit was still warm, steam rising from the moist linen in her palm.

Samael said nothing as he nodded, keeping his gaze fixed on the city below. The wind kicked up again, sweeping a lock of brown hair from his bun. Greer bit into the biscuit, almost groaning as the soft pastry filled her mouth.

"Your father wanted me to convince you to train with me."

Greer let her hands drop into her lap, the biscuit seemingly turning into shale on her tongue. "I knew it." She let out a mirthless chuckle, shaking her head. She lifted the biscuit above her head and threw it into the valley below. It arched through the air, hitting the apex just over the craggy rocks separating the palace grounds from the first switchback flanked by large houses.

"It's in your best interest to learn—" Samael started, but Greer had already stood.

"I don't want to learn anything. Especially from you," she replied, an impatient sneer curling her lip. She was careful to make sure she trod onto the edge of his wing as she spun back to the palace.

He hissed, both in pain and indignation, and shot up after her. "You should learn how to protect yourself. You should learn how to control your power. You—"

"Stop telling me what to do," Greer said, eyes wild. She paused to scoff, cursing under her breath before she shook her head again. Deep breaths filled her chest in an attempt to sway the river of power pulsing through her. "I'm going back to the city."

Samael rested his hand on the pommel of his dagger. "You weren't put back on the city accounts. There is no reason to—"

"I'm going for a walk. Just— just leave me alone."

Greer made to leave, pivoting on her toes to aim for the elegant staircase that led to the beginning of the switchbacks. She took one step forward and collided with leather armor in the same breath. Jaw clenched, she glanced up at Samael's stone-faced expression.

"There is nothing for you in the city right now," he started as Greer inched to the right, shoulders pushed back and chin lifted in defiance. "You don't know this world. It's dangerous for you. You aren't safe here."

"I will find out what is dangerous for me. Thank you very much."

Samael's fingers tightened around the hilt of his dagger, the bands of muscle in his forearm quivering under tension. "Just like you found out with Eligos?" A sigh escaped from his nose as if he instantly regretted what he said.

Greer's gaze turned cold and distant, her breathing slightly shallow. Her lips parted, then clamped together, then parted once again. She took a deliberate step back from him, and he watched her carefully. She shook her head before turning away from him again, giving him a wide berth this time.

The dagger whined, metal against leather, as Samael removed it from the sheath at his hip. "You should learn to use it. You should learn to use something." His tone was frosty, barely apologetic.

Greer dropped her eyes toward the blade. The emerald gemstones, embedded into the hilt just above the leather wrapping of the handle, glinted in the dim rays of the sun that managed to break through the thick line of clouds hovering at the peaks of the mountains. And the blade...the blade...

Samael's wrist twisted as he reached forward to extend the handle toward her, the silver metal gleaming with the motion, a sharp shine developing as the light caught the steel.

Suddenly, Greer was back in Oregon, back in the warehouse's parking lot. She was watching the blade in Eligos's hand, watching the light of the street lamps rebound from the dagger in a sudden jet. The same way it was rebounding from Samael's dagger now.

There was a heartbeat in her stomach, behind her eyes, and in the pads of her fingers. Her mouth dried as she stared at the blade, and she felt her throat constrict into a bed of knives as she tried to swallow. She needed to move. She needed to get away from the dagger, needed to step away from the blade pointed directly at Samael's abdomen. Her mind was disconnected as if it couldn't decide whether it wanted to remain blank or thrum through every thought she ever had. She couldn't move her feet, and they felt heavy and sluggish.

Greer's chest was tight as she scrabbled to reel in the power pulsating out with every beat of her heart, with every breath. Samael threw up a shield just in time for Greer to explode.

Afterward, they were wrapped in a dark gloom, a wave of blackness surrounding them. Greer had gone still, her knuckles white from clenching her fingers into tight fists, and she knew that her fingernails had cratered half-moon notches into the palms of her hands. The wind whipped around them, pulling her hair into tangles that lashed at her cheeks and brow. Her linen shirt *thwapped* like a flag during a hurricane.

Someone was saying her name, the voice steady and low. But it was garbled, as though she had dipped her head under the bathwater.

Greer opened her eyes in response, and the blasting roar ceased immediately, leaving nothing but a ringing silence in its wake. She had purged them both into darkness, the fog hanging between them distorting the markings encircling Samael's upper arms in a haze. She swept her gaze from his face, realizing that he had shielded them in a fully cased sphere. The whirling, dark gloom pushed against the barrier, creating murky swirls that danced around their arms and shoulders.

Samael released the shielded barrier, and a deluge of light, bright and white against the clouded sky, burst through the thinning haze. Greer's eyes narrowed against the sudden radiance, and she lifted her hand instinctively as a buffer.

"Your power is a living thing," Samael finally said. He had sheathed his dagger at some point, the emerald gemstones visible just at his belt line. "It will keep pushing back harder and harder until you find a way to control it."

Greer swallowed, and the motion felt raw against the back of her throat, proof that she hadn't remained as silent as she thought. She didn't know when she had started screaming or when she had stopped.

Before either of them could say more, movement flickered at the corner of her eye, drawing her attention toward the other end of the terrace.

A group of five daemons, a mix of pointed ears, sharp fangs, and leathered wings, stared at her. The leading female, her black hair falling in dreaded strands to her shoulders, shifted in discomfort, tucking her two books tighter under her arm. The second female, her snake-like eyes wide, inched closer to the male at her side, and she reached out to clutch his forearm in fear. Their stares flicked between her and Samael, seemingly unsure of the safest person to gawk at.

The right-hand man of Azazel or the daughter of the most powerful Primordial in existence.

The feeling returned to Greer's feet, and she could peel them away from the marble tile as she stumbled backward. Samael opened his mouth to speak, to say something, but she was already fleeing back to the innards of the palace, scurrying past him in a flurry of trembling muscles and a churning stomach.

Moonlight streamed in from the domed ceiling, illuminating the bronze chandelier suspended from the buttresses that held the glass into place. The soft glow cast long shadows against the wooden bookshelves, calm and quiet after a busy day of workers clad in olive green robes flitting in between the stacks. The library darkened momentarily as a thick cloud covered the stars, obscuring the moon in a halo of dim light.

The sandstone tile was gritty against Greer's bare feet, a change in texture from the smooth stone of the staircase. She walked slowly through the atrium, watching as the books shuddered and pulsed in her presence. They seemed to know someone was here after hours, darting and zooming from their shelves as if trying to get a glimpse of her. Greer could scent the leather covers and binding glue with every step. But otherwise, it stayed silent, and eerily so.

The library was once her refuge, a place for her to study during final exam week and a space for her to think when her line of research left her mind in knots. Remembering this, she paused in the center of the library, directly under the asymmetrical bronze chandelier, and stared at the mountain passes through the ceiling-to-floor windows that overlooked the mountain peaks behind the palace. For a moment, she imagined that she was back in the university library and seated at a table on the top floor. She imagined watching the Oregon mountains, the flowing river that split the city in the spring when the snowcaps melted in time for summer.

Greer shook her head. There was no point in pretending she was home. She would never see it again.

She turned to her left, entering an aisle at random between two tall bookcases. Brushing by the ladder propped against the sturdy shelves, she ran a finger over the rough leather bindings. The books shivered under her touch. On and on she went, weaving through each aisle with slow precision.

It wasn't until she had passed through her sixth aisle that Greer paused to actually pluck a book from a shelf. Carefully, she pulled the cover back, feeling the leather creak against her palm. The parchment was old, swirls of ink appearing on the page as if previously hidden by an invisible force. The words, originally in a language she didn't recognize, were reworked into English, and a few phrases caught her eye.

Greer sank to the sandstone tile, feeling the rough texture against her legs now, and leaned back against the bookcase. She took a deep breath, disbelief radiating through her at what she was about to do, as she extended a hand forward. Nerves flooded her system as she willed a flame to appear. Only when the light flickered like a match in her hand, warmly licking against her skin, did she relax again.

The dim light pushed at the darkness, its orange hue flickering against the parchment. She smiled at the only magic she allowed herself to perform and turned back to the book.

Greer was tugged into an adventure of three characters she had never heard of, written by an author who wasn't of her world. She didn't know how long she read for, pouring over the pages until her ass was numb and she could no longer comfortably shift her legs into new positions. Finally standing back up, she tucked the book under an arm and brushed away the loose grains sticking to her pants from the sandstone tile. The flame winked out, pitching her into shadowed darkness once again.

She had every intention of taking the book to her bedroom, tucking herself under the covers and reading by candlelight until the sun came up, but as she padded toward the atrium and ultimately the staircase that led to the balcony above her, she lurched to a stop as a second book sprang from the shelf above her and landed with a thud at her feet.

With her eyebrows furrowed, Greer bent down and wrapped her hand around the leather cover, pulling it into her arms. It vibrated under her touch, reminding her of the grimoire still hiding in the closet of her rented home. The vibrations grew faster and stronger until the book buzzed in her hand, sending tremoring shocks rattling her bones.

Hurrying toward one of the wooden tables in the center of the chamber, she let the book fall out of her hand. The vibrations vanished as soon as it was out of her grasp, and, for a moment, all was silent. In the next breath, the book flung open, and the parchment pages rifled as if on a phantom wind. They halted just a bit, the book stilling as it lay open on the table.

Cautiously, Greer bent over, placing a hand on the wooden surface to brace herself. She scanned the page once and then twice before her breath hitched in her throat.

Splayed before her was a map of Samsara.

Greer swept her gaze toward the north end of the map, pausing when it landed on Veritas tucked amidst the mountain range that edged along the sea. She spotted the lake where the city square was located and the second mountain range encapsulating the city in a protected valley.

Her eyes roamed downward, taking in the Meridians of Wrath, Gluttony, and Indolence. The markings of the forest turned into prairie and then into a bog. The seven meridians, each containing their own distinctive cities and terrain keys, were situated like four islands in a vast saltwater sea. Greer wasn't sure how long she studied the map, allowing the glow of the moonlight to illuminate the pages before her. She briefly turned the page, taking in a second map of an unknown, unnamed world, before returning to Samsara.

A rustle of wings and a door creak sounded from above her.

Greer's head shot up, her heart dropping into her stomach as her gaze darted intensely scrutinizing the library. The chamber had dropped into silence; even the books had ceased their shuddering as if intently awaiting the appearance of a second person. When no one appeared, and her ratcheted heartbeat finally calmed, Greer glanced down at the map before her. Without a second thought, she reached forward and tore the two pages from the bindings.

SIXTEEN

GREER

Greer hadn't been added back to the city accounts, but she realized one thing in particular on her adventures into the city square. Men, even in the afterlife, still loved attention. Send a quirky smile, look at them through her eyelashes, and she could have one eating out of her palm long enough to suckle a mead out of them.

Then, she would turn herself back to the bartender and never glance at them again.

There was enough of a revolving crowd throughout the week that Greer was able to hustle someone without overlapping, and even if she had garnered the attention from a knowing bartender, all it took was a glare for them to sidle up to the oak barrels nestled in the aging stands. That was exactly how Greer ended up cradling her third mead at the third new tavern of the night, hands wrapped around cold pewter. The band on the small corner stage was playing an upbeat tune, and the barmaids were weaving in and out of the tables, delivering pints of alcohol and bowls of steaming stew. The smell of roasting meat filled the hall, overtaken only by the honey wine whenever Greer lifted the tankard to her lips.

"Two glasses of red wine and— what do you want, Clem?" a woman asked to Greer's right.

From the corner of her eye, Greer spotted a group of three females plop down into seats at the bar. Who she assumed was Clem, sporting wings of black leather and curled horns at the edge of her hairline, leaned her forearms onto the wooden bar.

"What's special tonight, Georgie?" Clem asked the bartender as her two friends grasped the freshly delivered stems of wine.

"Don't toy with me, love," Georgie responded with a wink, wiping her hands on the stained cloth slung over her shoulder. "I know what you want."

A smirk spread on Clem's lips as Georgie turned away, and she smoothed back the loose, dark hairs around her horns.

"Did you hear the latest news, Mira?" The female seated closest to Greer asked. She paused to sip her wine, lips smacking, as she set down the glass. It clinked against the wood of the bar. "Another human made it out of the river."

Clem barked a laugh as the dark-skinned woman, Mira, raised her eyebrows in response.

"That's pretty rare, isn't it? For a human to make it out of the river?" Mira asked.

The unnamed woman nodded, her honey-blonde locks shifting with the movement. "I've only met a few of them, you included."

The three girls quieted as Georgie, the bartender, placed a pewter tankard in front of Clem, and her eyes darkened with hunger. "What is it today?" She asked, clamping a hand around the pint and taking a long sip. The substance, thick and red, dribbled down her chin. Greer swallowed back a grimace when she recognized it as blood. "Lamb? Venison?"

"Rare," Georgie replied, "Arachnid."

"It's delicious. I shudder to think how you got it." Clem took another deep gulp. "You can taste the fear."

"Gross, Clem," the unnamed woman chided, taking another sip of her red wine. "Have even a semblance of class, won't you?"

Clem wiped her lips with the back of her hand, smearing the blood across the top of her wrist. "Rich coming from your faerie kind." Her eyes flicked upward.

For the first time, Greer noticed the sharply pointed ears that the unnamed woman bore. Greer leaned back, pretending to stretch to get a better look at her back. It was bare, save for the linen shirt she wore. Clearly fae, even Clem had said so, but no wings. Greer took another sip of mead as the woman went on.

"My kind isn't stark raving lunatics like you, succubi," the woman reiterated with an eye roll.

Greer felt her heart jolt in her chest as she tried to get an even better look at Clem. She had never seen a succubus before, let alone been so close to one, and she was interested in discovering more. Her eyes dragged down her sensuous lips, the partially exposed breasts, and the tight shirt.

"Tania, do you think we would have been friends in the Gaian realm?" Clem asked, bypassing the insult with a wave of her hand. *Tania*. That was the third woman's name.

"No."

Clem turned toward the third woman. "And you, Mira? Would we have been friends?"

Mira flicked her eyes between Tania and Clem. "Somehow, I don't think so," she finally relented. "I think me being on your dinner menu would have deterred me from getting to know you any further."

Clem sucked a tooth, swirling the remains of the blood in her tankard before draining it. "You weren't on my dinner menu. No offense." The tankard hit the wooden bar with a *thunk*. "Going back to that new human. Mira, what was it like climbing from the river?"

"*Princes of Samsara*, Clem, take it easy," Tania clucked as she tapped on the rim of her glass with a slender finger. Georgie replaced the empty glass with a full one a moment later. "Maybe she doesn't want to talk about it."

Mira closed her mouth before opening it again, and whatever she had decided to say was drowned out by a group of fang-toothed males who burst through the tavern door. Greer didn't miss the haunted, hollow look that dulled Mira's gaze. The band's violin whined behind them as a roar of approval came from the dance floor. Georgie set a second tankard in front of Clem with a grin.

"It isn't often we get to talk with a human who made it through the river, Tania," Clem pressed on. "They usually come out looking like those things that crawl around south of the city."

"The devils?" Tania asked, her voice raising slightly as the band began another song.

Clem flicked her hand again. "Yes, those. Can you imagine staying like that for all of eternity?" She shook her shoulders in a dramatic shudder, taking a sip from the tankard.

"I think it's sad," Mira interjected. "All of those humans who never got the chance to atone for their lives."

"That's what the War of the Sixteen was about," Tania said. "I talked with a Lesser Primordial I met in a shop. Must have been fifty years ago now." She paused to take a sip of wine. "The King, Azazel, didn't want to torture souls anymore. He thought humans didn't get long enough in their realms to learn how to truly be good. The war started, Samsara and Elysia were split to create Gaian according to a treaty from the Ananke."

"And what about the ones that go to Elysia? What happens to them?" Mira asked.

Tania lifted a shoulder. "I'm not sure. I've never been."

"Us daemons would never be allowed to go to Elysia." Clem let out a soft snort of laughter. "We can't leave here even if we wanted to."

Mira lifted her head to look at Clem. "You can't go back to Gaian?"

"Do you want to go back to Gaian?" Clem retorted as a passing barmaid picked up the empty pewter tankard Clem had discarded to the side. "There are three other realms to choose from."

Mira bristled. "Of course I don't. Gaian existence was–" She trailed off, biting her lip as she seemingly searched for the right word. "Exhausting."

Greer almost tipped her own tankard of mead toward Mira in solidarity but didn't want them to realize she had been listening.

"Besides," Mira went on after taking another sip of her wine. "From what I understand, there is only one portal back to Gaian, and it's in the Meridian of Pride. You would have to be a fool to go through it. There isn't a way back. Your body is stripped away once you enter the human realm, and you're left as a spirit. Someone told me years ago that the only reason the dead have bodies here is because of Azazel's power."

Greer stilled, her stomach hardening, and the tankard slipped from her grasp, mead sloshing over the rim as it thunked against the bar.

There was a portal. And she wasn't dead. There was a way home. She could leave.

"That's if you can make it to the Meridian of Pride," Tania said, pushing her second empty wine glass away from her. It scraped across the carved surface, nearly tipping as it snagged against a gouge mark, but she righted it just in time. "There aren't many safe regions of Samsara, and if you get killed here, you will cease to exist entirely."

"Safe to say, I will not be–"

Greer didn't know what else Mira had said. She pushed the tankard away in a mad dash and hopped down from the barstool. The three women didn't even notice as she began to shove through the throng of wings and fangs, daemons and Lesser Primordials alike coming into the tavern for a nightcap. She accidentally knocked a wine glass from someone's hand, sending it soaring to the ground and shattering against the stone floor. A shout of frustration sounded behind her, but she didn't stop.

Spilling into the crowded square, Greer immediately turned toward the mountain and began to weave up the switchbacks.

Greer stumbled into the palace in record time, chest heaving and cheeks flushed. The entrance hall was empty, and her hurried footsteps echoed against the high ceilings. Her heart fluttered at the thought that this was the last time she would see this palace, but she didn't stop to take it in.

There were more important things to do.

Greer's lungs were burning by the time she reached the landing to her bedroom, and she was sure her legs would collapse if she took one more step.

She kept going anyway.

Ripping the door open, Greer made a beeline for the bedside table. Arista must have, at some point, come to light the candles as a soft glow permeated the darkness encompassing the corners of the room. The large, circular window, usually haloed by moonlight, was dark, and even the sky beyond, usually stained with a spackle of stars, was devoid of light.

She blew out a breath as she collapsed onto the edge of the bed, the retrieved map from a drawer in the bedside table held tightly in her hand. Leaning toward the candlelight, Greer's eyes raked over folded parchment, stretched tight to straighten out the fold creases. She took in the four islands, realizing for the first time that the small, spherical symbols located in precise placements across the maps were portal locations. Clem the succubus was right. Labeled with a tiny scrawl of handwriting, the word Gaian was printed next to the symbol in the Meridian of Pride. She would have never realized what it meant without the three females in the tavern.

To reach the meridian in the southeastern corner of the map, she would have to navigate three of the islands. The terrain was bereft of marshes, forests, and deserts.

But Greer had no choice. She needed to get home. And this was the only option she had.

A green rucksack was tucked in the bottom drawer of one of the dressers, nearly the size of a daypack for hiking. It was smaller than Greer wanted, but rolling up her clothes saved the smallest bit of space. Next, she tucked the fruit from a decorative bowl into the front pockets—enough for a handful of days, at least. She would still need to stop at the kitchen on her way out, and she silently hoped there was leftover cheese and dried meat that she could take.

She left just enough room in the rucksack for the additional food, locking the copper latches into place. She was ready to toss the straps over her shoulders when a knock at the bedchamber door made her stutter to a stop.

"Your high– Greer?" a quiet voice said from the other side of the threshold. "Are you back? I thought I heard–" Arista stepped into the room as her eyes fell on Greer, and she halted just as quickly, taking in the scene before her. "What are you doing?"

Greer was speechless for the first time in weeks, torn between telling the truth and making off into the night after a bald-faced lie. Arista's gaze, already sweeping over Greer and to the room beyond, had taken in the rucksack, the drawers of the dresser still open and empty, and the fruit bowl discarded upside-down on the bed, even though not a piece of fruit had been eaten since Greer's arrival.

"You're leaving," Arista breathed, her tone accusatory.

"Arista, I can't stay here," Greer replied, drawing herself up to full height. "I need to go home. I don't belong in Samsara."

Arista was quiet for a heartbeat, her fingers flexing at her sides. "I can't let you leave."

Greer felt a pressure tighten in her core. "You can't make me stay."

The flames of the candles flickered behind her, drawing Arista's face from the shadow. Her cream-colored wings snapped open to full attention, blocking the door with a barrier made of feathers. A flash of power, light and airy compared to Azazel's, brushed over Greer, and, at that moment, she knew that she had been underestimating the Lesser Primordial.

"I may not have the capability," Arista began, her shocked expression shifting into one of alert calm. "But I have already summoned the one who does."

Greer scanned the room, looking for a way around Arista. She briefly considered blowing the handmaiden off her feet, but under the sudden and unseen pressure, only sparks left her fingertips. Arista's smile was devastating, a crack in the outer shell built up over millennia of serving those more powerful than her.

But at that moment, Arista was the most powerful in the room.

The room rumbled, the floor beneath her feet shifting like an earthquake had hit the mountain. Greer fidgeted on her feet as she felt it, though Arista stood stark and still against the ongoing shakes and sways of the palace. A crash behind Greer made her jump, and she spun on the balls of her feet to see that the bathroom mirror had fallen from the wall. Shattered glass ricocheted across the floor, bouncing and jittering across the stone.

As suddenly as it began, the shaking stopped. Greer steadied herself on her feet, letting the rucksack fall from her shoulders. The room was strewn with flower petals, cracked picture frames, and knickknacks that had tumbled to the thick carpet.

Arista's expression had gone cold, and it took Greer a mere second to understand why. The flames of the candles winked out, and small curls of smoke danced toward the ceiling— the only indication of what came next.

A barrage of power filled the room, an explosion so forthright that it forced Greer to her knees. The magic didn't come in wispy tendrils like Samael's but in vast tentacles that seemed to cover every inch of her body. Her throat bobbed as she struggled to breathe against the power. The air ripped from her lungs with every ragged heave.

Greer coughed, her eyes stinging with tears as she clawed at her chest. She was drowning, drowning in a sea of fog, darkness, and power that she couldn't escape from. Her vision narrowed as she scanned the room, surprised to see three additional pairs of leather boots next to Arista's slippered ones.

The breath slammed back into Greer's chest as the power faded, and the stars pricking the backs of her eyes began to wane. Breath still battered and heavy, she lifted her head to peer at the three newcomers.

Azazel, she recognized immediately. It must have been his own terrible power strangling her. His blonde hair was pulled back, and his eyes were filled with fiery malice mixed with something she couldn't quite identify.

He stepped forward, his boot creasing the carpet fibers, and bent down to clamp his fingers around Greer's upper arm. She was hauled to her feet with an easy tug, her fingers tingling with the loss of blood to her hand. Greer couldn't help the whine of terror that curled in the back of her throat.

"Azazel."

Greer knew the second voice to be Samael, even through the sharp snap to his tone.

Azazel was still staring at her, his gray eyes studying every one of her freckles, as he remained silent. His breath, just as ragged as her own, fluttered the locks of hair framing her face.

"Azazel. She's still safe."

The leather of Azazel's armor creaked as he released Greer's arm, and she tumbled back to the floor, unaware that she had been standing on her tiptoes. From the corner of her eye, she saw Samael lurch as if he were going to come to her side but thought better of it.

Greer turned her attention to Azazel, a glare replacing her expression of shocked horror. "I can't stay here," she finally said, breaking through the strained air. "I need to go home."

Azazel was silent for another moment, but Greer watched the muscles in his jaw working with every clench of his teeth. "Did it ever occur to you that you are not safe and that I have a reason for keeping you?"

Greer pushed herself to stand, brushing the dirt that shook free from the cracked walls off of her hands. "You keep saying that, but I can take care of myself—"

"No," Azazel interjected with a curt shake of his head. "*You* are not safe. *You.*"

Greer blinked, but she may as well have been punched in the stomach the way her breath left her lungs for the second time in so many minutes. Pain lashed through her, and pressure built in her chest as she realized she had forgotten to breathe.

"Wh— what did you say?"

Not even a flicker of remorse from Azazel. "You can kill. You have killed." Arista flicked a stunned look toward Azazel. "You are not fit to live in a world with humans." He took a step forward, further closing the gap between them. Greer fought the urge to move. "You are dangerous, and you need to learn control."

Greer gulped back a stuttered sob, refusing to let a single tear fall. "I just want to go home."

"And how do you think you'll feel when you go home and explode again? When you go back to your ramshackle town and kill another friend? Will you believe me then?"

Greer stayed silent, hardening her overwhelming devastation into one of indifference. She wouldn't allow her eyes to drop from his.

Azazel slowly blinked, turning away from her. His hand rested on the pommel of a dagger, similar to Samael's, with three ruby gemstones lining the leather. "Baraqiel." The command came out as a bark.

The third male, dark-skinned with alarmingly pale eyes, stepped forward. One hand was crossed over the other, both resting at his beltline. "Your Grace?" Baraqiel's voice was low and smooth.

"You will stand guard at my daughter's door."

Greer opened her mouth to protest as Baraqiel placed an armored forearm across his chest in understanding. "You can't lock me in here!" She felt a shot of panic percolate beneath her skin. She made to move toward Azazel, but Baraqiel blocked the way with a single step to the left.

"You have proven incapable of making decisions regarding your safety and the safety of those around you. You will remain here until you have finished training with Samael."

Greer bit back the recoil that threatened to shudder through her at his words. "Holly would be ashamed of how you're treating me," she called to Azazel as he crossed over the threshold, Samael at his heels. It was a desperate, last-ditch effort.

Azazel paused at the doorway, and the peak of Samael's sword glinted against the moonlight, which was now spilling through the circular window. "Holly would thank me." His voice was calm, but he had a white-knuckled grip on the doorframe. "And I suggest you refrain from weaponizing your mother a third time. There are many things about her you will never understand."

The four Primordials left the room, and before Baraqiel locked the door, leaving Greer to the destruction of her bedroom, Arista sent her a deflated, apologetic stare.

SEVENTEEN

SAMAEL

It had been a long time since Samael had seen Azazel so shaken. Thousands of years, in fact. And he understood why. The regions outside of Samsara were dangerous on the best of days, and this woman had no idea what she was trying to get herself into.

If she knew, Samael was sure that she wouldn't set foot outside of the city.

He pursed his lips in thought. Actually, based on the little he knew about Greer, save for her unending and compounding desire to go back to Gaian, he was quite sure that she would rather be impaled by any one of the creatures that lurked in Samsara than stay in the city one second longer.

Samael leaned back in his seat, crossing his arms over his chest. He had deposited his leather armor in his own bed chambers before meeting with Azazel and the cool air through his thin, linen shirt was a relief.

"She's going to keep attempting to escape. Baraqiel will be able to hold her back for only so long."

Azazel let out a sharp sigh, and his own leather armor creaked as it shifted. "Do you think I'm being too harsh on her? By locking her away?"

Samael kept quiet. He tapped his fingers on the markings around his bicep as he watched Azazel. The man seemed to be working through his thoughts with eyes narrowed on the pewter tankard in front of him.

"We're friends, Samael–"

Samael scoffed. "No, you are a means to an end to keep me out of a locked tomb. That's different from friends."

"How do you think she'll escape, then?" Azazel asked, completely ignoring Samael's statement. "Baraqiel has been standing guard for nearly three days now and, so far, there's been no hint of trouble."

"And for the entirety of the three days, she's been requesting that Arista bring her bedsheets."

Azazel furrowed his brow. "And?"

Samael snorted. "You don't know as much about humans as you think you do."

"Are you going to answer my question?"

Reaching forward to grasp his own pewter tankard, Samael swirled the contents before taking a large gulp. Ale. It was not his favorite; he preferred the sour wine made in Parab, located in the Meridian of Greed, but it would do for now. "It's one of the easiest tricks in the book: making a rope out of bed sheets to climb out of a window." Samael didn't bother telling Azazel that Greer had already used the other oldest trick in the book on him in the tavern weeks previously.

"Bedsheets?" Azazel murmured, mostly to himself, as it was barely audible above the plinking of the freezing rain against the sheets of glass making up the domed ceiling. "Resourceful thing, isn't she? So very...human."

Samael unfolded his arms, leaning his forearms against the edge of the circular table seated in the middle of the meeting hall. He took a minute to sweep his gaze across the room, taking in the plush carpet beneath his boots, the warm wooden tones flanking the fireplace merrily crackling behind Azazel, and the painted portrait of a dark-haired woman nestled above the mantle.

Samael had never met Holly. When she had come into the picture, he was out of Samsara for a few centuries as he gathered intel on Elysia's forces and did his duty collecting souls for both Azazel and Michael. He hadn't returned until years after Holly had been killed when the son of Michael had amassed enough power to warrant Azazel pulling Samael back into Samsara. Now, he only used his limited power to collect souls and send them to their afterlife.

Samael missed the use of his sword. He hadn't used it since taking the soul of Greer's friend. He would visit the training pits with Abaddon, Prince of Wrath and Primordial of Vengeance and Retribution, and burn off some steam by sparring, but that certainly wasn't the same.

And it certainly wasn't the same as sparring with his brothers, but they were long scattered across the realms.

"Should I stop her, then? From collecting bedsheets?" Samael finally asked, carefully monitoring Azazel's reaction.

The king set down his tankard before clearing his throat. "No, she doesn't know how to get to Gaian, only that there is a way. I'm not too concerned."

Samael's mouth twitched upward, but he quickly hid it before Azazel eyed him. "She already has a map of Samsara. She knows where the portal is."

Samael had made sure of that, though he thought she should learn more about her native realm. He had been on the balcony of the library that night— it was his favorite place to see the stars. The silence of the dark hall, flourishing with the hustle and bustle of bookkeepers during the day, was the calm against the cries of the dead and dying who reached out for him from across the realms.

Greer had walked in, and Samael had watched as she took her time between each stack, slowly surveying the books before settling against the sandstone floor. It was he who had pulled the book from the shelf, where it landed at her feet as she made to leave.

Azazel's knuckles whitened against the handle of the tankard, and Samael knew imprints of the shape of his fingers had molded the metal with ease. "How?" Azazel asked from between gritted teeth.

Samael shrugged. The lie was easy and he knew better than to tell the truth to Azazel.

Azazel stood, wings tucked in tight against his back, and he turned to stare into the fire. "I want to see how this plays out. If you're so certain she will attempt an escape, I want to see how far she gets into Samsara before returning."

"You want her to enter Samsara? Alone?"

"Alone?" Azazel scowled into the crackling flames. "No. You go. Under the guise of helping her escape."

Samael still didn't know much about Greer, but he knew that *he* would rather be impaled by any one of the creatures lurking between the city and the Meridian of Pride than escort her all the way to the Gaian portal.

When Samael said nothing, Azazel picked up the insinuation of his silence. "She is quite stubborn, isn't she?"

That was certainly the understatement of Samael's immortal life-time. "She knows how to use weak spots against people. I wonder where that came from."

"I understand we aren't fond of one another, Samael, but without my help, you would be locked in the tombs along with your brothers. It is only by my intervention and benevolence that you sit here before me in true form."

"I'm not in my true form." Samael gestured toward the dark markings around his biceps, but he also felt them wrapping around his chest, his waist, his hips, and each thigh. They held him like chains, subduing his power like the prisoner he was. "And we both know the only reason you intervened was not due to your benevolence but a prophecy that involved us both. You needed me."

Azazel stilled, and Samael briefly wondered if he had stepped too far. He knew he could easily walk over any boundary with Greer, but with Azazel...being at a subdued power level, even with his own realm-creating magic, would not be enough to defeat the King of Samsara if it came down to it.

"If you go with her, I will free you."

It was Samael's turn to still, and when he finally looked up, he saw that Azazel was peering at him from over a shoulder. "That's impossible without defeating Michael. We both know that."

There was a *thunk* on the wooden table as Azazel rested both fists against the surface, leaning backward and forward as if in deep thought. "There is another way." He had gone pale, his dark leather stark against his whitened features. "The power of a demi-primordial."

Samael's eyes darkened as he, too, stood from his seat. "What did you do, Azazel?"

"What was necessary."

"There are only two demi-primordials in existence. You'll either have to use Greer's power against her will or kidnap Leander from Gaian. The latter will jumpstart the war between Elysia and Samsara, but the former will solidify the civil war that Greer will undoubtedly create."

Azazel pushed himself off the table, straightening to full height. Samael saw the tips of his white wings twitch with irritation. "Not unless we can get her to agree."

A log cracked under the intense heat and pressure of the flame.

Samael snorted with laughter, picking up his tankard to drain the last of the ale. "You can't get her to agree to training her own magic. You think you can get her to agree to open the tombs and clear me of my markings?"

"Not me. You."

Samael clamped his lips shut, swallowing his laughter as if it were something particularly foul-tasting. "Me? You think that I can get her to agree?"

"The clock is ticking for the prophecy. We need her in this, Samael. And you're going to be the one to get her there."

The plinking against the sheets of glass had turned into fat plops in the silence that stretched between the two males.

"Why me?" Samael asked, his low voice shattering the quiet as if it were a piece of thin ice.

"You know why."

Samael levied a warning stare at Azazel, feeling his power pushing at the chains that held it back. "Absolutely not. I will not be using *that*–"

"It's the only leverage we have. We've tried shoving her into her power, but that has not worked. If we aren't successful in leading her to it, the window will be gone, and you will be stuck in this form for eternity."

Samael felt his heart thumping against his chest as he dropped his eyes to study the wood grain arranged on the surface of the table. "Leander still could–"

"Leander was given less than one percent of Michael's power at birth. He cannot create enough on his own to open the tombs, and his stores are not large enough to source the needed power. Not without someone from whom he could siphon the power from."

Realization dawned over Samael. "And that is why you brought Holly to Samsara? Why you put obsidian in her and Greer's bones?"

Azazel raised a brow. "Among many reasons. Greer was given a third of my power upon her birth and when she becomes competent in using it, she will be stronger than nearly every Primordial in existence. If she is in the Gaian realm before she is ready, Leander will find her now that the obsidian has been removed."

Samael was deep in thought and, when he emerged, he hung his chin to his chest in defeat. "What must I do?"

EIGHTEEN

DELIA

The terracotta wall split vertically from the ground to dangerously near the flat roof as Kazzy drove Cian into it, showering the three of them with dust. Cian's teeth gnashed, fangs punching through his gum line as he struggled to bite any part of Kazzy that he could reach. His snarl echoed across the stone as he shoved his hand toward her and grasped her around the throat.

"Cian!" Delia cried out as he managed to lift Kazzy into the air, leaving her feet to dangle inches above the cobblestone alleyway. From the corner of her eye, Delia saw a curtain ruffle in a nearby window. Someone had seen them.

Kazzy kicked out her legs, landing a blow to the middle of Cian's chest. He let out a sharp breath, and his fingers slackened enough for her to peel herself from his grip. She spun on the balls of her feet as she dropped, canines lengthening in her mouth and her fingernails tapering into claws. She let out a low growl from the back of her throat as she leaped forward, tackling Cian and pinning him to the ground.

"Kazzy! What the fu–" Delia tried again, running forward to pry the woman from the vampyre. She clasped her hand around Kazzy's shoulder, sending Kazzy into a rampage, not knowing she intended to help her.

Kazzy twisted, swiping a clawed hand at Delia's cheek, and Delia let out a cry of surprise as she ducked, falling onto her backside with a sickening thud. A shock of pain missiled from her tailbone to the back of her neck, sending waves of nausea rolling up her throat.

Cian had wriggled from Kazzy's grasp and moved with a speed that Delia had difficulty tracking. He landed a punching blow between Kazzy's shoulder blades, and she pitched forward, her nose smashing against the cobblestone, blood dripping down the bridge and onto the front of her sundress.

Kazzy's eyes flashed dangerously, the pupils growing larger and then smaller as she pushed herself to standing, assessing Cian with an intense stare. She wiped the blood away from her chin with the back of her hand and began pacing in front of him with a wolf-like stride, her nose working as if she could sense his next move by his tang in the air.

Delia felt her heart stutter as she watched Kazzy, terror suddenly filling every cell in her body. Kazzy was a *werewolf*. No wonder Delia had that intuition regarding Kazzy's humanity. She didn't have any. She wasn't even human.

Kazzy was the first to lunge forward, bridging the gap between herself and Cian. Her feet were so forceful against the stone that it cracked, crumbles flicking from under her white sneakers. She wrapped her arms and legs around Cian, hanging off of him in a way that Delia would have found humorous if it hadn't been for the very serious situation she had landed them in. Kazzy was busy trying to clamber up Cian's trunk, reaching for his head to more easily snap his neck.

On the other hand, Cian was thrashing to the side to tear his fangs into the closest piece of Kazzy he could reach.

Delia's head lifted, her eyes darting around the alley to see if she could find anything to break them up. Kazzy and Cian were rolling around the cobblestone, knocking over vespas and fracturing the potted plants, sending soil spilling onto the stones. Delia's gaze landed on two loose bricks near the foundation of the building, and she lurched forward, crawling across the crushed clay on her hands and knees and ignoring the biting pain of the gravel sinking into her skin. She grasped onto both bricks and pushed herself to her feet.

Taking two steps toward the squabbling, Delia took quick aim and launched the brick at Kazzy. It rocked the werewolf in the temple, forcing her to release her grasp on Cian, where she fell to the ground with a crunch. Cian stumbled backward, tripping over an upturned stone, and crashed against the terracotta wall. He slid downward until his backside rested on his heels, his hand shooting up to probe the part of his skull that had slammed into the stone.

"Knock it off," Delia said between gritted teeth, her hands tightening into fists as she looked between them.

Kazzy had the decency to appear shame-faced, though Cian was glowering at the werewolf from his crouched position. He removed his hand from his head, wincing at the dark blood staining his fingertips. Delia dropped the second brick she had grabbed and glanced toward the alley entrance. Miraculously, no one on the main road had stopped to watch the fight, though the same couldn't be true for the residents of the buildings they were between. At the very least, she couldn't see any more faces peering out from the windows.

Delia turned back to Kazzy. "You're a werewolf?"

"We prefer wolf shifters." Her claws were already beginning to retract, returning to the dark purple polish that coated her fingernails. Chest still heaving, she looked at Cian, who was regarding her with an apprehended stare. "I've been searching for the Paladin Society for over fifty years."

Delia's brow cocked as she crossed her arms over her chest. "I thought you said you had been here for three years?"

Kazzy nodded, gently prodding the knot growing on the side of her head. "Yes, but it took me nearly fifty years to find them."

Cian slowly stood from his kneel, keeping his eyes locked on Kazzy. "Why?" He dusted off the front of his pants, smearing blood from his hand onto the fabric. "Why do you have an interest in the Paladin Society?"

Delia looked back to Kazzy in time to see her eyes grow glossy. Her lips parted, heat threading up her neck and onto her cheeks. She crept upward, sitting on her tailbone and, once again, twirling her loose ponytail with two fingers. It seemed as though it were a nervous tick.

"I was born as Katja Baltzer in the Austrian Empire in 1854," Kazzy started slowly. "I lived with my mother, father, four sisters, and two brothers until–" She stared at her bloody hands. "We were returning to Germany from New Zealand. We spent a few decades there to escape the World Wars. The Paladin assassins found my family." Her red-rimmed eyes shot up to meet Delia's. "I was gone for the night, hunting. It's harder to do as a pack these days. The world is smaller." She cleared her throat. "And when I returned...They were killed. Every single one of them. I found them all dead, each impaled with a silver stake to the heart."

Delia felt her chest constrict, but she hesitated to get too close to comfort the wolf shifter. Even Cian's contempt had softened to a general gaze of empathetic pity.

"I changed my name to Kazzy to hide my identity and set off as a lone wolf. It took me fifty years to glean any information on the Paladin Society." She swept her gaze over to Cian, who met it with conflicted resignation. "As you know, it's impossible for any daemons to get within a hundred feet of the building. The runes carved into the stone are binding. I've tried from every angle, including the sewers and the roof."

They were silent for a long minute before Cian spoke up. "Did you go to your council head? Your alpha?"

Kazzy snorted derisively, shifting so her forearms were resting on her knees. "Gawin? Yeah, I went to see him."

Delia tilted her head, studying the wolf shifter with a furrowed brow. "And what happened?"

"I requested a meeting with him a year after my family was killed, and it took another five for him to grant it. During that time, I traveled the world looking for anything to do with Paladin and came up short." She shook her head. "Once I was blessed with the opportunity to finally meet with Gawin, he was no help at all. His advice was to move on and find a new pack." Her hazel eyes slid between Cian and Delia before they fell and stayed on Delia. "Just move on like the murders of my family never happened. I— I just want the chance to work with you."

Delia and Cian exchanged glances. She wiped her palms against the front of her legs before shaking the dirt and gravel from the back of her pants. With an uplifted chin, she gestured toward Cian, moving them deep into the alleyway.

"We should let her help," Delia hissed as they got out of earshot of the wolf shifter. Cian was already vigorously shaking his head. "Come on, man. We both know we could use her assistance. We're at a dead end. Even outside of the whole 'Paladin killed her family' thing, it would cut our time down if there were three working this instead of two. And she's been trying for fifty years. Imagine how long it will take us."

"She's a wolf shifter," Cian retorted, his eyes wide. "She is my literal godforsaken enemy. We will kill each other before we learn anything more about Paladin."

"Grow up and calm your urges, then," Delia said, her lip curling in a sneer. "I'm calling in my favor."

Cian side-eyed her, his jaw ticking as he clenched his teeth. "You're what now?"

"When I changed my mind and didn't want to come, you promised that I would get a favor if I agreed to get on the plane. I'm cashing it in now. I want my favor to be you working with Kazzy without you trying to murder her every other minute."

Cian groaned, rocking back and forth on the balls of his feet. "When I said you could have a favor, I meant going out to a burger joint or something."

Delia smirked. "Your poor ability to clarify reflects you, not me."

He rolled his eyes. "Fine, *fine*. She can work with us, okay? Not too closely, but enough that she's helpful." Delia was readying to walk away when Cian grabbed onto her upper arm, holding her in place. "If she fucks us over and this blows up in our faces— and I lose out on my chance to find Greer in Samsara in the process— I'm going to kill you."

Delia looked him in the eye, grasping his fingers with her other hand and peeling them off her arm. "Even if you manage to find Samsara without me...if you kill me and Greer finds out," she whispered back, her smirk dangerously close to evolving into a triumphant grin. "You can kiss her goodbye for the rest of your miserable fucking life."

Cian released his hand as though she had smacked him, but his stare remained fixed and steady. "I realize what you're doing, you know, and who she reminds you of. The blonde ponytail, the can-do attitude...she's not Paige."

Devastation blanked Delia's face as she gaped at him in silence, and pressure began building in her chest from the breath she had forgotten to take. She shuffled back despite the sudden weakness in her knees.

"Delia—" Cian began to say, reaching out to grasp her hand, but she yanked it away.

She brushed past Kazzy, saying nothing as she marched from the alleyway.

NINETEEN

ODETTE

O dette was seated on the ground in the front garden, leaning against a canopy tree while she sharpened her blade. She pretended to be engrossed in the work, but she was watching the lower court members through her lashes. The hushed conversations, the side-glances toward certain guards, the scurrying footsteps when Caio or other high-ranking officials appeared.

There was already something afoot here. Odette just needed to figure out what it was.

"Beautiful day," a male voice said from above her.

Narrowing her eyes against the sun, Odette sheathed her dagger and stood.

"I didn't mean to startle you."

"You didn't," Odette responded, casually crossing her arms across her chest. "What can I do for you, Kaique?" Behind him, a female servant was picking herbs from the kitchen garden. The basket that was dangling from her forearm slid to her wrist.

Kaique waved her off, his dismissively signature move that Odette had grown to hate in the days she had been in the Court of Mist and Tide. "I wanted to formally announce your return with a special dinner this evening. I already have everything prepared."

Odette bristled, remembering the last formal dinner, and glanced to her left to watch the jungle canopy sway with the wind over the top of the basalt stone walls. Taking in a deep breath, filling her nose with the scents of saltwater and the ripening tomatoes hanging on the vines near the kitchen, she finally said, "Do you think that's a good idea? Your court—"

"Only do what I want," Kaique replied with a firm smoothness that echoed his father more than Odette wanted to admit. "Your return has been whispered for nearly two weeks now. I think it's about time that we show them our united front." His stare was pointed, dark eyes penetrating her own amber ones.

"We *don't* have a united front," Odette shot back, leaning against the tree trunk once again. She propped a casual foot behind her. "You have enough slaves to remind me of that."

Kaique's sinister smile curved onto his lips. "Are you unhappy with Luisa already? I'm sure I can find someone else for you. I certainly remember your inclinations when we were younger. But I can assign a male this time, perhaps? Or are you not quite ready to indulge the pleasures of a cock?"

Odette stared boldly into Kaique's, ensuring it didn't flicker away. She had steered clear of Luisa since the first day they had met, deciding once and for all that she didn't want any knowledge of the escape Luisa had planned. They wouldn't survive anyway, and Odette did not need to go down with her.

She was already a political prisoner, whether or not she wanted to admit it.

Regardless, Odette knew exactly why Luisa was sent to her. Kaique had made advances on her when they were young, around sixty years old or so, which were promptly shot down. Not because of her *inclinations*, she enjoyed men just as much, but because he was...*Kaique.*

Seems he still harbored some of those feelings.

"Luisa is a fine gift," Odette said, tempering the shudder of disgust that started at the base of her spine. "I'm perfectly happy with her companionship." Lies. She would never, the thought unfathomable to her. But she knew what Kaique wanted and refused to give it to him.

"Have you tasted her on your tongue yet?" Kaique went on, a passing cloud casting half of his face in shadow. "It doesn't happen often, but sometimes I want the pleasure of a newly spent cunt on my lips. And hers is far sweeter than anyone else I've had since I became the Lord of Court and Mist."

"And when was that again?" Odette shot back in an attempt to change the subject, afraid that her twitching fingers would grasp the hilt of the dagger she had sheathed at her hip.

Kaique's smile quirked at one corner. "She's the one that's lasted the longest. The others don't matter. But Luisa is something quite special, isn't she?" He stepped forward to lower his voice. "Just last night, I had her riding my cock until the early hours of the morning." He reached into his pocket to pull out a chunk of long, brown hair, twirling it between his fingers.

Odette felt the anger roil within her. Her mind drifted to the prison cell she had been held in for all those centuries. Of Adair coming to *visit* her. Her lover, Egohann, had to listen to her being taken by that monster who called himself king. How it took her decades to be touched without the jolting reaction she recognized in Luisa, how it took Nerea just as long to convince her that she was whole despite her fractured soul, or how, even now, she didn't let anyone get too close.

"You should hear her moans when she comes," Kaique went on, letting Luisa's hair drift away on the humid morning breeze. "She has this little squeak when she tightens around my–"

"Enough," Odette snarled. She pulled on the molecules in the air, tugging them into a lasso that she could lash, catching Kaique around the throat. His chin lifted at the phantom magic, his smile growing wider despite his position. "Do not speak of her that way."

The water churned in the pools around them, waves cresting over the sides of the marble like small tsunamis. "Careful, general," Kaique warned through choked coughs. "We are matched in our power. And I, unlike you, have no issue with using my servants as a shield." He gestured with a jerk of his chin over his shoulder, a servant behind him suddenly straightening.

Odette glanced past him, horrified to see the woman with a bubble of water wrapped around her face as she writhed on the ground, unable to breathe. The basket had been dropped to the stone pathway, and herbs splayed onto the tile. Her lips had already begun to tinge blue as she struggled to free herself. A second servant, a younger male, was screaming as he was being held back by one of the palace guards.

"Let her go," Odette said through gritted teeth, pulling deep inside of her to let loose another gust of wind that only managed to separate the water long enough for the woman to take a deep, gasping breath before she was plunged back inside. "Before I kill you."

"You work under the assumption that I haven't thought of that the moment you stepped foot in my court," Kaique spat back. "As if I don't have a letter addressed to Adair ready to be sent when my death occurs. *Tick-tock, general, she doesn't have much time left.*"

Odette freed her magic, releasing Kaique from her hold, who then freed his. He stumbled once before straightening, adjusting his tunic and royal robes back into place. "I look forward to seeing you at our dinner tonight," he said with a bow of his head as though nothing had transpired between them. "Someone will be along to collect you, as it won't take place in my private dining chambers."

Behind him, the woman was propped on her elbows as she spewed water from her lungs, face pale and hair tangled into a wet, matted knot. The man was still sobbing, held aloft by the blank-faced guard.

Luisa came to collect Odette that evening. Her demeanor was cool and indifferent despite the hatred Odette knew pulsed from her. They said nothing to one another as they walked past the empty guest chambers that had once been filled to the brim with emissaries from other courts. Odette felt her stomach flop as Luisa turned the corner toward the east gardens, where Odette knew the colosseum now sat. They walked along the stone path, flanked by marble pillars and curved trees that held bundles of acai. Servants perched on tall ladders plucked the fruit from the branches, plopping them into backpack-style baskets they had strapped to their backs.

The pathway ended at the entrance of the tall bushes, and, in the daylight, Odette noticed there were actually two entrances. The one on the left was sharply manicured with a continuation of the garden tile. The one on the right contained bloodied thorns and ripped fabric. The slave entrance.

"You'll go that way," Luisa said at last, gesturing toward the entrance on the left. "Follow the path to the wooden stairs. The Lord has already set up the dinner in the viewing box." She turned toward the servant's entrance and, without another word, disappeared into the brush.

Odette took in a deep breath, the air heavily scented with orchid and cinnamon, before lurching over the threshold and into her side of the shrubbery.

Kaique had made sure to send a new dress to her royal apartment, this one fit for an emissary of a foreign court. Dyed a deep shade of blue that complimented the growing number of freckles on her cheeks from the constant sun exposure, the dress was long and covered her from shoulders to ankles. It was surprisingly light, despite the length, and slits for her wings had been cut into the back. But Odette knew that Kaique wanted her to appear as his ally, so he would have never dared to pull a stunt like the first dress in a public setting.

The walk to the viewing box was a gentle, uphill grade that took her nearly ten minutes. Odette contemplated flying in but knew that it would be frowned upon to upstage the Lord of Mist and Tide. Although Nerea's father would have found it amusing— Kaique, however…Odette wanted to protect the other slaves from his wrath, and one of the easiest ways to do that was by not provoking it.

When she decided to settle into the viewing box, Luisa was already seated at one of the stone benches nearest the platform's edge. Her fingers were threaded tightly together against her lap. The women she was seated with were dressed just as sparingly as Luisa was, prompting Odette to believe there was more than one courtesan in Kaique's land.

Renan stood guard behind Kaique, his hand resting casually against the pommel of his sword. He was dressed in his finest fighting leathers, and Odette figured they had never seen action before, given the lack of creases or slash marks in the breastplate.

"Ah, my honored guest," Kaique said with a sweeping smile as he stood from his seat, centered in the rectangle table. "Please, Odette, have a place next to me."

The males gathered around him shot Odette scathingly jealous looks as they each shifted toward each end of the table, making room for her. More faces turned upward at her arrival, mostly villagers from what Odette could see, but after a quick glance around the colosseum, she recognized some of the kitchen servants on one side and some of the palace guards on the other.

Below her, chained to the wooden platform built on the pit's dirt floor, were three human men. They shook with anticipation and nerves, their shoulders trembling as they struggled to hold steady against coursing adrenaline. Odette knew that feeling well—the pre-jittery feeling of a pending battle.

"What is this?" Odette asked, gesturing toward the three men. Princes, she hoped she was wrong. She hoped this wasn't a battle. "What are they doing down there?"

Kaique snapped his fingers, and four servants appeared, one of them Tomas, who had gleaming trays of roasted garlic pork and squash. The food would have smelled delicious had it not been for the scene before her. Now Odette just found it repulsive.

"I found the best way to keep my servants in order is to cull them when I find it necessary," Kaique said as Tomas placed a heap of pork onto his plate. "And considering we are coming up on the summer solstice soon, it's time for me to bring new blood into the palace. To make room—" He trailed off to gesture toward the three men with his fork. "I picked three that I thought would give us a good performance."

"Performance?" Odette asked, her face growing pale with the words, but she didn't need to wait for Kaique to explain further.

The platform rumbled as heavy chains clanked below her, and the eyes of everyone in the colosseum fixed their eyes on what lay beneath. The three men's trembles deepened as shouts from the guards working in the pit were heard over the crack of their whips. A roar sounded just as a guard hurried over to unlock the chains of the first man, shoving a sword into his hand.

Silence fell over the colosseum, save for the whisper of a large body gliding along the sandy dirt of the pit. A massive snake head appeared from the door beneath them, the forked tongue darting from its mouth to taste the air around it. The body was as thick as one of the jungle trees and nearly twenty feet long, with green and brown scales covering the trunk like armor. And, had it not been for the flames licking along the scales, one may have thought it was just an ordinarily large snake.

"The Serpent of Fire," Odette murmured under her breath as the male official beside her took a bite of the roasted pork, fat dripping down his chin. "What did you do, Kaique?"

"What should have been done by my father centuries ago," Kaique replied, tossing a piece of mango into his mouth. "These creatures were in our jungle, protecting the lands from those who meant us harm." He paused to chuckle, taking a gulp of wine. "I harnessed their natural instincts and trained them into seeing humans as the invaders instead."

Caio, nestled at the table three seats to her left, smiled at the scene playing out before her.

Odette's lips parted as she turned back to the serpent, the brilliantly bright eyes fixed on the man with the sword. The soldier standing guard over the two chained slaves stepped forward to shove the man from the platform. He landed on his belly, a painful *oof* sounding as the breath was released from his chest. A cloud of dust formed around him, momentarily obscuring him from sight.

The sword slid away from him, a groan resounding from the crowd as the man shuffled forward to pick up the blade by the hilt and swing it toward the bobbing head of the serpent. Tongue lashing, the serpent let out a second terrifying hissing roar as it lunged forward. The man rolled to the side, whipping the sword over his head and slicing the serpent's cheek open. It reeled back, the bulbous eyes flashing with anger before lunging again.

The man staggered backward, thrusting the sword forward and catching the serpent underneath the chin. The serpent stilled, swaying steadily as it held its head in the air. The crowd bellowed out its cheers, the villagers clapping and chanting their approval. For a moment, hopefulness swelled within Odette as she thought the slave had pierced the serpent enough to kill it.

Instead, she watched in horror as the serpent snapped its tail behind the man's knees, sending him tumbling backward. And, in the next breath, the serpent darted forward and sank its forearm-long fangs into the man's gut. Blood spurted as the man let out a blood-curdling scream. The serpent ripped its fangs from his body, spilling his intestines onto the dirt floor.

The courtesans and various other servants who had been forced to witness the inevitable death of their friend had scores of reactions. Some had squeezed their eyes tightly shut, placing their heads in their hands. Others had covered their mouths to keep from crying out, knowing well that the guards stationed around them would have easily beaten them for making a sound. More had silent tears streaming down their faces, watching in grief-filled terror as their friend began to drag himself away from the snake, his intestines trailing behind him.

Kaique snorted into his wine glass. "Pathetic showing," he said with grim dissatisfaction. "I certainly thought he would last longer than that." He lifted his hand toward the guard on the platform, who immediately descended the stairs and lopped off the head of the dying slave.

A silence blanketed the colosseum as many struggled to comprehend the scene before them. Kaique, on the other hand, merely snapped his fingers for more wine. Tomas stepped forward, his hand rocking with tremors as he struggled to pour from the glass carafe. Odette lifted a subtle hand to steady his elbow, and from the corner of her eye, she saw Renan's eyes glide down to watch.

"Bring out the second," Kaique called over the cracking whips that struggled to contain the Serpent of Fire, who was letting out roaring hisses once again.

But Odette had seen enough.

The chair's wooden legs scraped against the platform as Odette stood, commanding the attention of the men surrounding the table. "Leave him," she shouted to the guard on the platform who was readying to unlock the shackles from the second slave's ankles.

Another chair scraped, and from the corner of her eye, Odette saw Caio stand. "We didn't ask for your input, you traitorous bitch," he spat at her as he reached for the sword sheathed at his side. "But I'm happy to remind you of your place."

Planting a hand on the back of his chair, Caio lunged toward her, but Odette was quicker. With a movement that was nearly imperceptible to humans, Odette pulled out the dagger she had hidden under her dress and threw it toward Caio with expert precision. She knew it hit its mark as she turned away from him, Caio letting out a sharp shout of pain as the dagger sunk into the back of his hand and pinned it to the chair it was resting on.

Odette had already cleared the table, Renan stepping toward her with his own sword drawn. She side-stepped his half-hearted swipe easily, sending a jabbing elbow into his nose before reeling back and punching him across the jaw. The double blow sent blood pouring from his nose, but Odette was already past him.

Gasps and cries rattled the crowd as Odette launched herself off the platform, letting her wings flap open. Soldiers yelled, struggling to shepherd the slaves from the stone benches amongst the chaos. She soared over the colosseum, banking toward the second platform that still held the two slaves. Kicking the guard off the edge with relative ease, she grasped the bow and quiver filled with arrows the soldiers had leaned against the far post.

Rocketing into the air once again, Odette pulled a single arrow from the quiver, letting it fall back to the pit below her. Nocking the arrow, she pulled back on the bow and took a steady aim, despite the rise and fall of her body as her wings beat at her back. She let the arrow loose in the next breath and it arched through the air. Odette watched the arrow fall, seemingly in slow motion, before it pierced one of the bulbous eyes of the serpent. More screams echoed against the stone as soldiers spilled into the pit, swarming toward her while attempting to evade the serpent's lashing tail.

The serpent's head thrashed as its thick body slithered along the floor of the pit, slamming against the wooden fence hiding the stairs. The planks splintered under the pressure, shooting outward like bullets and implanting into the exposed skin of the soldiers. Odette dropped the bow before swooping down to scoop up a forgotten sword, maneuvering around the distracted guards.

She rose to face the back of the serpent's head and grasped tightly onto the arrow with her empty hand. The head thrashed again, but she held it steady. The flames licked against her skin, hot like a breeze in the desert, as she forced the head back and sliced the blade across its exposed throat.

Black blood spurted from the wound as it let out a final hissing roar before crashing to the ground, finally unmoving. The flames winked out, leaving the scales to dull under the setting sun. Arms dripping with the viscous black, Odette landed on the pit's platform, chest heaving. Planting the sword into the wood beneath her like a flag on a new land, she waltzed over to the two slaves and ripped their chains off with quick tugs against the iron.

"These two are mine," Odette said, finally looking up at the viewing box where Kaique was still seated. Caio had managed to rip the dagger from his hand, flexing his fingers against the puncture mark that had surely severed a few tendons. "And they will be under my protection while I am in your court."

Kaique leaned forward in his seat, placing his forearms on the edge of the table. The colosseum went silent as they awaited his words, a shiver of tension flowing just beneath them. "Welcome to the Court of Mist and Tide, Odette Milne," he said, tilting his head in her direction. "I'm sure you'll find welcome accommodations here."

But Odette saw the sinister wrath hidden behind his eyes. And she knew, at that moment, she had punched her ticket to meeting Adair once again.

TWENTY

GREER

For the first few hours of her imprisonment, Greer allowed herself to fall into a mess of depression that included pounding at the door, screaming at the top of her lungs, and allowing her power to escape in brief yet forceful explosions that shook the paintings on the walls, before finally sinking into bed to cry into the covers.

The next morning, as the sun rose and the rays lit up the plum-colored room, Arista had come in with breakfast and a pile of freshly laundered bedsheets. They had both been set on the corner table before Arista bowed from the room, not once bothering to look over at Greer, who watched her with narrowed and hardened eyes.

When Greer unfolded the sheets to change the bedding, she had the idea. She had fooled Samael once by sneaking through a bathroom window. Who was to say she couldn't do it again?

With that thought, Greer padded to the large, circular window overlooking the city. Running her fingers against the seams where the glass met the metal, she felt her heart drop to her feet when she realized no latch accompaniedcould the panes. She stepped back with a sigh, knowing that the Primordial standing guard at her door would surely hear the shattering of glass if she opted to break it.

Greer glanced to the much smaller window on the right wall near the four-poster bed. It was too small to fit her hips through the frame. The window was high on the wall, her head barely approaching the sill. Even if she was able to fit through, there wasn't a chair or table tall enough that enabled her to hoist herself through.

But...there was still a third option. Eyes sweeping across the room, they finally landed on the bathroom window. Her power-walk turned into a jog, and a shiver went up her spine when her feet hit the cold tiles, the mirror fixed, and the glass cleaned up from the day before.

Only when she spotted a latch nestled between the pane of glass and the windowsill, locked tight, her heart leaped from her feet back into her throat. The glass was frosted, possibly sandblasted based on the patterns etched into the window, and Greer was forced to reach upward to tug the latch from the position. Luckily, it came loose after two quick pulls, and the bronze pin was left to hang from the chain, dangling against the tiled wall.

The only problem was that the window was directly to the left of the tub, almost out of reach, and would require some hefty maneuvering.

Carefully, Greer placed one foot on the edge of the claw-foot tub, using her toes to wrap around the rounded, porcelain edge. She pushed herself up, balancing on the balls of her feet and using her fingers against the wall as a counter. She side-walked on the edge, pausing briefly when her knees threatened to give out with nerves, until she reached the window. Greer leaned forward to push the pane outward, and she felt the fresh mountain breeze coat her face.

Maintaining her steady foot on the edge and leaning forward enough to peer through the window was difficult, but she could do it long enough to stick her head out and look downward.

Greer estimated that the drop was about fifty feet, too far to just free fall from the window, and she certainly didn't trust her power enough to ensure she would survive if she did decide to jump. Grasping the sill, she hopped down from the tub's edge and hurried over to grab the bedsheets she had thrown in a haphazard pile on the mattress.

Greer unfolded the fitted and flat sheets and spread them on the thick carpet. She rolled them down into a long bundle, tying the top end of one sheet to the bottom end of the other in a tight knot. Pulling them taut once again, Greer lay on the floor parallel to one of the bundles and used her height to measure the length of each piece.

With Greer's approximation, she calculated she would need eight bedsheets to tie into one long rope and escape through the window. She kicked the bundled sheets under the bed, tucking them safely in the corner, where they couldn't be seen unless someone bent down to look.

"Baraqiel?" Greer called through the wooden door as she approached the threshold, slamming her hand against it and shaking the door in the frame. "Baraqiel! I know you're there!" Silence followed, as it had for the last twelve hours or so. "Baraqiel, can you tell Arista I spilled my tea on the new sheets? And ask if she can bring more?"

Baraqiel said nothing in return, but ten minutes later, Arista showed up with a fresh set in her hands.

"Where is the dirty set?" Arista asked as she set the pile on the table. Greer had faked the tea spilling by dumping the full pot onto the silver tray. The tea dripped through the tray's handles onto the table, creating puddles of aromatic liquid she smeared with white towels.

"I burned them," Greer lied with ease. "Just exercising my power, getting the kinks out."

Arista's stare was wary as she said, "I didn't feel...I guess I must have missed it. Is there anything else I can bring you? A replacement pot, perhaps?"

Greer sent her a dazzling smile. "I'm okay, thank you. Would you put some extra fruit and dried meat on the lunch tray? I've been getting hungry in between lunch and dinner."

Arista's wariness cleared with Greer's smile, and she enthusiastically nodded as she backed from the room. Greer's smile slid from her face with a comical speed as soon as the lock clicked shut.

After fishing the knotted sheets from under the bed, she grabbed the new pile from the table, unraveled the fitted and flat sheets on the carpet, and tied them together. The makeshift rope doubled in length, and Greer let out a satisfied sigh as she sat back on her heels.

The pattern repeated for two more days. Greer slowly repacked the canvas bag Samael had conveniently left behind, rolling her clothes into tight wads to conserve space. In the extra pockets, she stored the dried meat and cheese wrapped in linen and the fruit she managed to pull off the tray. She requested a new set of sheets both mornings as well, and Arista brought them with only minimal questions asked...questions that Greer was able to skirt around with little issue.

Greer stored the rope under her bed, out of sight, and pulled it out to work on the knots in between the times Arista would come in to deposit meal trays on the table. The task gave her something to focus on instead of how Azazel had locked her up or how Samael let it happen. How Arista had betrayed her and how Baraqiel had stood guard at her door for nearly four days now.

At the end of day three, Greer felt ready for her prison break, so she pulled the bundle of bedsheets from underneath the four-poster as soon as Arista cleaned up her dinner tray. Knowing the schedule now, the handmaiden wouldn't be back until breakfast, giving her at least ten hours to get ahead of the search party that would surely be after her.

Greer dropped the bundle on the bathroom tiled floor just as the sun set over the lake, pulling the rays back and shifting the cloud color from a deep orange into dark navy. It would barely be light enough for her to navigate the rocky terrain, but it was her only chance of not being spotted by those leaving the palace for the evening.

Swallowing back her nerves, Greer felt her fingers trembling as she tied one side of the bedsheet-rope to the claw foot of the tub. Wrapping her hands around the linen, she tugged on it as hard as possible, ensuring the knot wouldn't slip loose.

During her anthropology trips in graduate school, Greer prided herself on learning how to tie knots and the basics of living off the land, which she was taught in the remote areas of the dig sites around the country. She had little doubt she would be okay in the wilderness of Samsara as long as she could move under the cover of darkness to avoid detection.

Reaching up, Greer unlatched the lock from the window and pushed the pane out, feeling the wind chilling under the night sky through the mountain pass. She had measured the angle of the pane against her hip size the day before, and although it would be tight and require her to tie the canvas pack to the end of the rope before climbing out, she knew it was doable if she wriggled as close as she could to the outer stone wall.

Gathering the bundle in her arms once again, she watched to make sure the bedsheets didn't tangle as she fed the rope through the open window, letting the canvas bag at the end lead the drop until the column of bedsheets was taut against the claw foot of the tub. Greer tugged on it again, a sigh of relief escaping her nose when the knot remained tight and unmoving.

Next, Greer climbed onto the lip of the tub. The sneakers she chose assisted in her grip, and she clambered over to the windowsill with relative ease. Her body trembled as she hoisted herself onto the windowsill. As soon as she settled herself onto the sill, glancing behind her to see the makeshift rope dangling tens of feet below her and held steady by the canvas pack, she wiped her sweaty palms on the front of her leggings. She spun onto her hip, slowly and carefully, until her feet dangled from the window, heels resting against the outer stone.

The weather was colder than she had anticipated, cutting through the tall turrets of the palace with sharp whistles. Greer cleared her throat as she grasped the bedsheets with a white-knuckled grip, trying to forget the empty, swooping feeling in the pit of her stomach as she slowly lowered herself out of the window.

The whipping wind lashed through her sweater, prickling the skin at the back of her neck. The force of it shoved her to the side of the tower, and she held on tightly as the gust blew her over the side of the mountain, swinging her back as the gust died back down. Greer let out a squeak of anxiety as she settled back against the wall, the bedsheets tightly clamped between her knees.

She waited for a beat, just in case a second gust was imminent, but began slowly descending down the rope moments later when nothing came.

The canvas bag swung below her, rocking the bedsheets back and forth as she lowered herself. *Hand. Hand. Unclamp knees and move lower. Hand. Hand. Unclamp knees and move lower.*

Greer wasn't sure how long it took her to reach the bottom of the rope, and her heart rammed against her chest with her movements. Every second, she anticipated that someone would stick their heads out of the window and pull the rope back up. It wasn't until her feet were firmly on the rocks that she let out a breath of relief, and it was in the very next breath that she fumbled with the knot holding her canvas bag. She didn't lift her head to look at the window as she tossed each strap over her shoulder, tightening the bag against her back.

The rocky terrain wrapped around the stone tower, large boulders half buried in the loose earth making up the steep cliffside. Instead of making her way toward the terrace and, inevitably, the city where Azazel would assume she go first, Greer turned to her right and slid along the outer wall towards the mountain pass. She had studied the way at large, both from her window and by staring at the map spread across the small table in her bedroom.

Greer followed the curve of the wall until it ended against another sharp cliffside that climbed high above her. Leaving the confines of the palace shadows, she swept her gaze along the caves and crevices carved into rock above the city. Each stone was cold and slick, freezing rain misting from the clouds stuck at the peaks. The path below her sneakers was so precariously narrow that she knew if she stuck her arm out to the side, it would float over the vast nothingness that plunged into the valley hundreds of feet below.

Shuddering at the thought, Greer pressed on. One foot in front of the other, careful not to trip, she kept her left hand firmly planted on the wall. She followed the cliff until she reached the end of the narrow path, and she took a moment to look up.

Squinting against the misty rain, Greer took a small step backward to better assess how she would need to take it. Taking the path leading down was a near-straight drop from her position on the mountain, but the way up would require a rock scramble at an anxiety-inducing angle above the valley. She glanced upwards toward the outcrop twenty feet above her and watched as a head peeked over the cliff's edge, then disappeared again.

Greer froze in place, staring into the darkness above. Even though she craned her neck to chance a peek over the edge of the outcrop, there were no sounds, save for the rain against the empty branches of the trees. She felt a panic build in her stomach. She could see two choices: turn back and admit defeat the moment she set foot on the terrace or face the unknown creature at the top of the cliff. Greer knew it would be a bad idea to continue on, but she couldn't imagine returning to the locked bed chambers guarded by Baraqiel.

This was her only chance at escape. Azazel would make sure she didn't have another.

Reaching out a hand, Greer wrapped her fingers around a crevice in the rock wall, pulling herself upwards. Steadying herself, she placed a foot onto a small ridge and pushed. She continued her climb, scrambling over the large boulders when the wall began to even out to a horizontal plane, and used the ridges and holes like a ladder when it straightened out again.

Dripping in cold sweat by the time she reached the edge of the cliff, Greer crawled over the top and rolled onto her side in a poor attempt to catch her breath. Using her shaking arms to push herself up, she could see the flickering candlelight from her small bedroom window, the bedsheet rope still billowing in the breeze, and the first winged statue perched on the end of the terrace.

No one had realized she escaped yet, at the very least.

A low and threatening growl echoed behind her, and Greer felt her face pale. Blood drained from her cheeks as she slowly spun on the balls of her feet. A dog-like creature appeared on the outcrop from behind a large boulder.

Even as she thought it, Greer thought a dog-like description seemed like a terrifying understatement, as the massive animal was unlike anything she had encountered before. The head of the creature came to her waist, and the body was bare of any fur except for a black mane that grew from its pointed ears to between the muscled shoulders of its back. The skin was leathered as if the old flesh had been pulled taut over too long of a time. On each spinal notch extending down the back was a spike, sharp and lethal, eight in total.

Whatever it was, it crept toward her, snarling its lips and baring its finger-length fangs. Despite the size of the paw pads and claws digging into the loose rock of the outcrop, the creature was nearly silent in the footwork. The head dipped low, its dark eyes connecting with hers as the snout worked, sniffing and assessing her.

Greer took a step back as it approached, the heel of her foot slipping over the edge of the outcrop. Glancing over her shoulder, she saw the gravel bounce off the rock face as it fell to the path below her. She had to get away, had to move from the outcrop before this thing chased her right over the edge.

In slow and controlled movements to keep it from being startled, Greer slid along the edge of the outcrop, edging closer to the interior to shift away from the drop-off. But that didn't seem to deter the thing any less. The creature snapped at her, teeth bared and saliva dripping from the corners of its mouth. She slipped on the slick rock, landing painfully on her hip before she managed to scramble behind another large boulder.

In that instant, Greer knew it was a bigger mistake than she had calculated. The dark side of the boulder was narrowly nestled to the other edge of the cliff, and she felt the toe of her sneaker catch against a crack in the rock in her attempt to keep herself from falling, which only sent her tumbling head over foot down the cliff face. The crags and ridges in the wall snagged at her arms and legs, tearing her leggings and sweater, leaving a bloody trail down the mountain as she fell.

Greer landed on her back, pack still strapped to her shoulders, and let out a breathy moan of pain. She realized her luck landed her just on the other side of the cliff wall she had scaled. Gravel punctured her skin as she opened her eyes, watching with blurred vision as the creature steadily leaped down the bluff, its eyes still locked on her in a territorial snarl.

Greer pushed herself to her feet and limped down the narrow switchback, but it was useless. She wouldn't make it down the mountain in time with the creature easily stalking her. She turned to face the creature, who had just skidded to a halt at the beginning of the switchback and let out a loud, strangled yell. She had been taught by a nature guide once that when faced with a wild animal, like a bear or mountain lion, when working in the backcountry, you need to make enough noise to scare it off.

But this wasn't a mountain lion, and she certainly wasn't in any backcountry that she was comfortable navigating. The creature took another step closer, curling its paws into the dirt.

Oh God, someone...anyone...

A shuddering boom ricocheted over the mountains, sending loose gravel plunging down. The creature in front of her screeched with terror as it about-faced to scramble back up the cliffside and disappear from sight. Greer thought her stomach would fall out of her ass as she spun to look behind her, expecting a more terrifying creature. Instead, relief flooded through her body as she spotted Samael, his dagger drawn from the sheath at his hip.

In the next breath, Greer's relief shifted into an overwhelming feeling of panic. She reached down to grasp a large stick that had slid down the cliffside, holding it in front of her like a weapon. "I won't go with you," she said in the most calm voice she could muster. Her back barked in pain with every movement she made, and she briefly wondered whether the bleeding cuts where she had hit the rocks were more or less intimidating.

"Relax." Samael paused to place his dagger back in the sheath, the emerald gemstones glinting under the pelting rain and moonlight passing through the cloud coverage. "I'm not going to take you back."

Greer didn't lower the stick as she asked, "You're not?"

"What are you doing up here? Taking the stairs not your cup of tea?"

"I went exploring, and I found a friend."

Samael snorted, pushing his wet hair from his forehead and slicking it back toward the bun behind his head. "That's not a friend. That's Orthrus."

Greer paused. "Orthrus? Brother of Cerberus, Orthrus?"

Moving forward, Samael placed himself directly in front of Greer. "Orthrus is one of the guard dogs of Samsara, a hellhound." He arched an eyebrow. "You should be splattered against the mountain right now. I'm surprised you made it this far." He gestured toward the palace. "I won't make you, but you should go back. He's the least of your worries out here."

Greer scoffed, skirting around him the best she could on the narrow switchback and continuing down the mountain. She heard him swear behind her, and the scent of his leather armor overpowered the heightened smell of wet soil and fresh pine needles. "I'm not going back to that...prison. And how did you even find me?"

His boots crunched against the gravel. "I heard you."

"Heard me?"

"Your fear. It reached out to me, and I heard it."

Greer wrinkled her nose as they turned the corner of the switch-back, now facing the palace once again. From the distance, she could still see the bedsheet rope whipping in the rain that lashed through the mountains. "That is...concerning, to say the least. Could everyone hear me?"

"No, I was the lucky one." Greer felt Samael glance down at her as she covered the top of her head with the canvas bag. "I assume you're going to the Meridian of Pride."

Greer tripped over an exposed root in the trail. "How— how did you?"

Samael said nothing, merely tapping his nose in response.

Greer huffed a sigh of irritation. "Yes, if you must know. I need to go back home."

"It's a dangerous road to the Meridian of Pride," he relented, with the air of someone commenting on the weather. They turned another corner. Their backs turned to the palace as they faced the dark banks of the lake. "Orthrus is tame compared to the other creatures of Samsara. I don't think you'll get through alive."

"Thanks for that," Greer retorted, peeling a lock of hair off of her cheek and tucking it behind her ear. Rainwater dripped from the end of the lock, landing on her neck and running under her soaked, torn sweater. "I'll be fine."

Samael was quiet for a moment, rocking his head back and forth in contemplation. "You convinced me. I'll accompany you. I'm going to the Meridian of Pride, anyways."

Greer halted in her tracks, lurching with the slope of the switch-back. "I don't believe I asked you to come with me."

"I don't believe you prepared enough." He flicked the bag, still covering her head, and Greer heard the *thunk* emanating through the canvas. "What did you pack in there? Six pairs of shoes?"

Greer bristled, pushing away the feathered wings that had brushed over her arm. "Food. Dried meat. A water pouch. Extra fruit. Dry clothes." A shot of irritation rumbled through her. "I know how to pack for a hiking trip. This isn't my first rodeo."

Samael scratched at the stubble on his chin in mock thought. "Were your other proverbial rodeos six to eight weeks long?"

Despite her chest clunking uncomfortably, Greer sucked a tooth. "I studied the map for over a week. I calculated how many miles I need to walk daily and how much food and water to consume. How to cross the strait from the Meridian of Greed into the Meridian of Pride—"

"And did you take into account the creatures you'll meet? The ones who will try and get you off track? How the Meridian of Indolence is a bog that you'll move slower through? How the Meridian of Greed ends in a city before the strait? What happens when you come across another Primordial and are dragged back here?"

Greer was quiet, stewing in her discomfort. "I'm not sure how you expected me to find that information."

Samael snorted with laughter again. "Well, for starters, you could have taken the entire book rather than ripping a few pages out of the middle."

Greer's lips parted in shock, head darting upward to look at Samael. "That was you? In the library?" She paused for a moment, her eyes narrowing. "Were you spying on me?"

"That's rich. I was there first."

Greer felt smug at his evident annoyance at her question. "I didn't know you could read. I thought you just inserted yourself physically into different situations—"

"I don't *insert* myself—"

"Just running into places and swinging your sword around with no clue as to what you're getting into—"

"I'll have you know, I am an expert swordsman."

"Smashing things around, running people through with your dagger—"

"Okay, I get the hint." Samael stopped in the middle of the trail, allowing Greer to walk a few steps ahead of him. She turned to glance behind her, a smirk quirking the corner of her lips, and her brow rose in surprise to see his wings spread wide behind him. "You don't need me, I'll just go."

Greer watched his knees bend, and he readied to rocket into the air when she stepped toward him, holding out her hand to stop him. She didn't know why she did it, didn't even realize she had reached out to him until she glanced down and retracted her hand back to her side. She groaned, tilting her head toward the sky to let the rain drip onto her cheeks and catch in her eyelashes. "You know how to get there?"

Samael relaxed, crossing his arms over his chest. "I've been there many, many times."

"And you know what creatures we're going to encounter?"

Samael shrugged. "A fair few of them, anyway."

Greer narrowed her eyes as they continued down the switchback. "Why are you helping me? Why not drag me right back to Azazel?"

"You don't want to be here," Samael started with a shrug. "And I don't want you here."

Greer cleared her throat. "Wow, you're a—you know what, I'll take it. Whatever it takes to get me out of here."

Samael gestured down the switchback, a wide, shit-eating grin nestled on his face. "Lead the way, then. We only need to make one stop."

TWENTY-ONE

GREER

The misty haze sliding over the lake, barely penetrated by the moonlight that managed to escape the thick cloud coverage, combined with the unpleasantly wet clothing that stuck too close to her skin, made Greer feel uneasy. A shiver ran up her spine from the cold, and goosebumps spread along her arms as she walked alongside Samael.

Greer wasn't particularly excited to have an escort to the Meridian of Pride, let alone an escort she couldn't trust, so she kept a steady five paces behind the Primordial to ensure she had room to run if needed.

The two clambered through the rocky terrain, the palace turrets barely discernible over the cliffs jutting upwards into the mountainscape, and made it to the banks of the lake. The pelting rain plunked on the surface of the water, and the blocks of ice scraped against the shingle beach, sending crisp scents of decaying algae into the air. Opposite the lake, Greer spotted the square, lit and thrumming with activity, and live music danced over the lapping waves, echoing across the valley.

"Where are we going?" Greer asked. Pebbles and thin layers of ice crunched underfoot as they skirted the bank. "We have to go that way." She gestured vaguely toward her right, where the falling rain cut the misty steam curling lazily from the water.

"I told you we have to make a stop."

Greer scowled as Samael turned away from the lake and entered the sea of wilted grass, brown from the cold. She flexed her fingers in an attempt to move her frozen joints against the sleet and felt another bone-deep chill shiver up her spine. Sneakers sloshing with every step, she followed him. Her clothing grew heavier, drenched in the rain, and she opened her mouth to voice her complaints when she spotted Samael standing still at the edge of an empty field.

Samael lifted his hand to his mouth as she approached and, sweeping his gaze into the dark valley, let out a sharp, ear-splitting whistle.

"If Azazel doesn't know where I am, he does now," Greer said through gritted teeth, rubbing her left ear with the palm of her hand.

Samael sent her a glowering side-eye. "Just wait. You'll see."

Crossing her arms over her chest, Greer shifted her weight to her left hip and watched. And waited. And waited. Two minutes. Five minutes. Eight minutes. With her eyes adjusting to the blackness covering the field before her, she straightened when she caught a shadow racing across. It drew closer, hooves cantering in thick mud, and Greer swallowed back the urge to step behind Samael.

When the creature came into clearer view, Greer did a double take when she realized it was a large, black horse. Samael walked forward and reached to greet it with a hand gliding between the bulbous eyes. The horse whinnied in response, tossing its head back with a flick.

"His name is Egyn," Samael said, gesturing for Greer to come closer. "He'll be accompanying us."

Egyn was the largest horse that Greer had ever seen. The mane was long and black, matching the slick, drenched coat. A simple saddle sat atop his back, and leather bags bounced on his flanks during each squelching step. Egyn blinked away the raindrops gathering in his lashes, and Greer lifted her gaze, gasping with surprise when she noticed his pale, ashen eyes.

"You can touch him," Samael said, a faint smile pulling at the corners of his mouth as he ran a hand down the beast's sopping mane. "You should get used to one another."

Greer lifted a trembling hand to touch the end of Egyn's muzzle, chuckling when the whiskers twitched under her fingertips. The horse let out another nicker, misty breath unfurling from its nostrils. "Is he blind?" she asked as Egyn nudged her hand further up the muzzle.

"No," Samael said from the other side of Egyn. The straps of the saddle pulled as Samael tugged at the saddlebag. "He was created that way. He can see just fine." He paused to rest his forearms on Egyn's back. "If you prefer to ride over walking, I can help you."

Greer withdrew her hand, much to Egyn's chagrin, and she quickly shook her head. "No, I would still prefer to walk."

Samael's brows rose as he took in her hair lying flat against her head, her cold-burnt cheeks, and the soggy sleeves of her sweatshirt that were pulled taut to cover her fingers. She lifted her chin in defiance under his scrutinizing look. "Do you want help securing your bag to his saddle?"

Greer's hands lifted to the straps of her canvas bag, and her stiff fingers curled around the buckles as if he would rip the bag from her at any moment. She wanted the bag to stay in her possession in case she needed to take off.

Samael snorted with derision, shaking his head. "We'll have to trust each other eventually." He paused as if waiting for her to interject. When she didn't, he said, "Suit yourself." Clicking his tongue, Egyn followed Samael from the marshy field and back toward the lake shore.

Greer briefly hesitated, Egyn's long tail brushing against her as he walked by, and she glanced toward the palace in the distance. Still imposing and starkly lit against the mountain, she knew that she would not have a second opportunity to escape if she turned back now. With a small sigh, she adjusted the straps onto her shoulders and pulled her sneakers from the mud as she trudged back through the grass.

Egyn had paused at the shore, and his head ducked toward the water to drink. The rain had begun to freeze, pelting the back of Greer's neck with half-melted chunks of ice. Samael watched her closely as Egyn picked up a back leg and kicked his hoof into the beach pebbles.

"There's a series of caves at the border of the Meridian of Wrath. It'll take a couple of hours to reach them," Samael said. Egyn lifted his head, water dripping from his muzzle, and turned his pale eyes toward the Primordial. "We'll stop there for the night. You can dry your clothes, and then we'll leave at first light."

"Why don't we get as far as we can?" Greer asked, her eyes narrowing against a blast of icy wind. She was desperate to put as much distance between herself and Azazel as possible.

"I'm not crossing the river or entering Dead Man's Brush in the dark, and neither should you."

Should. That word caught Greer's ear. It wasn't a demand but a suggestion—a choice. And, though there was nothing more she wanted to do than sprint to the Meridian of Pride, she nodded.

The walk was a slog through the rain-slicked valley, the cold mud settling deeper into Greer's shoes. She used Egyn as a barrier against the whistling wind, but he gave her little comfort against the deluge of rain. The boulders dotting the terrain were smooth from the constant battering of weather, making it easier to slip, and the only thing Greer could be thankful for was the absence of bugs.

Teeth clattering loudly and arms wrapped as tightly around her chest as they would allow, Greer was chilled and wet. She kept her head down, attempting to ignore the water sluicing down from her hairline and dripping off the tip of her nose, but with every breath, she felt her throat painfully constrict. She didn't know how far it was to the caves, nor how she would possibly dry her clothes when she got there.

Unfurling her arms, Greer cupped her hands in front of her and concentrated on the pruned palms and fingertips. With every shiver that dug into the spot between her shoulders, she tried to summon a small flame like she had in the library. However, the one she had managed to create was blown out with a gust of wind a moment later.

Greer bit back the groan of frustration, cold agony ripping through her. But in the next breath, a warm, calm trickled down the top of her head and onto her shoulders. Her water-logged clothing dried, the mud drained from her sneakers, and she could at least straighten her spine though her fingers were still stiff. Greer hadn't realized how much she had hunched against Egyn, and her back was sore from it.

Jaw slackened in amazement, Greer lifted her gaze to look at Samael. He said nothing, eyes squinted against the blasting wind and hair drenched flat against his head. He didn't bother to look at her. Greer faced the tall cliffs in the distance, and if she hadn't felt the tendrils of his power pulling back, she would have thought she warmed herself.

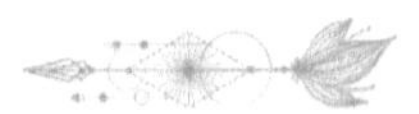

Greer could have sworn that, no matter how long they walked, the rock faces of the caves didn't get any closer. By the time the city was no longer in view behind them, the freezing rain was coming down in sheets, making it nearly impossible to see in front of them. Egyn kept a steady pace despite his size, and Samael dried off Greer three more times before they reached the caves. They hadn't said a word to one another in hours.

The open valley gave way to tall rock formations, layered by rain and old river activity, where the caves were nestled inside. Animal scat and small bones marked the front of the first slotted opening, but Samael ushered her to a smaller one nearly half a mile down. The uneven, crumbling rock at the entrance was slick, and the wind howling through the narrow caverns covered the noise of the pelting rain. Tiny rivulets ran down the cave walls, following the path of the veins of quartz hidden deep in the stone.

Greer knew if she ran her finger along the wall, it would be slimy with condensation, and the water dripping from the ceiling formed puddles in the crevices carved in the ground. Something skittered deeper into the cave, and she tried to ignore the smell of musky, wet fur that told her rats were around.

There was a rumble of breath behind her, one that echoed off the stone, and Greer glanced over her shoulder to see Egyn in the entryway, shaking the excess water free from his mane. She felt the pricks of droplets against her cheeks as Samael shoved past the horse, his arms filled with wet sticks. He dumped them unceremoniously onto the ground, where they bounced every which way before flapping his wings.

"The rain and wind will hide the smoke from our fire," Samael started as he bent down, holding his hands over the wet sticks. Under his power, the water evaporated, first from the sticks and then Greer, and, with the wave of a hand, a small, crackling flame appeared under the pile.

"And what about the light?" Greer asked, and she could have sworn a ghost of a smile flitted on Samael's face.

"Any flicker of it will only be seen from above, and the wind is too strong for anyone, or anything, to fly right now. We'll be safe tonight." He straightened just as the small fire popped, sending a smattering of sparks to land in the puddles. "You should get some sleep. It'll be a long day tomorrow."

Slowly, Greer let her canvas bag drop from her shoulders. She reached into the bag and pulled out two apples tucked deep between the folds of her clothes. Stepping toward Egyn, she held her hand and let the horse sniff the apple. His muzzle twitched twice before he scooped the fruit up with a crunch, his whiskers tickling her empty palm.

"He likes you."

Greer's eyes darted up, unaware that Samael had been watching again. Clearing her throat, she took a quick bite of the second apple in her hand, ignoring Egyn when he moved to inspect it. She scratched the region between his eyes. "He's sweet."

"He's been in battle. He's not sweet."

Greer shrugged her shoulders, taking a second bite of the apple before holding it out for Egyn to take. "Just because he's been in battle doesn't make him any less sweet." She wiped her hand on the leg of her pants. "What will you do if I go to sleep?"

"Keep watch. Make sure the fire is going. Gather water."

Greer settled on the stone floor, positioning herself closest to the wall. She rested her head on the canvas bag, and it took a few punches to the over-packed knapsack to flatten it enough that her neck wasn't kinked. She felt wired, a nervous anticipation thrumming through her body. She didn't know how long she stayed awake, watching the shadows from the flames dance across the ceiling, but she and Samael didn't say another word to one another until morning.

A sizzling woke her. Bleary-eyed, Greer groaned as she pushed herself up to sit, rubbing at the sore spot near the base of her back. The wind died overnight, and the rain stopped, though it was hard to tell whether there was sunlight through the thicket of trees growing atop the rock formation.

"Here."

Greer started as a stick appeared before her, a partially burnt carcass impaled on the end. That must have been the source of the sizzling. In the next breath, she caught the scent of roasted meat.

"What is it?" she asked.

"Rabbit. Don't tell me now that you're afraid of roughing it."

An impatient frown pulled at Greer's mouth as she reached up to take the stick from Samael. She said nothing, biting back the scathing remark threatening to lash out of her. Greer had been to several dig sites between her undergrad and graduate years and was confident in her outdoorsy skills. Though...this would undoubtedly be the most prolonged period she would need to use them. She picked at the shoulder of the rabbit, pulled off a piece of meat, and slowly chewed. It was dry and unseasoned, but it was still hot and fresh. And, though Greer hated to admit it, it was wise to conserve the stable food she had packed in her bag.

"The rain is gone. Crossing the river, as well as the brush, will be our priority today." Samael paused to blanket the fire with water from a leather pouch. Smoke rifled off the charred branches in a sharp hiss, filling the cavern with the acrid scent of burnt wood. "Egyn is grazing." When Greer continued to stay quiet, Samael went on. "Is your plan to remain silent for the rest of our time together?"

Greer swallowed before casually lifting her gaze to connect with his. "I was hoping that would be the plan, yes."

Samael reached down to peel the meat from the rabbit's back leg, popping it into his mouth. "That's a change from the woman I had to pull from a stranger's bed two weeks ago."

Greer bristled. "Now I can't escape you. And my mother always taught me not to say anything if I can't say something nice." She leaned over to dip her oily fingers into the nearest puddle before wiping them dry on the canvas of her bag. "And considering you're escorting me across Samsara, I figured staying quiet was best."

He made a noise of disagreement at the back of his throat. "The spitting anger was more fun. We're going to need some entertainment these next couple of months."

At the mention of months, Greer's stomach flip-flopped. Oh, God. Months. She stood quickly, tossing the stick and rabbit skeleton into the corner of the cave, and grasped the straps of her bag before hauling it onto her back. "Best get a move on then, shouldn't we?" She brushed past him, carving a path away from his broad wings.

The layers of the rock formation containing the cave system were covered in lichen and moss, something Greer had missed in the darkness the night before. The morning light was hazed in gray, and the skies looked as though they were threatening to release more rain at any moment. There was a cold humidity in the air, one that immediately dampened clothes and stuck in the chest.

Samael ducked as he emerged from the cavern, and Greer immediately took off toward Egyn, his swishing tail barely discernible around the corner from the cave entrance. The horse lifted his head on her approach, grass and tangled roots hanging from his mouth, and he continued to chew as he looked at her. The bulbous and pale eyes were even more disturbing in the light.

"Come, Egyn," Samael commanded as he passed, slapping a hand on the horse's left haunch. The primordial didn't bother to see if Greer was following, but she trudged forward regardless.

Though it remained cold and the grass was dewy, the walk was better today than the night before. The thick mud was easier to avoid, at any rate. They walked silently, birds chirping and the whooshing leaves in the breeze filling the space between them. At one point, a low growl followed by a shriek sliced through the forest and Greer's breath hitched in her throat at the suddenness of it. Egyn, the battle-torn warhorse Samael claimed he was, barely lifted his head to study the noise, but Greer saw his ears twitch back, then forward once again.

By tracking the rise of the sun, Greer approximated it was just past midday when she heard the gurgling of a river, and it wasn't long before she smelled the rotting deadfall and fishy compost that flanked it. The eddies and whitecaps of the water came into view a few moments later, and despite the rush of the current, a sour smell emitted from the water. Tree branches dipped into the murky rapids, and white foam surrounded the boulders, breaking the surface. She could imagine wildflowers dotting the bank during the spring and summer.

Greer peered down the muddy bank, left and then right, to see if the current slowed to a creep. As far as she could tell, the rapids continued down the wide river with no bridge, log, or series of large rocks to help ford it. Sidling up to the edge of the bank, the toes of her sneakers sliding in the silt, she bent down to dip her fingers in to test the temperature of the water. She sighed, resting her forearms on her thighs as she stayed crouched down. Crossing the icy depths certainly wasn't going to be fun.

"I can bring you to the other side," Samael stated over the sound of the water crashing against the river's boulders. "Egyn will be fine crossing alone."

Glancing over her shoulder, Greer spotted a dead tree. She stood, catching her balance with her fingertips in the stinking mud, and placed a sneaker against the trunk. With her foot placement, the dried bark shed onto the bank as she grasped both hands around a branch above her head and tugged. With a crack, the branch broke away from the trunk. Greer stumbled back and fell to the mud with an *oomph*.

"This is unnecessary," Samael drawled, his tone bored. He casually picked at the leather armor he wore.

Greer ignored him.

Scrambling to her feet, she took a moment to collect herself as Egyn trundled toward her, sniffing at the bank with sweeps of his muzzle. His breath was visible against the misty afternoon.

Greer approached the edge of the river again, branch in hand. Hinging at the hips, she leaned as far over the icy water as possible before sinking the branch into the depths. The branch, nearly her height, sank to over three-quarters of the way down. She let out a soft groan as she let the stick go. It briefly sank below the rapids before floating to the surface, rushing with the current, and disappearing around a bend.

"You can't be thinking of going in there." Samael's voice was sharp now, a warning reflected in his tone.

Egyn nickered in surprise as if on cue and jolted backward, his ears flattening against his head. Greer glanced down, following his stare, and let out a shriek of shock. A hand, ghostly white and rotten, had clasped the toe of her sneaker and was using her as leverage to slowly drag itself from the water.

She launched herself backward, her heart bounding in her chest. The fingers scratched at the bank, desperate to cling to something tangible. The current pulled at the hand and whatever it was attached to and tugged it back under the surface, disappearing without a trace.

Greer could feel her pulse in her ears as she took another tentative step forward, this time looking closer at the cloudy, rushing water. She bit the inside of her lip to hold back a second shriek. The water, which she had previously thought was murky due to the silt on the river bed, was filled with souls. Hundreds, if not thousands, of souls.

A flop on the river, water squelching against flesh and rock, sounded like thunder on a quiet summer night. Greer's stomach sank as she watched one of those souls pull itself from the river, water sluicing off the rotten sides of the body. Before her eyes, it transformed from the translucent, murky color of the river into a fully-fledged devil. The soul contorted as if in immense pain, the spine lengthening and curving into that of one of the spindly-legged demons she had come across in the warehouse all that time ago.

Panic flooded Greer's senses, and a cold sweat broke out on her brow. Her eyes grew wide as her mind brought her back to that night. To Paige on the asphalt, blood seeping out of the wound in her gut. The empty, open eyes when Samael had cleaved her soul from her body.

Greer was frozen in terror as she watched the devil struggle to find its footing.

The feeling of whiskers against her hand finally jolted her from the memory, but Samael's voice still sounded as though he were underwater when he spoke. "It would be a poor decision to enter the water."

Greer darted her eyes up to his, lip curling into a sneer. "I would rather get in that water than let you fly me across the river."

A flash of anger sparked across Samael's stare before he masked it in cool indifference. The corner of his mouth quirked into a smirk as his wings snapped open. "Suit yourself then. It's your funeral." He leaped into the air, wings flapping, and paused mid-way across the river. His body bobbed up and down with every whoosh, and Greer could feel the draft sweeping at the locks of her hair.

Egyn had already entered the river, and though the souls still flowed in the water past him, they kept a wide berth around the beast's legs. The circle, visible from the bank, shifted with every step he took. She watched for a beat, feeling the anxiety weaning as she studied the ease with which he crossed.

Greer took a tentative step into the icy water. Then another. And another. Only, for her, the souls did not keep a wide berth. Their slimy hands clamped around her ankles, calves, and thighs, pulling her deeper into the rapids. Her breath was ragged as the water flooded her sneakers, encircling her hips and waist as she moved into the depths.

Greer's brain was numb. Her body had gone into shock, the water plummeting her body temperature as if siphoning it straight from her core. She kept walking, her canvas bag high above her head, as she squared her attention on Egyn, who had emerged on the opposite bank unscathed.

Hands tugged at her, ripping at the hem of her sweater, as they struggled to pull themselves from the water. One rotted hand clasped tightly onto Greer's shoulder, and though she fought against it, she was yanked under the surface, the strap of her bag tangling with her arm. She sucked in an unwanted breath, thrashing against the hands and faces that kept her down. Sinking to the bottom of the river, she found the silt foundation and used the last of her strength to kick herself upward, rocketing toward the sky.

Greer broke through, coughing and sputtering, the hands still clamped tightly around her. She was depleted, utterly and entirely spent. And, though she tried to summon even a wink of the power she possessed, nothing answered her call. She thought about sinking back to the depths, allowing the souls to overtake her. She would be with Paige, and this would all be over.

It would be so, so easy to...float away.

Eyes snapping open as though Paige had admonished her, Greer caught sight of Egyn on the shore. He tossed his head in agitation, hair still matted and wet, ashen eyes still fixed on her. He entered the water, and, once again, the souls parted from him as though he were poison.

And, when he was close enough, Greer gave it everything she had left and moved toward the horse. She threw the hands off her arms and shoulders as she ascended from the river bed. Her waist was free, then her hips and her thighs, but she struggled against the souls using her legs as an anchor. She ignored their screams as their faces broke through the water and grasped onto Egyn's saddle.

Finally, when the horse assisted to haul her ashore, she stumbled in the mud, falling to her hands and knees.

Crawling up the bank, she coughed a lungful of water and collapsed onto her back. Her chest heaved with the effort it took to breathe, and her throat burned from the icy water that had sawed through the sensitive tissue only moments before. Lifting her hands to try and straighten herself out, she noticed the nail beds had turned a sickly blue.

Egyn nudged her head, soft brays echoing into her ear as she shivered on the cold ground. Greer wanted to stay there; she wanted to lay there until sleep took her. The forest was so dark with night that her hand was indiscernible, even if it were in front of her face.

A squelching thud sounded next to her head, and Greer glanced up to see Samael kneeling at her side, with a look of utmost fury on his features.

"Welcome to the Meridian of Wrath," he said through gritted teeth. Her eyes flicked down to see his fist white-knuckled on the hilt of his dagger. "Congratulations. You've used your energy, and we still have to get through the brush. It would be merciful if I left you here to die."

TWENTY-TWO

O dette walked on eggshells for two days following her interference at the arena, and though Kaique had been eerily silent on the ordeal, she wished he had run her through instead. The smiles, the quiet moments at meals, and the calmly asked questions regarding the other courts only heightened her senses around him. She half expected him to appear in the shadows of the hallways, the dagger she had thrown at Caio wrapped tightly in his hand. Instead, all she got was an unreadable coolness that seemed more manipulative than Kaique's exterior let on.

But, despite that, Odette couldn't quite shake the nagging feeling of guilt in her gut. She barely recognized this kingdom, *her* kingdom, and couldn't help but remember how beautiful it was to live here before Adair. Everything happening to the humans in the Court of Mist and Tide...their blood was on her hands, too. She should have done more.

Eoghann would have done more.

In the days when Adair had imprisoned her, she would spend the long nights tending to the stumps left of her wings. The bloody scabs would itch as they healed and formed again, but Odette would still manage to bite back the frustrated sobs that caught in her throat.

Eoghann noticed, though.

It started with him talking to the space between them, twisting the tip of his blade into the stone floor of the dungeon. He would mindlessly gab about his day, family, or life before becoming a guard to the dungeons.

Before Odette had ever said a word to him, she learned he had trained with the Court of Cedar and Sand before being ordered to the dungeon after Adair became king. She knew he had two brothers, a rarity amongst the Fae who usually never bore more than one child. She also knew that his mother was a healer in the village he grew up in.

It took him time to build her trust, but the first time Eoghann brought a salve for Odette's mutilated back, his fingers were so gentle against her skin that tears rolled down her dirty, mud-caked cheeks. It was the first time in nearly ten years she had been touched by another person who wasn't Adair, and she fought against the rushing need to jerk away from Eoghann every time he reached his hand through the obsidian bars of her door to help her.

The first time she opened up to him was six years later when she voluntarily reached through the bars with trembling fingers to brush his blonde hair from his forehead. Her heart rattled in her chest the whole time. She had never been with a male before, having previously preferred the company of females. And while she and Eoghann hadn't been able to do much more than briefly kiss if they wedged their faces between the thick metal bars, Odette thought their bond was deeper that way.

They would daydream by torchlight about how the world would look if Adair were gone. They would lean on one another to distract from the blistering chill of winter or the unimaginably hot summer days. When Adair took Odette as his own, she would stare into Eoghann's eyes and pretend they were together. But as soon as Adair was gone, Eoghann would make her promise that she would make the world a better place when she escaped.

Instead, Odette spent almost two hundred years huddled in the Pacific Northwest with Nerea, professing she was healing when, on the contrary, she was devising a plan to hide away from the Fae realm for the rest of her miserable existence.

Her people suffered all the more for it, and Eoghann would have been livid. That thought kicked Odette into high gear, along with the colosseum, where she saw firsthand how Adair's cruelty bled into every facet of every realm. She still didn't have an army, and they would probably all die trying, but the least she could do was help the humans escape on her way back to the Gaian realm.

Even if it cost Odette her own life. As Eoghann had done for her.

She thought about all this as she watched the gardens from the cutout window. Rain fell from the dark, cloudy sky in droves so heavy that the clouds appeared to smear. The petals from the flowers that had just recently bloomed were strewn across the lawn, tumbling across the wet grass with the rolling wind. The jungle air was heavy with moisture, the scent of freshly dug earth clinging to every drop plunking into the fountain pools.

A bang resounded from the hallway so loudly that Odette thought it was thunder at first. When a second bang echoed a series of heartbeats later, curiosity got the better of her. Brow furrowed, she uncurled herself from her seat on the windowsill and padded to the foyer door. A third bang shuddered the door in the frame, and she turned the handle to crack it open and peek into the long hallway.

"Odette?" Luisa asked, her voice small and weak. Her eyes rolled to the back of her head as she fell forward.

Odette flung open the door, catching her around the waist just before Luisa's knees hit the ground. "Luisa? Luisa!" She swept her gaze along the empty hallway, seeing nothing and only hearing the sound of rainfall from the courtyard beyond. Turning her attention back to the woman on the floor, Odette noticed injuries littering her neck and face. She ran a gentle finger over the hand print shaped bruise around Luisa's neck, the swollen eye, and bleeding nose.

Scooping Luisa into her arms, Odette carried her into the foyer of her apartment and kicked the door shut behind them. Luisa groaned as Odette laid her gently on the bed and lifted the lid of the swollen eye. There were a few broken vessels, but the pupil was reactive and intact.

Luisa was certainly going into shock, though, and there wasn't much Odette could do without a healer. She grabbed the second dagger from the canvas bag and pulled up a seat— just in case Kaique came looking for his favorite toy.

The evening stretched into night, but Odette stayed put. The rain had finally ceased, leaving a hazy blanket of humidity over the palace and surrounding jungle. Low-hanging clouds threaded into the canopy leaves, and the dimmed moonlight barely made its way through to the underbrush below.

At one point, Odette mistook an unlucky lower court faerie who had attempted to deliver dinner as Kaique and was met by Odette's blade to her throat. The woman was shocked, but after spotting Luisa's unconscious form in the bed by peeking under Odette's arm, the color drained from her plump cheeks.

"Yarrow," the woman said quickly, her eyes darting up to meet Odette's in a plea to stop Odette from slitting her throat. "For the bleeding. And willow bark for the pain. I can get some clean clothes and fresh water, too."

Odette hesitated for a long moment before slowly releasing the woman from her grasp. She immediately picked up her skirt and hurried down the hallway, her bare feet slapping against the stone and the tray of food still precariously balancing in her palm. After what felt like ages, she was back with a second servant, who was already stuffing a bundle of yarrow flowers into her mouth and chewing. Odette stepped back as the women hurried into the bedroom and mopped up the bloody nose.

The two women worked for nearly an hour under Odette's intense scrutiny but never wavered. Fresh cloth to cover a wound at the back of Luisa's head that Odette hadn't yet noticed and padding soaked in cool water to stemmy inflammation expanding a turned ankle. The second woman made to place a folded cloth between Luisa's legs, but Odette stopped her with a slap of the broad edge of her blade against the woman's wrist.

"She can decide how to care for herself there when she wakes," Odette stated, her brows lifting in warning as she surveyed the servant.

The woman nodded but said nothing before moving on to tend to the eye. Odette slid the dagger into her sheath and leaned forward to grip the end of the bed frame, running her hands along the rough wood.

"We've helped her before when the Lord has been rough. He's going to come looking for her," the first woman said softly, tucking a lock of hair behind her pointed ear. "He always comes looking for her."

"What's your name?" Odette asked, lifting her stare from Luisa to study the woman's thin lips and soft jawline.

"Yara," the woman said, removing a cloth from the back of Luisa's head and replacing it with a cool one. Odette watched as water ran like small rivers down the side of her face. "And this is Aldonza." The second woman, eyes a dark brown and deeply hooded, nodded her head but didn't glance upward.

"Aldonza. I've heard your name before." Odette narrowed her eyes on the woman's pointed ears. "You're both Fae." She paused to slide her gaze back to Yara. "And you're helping a human."

"We help many humans," Yara said, handing another set of clean clothes to Aldonza, who looked over Odette with suspicion. "They come to us in the early hours of the morning for Aldonza's salve to put on their backs, especially those who work the gardens and the fields-"

"Yara," Aldonza warned firmly as she shook her head.

"She saved Ilyapa and Micos from the Serpent of Fire," Yara replied sharply. She swallowed thickly, and Odette watched the column of her throat bob. "I was sorry to see what happened to Urpi, the first man. He was always so sweet, bringing me wildflowers from the jungle when he went to work in the fields. Micos and Ilyapa— where are they?"

Odette shifted on her feet, the floorboards creaking beneath her. "As guests of mine, they are officially guests of the court. I arranged for them to share a royal apartment down the hallway. They will be escorted back to their families during the solstice."

"That's kind of you," Yara said. She quieted to watch Aldonza work.

Odette's heart hammered in her chest as she grew the courage to ask her next question but was too curious to keep it in. "What happened to Kaique's father, Quenti? How long has Kaique been Lord of Mist and Tide?"

Yara's hands halted over Luisa's eye, but Aldonza answered, much to Odette's surprise. "Kaique killed him nearly six years ago now. When Quenti was still Lord of Mist and Tide, my mother was a member of the lower court here at the palace." She paused to clear her throat, her voice beginning to wobble. "Kaique didn't want a single lower court member to be the same. He was deeply paranoid. I was living in a village near the coast with my father, learning the craft of healing. I was called up to the palace shortly after his coup."

"The colosseum was built soon after," Yara continued as Aldonza wiped the tears staining her cheeks. "He executed every single member of the lower court who served under his father, including my eldest friend. It was turned into an entertainment center following that."

Luisa groaned the first sign that there was still life inside of her.

"We'll take our leave," Aldonza said, folding the clean clothes and stacking them on the bedside table. "I've done all I can for now. I'll come back tomorrow to clean the bandages. In the meantime–"

Odette lifted her dagger by the hilt, showing off the sheathed blade, and nodded to confirm she understood she would need to be ready to protect Luisa.

Yara nodded, but Aldonza spoke up one last time. "There were tales of your prowess in battle, that you were one of the best warriors to ever serve in the Fae King's armies." Her gaze hardened. "I hope that continues to be true. You're going to need it."

Midnight came and went before Luisa shifted in the bed, a soft moan escaping her lips. Odette glanced up from watching the dagger's point twirl a hole into the arm of the chair, something that Eoghann once did while he was awaiting her.

Luisa's eyes cracked open, her brow setting in confusion as her gaze cleared. Suddenly, she shot upward as she took deep, heaving breaths, as though she couldn't get the air in fast enough. Wild-eyed, she looked around—first at the room she was seated in, then at her elevated ankle, finally at Odette nestled in the corner of the room. Luisa lifted a hand and gingerly touched the bandage at the back of her head and then her eye, still nearly swollen shut.

"Willowbark tea?" Odette asked, pushing herself out of her seat and padding toward the foyer table where Aldonza had set it up before taking her leave. "It's probably cold by now, but—" She trailed off when she lifted the cup, forcing the air to swirl around the contents of the cup to heat it. "It would be easier to boil it, but water manipulation isn't my type."

She reached Luisa within a few steps, handing the lukewarm cup of tea to the servant, who held it hesitantly.

"You got Yara and Aldonza here," Luisa said, keeping her eyes trained on Odette as she took a small sip from the cup. "I recognize the bandages."

"It was by happenstance if I were honest." Odette took a seat in the corner of the room once again. "Aldonza put more bandages on the bedside table. You can use them for between your legs if you'd like."

Luisa glanced down at her lap, her face flushing a dark red. "You didn't change my clothes."

"I wouldn't have wanted someone to change mine while I was unconscious. Not after—" Odette trailed off before clearing her throat once again. "We don't have to talk about anything. I can just be here to protect you while you heal."

Much to Odette's surprise, Luisa clamped a hand over her mouth and let out a muffled sob. The clanking of chains from the slaves working the garden entered through the window, the scent of newly tilled earth coming on the next breeze. The sound of a whip cracking pierced the air, followed by the grunting groan of the victim it had snapped against.

"I was the general to the Fae King's army for centuries," Odette started quietly, tucking a stray lock of her red hair back into the bun at the base of her neck. Luisa continued to sob, both eyes squeezed shut as tears leaked from the corners. "My father's armies. A coup was led against him by his right hand, the current king, Adair. I was kept locked up as a political prisoner, but Adair...he took his liberties with me."

Luisa lowered her hand, swollen lips wet and gleaming in the candlelight, the tea lay unforgotten in her lap.

"He cut off my wings and, for nearly two hundred and fifty years, he tortured me. I've been on the run ever since." Odette leaned forward, resting her forearms on her knees and letting her hands dangle toward the floor. "You don't have to talk to me. Just know that I understand. It took me a long time to understand."

There was a long moment of time where neither woman spoke. Odette focused on the thrum of bugs buzzing over the faint rumble of thunder that whisked from the open sea and over the swaying canopy trees. Luisa stared at her feet, eyes unfocused and unseeing, but it was she who broke the silence first.

"I was on a girl's trip from Colombia to celebrate one of my friends graduating from medical school. I was a primary teacher." Luisa paused to wipe her eyes, gently prodding the tears from the swollen one. "I saw Kaique on the boardwalk of Iguazu Falls during a midnight hike. He was handsome and sweet. My friends saw how we eyed one another, so they were excited when Kaique and I went off into the jungle and spent an hour together. I thought it was just a fleeting moment of passion between two strangers, but when we were finished, he knocked me unconscious, and I awoke...here."

Odette shook her head, her heartbeat throbbing in even the smallest of places— the tips of her toes, the underside of her knees, and at the points of her ears.

"He has taken me to his bed every single night since then," Luisa spat with such anger that more tears leaked down her cheeks. "Sometimes he's soft and sensual. Other times he's–" She stopped to draw in another shaky breath. "Tonight he was out of his mind with rage when I entered his chambers. He grabbed my hair and bashed my face into the corner of his bed frame." She reached out to touch her eye, the swelling still red and splotchy. "He choked me over and over while he..." Luisa began sobbing and Odette wished to not hear any more.

Luisa curled herself into a ball on the mattress, the cup of tea spilling onto the floor. Odette stood from her seat and sank onto the corner of the bed, reaching over to touch Luisa's shoulder. When the woman didn't flinch away from her, Odette rubbed Luisa's bruised arm.

"I cried for the first three months I was here," Luisa went on through her tears. "I begged him to let me go home— begged him. I told him that my family was missing me, that my friends were out looking for me, that they had seen him. I tried everything. And when he left for the winter solstice and was gone until spring..." She chuckled, low and throaty. "It was the best three months we've had here in years."

Odette closed her eyes, knowing the worst had not yet been revealed.

"I was called to his chambers the morning he returned. He said he brought my family with him. I was so excited to see them again, so excited that I wouldn't be here alone." A single sniffle sounded through the room. "He gestured for the guards and they came into the room, each carrying a jar that contained the heads of my mother, father, and brother."

Bile clawed up Odette's throat as her hand paused on Luisa's back. Her jaw clenched, so tight that her teeth cracked together. Rage flooded through her from the cruelty of Kaique, so different from his father, but so like many of the other Fae members she had encountered through the centuries.

"He told me that they would be here watching over me," Luisa went on, her voice monotone. "And he spiked their heads to the wall in my bedroom, where I was forced to look at them every day until they were so badly decomposed that their flesh fell off the bone and splattered to the floor."

"My father did not allow for slavery while he was king," Odette said softly. "And he would be ashamed of how I've stood on the sidelines and allowed this to happen to my realm." Luisa rolled onto her back, looking up at Odette with red-rimmed, tear stained eyes. "I want to help your group get out of the Court of Mist and Tide."

Luisa's eyes steeled before she pushed herself from the bed and hobbled to a stand. "I don't know what you're talking about," she said as she attempted to straighten out the ripped tunic she wore. "And that is a very dangerous accusation."

"The dagger is dull," Odette said, casually picking at her nails. "It needs to be sharpened before it can be used." She turned to glance over her shoulder, where Luisa had a hand planted on the door frame. "You know. The one under your mattress."

Luisa whipped around, her face curving into a grimace when she put too much weight on the sprained ankle. "Are you threatening me?"

Odette stood, squaring herself to face Luisa. "No. I'm offering to teach you how to fight the Fae. And you can't do it with one dull blade." She tilted her head, assessing the woman in front of her. "It took me decades of prep, finding the right guards, and well-placed weapons to break out. You will not be able to do it on your own and if you are caught, you will not be killed for your effort. There are worse things than death to the Fae."

Luisa seemed to deflate, her hand sliding from the frame. "I can't do this for decades," she whispered in horror. For a flicker of a moment, Odette saw the wounded, terrified woman underneath the steel exterior once more.

"I know," Odette replied. "I will train you and any humans you wish. I will assist in supplying you with weapons and, when the time comes, I will help in getting you all back to the human realm. You have a voice in this place that I do not as an outsider. We're going to need an army and we're going to need one fast." When Luisa didn't say anything, Odette went on. "You showed up at my door when you were injured. Why did you come here?"

Luisa's lips parted as she looked down, sweeping her stare across the floor. "I— I saw what you did for Tomas when his hand was shaking. And I saw what you did for Micos and Ilyapa. When Kaique allowed me to leave I just...thought of you." Luisa shook her head, snorting through her nose. "I know of a network of lower court faeries who are still loyal to Kaique's father. I'll— I'll do some investigative work to see who is willing to help."

The corner of Odette's mouth quirked as she waltzed forward to extend her hand. Luisa looked at it with trepidation before gingerly taking it.

"It'll be nice working with you," Odette said, retracting her hand back to her side. She still didn't quite enjoy the feeling of someone touching her. "I like your energy."

TWENTY-THREE

GREER

"Do it, then. Leave me here to die," Greer groaned, letting her cheek fall back into the cold mud. She heard nothing from Samael save for the tight, nasal breathing that flared his nostrils. She glanced back up at him. "What are you worried about? We got past the river."

"You barely got past the river," he corrected her as he turned to fix the saddlebags strapped to Egyn. "And we'll be lucky if we get through the brush alive."

"Give me ten minutes, and I'll be ready to go," Greer retorted. Her breath had finally begun to calm, turning from pants to deep heaves, though the bone-chilling cold had returned. They had spent longer than she thought getting to the river— the sun had marched across the sky, painting the clearing clouds in deep gold and lengthening the shadows cast by the trees.

Samael knelt beside her, his knee sinking into the thick silt coating the bank. "If we wait much longer, they will know we are here." He paused to reach forward, extending his hand toward Greer. "We have to move." Despite his calm demeanor, a pointed alarm was hidden in the underbelly of his voice.

And Greer knew it said, *hurry, hurry, hurry.*

Greer ignored the hand and the warning as she took her time to stand. "Everything is fine, Samael." She tossed the canvas bag to her back once again, tugging at the wet straps to tighten them into place. "You're being to–" And that's when she heard it, or rather, didn't hear it.

There was no chirping of birds or buzzing of insects. The river seemed too quiet, the once-roaring rapids a mere gurgle. Even the leaves, once rustling with the breeze, had ceased to make any sounds. Greer turned toward the forest. Her power guttered in response to whatever was beyond the shadows of the tree line, attempting to flicker to life inside of her.

A haunting hum had begun to weave through the trees.

"What's in there?" Her voice was a petrified whisper, a frightening chill snaking down her spine.

"The Sisters of Fate," Samael answered, unsheathing the sword strapped between his wings smoothly. "They won't be something you'll have seen before. Stick close." He stood, sword still in hand, stepping up the river bank and onto the grassy plain leading to the forest edge.

Greer swallowed, starting when Egyn nuzzled her hand. The horse clopped by, heaving his monstrous body after his owner. With a sharp inhale and against her better judgment, she followed them both into the thicket.

The tall trees rose from the earth, brushing against the golden sky. Where Greer expected to see animal trails disappearing into the undergrowth or scat along the beds of moss and mushrooms blanketing the forest floor, there was...nothing. No deer grazing along the bright berry bushes. No insects scurrying along the rotten, fallen logs. Even the trees that greeted her refused to groan as they swayed in the wind. Her footsteps fell heavy against the spongy layers, snapping the twigs and crunching the dead pine needles, and her heart pounded with each step she took.

"What do you mean they won't be something I've seen before?" Greer asked in a low voice that was still too loud against the silence. Before Samael could answer, there was a flutter of pink in the periphery of her vision. Whirling toward the movement, Greer's jaw slackened at the sight before her.

It was a girl or had been a girl at one time. Her skeleton was splayed across the forest floor, picked apart by animals Greer had yet to see. At least, she thought to herself, she hoped it was animals. Clothes still covered the corpse– a pink dress, dirty and half-hidden by the dead leaves that had fallen from the branches above, and one white shoe that lay forgotten next to the foot. A pink ribbon to match the dress had caught in the bark fraying from the tree trunk nearest the body.

In an attempt to avert her eyes from the young girl's body, Greer's gaze landed on a second skeleton. Based on the brown boots and the linen pants, this skeleton was that of a man. Perhaps the young girl's father. He reached for her in death, in permanent death, but they had been ripped apart.

"Dead Man's Brush is not figurative," Samael said softly in response, "It was aptly named."

"Why did we come this way?" Greer asked, peeling her stare away from the second body and sidling closer to Egyn. Even the horse seemed alert, his pointed ears flexed against his head.

"It's the fastest way through the Meridian of Wrath, as well as the least expected. There is a reason I wanted to fly." Samael twirled the sword in his hand as he frowned at the golden sky barely peeking through the tops of the trees. "The sisters were in this realm when Samsara was ripped apart from Elysia. Many things were. Azazel carved out regions so that they could reside peacefully and forbade his people from going. Some didn't listen." He paused to point to a third skeleton with the tip of his sword, this one much older than the two they had passed minutes before. Horns curled from the skull, the one on the left fractured nearly in two.

"This forest is huge on the map," Greer continued. "Is it possible we just...walk by them? Unnoticed?"

"They already know we're here."

Another haunting hum was on the wind, closer this time, and she felt her power flicker to life once more. Samael's shoulders stiffened, the muscles in his back pulling taut to flex his wings as he stood at attention in front of her. Egyn shifted unhappily on his hooves, braying in warning. Samael jerked his chin toward his right, and Greer saw his cerulean eyes darken as he watched the shadows of the trees.

"How can you be certain?"

"There."

Greer followed Samael's gesture, and her stomach turned to lead. A head, covered in black robes, peered out from behind a tree trunk, a wrinkled hand with gnarled fingers wrapping around to the front. She couldn't see the face of the on-looker, the features veiled beneath the hood, but she could tell the figure was shrunken and contorted, as though the person hadn't consumed a meal in quite some time.

It disappeared just as quickly as it arrived, the silhouette darting from behind the tree and deeper into the wood. It didn't make a sound, not a swish of a robe or a rustle of branches. And, though the sister was out of sight, Greer had the distinct feeling that she was still being watched.

"Deino the Terrible," Samael said, answering a question Greer hadn't posed aloud. "The other sisters will be coming. We need to hurry."

Greer picked up her pace, tromping through the thicket with no regard for the noise she was making. According to Samael, it didn't matter. The Sisters of Fate, whatever they were, already knew of their presence. Egyn trotted behind his master, black mane billowing on a phantom wind.

After nearly an hour of running through the forest behind Samael and Egyn, they reached a clearing at dusk, and Greer was exhausted. Past exhausted— she was bone-weary, desperate to rest on the bedding of moss and dead leaves. Still covered in silt and smelling like river water, she knew she sported red-rimmed, puffy eyes. The jolt of adrenaline from seeing Deino the Terrible had long since worn off, leaving a hollow feeling in her chest.

"Ten minutes," Samael huffed as Greer collapsed onto a tree stump, "I'm taking Egyn to the stream, and then we leave again."

Her nod was lost on him, and his wings had already turned to face her. Greer shrugged the canvas bag from her back, feeling an instant rush of relief on her sore shoulders. She groaned as she prodded the top of her shoulder, red and rubbed raw from the wet strap chafing her skin. Unbuckling the top of the bag, Greer reached in to retrieve the leather water pouch and a piece of dried meat. She took a deep drink. The water was warmed from the layers of clothes in her bag. Still, it filled the empty space of her stomach, an uncomfortable hunger rumbling through her.

Greer went to replace the cap, fingers enclosed around the cool metal when she stilled. The haunting humming had returned, echoing across the clearing. She stood, twisting around in an attempt to find the source. "Samael?" she called nervously, hoping he would be close enough to hear.

The Primordial didn't answer him, but another voice did.

"I left my sisters in the wood, in the wood, in the wood. I left my sisters in the wood to fetch a pail of water."

The singing was female and cold, the high-pitched tone skittering along Greer's skin. It seemed to mirror itself, playing off the trees. She spun on the balls of her feet, pivoting in place to see if she could locate the source of the song. Curiosity rose within her.

"I found the stream, found the stream, found the stream. I found the stream with my sister's corpse afloat in the water."

Greer shoved the water pouch back into her bag as she peered into the darkness of the surrounding forest. Stepping over a small pile of pinecones, perhaps placed there by a woodland animal, she entered the thicket, following the song deeper into the shadows.

"Her soul had fled, soul had fled, soul had fled. Her soul had fled, stuck in the stream, corpse still in the water."

A flame danced far beyond the trees, the orange hue blending with the golden sky, sending vast swirls of smoke into the clouds. And there, seated on a boulder, her hands swiftly working in her lap, was a woman.

She wore black robes, and the hood pulled above her head. By the shape of her spine and the hunch between her shoulders, Greer knew it was the silhouette of the woman she had seen peeking out from behind the tree.

"I followed the trail, followed the trail, followed the trail. I followed the trail, found her soul, and ate it out of the water."

The woman let out a sudden cackle that made Greer jolt in surprise. Breathing deep to calm her erratic heart, Greer quietly circled to the front of the woman for a better look. Her gnarled hands, fingers bent and broken, were weaving a net of...Greer swallowed back the bile that crawled up her throat.

A large spider with pincers the size of a child's fingers was perched in her lap. Thick, white strands appeared between the spider's back legs, and the sticky fibers became entangled in the woman's robes as she worked to knit them. When Greer looked around, she realized what the woman was knitting it into.

Bodies hung from the trees, some bloated and swollen, wrapped in tightly woven nets, their chins lolling against their chests. Others had already been crudely sliced open, intestines dangling toward the forest floor like macabre ornaments. At the base of a tree, Greer spotted a small, white shoe identical to the one near the skeleton child at the river. Her heart palpitated, tingling in her chest, and instant nausea clenched at her.

"A beauty I once was, Greer Myers. My sisters and I together." The old crone's voice was sickly sweet— directly opposed to the cold voice she had been singing with. She kept her head bent low in concentration, and her chin turned toward the tangled web in her lap.

"How do you know who I am?" Greer began to back away. Fear washed away the remaining curiosity, tugging at every thought telling her to run. The creature in the old woman's lap turned its eight eyes toward Greer as she moved, a deep, throaty whine purring between the pincers.

"We know many things and can see many things." At that moment, the old woman's head snapped upward, the robe hood falling back, and Greer couldn't help the horror gasp that escaped her.

Skin sagged on bone, deep pockets of wrinkles carving notches into the horrible face. Her gray hair was thin, delicate patches of locks falling to the top of her shoulders. Judging by the shape of her jaw and how her lips buckled inward, the woman had no teeth. The square chin, covered in minuscule hairs and warts, was sharply disfigured. And, where a pair of eyes should have been, there were two dark sockets, the skin caving in to cover the skull.

Greer's breathing was ragged as she struggled to catch it. She stumbled on a tree root as she surged back, landing painfully on the forest floor with an *oomph*. Any soreness from the fall was drained away, replaced by bone-deep fear filling every spot in her body as a gnarled hand clamped onto her shoulder. Head whirling up, she caught a glimpse of the second sister, hood pulled down, revealing a similar sight: eye sockets empty, sunken lips quivering.

This sister, though, cupped a single bulbous eye in her hand. The eye darted its gaze around, taking in the scene before it.

"Not this one, Enyo," the seated sister chortled as she turned back to the web in her lap. "Not yet. It's not time to cut her cord."

A chill went down Greer's spine as Enyo ran a long, dirty fingernail down the side of Greer's cheek.

"She doesn't need all her life force, Deino," Enyo retorted as she smoothed the flyaways near Greer's brow. "And it's been so long since we've had a fresh meal." The eyeball was still stirring in her hand. "Even longer since we've felt young."

Enyo clamped her hand around Greer's cheeks, inhaling noisily through her wide nostrils. Greer felt a pull behind her navel, and her knees knocked weakly together. In horror, she watched as her fingertips wrinkled into prunes before returning to normal.

There was crashing from the brush before Greer, branches rustling and snapping as footsteps thudded toward them. The noise distracted the two sisters long enough that Greer could right herself, stumbling away from the clutches of the twisted fingers, but not before snatching the eye from the palm of Enyo's hand. The sister lunged after her with surprising agility, a roar of anger flooding the wood.

Samael leaped into the space, jumping over a thicket of bushes, his wings furiously beating to keep himself airborne. He clutched his sword in one hand and his emerald-encrusted dagger in the other. His power, trembling and terrible, doused Greer like a wave. She felt his strength and anger in it, mirroring the harrowing expression pulling his mouth taut. But, surprisingly, she also felt a kernel of fear tunneling beneath his strength and anger, thinning the lines separating them.

"You have no power here, Samael," Deino cackled, slowly rising to a stand as she unceremoniously dumped the spider from her lap. It skittered into the shadows of the forest. "What was stolen from us cannot be used to harm us."

Samael had opened his mouth to speak when a singsong voice echoed from behind them. "*An Ananke of Time and Death and Pestilence and War and Famine and Thought and Ether and Peace. Each destined to march across the land of the mortal. Each bound to fight their thread.*" A third crone appeared, her black robes sweeping silently across the pine needles and leaves. "You charged us with knowledge, Samael, or have you forgotten so easily?"

Samael snapped his wings inward, his boots loudly landing on the soft ground. "Your creation hinged on your usefulness, Pemphredo, which hasn't been called on for thousands of years. What was once charged can be undone."

The third sister, Pemphredo, hissed a low warning. "Death has always been cunning." Her square chin, nearly identical to her sisters', lifted. "She has something of ours. We want it back."

Greer felt the eye shift between her fingers. "And what will happen if I don't give it back?" She tightened her grip against the eye, and it shivered in protest.

Enyo was the first to respond. "It would be quite foolish, child, for you to deny us what we seek." She made to bare her teeth, revealing a set of fleshy, pale gums and one singular tooth. "We have a duty to Death."

"A duty that has been stripped from you and given to someone else," Samael growled, the dagger's hilt twisting in his palm.

"Not for long, Samael, as we both know," Pemphredo interjected. "*An Ananke of Time and Death and Pestilence and–*"

"You've already said that," Greer bit back. "But what does it mean?"

The three sisters remained silent, and all Greer could hear was the rustle of leaves in the brush. Deino waved a hand in a long and slow arc. A black mist appeared before her, writhing as if in a great deal of pain. It twisted and pressed against the bond holding it together, and before Greer knew what was happening, Deino inhaled deeply before blowing it toward her in a plume of magic.

The mist hit Greer in the chest, infiltrating her senses and sinking deep beneath her skin. She let out a yelp of surprise as she dropped to her knees, the eye falling from her limp hand. From far above her, Samael's outcry was muddled and broken.

"*There was Time, and there was Death, Greer Myers,*" one of the sisters whispered within her mind, the voice echoing through her brain like a passing thought. "*And, in the beginning, they were together as one. Mortals came and, because there could be no time without death or death without time, they split.*"

In a sudden rush, Greer's eyes burst open, but she knew she wasn't truly awake. Deino had taken her somewhere. The universe surrounded Greer, stars, planets, and dust swirling around one another in a cosmic dance. She reached out a hand to run her fingers along the closest galaxy. Icy pins pricked at her palm as each star passed through.

"Primordials woke, the gods of the realms and protectors of life. They created mortals in their image, people to watch over the land. But with Time...comes Death."

As though speeding downward, the galaxies swept past Greer, and she fell. She fell until her scream could no longer rip from her chest. She found herself on a battlefield, creatures made of smoke and darkness falling around her. Swords, blood, and limbs littered the clearing. In the background, sweeping through each body was a sinister shadow.

Greer felt her heart lurch as she watched it. The image flickered, from a battlefield covered in djinn to intricately made wooden ships crewed by shouting men in a storm, their sails battered against the winds and waves. The shadow swept through once again, and all of the men dropped. A wave overturned the ship, sending the bodies sinking into the deep.

As before, the image flickered to a volcano splitting open, liquid rock and fire rocketing upward into the ash-filled sky. Clad in thin dresses and bare feet, women clutched their children to their chests as they ran through the streets of a clay-built city. Men bellowed commands, shuttering their houses. Balls of flame ricocheted through the clouds, landing on the dirt pathways and the wooden carts that lined them. Again, that shadow wove through the alleyways, striking down anyone it encountered.

"Death was free to reign, and so were his brothers. It was not until the Primordials rose into battle against one another that the fallen

were bound. And slowly, Death and his brothers were stopped. That is...until–"

The image shifted one more time, a woman appearing before her against a backdrop of that sinister shadow. She had wavy brown hair and a nose covered in a light smattering of freckles. She was smiling, her front teeth slightly crooked, and her blue eyes wrinkled at the corners. Her hands covered a swollen belly, lovingly rubbing it.

Holly.

Greer's breath hitched in her throat as she reached a hand forward again, expecting to feel the woman's soft locks between her fingers. Instead, her hand went right through as though she were a ghost. Holly didn't seem to notice. A smile still spreading her lips, she blinked and continued to move her hands along her belly.

"Enough!" Roared a voice different from the sisters. Male, low, and angry.

Greer was wrenched from her mind with a startled gasp. She clutched at her heaving chest, coughing as though she had been plunged into a pool of cold water. When she managed to flick her eyes upward to find Samael, they instead landed on Deino, who was cradling a blackened hand against her heart, the eye clutched tightly in her other fist.

"You go too far, Samael!" Pemphredo cried out in return, thrusting a hand forward to force Greer back into her own mind.

With a frightened kick backward, Greer rolled out of the way, and Pemphredo's blast of power embedded into a nearby tree trunk instead. Greer felt weak, barely alive, and it was when she glanced down to see her pruned and skeletal arms that she knew why.

Deino had been feeding off of her. Quietly taking her fill of Greer's soul, she gave Greer the images of what she had been looking for. And, for a brief moment, Greer wondered what images the sisters had given the small child before feeding off her soul, too.

"Run, Greer, *run now*! Find Egyn!" Samael shot at her, lifting his sword to fight off Enyo, who had stepped forward to send another blast of power toward her.

Greer's sneakers slipped against the dead pine leaves as she bolted upright, grasping the loose eye from Deino's outstretched hand as she stumbled painfully into a low-hanging branch. The bark lashed at her cheek, cutting a deep laceration underneath her eye. She could feel the blood trickle along her jaw and down the curve of her neck as she ran.

Shouts from the sisters rang behind her, but Greer didn't look back. Her breath was loud and harsh in her ear, and she focused solely on the pounding of her feet against the packed earth. Lungs burning and thighs aching, she didn't stop until she scampered into a second clearing.

Egyn, merely a shadow against the dark background of the forest, brayed at her sudden appearance. He reared onto his back legs, eyes shifting as he watched for Samael to appear behind her. Greer forced herself forward, a feeling of gratefulness penetrating her fear when she realized Samael had tied her canvas bag onto Egyn's saddle when they returned from the river.

Egyn settled when Greer grabbed his reins and dipped low to the ground to facilitate her climbing onto his back. There was a moment of hesitation before she heard crashing in the trees behind her. Whipping her head to look over her shoulder, Greer balked in horror when she spotted hundreds of spiders rushing toward her in a mob of hairy legs and pincers.

Deino must have called her pets to follow Greer. Or, to Greer's chagrin, to follow the eye that Greer still clutched in her hand.

Egyn brayed once more, tugging Greer into action. She pulled herself into the saddle, tucking herself tightly against Egyn's frame. She was barely situated when the horse took off, thundering through the forest and weaving through the trees.

More branches lashed at her as they passed, cutting at her face and exposed chest. Despite the roaring of wind and whipping of Egyn's black mane, Greer could still hear the spiders cantering after them, their dulcet purrs vibrating across the foliage littering the forest floor. Greer tried to send a blasting power toward them in a desperate attempt to fend them off. Fire, ice, anything she could think of to slow down the mob.

But nothing came, her power shuddering to a close as it reached the tips of her fingers. Sparks were the only things that flew, landing pitifully on the back of the saddle as they ran.

One spider, coming close enough to leap onto Egyn's rear, began to claw up the beast's spine. Greer heard his cry of pain as the pincers sunk into his flesh. She twisted in the saddle and, using a loose saddle bag she had yanked from its place, she swung it at the spider. The bag collided against the hairy body, and with a second cry of pain from Egyn, the pincers pulled from the horse's flesh and fell.

"Use your power!" Samael bellowed, appearing above the tree line as he expertly wove in between the bare branches. His sword and dagger, both still in each hand, were painted with a thick, dense black.

"I– I–" Greer stuttered as a second spider leaped forward. She swung the bag at it, sending it flying into a nearby tree. It crunched sickeningly against the trunk, sliding to the exposed roots. Dead. "I can't!"

Samael banked toward the ground, swinging deftly around another tree, and landed between Egyn and the swarm of spiders. They gathered around him, forming a circle of clicking pincers and throaty purring as Samael raised his sword in answer.

Egyn burst through the trees, entering a field just outside the forest boundaries, and Greer's vision popped with moonlight and speckled stars in the night sky. The horse climbed up a grassy knoll, and Greer dismounted from the saddle as soon as they reached the apex. No spiders had followed them, whether because of Samael or because they couldn't leave the tree line, Greer wasn't sure.

Ignoring the blood dripping from the deep cuts in her cheeks and chest, she watched with bated breath, eyes sweeping along the dark forest for any sign of Samael. Two minutes, five minutes, ten minutes went by.

A thump of earth behind her made Greer jolt in shock. Whirling around, she glimpsed Samael, his arms and hands covered in a thick, black goo. He sheathed the sword between his wings with a zing of metal against leather, glowering down at her with narrowed eyes, the dagger still held tightly in his fist.

"I told you to stay put."

Greer opened her mouth to respond, but just as quickly, clamped her lips shut.

"You need to learn how to use your power." Samael brushed past her, angrily tugging at Greer's canvas bag before tossing it onto the grass. "If you can't get past Deino's spiders, how do you expect to fight off the Primordials who will come looking for you in Gaian?"

Greer bristled, anger thrumming through her. "I was doing just fine on my–"

"Don't finish that." Next, Samael opened up his water pouch and took a deep gulp.

Greer turned her eyes away from the column of his throat, working with each pull.

"You were far from doing just fine." He capped the pouch with a twist from his wrist. "You'll die the minute you step foot in Gaian." He sank onto the grass, wiping the sweat and blood from his brow.

Greer shifted awkwardly on her feet before saying, "I can take the first watch this time. You know, so that you can get some rest."

Samael let his arm drop, settling onto a bent knee. He glanced up at her, a humorous expression of doubt pulling a smirk on his mouth. "And do what, exactly, if something shows up? Stare at them?"

Bending down, Greer snatched her canvas bag from the grass and swung a strap over her shoulder. "You're an ass," she retorted, marching as far away from him as the apex of the hill would allow.

"You're right," he called back. "But I'm right, too."

Greer didn't respond. She threw the bag against the tree trunk, thin branches swinging in the chilled breeze that floate over the grass plain. Punching at the canvas bag twice, she settled her head against the lumpy fabric and let out a sigh of irritation from her nose.

"I'll wake you in the morning for breakfast, then?" Samael said as Greer shivered from the cold, her arms wrapped tightly around her chest. "What would your majesty prefer?"

Greer ignored him for a second time, incensed that he was attempting to get a rise out of her.

"I'm going to the river to wash up. Egyn will stay with you this time since you can't be trusted not to run off on your own."

Clicking her tongue against her teeth, Greer settled deeper into the earth, keeping her back turned as she listened to Samael's leather armor swish against the long grass.

TWENTY-FOUR

GREER

"**S**top looking at me."

"Greer, I am not looking at you."

"I can *feel* you looking at me."

Samael let out a sigh. "My back is to you. My wings are expanded. I cannot see you. I have not peeked in the last four times you've bathed."

Hesitantly, Greer, still covering her chest with her arms, glanced over her bare shoulder. His wings were snapped to attention, and he was facing away from her. Shivering from the cold water, she dipped low one more time to wash the soap suds from her neck.

"I still don't know why you wouldn't let me get rid of the dirt."

Greer rolled her eyes. "Because I still feel grimy if I don't scrub myself with soap." Planting her feet into the stones lining the river bed, she slowly returned to the bank.

"Who brings soap on a trek like this, anyways?"

It was Greer's turn to let out a sigh. "Women, Samael, women do. Or people who prefer not to smell like a dirty turtle tank." Though the breeze was humid and warm against her bare skin, a wave of goosebumps still appeared on her limbs. "Towel me." The rivulets of water soaking her hair and skin dried up instantly. Greer let out another sign of irritation. "What did I tell you about drying my hair?"

Samael's arms splayed out to his sides. "I don't know what you want, Greer."

"It gets poofy if I don't braid it, and argh–" Greer was cut off by a rogue wave of river water hitting her from behind, thoroughly soaking her from head to toe once more. "Are you serious? There's dirt in my hair again!"

"We're two weeks into an eight-week journey. Dirt in your hair is the least of our problems."

The last two weeks had been long and exhausting, made even longer by their constant bickering. If Greer said the sky was blue, Samael would swear it was green. If Samael wanted to go east, Greer would pick a fight until they went west, ensuring her map was more accurate than his knowledge. And on and on it went.

Even so, it had been smooth sailing through the Meridian of Wrath since meeting with the three sisters in the forest. The landscape was primarily plains filled with long grass and pebbled by abandoned stone castle ruins. The longer they walked, the warmer and more humid it grew. In the last day or so, Greer had opted to remove her sweater and wear only her tank top, soaking in the sun's rays on her bare shoulders.

On the other hand, Samael had strapped his leather armor to Egyn. Greer would glimpse the straps of muscle beneath his linen shirt when she knew he wasn't looking, taking in the large wings and the gentle hands he only reserved for his horse. And then she would find another reason to argue.

A butterfly ambled by as Greer grumbled, pulling on a clean shirt over her sopping wet hair. She continued to grumble as she wrung out her locks and promptly braided them into place. She even grumbled as she slung her canvas bag, dirty and covered in muck, onto her shoulders.

"What are the chances you stop complaining before we get to the Meridian of Indolence?" Samael said through gritted teeth.

"Slim," Greer replied with a sweet smile, eyes narrowed against the blazing sun as she looked up at him. His back was still turned, but by the stiffness of his shoulders, she could imagine the flash of irritation in his gaze.

Bees flitted through the wildflowers lining the muddy bank, and frogs hopped back into the calm waters as Greer hauled herself onto the grassy ledge overlooking the river. Shafts of morning sunlight pierced through the clouds drifting across the blue sky, illuminating patches of long grass and tall trees. The mountains in the distance behind them were barely discernible.

She hadn't expected to make it this far...though she would never admit it out loud to *him*.

"When will we get to the Meridian of Indolence?" Greer asked as she circled to Samael's front.

He glanced down at her, cerulean eyes bright against the sunshine, as the soft wind brushed his dark hair from his brow. He pulled his wings back into place, ruffling the feathers until they lay smooth. "This afternoon. We'll spend a few days getting through." A wicked smile formed. "The entire Meridian is a bog. No point in bathing when it's all mud."

Greer bristled. "Do you have to preen yourself? Like parrots do?"

The smile slid from Samael's face. "Get a move on. Egyn is in the meadow."

The horse lifted his head at Greer's approach, a stalk of long grass hanging from his mouth. His ears and tail twitched against the onslaught of flies attempting to land on his black hair. Mosquitoes whined past Greer's ear, shooting upward with every step she took.

Upon reaching him, she ran a hand down his long neck and tipped her head back to soak in the sunlight. It had rained the past three days, leaving all three of them drenched and miserable, and it was the first time the sun had made an appearance since.

"Come on, Egyn," Samael said, slapping the horse's saddle, "no more time to eat."

Greer could have sworn Egyn's pale, ashen eyes turned wary as he looked over Samael.

As they crossed the meadow, the sweet smell of wild berries wafted on the breeze, reminding her of the perfume Paige preferred to wear. Greer felt a lurch in her gut. She had been so consumed with Samael, Egyn, and getting out of Samsara that Paige had left her mind. She hadn't realized it until now.

Guilt consumed her, spreading like a fire and flushing her neck and cheeks pink. Clearing her throat from the sudden lump, she blinked away the tears that formed in the corners of her eyes.

"Is everything okay?" Samael asked gruffly, and Greer felt his gaze on her face.

Not looking up, she merely nodded. "I was just thinking whether you would pick at your feathers to clean them or whether someone else picks through them." She paused, letting out a shaky breath to steady herself. "And if you let someone else pick through them, do you Primordials form a giant line like gorillas?"

Samael looked away with a shake of his head, not bothering to indulge in her question.

By lunchtime, the meadow had shifted. The earth gave way to scummy waters. Slugs and bloated leeches rested on tree roots, dripping with condensation. The humidity and the briny smell of algae had even changed, and Greer found herself drenched in sweat by mid-afternoon.

And that didn't help the bugs. Gnats hovered over the standing water, and the thick throng of mosquitoes landed on her sticky skin, biting through the layers of clothing she had placed back on for protection.

The three of them trudged through the slime-coated muck for hours. Greer watched the snakes curl on wet branches, the turtles parting the algae as they passed through the water, the water birds carefully navigating the swamp. She kept her eyes trained on the animals around her with fascination and intense focus. Mostly to try and make herself forget how utterly shitty she felt. Both physically, sweaty, and covered in muck, and mentally, from having forgotten about the death of her best friend.

She thought she would see Paige when she reached Gaian for that brief period. Now, it felt like Greer had lost her all over again. She pushed back her thoughts as she pulled her foot from the sludge with a loud *thwap*.

As they neared evening, a curling mist swelled above the murky water. The trees hung crooked into the swamp, thick moss blankets covering their roots. A ripple of water and a pair of yellow eyes slipped just above the surface and caught Greer's eye.

With a surprised gasp, she caught herself against the saddlebags tied to Egyn. His huffing snort echoed through the darkness, cutting into the chirp of bats and the whoosh of owls navigating the tendriled branches swaying in the breeze.

"Nakki," Samael said in a hushed whisper, pointing toward a second set of eyes peering toward them. It tilted its head as though curious and beckoning. "Many things here will try and lure you into the water."

From what Greer could see of its brow, the creature was humanoid. Skin mottled blue with a shine that reminded her of reptilian scales, the Nakki also possessed a tangle of matted, black hair. The locks floated on the surface, dancing in the ripples created by bugs landing on the water. The brow dipped below, and the Nakki was lost to the muddled silt.

"Don't stare in the water," Samael went on, holding a hand to help Greer out of the mud. "We'll stay on this piece of land for the night. No good in getting lost here."

Greer shoved past him, squelching through the muck until she reached a bank rising from the swamp. Samael followed her, saying nothing about her refusal of his help, as she sat on the soggy moss and dumped the excess water from her sneakers.

Greer's feet were pruned and uncomfortable. Her wet clothes chafed against her moist skin, rubbing the fresh mosquito bites raw. Dead leaves stuck to her ankles, and she swallowed back a gag as she plucked an attached leech from under the hem of her pants. She tossed it back into the water, where it landed with a soft *plunk*. From the immediate ripple— aside from the leech's— she could tell something below the water darted toward it, and a flash of fins told Greer the leech was no more.

Greer had camped a decent amount growing up in northern California and again at dig sites through college, but this was easily the most miserable she had ever felt.

Leaning against a mossy tree, the smell of wet bark and rotting vegetation curling around her, Greer pulled a book from the canvas bag. The pages were wrinkled from being dunked in the water, and the leather binding was peeling at the spine, but it was, surprisingly, still readable. She settled into a nook between roots to read.

"Are you reading that again?"

The question came after a few minutes of silence.

Samael had made his way to the bank, sat on the mossy bed's edge, and pulled off his boots to dry. The sheathed sword and dagger lay next to him. It was the first time Greer had seen him without his weapons strapped to him.

She raised her brows in response. "I...yeah, I guess I am." She made to return to the open page in front of her when Samael spoke up again.

"Haven't you read it three times over by now?"

Greer shrugged a shoulder, turning the page. "It's a good book, and it takes me away from...well, it's a good book." She had almost slipped up, had nearly said something personal. She peered over the top, spotting Samael with his foot dangling toward the swampy water below.

He played with his dagger, emerald gemstones glinting in the evening light. He tossed it in the air, watched it rotate end over point, and caught it at the hilt. "Are you hungry?" he asked, glancing over at her.

Greer ducked behind the book, digging her toes into the moss under her feet. "I could eat," she replied simply, pretending to be absorbed in the pages of her story once again.

Samael stood, flexing his gray wings behind him. He bent down to unsheathe his sword and slowly dipped each foot into the water, making sure not to cause any ripples. He stilled for a heartbeat, his gaze raking over the murky surface. With a swift lunge, he plunged the tip of his sword into the swamp and retracted it just as quickly, a flopping fish speared on the end.

"Do you want to do the honors?" He asked with a grin as he clambered out of the water. "I'm not sure I know how to gut a fish."

Greer knew he was lying, and she was sure that Samael knew that she knew that he was lying. But she bit her lip against the silliness of his bare feet still covered in muck, the feathers of his wings dirty and crusted in mud, and the boyish smile that lit up his eyes. With a sigh and a fake groan, Greer pushed herself to stand and took the sword from him.

It was heavier than she expected, and the sword tip fell against the moss with a muffled *thunk*. Samael's chuckle, low and breathy, skittered across her bones. Glancing over her shoulder, she was surprised to see him so close. Less than a foot apart. He was still standing on the bank of the river, and the difference in their heights evened. The flecks of green in his eyes were brighter than she thought, and he had a single freckle under the stubble on his upper lip.

They stared at one another for a long moment, unmoving and silent. When Egyn neighed, tossing his head back against a new swarm of flies, Samael blinked and pulled back.

"I'll get a fire started," he said. "It'll take a good dose of power to light wet wood."

Greer nodded, swallowing thickly as she bent down to tug the fish from the end of his sword. Despite knowing that his power would drain quickly against the dark bonds holding him together, she noticed tendrils of magic shooing the flies away from Egyn, who had finally settled back into resting.

They got through the cooking and eating of the fish, and Greer took her time to show Samael how to gut it. It was the first night they hadn't fought and the first night Greer had seen Samael relaxed enough to lean against a tree trunk, forearm resting against a bent knee. He asked about the book she was reading: her favorite parts, why she kept diving back into it, and the characters that resonated with her.

And, despite her mind tugging at her to pipe down, Greer answered them. She managed to work up the courage to ask him a single question: if all of the Primordials had the same dagger. She had noticed Azazel sported a similar one.

Samael had glanced down at his, where it still lie on the ground, before taking it into his hand and, when he extended his arm toward Greer, she grabbed the hilt to inspect it.

"It's a beautiful piece," she said, smiling softly as she ran her fingers delicately over the emerald stones. "The etchings are stunningly intricate." She could feel his gaze on her, studying the contours of her face and the color of her eyes in the darkness.

Greer didn't look up, but that night, she fell asleep imagining what it would have felt like if she had.

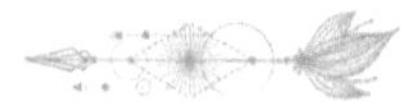

Greer didn't know how long she had been asleep, but the crescent moon had marched halfway across the sky in the same amount of time. The crickets chirped, and the *gloop* of frogs jumping into the water sounded through the swamp, softly infiltrated by Samael's snores.

She looked over at the Primordial. He had seemingly fallen asleep against the tree he leaned on, his chin tucked against his chest. His wings were cramped behind his back, kinked at an odd angle. She didn't know the last time he had slept, let alone so peacefully.

Stretching her arms above her head, Greer shifted to her other side, curling her hand underneath her cheek. The moss was a cushion against the mud-slick swamp, and the humidity settled on her like a thick blanket. She was readying to settle back into sleep when movement caught her attention.

Greer opened her eyes further, focusing them on the ripples of water cresting over the algae and lily pads. She vaguely remembered Samael's warning in her half-sleep, but she couldn't seem to remember why. An image appeared beneath the surface. Ghostly white and flickering.

With a lurch, Greer rolled onto her hands and knees, crawling over to the edge of the moss-covered island. Her fingers dug into the mud of the bank as she leaned over to sweep her gaze over the water. She saw nothing at first, save for the water bugs skating across the surface.

That was, until Paige's face appeared, her body pale and naked, settled on the silt bottom of the swamp. Greer felt her heart fly into her throat. She pushed herself away from the bank, a wave of dizziness washing over her.

Breathe, breathe, breathe, she told herself through spotted vision.

Behind her, Samael stirred but remained asleep. She swallowed the panic rising in her throat before returning to the murky water. She stared into it once again. It was impossible. There was no way it could have been– but there she was. Paige. Her hair bobbed in the water, smooth and untangled. She sported the familiar crooked grin on her face.

"Paige?" Greer whispered, resting her head against the palm of her hand. "Is that you?"

Paige nodded her head, still smiling.

Greer thought her heart would burst. "Can you– can you get out of the water? I want to talk to you. To...to..." To apologize. She couldn't finish the sentence.

Paige nodded again, this time raising a pale hand toward the surface. Greer reached forward to grasp Paige's wrist to help her up, but a shout had her ripping her arm to her side.

"Greer! No! *Get away from the water!*"

Greer whipped her head around to look at Samael, who had shot to his feet, sword in hand. She blinked, tilting her head in confusion. Opening her mouth to respond, Greer turned back to look at Paige.

But she had disappeared.

In Paige's place was a yellow-eyed, mottled-skinned nakki. The dark lips were pulled back, revealing black teeth sharpened into points. Greer gasped in horror as she tried to move, but she was too late.

The nakki leaped from the water and clamped its blue-tinged hands around Greer's throat. She felt the biting sting of the dirty nails wrench through, breaking skin. Then, she was pulled forward, plunging and disappearing beneath the water, sucking in a lungful of water in surprise as she went.

Despite the warm humidity of the swamp, the water was still cool and might have even felt refreshing had it not been for the circumstances. The moonlight above went dark, hidden by the layer of scum and algae floating above her. Greer thrashed, remembering how, just two weeks ago, she had been forced under by the souls crossing the river.

This time, the adversary was stronger and faster. The nakki yanked Greer deeper into the swamp and through the swaying vines of seaweed growing up from the muck-filled bed. There was a muffled splash from somewhere above, and Greer felt a second nakki dart past her, heading off the intruder who had entered the swamp. Bubbles whirled around her as she fought against the hand wrapped around her throat. Her head was spinning, her chest burning, as the nakki dragged her toward the pitted roots of the trees.

And Greer knew that if the nakki were successful in getting her there, she would be dead.

She kicked at the creature and felt her heel collide with a hip. Foot slipping against the slick skin, it forced the nakki to release its death grip on her throat. Greer could slide her hand underneath the nakki's second claw and pry the nails out of her flesh.

Her thrashing slowed, and her thoughts became muddled and fuzzy. Greer was running out of air, and she knew it. The nakki, who had dug its nails into her arm once more, knew it too. All it needed to do was keep her below the surface for a final minute. Her chest was on fire as pained and involuntary gulps forced the water into her lungs. She didn't want to breathe, but her body betrayed her, and she tasted the earthy silt as it slid down her throat.

A hand grasped Greer's shoulder, violently shaking her in an attempt to pull the nakki's hand away completely. The motion pulled her back to consciousness one last time, and she clamped her fingers around the nakki's wrist, desperately straining against the nakki's tightening grip.

It happened instantly, the force of power Greer had tried so hard to keep down. It rose in her chest, swirling the water around her and the nakki like a whirlpool. The magic jetted out of her like a rocket, whipping through the murky water and slamming the nakki square in the chest.

Greer felt the slimy fingers finally loosen before letting go entirely. The nakki floated away from her, bumping against the slime-coated rocks before settling dead in the shadows of the tree roots. She felt the strong hand, still grasping her shoulder, tug her toward the surface. The last thing Greer saw was a crowd of nakki swarming the dead one, breaking through the mottled skin and burying their teeth in its intestines.

Her head broke through the algae, covering her hair in swamp scum and dead moss, but she was alive. Greer took a garbled breath of humid air, forcefully coughing the water from her lungs.

Greer was exhausted down to her very soul. Her arms and legs felt heavy, and it took the rest of her energy to loosely pull at Samael's water-logged shirt as he carried her. She felt another wave of magic coming, but she didn't have the energy to fight back the power that was building. She had let it pool inside of her, had refused to unleash it, to exercise it. Now, there was nothing she could do to stop the blasts that shot through her, each rush ricocheting loudly off the deadfall and swollen logs nestled in the swamp. She tried to push Samael away, make him drop her, and protect him from the panicked magic she couldn't control. But he held on until they were a safe distance from the swamp.

Once they were, Samael dumped her on the moss, and Greer rolled onto her back, locks of hair glued to her face. She didn't have the fortitude to peel them away. Instead, she stared at the stars through the roiling mist that twisted toward the sky.

"I told you not to look in the water," Samael said through panting breaths.

Greer slowly turned her head, the only movement she could do, and looked at him. His wings were limp against his back, and his shirt, stained with slime and goo, was drenched. She felt another blast of power tug at her navel and cried out as it painfully launched out of her, spine arching off the moss.

"You don't listen to a damn thing anyone says," Samael continued. He managed to straighten, despite his heaving chest, and planted his hands on the crown of his head in a further attempt to catch his breath. "Are you going to say anything?"

Greer turned away from him to look toward the sky again. She thought she was being given the chance to talk to Paige and apologize. She had been a fool, and she knew it.

Nothing Samael could say would have made her feel worse. She deserved to die. She deserved to take Paige's place. And she wished the nakki would have taken her, so she didn't have to relive it all over again.

Samael shook his head, jaw clenched and eyes hardening. "If you think you can get to the Meridian of Pride on your own, then so be it. Making sure you don't kill yourself has become a job I'm not interested in keeping."

Greer didn't respond as he snapped his wings open, water smattering her and the moss she lay on before jumping into the air. He beat his wings once, twice, and three times before soaring over the treetops and disappearing from view. Egyn's nicker was low, as though he, too, was disappointed in her.

TWENTY-FIVE

Odette

"No, absolutely not," Anaise said, her arms crossed tightly over her chest. "You have gone too far, Luisa. Us work with—work with her?" She vigorously shook her head. "No, I won't have it."

Odette sat on the pit platform, legs dangling over the edge, as she sharpened the blade Luisa had brought for her. There were five humans that night— two men and three women— debating the merit of allowing Odette to help them. So far, it was split evenly between the four newcomers. And it still took Luisa two weeks to convince them to meet with Odette in the vicinity.

The serpent's corpse had been cleaned up, but the blood staining the dirt floor remained. Splinters of wood from the fence littered the space around them, and the barefoot humans steered clear of the wreckage.

"She helped me," Tomas interjected. "During the cull. She made sure that I didn't spill the wine onto Kaique–"

"She didn't want you to spill it on her–" Anaise cut it with a roll of her eyes.

"She also saved those two men from being killed by the snake," the third woman said as she brushed her blonde hair over her shoulder. "There was a rumor going around the barracks that she had them set up some royal apartments until the solstice."

"That rumor is true," Luisa said, glancing at the third woman. "I have seen them myself. They are being treated as guests."

From what Odette had learned about her in the hour she had been seated on the pit platform, the woman's name was Karina. She was dressed in the same risque attire as Luisa, however, her duties were reserved for the soldiers living in the guard barracks just outside the palace grounds. On the walk over, Luisa mentioned that, though Kaique had violent fetishes he preferred to play out during their time together; at least she wasn't being passed around. Karina, on the other hand, thought the opposite.

The stars in the clear sky above them were the only things illuminating the colosseum. Luckily, the grounds stayed quiet during their meeting, but Odette didn't want to push their luck by lighting a fire and attracting a wandering soldier's attention. Most of them spent the evenings drinking themselves into a stupor since the rift had closed, frequently employing Karina, but still, they couldn't take the risk.

"And she's probably saving them to carve up for a late-night snack," Anaisa shot back. "With the dagger you just handed over to her."

Odette snorted with laughter, garnering the attention of the five humans below the platform. Sighing, she tossed the dagger to the earth, where it embedded in the dirt at their feet.

"You can have it back," Odette called down, unable to control the amused tone in her voice. "I was just sharpening it for you." She adjusted her wings to lean back on the palms of her hands. "You can use it to carve me up if you like. It won't be the worst thing that's happened to me."

Anaise scowled at the blade, but Luisa called a quick *"you aren't helping"* up to Odette.

Odette shrugged her shoulders, stretching her neck back and forth to rid the kinks from sharpening the blade for so long. "It sounds like their minds are made up. Maybe we should move on to another group."

Luisa slid an angry look to Anaise. "You trust Aldonza and Yara," she started again, unwilling to relinquish the fight. "Why not trust one that I bring forward?"

"She's a guest of Kaique," Anaise said for what seemed like the tenth time. She sighed with frustration. "That means she's loyal to Kaique."

Odette hopped off the platform, spreading her wings to slow her fall to the ground. Reaching down, she picked up the dagger and sheathed it. "The only reason I'm here, in this realm, in the first place, is on behalf of a friend. If it weren't for her, I would have happily been in hiding for the rest of my life. Now I'm staying to help you."

"Don't do us any favors," Anaise clucked in return. "We could have easily gotten out of here without you."

"I'm not arguing that you couldn't. There was always a possibility," Odette replied, feeling her magic rising, along with her temper, just under her skin. "I'm just saying that you'll have an easier time with my assistance. I trained Fae like them and spent centuries doing it. If you don't have a plan and a good one, you're all going to die."

An unsteady shudder ran through the group at her words.

"You said that you were here on behalf of a friend," Tomas said, running a hand over his buzzed hair. "Who is that friend?"

Odette shifted on her feet. "I can't tell you that."

Anaise gestured wildly toward Odette. "See? She's keeping secrets from us. Another reason to not trust her–"

"You must earn my trust as much as I must earn yours," Odette hissed, a blast of wind ruffling their hair and flapping their clothes like flags on a pole. "And this friend isn't known to exist in this realm, and her death will be swift if it is uncovered."

"Is she–" Gael trailed off, rubbing the back of his neck. "Is your friend half Fae?"

Odette went preternaturally still, a blank expression drawing over her face. She rifled through her comments, trying to see if she said something that gave it away.

Seeing her worried confusion, Gael quickly went on. "It's just that there aren't many reasons why a death would be swift here– Kaique likes to play. Just last week, we found out that a soldier had impregnated a human...a human who had a secret relationship with the soldier. They executed her on the spot."

Anaise's throat bobbed when she swallowed. "She was a fool. A sweet fool but a fool nonetheless. We warned her every step of the way not to get involved with the men here–"

"You cannot possibly be blaming her," Tomas said, his nose wrinkled in disgust and horror. "She fell in love–"

"Falling in love with these captors should be a death sentence, and as you can see, that's what it always turns out to be," Anaise shouted back. It echoed over the stone in the colosseum, rising above the tall hedge walls.

The group went silent again. Odette pricked her ears, waiting to see if there was a rustle against the walking paths or a call from the soldiers in the gardens. Nothing came, save for the humming of insects and the chittering of small animals in the jungle underbrush.

"Keep your voice down," Gael admonished Anaise. "Now isn't the time to start—"

A bellowing laugh from the gardens above them cut Gael off, and the group stilled again.

"We've pushed our luck," Tomas whispered. "We should go before the wandering guards find us here."

"I'll be here tomorrow night for anyone who wants to learn from me," Odette said quietly as the group dispersed. Anaise didn't bother glancing at her, but Tomas, Gael, and Karina nodded in understanding.

Odette sighed as they scuttled back into the shadows of the colosseum. As it stood, they didn't have the numbers to take on Kaique and his soldiers.

And it didn't seem like they would before time ran out.

"Good, Tomas, good," Odette said as the man lunged forward and sent two quick jabs to Gael before retreating. "Beautiful form. Again." He lunged again, punched Gael's open palms, and dropped back.

Odette kept her promise of coming back to the colosseum the next night. There may have been more secluded places on the grounds to gather, but the stone steps allowed them to train for cardio, whereas the long benches were perfect for balance and hand-to-hand combat. They stayed near the hedges in case a wandering guard decided to peer down toward the pit. At the angle Odette had chosen, they would be in the shadows long enough to make a quick getaway.

It was easy enough for Odette to keep Kaique entertained during the day, which led to him being occupied during the evening. Mention a couple of quirky facts about the other courts, and he was distracted in his personal library for a few more hours after that. At the very least, it kept him away from Luisa until nightfall.

And, in the meantime, Odette was busy stockpiling weapons. She smoothly took daggers off the hips of guards, slid large knives from the counters in the kitchens, and knabbed a sword from the barracks when she could sneak into the artillery room just before dinner.

"Luisa, come this way," Odette said in a hushed call. "Tomas, step aside for just a moment." Anaisa, much to Odette's surprise, and a last-minute recruit named Yasmin, taller than average with a mouth to match, stopped what they were doing to peer over. "I just want to do a form check for your punches. You'll be paired with Gael."

Gael, who was in athletic shape himself, gestured toward her with two fingers, a smirk tugging at his mouth. "I'll try to go easy on you," he said in Portuguese, getting himself set into a hip-wide stance with his hands splayed on either side.

Luisa merely smiled sweetly back. "Thank you, Gael. That's very kind."

In a flash, she kicked out a leg, catching Gael hard in the chest. He buckled to his knees under the surprise, and before he had a moment to recover, she swung onto his back and twisted toward the ground. He flipped over the top of her and landed flat against the stone bench, a whoosh of breath escaping from his throat.

The pairings surrounding them let out a mixture of low gasps and chuckles. Luisa bent down and held out her hand. Gael, grinning, grasped it and pulled himself up.

"That was unexpected," Odette said, though she couldn't help the smile that crept onto her face. "You've been holding out on me."

Luisa nodded in agreement. "My parents had my brother and me trained in Jiu-Jitsu when we were growing up. We lived just outside of Bogota, and they wanted me to be able to protect myself."

Odette and Tomas exchanged looks before she spoke. "Luisa, I want you to train with the dagger. If you become competent, I'll train you to use a sword."

She paused to reach down to her waist, removing the sheathed and freshly sharpened blade from its leather casing. The humans stilled as she approached Luisa, but Odette flipped the dagger and held out the hilt. Luisa grasped her hand around it without hesitation.

"This is much sharper than when Tomas stole it," Luisa commented, turning it over to look at the engraved pommel. The blade glinted under the soft glow of the moonlight.

"Yes," Odette replied. "And I want you to learn to use it. You'll work with me every day. Give the blade back to me when you're done for the evening. We don't need you getting caught with it by accident."

Luisa glanced back up at her. "Aren't you afraid of me learning to use a dagger?"

Odette nodded, a mischievous grin splitting her face. "Yes, I am. That's why you need one."

Luisa returned the grin before peeling off toward the opposite side of the stone benches, her gaze down at the blade again with intense focus. Odette looked back at the group only to find them staring at her in awe. She cocked a brow in question.

Tomas stepped forward in Luisa's wake, a squinting curiosity wrinkling the corners of his eyes. "We've never seen a member of the Fae give a weapon over to a human willingly." He swallowed. "When Luisa told us of your offer, we thought it too good to be true." A chuckle rumbled deep in his chest. "We've been half-expecting Kaique and his soldiers to ambush us on sight."

"No, I will not turn you in." Odette shook her head, her braid shifting between her wings. "My deal remains."

It was Gael's turn to step forward, and he planted a steady foot against the stone bench before him. "Luisa, she needs this. We all suffer the wrath of Kaique, but no one more than her. He's done more than give her a few bruises in the two years she's been in the Court of Mist and Tide. He–" Gael paused to take a deep, shaking breath. "He's obsessed with her. No one else can touch her. His gifting her to you was a sick joke of sorts. No one else can look at her. It's disconcerting."

"*He* is deeply disturbed," Yasmin piped in, reaching up to adjust the red scarf that tied back her hair. "The violent things he does to her. Yara and Aldonza have been fixing her up for years now." Odette saw a shudder run up her spine, goosebumps prickling the skin of her arms. "And she walks around with her head high like it doesn't matter. From what we know, and it isn't much, the last human woman who had caught Kaique's eye lasted four months before she hung herself from a tree in the garden."

"And the woman before that stole a guard's dagger and slit her own throat in the dining hall at dinner," Gael said, shaking his head.

Odette swallowed. "How long have you all been here then?"

They were quiet for a long minute before Tomas answered.

"I have been here for the ten years he's sat on the throne. I owned an architecture business in Buenos Aires, focusing mostly on landscaping for upscale companies. Kaique must have liked my work when he came out of the rift because he kidnapped me and brought me here." He gestured toward the top of the stone stairs. "All of that is my work. The fountains, the pools, the gardens."

"Tomas and I came through together," Gael said as he rubbed his salt-and-pepper beard. "I was a chef for a five-star restaurant in Sao Paulo. Kaique killed my business partner and left his body in the refrigerator in our kitchen. I had the choice of being charged with murder or coming here." He let his hand drop to his side. "I should have taken my chances in a Brazilian prison."

Anaise reached out, grasping Gael's forearm. She squeezed gently in support. "I've been here six years. I was a maid at a hotel in Lima. I think he was just bored and left the rift. He brought me back with him, and I've been serving him dinner ever since."

Odette glanced over her shoulder to look toward Luisa, who was working with the dagger, attempting to get her footing in the right place to have a more powerful strike.

"Every human here would step in front of a bullet for that girl," Yasmin said, her gaze sliding over Odette's shoulder toward Luisa. "She's been protecting us from Kaique for the entire two years she's been here."

Odette couldn't help but think about her imprisonment and what Adair forced her to do. She glanced back at Luisa again, wondering how much more the woman could take before Kaique broke her completely.

It was late at night when Odette returned to the apartment, the moon having marched to its apex and beyond. Lounging on the cushion on the window's ledge overlooking the gardens, she was gazing at the grounds Tomas had so beautifully designed. The summer breeze wafted in sweet scents of blooming flowers, trickling water from the fountains in the air.

There was a knock on the door leading to the hallway, and Odette lifted her head as she untangled her crossed legs and pushed off the windowsill. A female kitchen faerie bustled in as soon as Odette cracked the door open, pushing a cart over the threshold.

"I heard you wanted a snack, miss," the female said as Odette closed the door. She parked the cart in the middle of the room before striding to the window and poking her head out, checking the courtyard underneath the apartment before she whipped the curtains closed with a quick tug.

The female shuffled back over to Odette, who was watching the scene unfold before her with wide eyes, and stopped just as she reached the cart. Her pointed ears perked as if she was listening, then said, "There is something under the dinner plates for you." The whisper was so low that Odette had to crane her neck to hear. The woman released her grip on the cart handles, patted Odette's arm twice as she passed, and sashayed from the room.

Odette slowly stalked to the cart and picked up the gold-coated plate cover. She spotted an envelope lying flat against the wooden plate. She set the cover aside, and the underside was still warm from the freshly baked pastries that circled the outside of the plate. Sliding a finger under the slit of the envelope, she sliced open the thick parchment with a quick pull and began to read the note within.

We are here, your Grace, and awaiting your command. Long live King Tor.

Odette felt her cheeks flush, red and hot. She lifted a hand to her neck, feeling her pounding heartbeat against the column of her throat. For the first time in centuries, Odette allowed the warming sensation of victory to radiate through her core, the drumming of joy in her chest, the teary breathlessness that tightened her lungs.

She reached for the candle in the middle of the table and placed the edge of the parchment into the fire. She watched the flame slowly spread, engulfing the note and turning it into ash and ember that drifted toward the wooden surface. The jungle breeze through the cracks between the curtains blew the cinder away.

The following day, the kitchen attendant sent her a subtle wink as she set a bowl of fruit in front of Odette for breakfast before taking a pile of dirty dishes into the back room. Odette couldn't help the smile that crept onto her lips.

The time was now.

TWENTY-SIX

GREER

Greer was utterly and entirely alone for the first time since she was brought to Samsara. The first time no one lorded over her, the first time no one followed her to ensure she wasn't getting into trouble. And, while she had begged for this at one time or another, now she felt...empty.

She was thankful to at least have the horse's companionship, but when Greer finally had the strength to lift her head, she realized Egyn had taken off after his master. She imagined him trundling through the marsh, stopping to snack on tall grass, his tail swishing away the flies. She already missed his warmth, the exact opposite of Samael, and how she would use him to guard against the wind and rain.

Staying where she was, Greer allowed the sleep to take her.

When Greer woke, the sun was high above the trees. The mist had dissipated from the heat, only making the humidity more unbearable. Sweat dripped between her shoulder blades, pooling in her lower back, and she immediately stripped off the sweater she wore to protect herself from the bugs. Standing, she took a few steps toward where they had stayed the night before.

Samael had, fortunately, left her canvas bag behind. The food scraps were dwindling—a few pieces of dried meat and two wrinkled apples. Greer removed the apples and tossed them into the swamp, where a surfacing fish scooped them up. She popped one of the pieces of dried meat in her mouth and chewed slowly, ignoring the stabbing pain in her stomach as she folded the rest back into the linen.

She desperately needed more stock.

Greer shouldered the canvas bag and glanced around the small clearing. Her studying gaze landed on a branch low hanging against the trunk it was attached to. It only required three hard tugs and a twist for the branch to come free. She had studied ancient hunter-gatherer societies and seen the weapons they used to capture prey.

The vined seaweed could work if laid out to dry and then tethered to a sharp river rock at the branch's end. It had to work.

She was alone, and she had to try something.

Greer walked through the afternoon with nothing to keep her company except her thoughts and the sun marching across the cloudless sky. And the sun was worth chasing rather than pondering what lay in her mind because her thoughts were as damaging as ever. When she did allow them to surface, they were filled with guilt and regret. Not knowing Celeste as well as she should have, not having the chance to be honest with Delia, missing out on her opportunity to go to Greece and participate in the dig. Something she had been working toward for the entirety of her career.

And Paige. Seeing her body under the water, at peace and reaching for her, was nearly enough to break her for a second time. Maybe it already had.

When the sun disappeared for the day, Greer decided to try walking through the night. She was keen on spending less time in the Meridian of Indolence than was already necessary, and, according to the map she managed to save, the strait was just on the other side of the swamp. She would need another few days of walking, less if she could help it.

The marsh mist encircled the moon in a hazy orb, and bats swept across, their silhouettes like shadows across the reflecting light. Dew beaded on the spider webs spanning the trees. Greer shivered at the thought of those spiders scuttling through the Meridian of Wrath.

The eye was still stored in the front pocket of her canvas bag, and it glared at her every time she took it out. Greer was pleasantly surprised that the sisters hadn't come after her. She also considered that perhaps the sisters couldn't go after her, and it would be best if she never set foot in the Meridian of Wrath again.

Greer sat to rest for the first time since that afternoon. Leaning the back of her head against a tree, she swallowed back the bile that rose in her throat from her clenching stomach. Resigned to the realization that she wouldn't be able to eat much in the coming days, she popped another piece of the dried meat into her mouth. As she chewed, she assessed the swamp's shadows, the trees swaying, and the light in the distance.

Greer went still, nearly dropping the last bit of the meat into the muck—a light. There was a light in the distance. She shot to her feet, readying to tromp into the darkness toward it when she lurched to a stop.

Samael's words rang through her. How she didn't listen, how she was going to get herself killed, and he wasn't going to watch her do it any longer. There were things in the marsh.

But Samael had told her not to look in the water, and the light wasn't *in* the water. Greer briefly wondered whether it was a Primordial or daemon. She also wondered whether they had food. And it was the latter thought that had her pressing forward.

The light dipped between the trees, illuminating brighter and brighter before dimming again. Greer followed it as quietly as she could, stick still in hand and canvas bag strapped to her back. The light bobbed as it moved like a lantern, and Greer squinted against the darkness to see if she could make out a wing, horn, or pointed ears of the daemons she was accustomed to.

She followed the light deeper into the bog, past the standing water snaking through the tall grass, through the thick swarms of mosquitoes that followed her like a miserable cloud, into the rolling mist that swirled along the banks.

The stagnant air was thick with rotting wood and mildew as Greer trained her eye on the light, ignoring the blisters rubbing her heels. She peeled back the tall reeds growing out of the marsh, the thick cattails sticking to her damp clothing, and took one more step.

Then, she fell.

Head over feet, Greer tumbled down a muddy slope. Slipping and sliding as she struggled to catch herself on the broken logs and low-growing shrubs that made up the bank. A shout elicited from her as she landed squarely on her arm, followed by a sickening crack and a sudden flood of white, hot pain in her forearm. She finally came to an abrupt halt at the base of the hill, groaning as she clutched her wrist to her chest.

Greer rolled to the side, bursts of stars clouding her vision and roils of nausea, making it nearly impossible to move. When the first wave ended and her mind cleared enough for her to think straight, Greer went to lift her leg toward the slope but found herself stuck in a pool of thick, viscous mud.

In her pain, Greer hadn't realized she had sunk hip-deep into the marsh. The mud squelched as she tried to haul herself forward, but the sudden motion sent another wave of blinding pain through her arm. She slipped further into the sludge, letting out a cry of frustration and pain.

The same flicker of light danced in the corner of her eye, drawing her attention into the shadows of the darkened trees. It winked as it wove closer, and Greer wrestled with the muck, fighting to free herself as it dashed toward her.

She threw her uninjured hand forward and made a last-ditch effort to pull a shard of her power forward. The magic seemed to nestle deeper within her, refusing to surface.

The orb halted near the sloped bank, illuminating the gouging mark Greer had carved through the earth as she fell. The light was indeed cast from a lantern, black and rusted, and the flickering candle from within dripped wax onto the grass lining the marsh. A ghostly hand, misty and white, held it aloft.

Greer let out a shrill scream when two bulbous, white eyes peeked from behind the lantern, the body seemingly made of smoke. The creature ducked behind the lantern again, its hand trembling with fright.

"Out of all the creatures you've encountered, *this* is the one that makes you scream like you're dying?" A voice from behind her drawled. "It's a phouka."

Greer started and twisted at the waist, glaring over her shoulder at the Primordial kneeling on the opposite bank of the marsh. Face half-hidden by the swaying lantern light, she could still make out the quirked corner of his lip. She let out a sharp sigh and cradled her arm back into place against her chest. "What are you doing here?"

"I thought I was saving you, but you're doing just fine." Samael stood, leaning on his sword to lift himself upward. The tip sunk into the mud, and he left it there as he stepped toward the marsh's edge. "Nice stick."

Greer momentarily darted her gaze toward the branch near her canvas bag, which she had lost possession of during her tumble down the hill. "It was supposed to be a spear handle. But it would have been better if you had left me something to use to sharpen it." Her eyes flicked to the dagger at his waist, still sheathed in the leather casing.

"I've been trying to teach you for weeks."

Greer bristled. "Are you going to help me out of here or not?" She lifted an elbow in gesture toward her throbbing wrist, still tucked tightly against her chest. "I can't get out alone."

"Not." Samael shifted on his feet, the mud beneath his boots leaking water. "Can't. You've gotten yourself good and stuck. Again."

"Why are you here then?" Greer pressed again. The drying mud had glued her linen shirt to her torso, making the skin beneath itch. "I thought you left."

"I did," Samael replied simply as he lifted his shoulders in a shrug. "And then I realized...it does me no good to let you die out here." He lifted an eyebrow as he studied her. "It doesn't do you any good either. The wounds you attempt to inflict on others are merely the defensive projections to keep yourself from fully feeling the death of your friend."

Greer thought it would have been better if Samael had rammed his dagger into her heart. "That's bullshit," she said instead, swallowing back the snide and insulting comments that had threatened to explode out of her.

Samael shrugged again, his wings bobbing with the movement. "It's too bad you won't recognize it. Admitting the truth is the only thing to get you out of this mess." His eyes dropped to the phouka still hovering behind her.

Greer had forgotten the creature was there. She glanced at it, blinking at the phouka peering around the lantern. "What does he have to do with you helping me out of the mud?" Irritation began to bubble, anticipation stiffening the muscles in her jaw. It quickly overtook the throbbing pain in her wrist.

"Phoukas are entities meant to lure travelers deeper into bogs by the light of their lantern. You fell right into its trap. Plus, it's not like you would have listened to me even if I had given you that advice. As you've shown."

"You told me not to stare into the water. You didn't say anything about—"

"Did I have to explain in depth that you shouldn't follow ghost lights at night through a marsh in the underworld? I thought you were intelligent."

Greer clamped her lips shut and imagined strangling him the moment she was freed from the mud. "What do we do now, then?" She asked through gritted teeth. "How do I get out of here?"

Samael turned away from her, facing the phouka, who was still observing them from the opposite bank. "Two," he said, crossing his arms over his chest. His markings seemed to swallow the dim light from the phouka's lantern, the muscles in his forearm flexing as he tapped his fingers on his bicep.

The phouka shook its ghostly head. Releasing a hand from the lantern, it held five misty fingers into the air. Tendrils rolled off the hand like fog.

"Five is outrageous," Samael countered, shaking his head. "We would rather take our chances with the rougarou you work for. We'll do three."

The phouka ran a pondering hand down the front of its face. Bulbous eyes lifted, and it gestured between Greer and Samael.

"You want us both to give you three? That's six in total."

Grasping the handle of the lantern, the phouka began to twist away, floating further into the bog.

"Okay, okay," Samael said, throwing up his hands in surrender. "Three from each of us it is." Undertones of panic littered his voice, something Greer had only caught due to the time they spent together. Whatever the rougarou was, she was sure that Samael had no interest in meeting it.

"Three of what?" Greer asked, her stare bouncing back and forth between the phouka and the Primordial.

"Truths," Samael replied with a sigh. "It wants three truths from both of us."

Greer snorted, relief blazing through her. "That's easy enough. I want to leave Samsara, I want to go home, I wish my best friend weren't dead. Can you let me out now?"

The phouka blinked its bulbous eyes at her.

"It wants your secrets, Greer." Samael scrubbed a hand over his jaw. "The deepest truths you hold for yourself and only for yourself." He was quiet for a moment, staring at the emerald gemstones embedded in his dagger. They glinted in the light of the moon. "I hate being chained to Samsara. I wish I were set free, even though I know what it means. My selfishness would end mortal life, yet I still yearn for the bond to be broken."

The phouka nodded its misty head in response before turning its lantern toward Greer.

She felt her mouth go dry. She knew she wasn't ready to sift through the memories she had worked hard to force down. "What's a rougarou?" It didn't matter what it was. Greer was sure she would prefer it.

"Half devil, half wolf. It haunts the wetlands and marshes, using phoukas to lead travelers into the mud pits of the bog. Once there, the phoukas give the travelers a choice: reveal their deepest truths or face the rougarou. The phoukas feed on your deepest fears either way."

Greer mumbled a string of clipped curse words under her breath. She couldn't fight a rougarou, wedged and half-buried in mud, sporting a broken wrist. She sent a pleading gaze toward the night sky, praying that the swamp would open up and finish swallowing her whole.

When that didn't happen, Greer cleared her throat and, with a shake of her head, said, "I miss my mother, Celeste. Or Anna. I...I don't know what to call her. And I know she did some horrible, horrible things, and our relationship was complicated, but I could use her right now."

Greer kept her eyes trained on the mud, watching a water bug skate across the pooling water.

"I feel cheated that the universe created me to bring about death." Greer's head snapped up at Samael's words, but his stare was fixed on the phouka and its lantern. "To listen to their pleas, to watch them beg for their lives when they see me. To know what will be released into the world if I don't comply. I feel resentful of my existence."

Greer opened and closed her mouth several times, unsure what to say. A soft flood of despair and shame crept up her spine as though she could sense him through an invisible thread that connected them. A surge of pity rose in her gut, and Samael shot her a look in return.

"Paige's death is my fault." Greer lifted her chin as the phouka turned to look at her, the glow from the lantern illuminating its round eyes. "One of my best friends. Her death is my fault, and I didn't have the chance to tell her wife what I did. I–" She paused to pick at the cuticles of her fingernails. "I wish it was me who died instead."

There. Greer had said it. The recklessness. The bad sex. The drinking. It was a culmination of everything she could control and the things she couldn't.

Like dozens of times before, she wished death would come for her, for Samael to take his blade and sever her soul from her body. And Greer wished he could bring Paige back when he did.

"There was nothing you could have done," Samael said quietly. "Fate sealed her life before she was born."

Greer swiped a tear from her cheek, smearing muck from her fingertips.

"I regret the part I played in the War of the Sixteen," Samael said in Greer's silence. She lifted her gaze to see he had turned his cerulean eyes from her to the phouka. "My brothers were interred from my decision, and they paid the price. If given a second chance, I would let the mortal world fall to Michael."

One final admission. One more, and she would be free. Greer listened to the sweeping of the reeds in the wind and the croak of the frogs seated on the dead logs, reveling in the simplicity surrounding her.

Finally, she returned her gaze to the misty figure and its lantern. "I'm afraid of my power. It killed Holly. It killed Paige. It hurt Delia and Arista. I'm unsafe and dangerous. I'm better off alone."

The phouka's lantern winked out, shrouding the creature in darkness, and it was only by the light of the stars above them that Greer saw him float into the marsh once more.

A squelching sounded behind her, and Greer turned to watch Samael wipe the blade of his sword on his linen pants. "I'm going to fly over to you and pull you up from the mud," he said. The tightness of his voice marred his attempt at cool indifference.

Greer nodded, clutching her broken wrist tighter to her chest. The throbbing pain returned, sending dull shocks reverberating across her bones and up through her shoulder. Strands of hair brushed across her brow at the wind created by the *thwap* of Samael's wings.

He hovered above her, bobbing up and down in the air. Greer looked up, squinting against the mud and water flecks displacing from the pools around her, and locked her eyes on his hand extended down toward her.

"Grab onto me with your good hand," Samael said, firmly grasping Greer's upper arm. "This won't feel great, but I can't do anything until I get you out."

With the corners of her eyes wrinkling into a grimace, Greer let out a hiss of pain as Samael hauled her out of the mud. He was quick to wrap one arm around the back of her knees and another around her waist the second they were free, being careful to avoid putting any pressure on the broken wrist.

Tucked against his front, Greer found it comforting to feel his chest rise and fall without the armor's hardness or buckles. For a moment, she was lost to the first time he held her like this, remembering the sweeping rage that flooded every piece of her. A great deal had changed since then. An unexpected tide of gratefulness rushed over her, and, as though he could sense it, Samael drew her closer to him.

After a long minute, they were on the ground, Greer's feet planted next to her canvas bag on the sloping bank. Samael immediately took her wrist into his hand, the coarseness of his calluses in opposition to the gentleness with which he touched her. She let out a soft cry as he turned her hand over to study the misshapen form of her wrist.

"Are you okay?" Samael asked, eyes still fixed on her arm.

Greer cleared her throat. "It'll be okay. It's just broken." She lifted her eyes, her heart stuttering in her chest, to see his gaze piercing her own.

"I wasn't talking about your arm." A warm vibration tickled at her fingertips, spreading along her palm, wrist, and forearm. The pain vanished as her arm straightened out.

But Samael kept her wrist in his hand, his thumb running along her palm. Greer's stomach flipped, and she allowed her hand to rest there for reasons unknown to her.

"Thank you for coming back," she said softly.

Samael's gaze searched hers before he withdrew his hand from her own, sliding his fingers along her newly-healed wrist. "I will always come back." He bent down to grab the handle of her canvas bag, slinging it over a shoulder with one smooth toss. He held out his hand again to assist her up the hill.

Greer had many reasons not to give out her trust easily. Celeste's secrets. Cian's betrayal. Azazel's general existence. But Greer swallowed back the fear threatening to engulf her. Samael continued to show up and tried to reach out repeatedly. She had been the one to push him away, and he had, indeed, always come back.

The phouka forced her to voice things she had tried hard to push down. She had wanted to forget. But now, the world had been lifted from her shoulders, and there was a lightness to her that hadn't been there for months. And it seemed like there was a lightness to Samael, too.

At the very least, they shared an experience that connected them to a better understanding of one another.

This time, Greer took Samael's offer and clasped her hand into his instead of pushing him away.

TWENTY-SEVEN

GREER

For a few days, the bog Greer, Samael, and Egyn had been tramping through slowly turned into an open estuary. Saltgrass replaced the slime-coated algae, and the stagnant air turned briny. The river was cleared of mud, water streaming through an unobstructed bed of rock and sand. Squawking birds soared across the cloudless sky, dipping their thin legs into the bands of water before skating to a stop in the gentle current.

The breeze blew Greer's hair out of her braid, the strands thick with dirt and oil. Samael had been right. There was no use in bathing while they crossed the swamp. Her skin, grimy and itchy, was paying for it. And while she was anxious to reach water fresh enough to bathe in, she was equally as anxious to find a new source of food that didn't include flame-broiled frogs.

And, sure enough, her wish was granted when Samael pointed out a blueberry bush. At the sight of it, Greer thought she was going to cry. They picked through the thicket, eating the berries until their lips turned blue and feeding Egyn fruit by the handful. The horse would nudge Greer's shoulder, tickling her arm with his quivering muzzle, and she laughed before picking more berries off the bush for him to enjoy. Greer pretended that Samael wasn't watching them from the corner of his eye.

In the few weeks Greer had been on the journey, the easy days and nights of the bay were, by far, her favorite. They followed along the shore, moss-covered rocks breaking into pebbled sand. Greer removed her sneakers every afternoon, tying them to Egyn's saddle, and rolled up the legs of her pants to walk through the calm, lapping waves. Greer would start a small fire at night, and Samael would use his sword to spear a fish. She would sit on the beach, listening to the waves crashing against the uneven shore and the foam fizz as the water spread across the sand.

The sun would set, giving way to a blanket of stars above them, and they would lay on the dune, still warmed by the last of the daylight. Greer and Samael sat in awkward silence on the first day following their encounter with the phouka. She would peer at him through the darkness, thankful for her cover, before turning away when she saw his silhouette shift. She swore she could feel his gaze on her cheek but never dared to look.

By the third night, they had migrated toward one another: Greer, lying on the canvas bag beside him, and Samael, seated with his wings sprawled behind him. He must have thought she was asleep because he gently brushed the hair from her brow that night before daring to trail his fingers down the back of her neck.

Greer thought she stopped breathing at that moment, and it took a few heartbeats to remember her name.

By day four, the bay had narrowed into a channel, a thin strip of land discernible at the horizon. As the current carved through the rock beneath the surface, the water deepened from sea green into a sapphire blue. Seven docks, wooden and long as piers, jutted into the water. Waves crashed against the posts anchoring the docks to the rock, and the whipping wind churned the water into a murky frenzy. The barges and boats, tied to each post with thick ropes, bobbed and swayed.

A thunderstorm was blowing in— Greer could scent it on the breeze. She eyed the darkening skies in the distance, watching the clouds gather above the open bay.

"We have to pay the ferryman," Samael said, his voice barely heard over the low rumbling of thunder that skittered over the water. He pointed toward the derelict stone building at the base of the seven docks.

"A ferryman in the underworld?" Greer asked, a smirk creeping on her face. She reached toward the iron handle of the door, still studying the weather-worn stone exterior. "How cliché."

Samael snorted, grasping the door above Greer's head to hold it open for her. "We were here first. Perhaps it's you mortals who are cliché."

Greer made to cross the threshold, relieved to see the first hint of civilization in nearly three weeks when a crowd of males stepped in front of them and burst through the door frame as they exited. She hopped back to allow them passage, surprise flitting over her face to see each carting stacks of wooden crates.

"—Doesn't want to cross the channel." The first male, short and squat with a crooked nose, said. "What kind of ferryman is afraid of a little rain?"

"We've seen worse weather." Fourth in the line replied. He was just as short and squat as the first, hair sprouting from his wide nostrils.

"If we leave now, the storm will hit after we cross," the fifth in line grumbled as he adjusted the crates against his hip to scratch the mole growing from his forehead. "If our shipment is late, Mammon will nail us to the barge."

Greer caught sight of the sickly green skin and the thick tusks protruding from under his upper lip. She had just enough time to briefly wonder who, or what, they were when she felt Samael's breath tickle the crook of her neck.

"Orcs," he said, pinching the back of Greer's shirt to pull her further from the door. "They ship cargo between the meridians. Meat and produce mostly." His arm brushed against hers as he gestured toward the far dock. "Sometimes daemons or mortals— if they make it through the other meridians, that is."

Greer spotted a group huddled at the end of the dock, and their backs turned to the wind howling through the channel. Two females and one male for sure, none sporting wings and all staring at the wooden dock with stony faces.

"He's not going to leave now, Rodagog," the first orc grunted in displeasure, dropping his crate to the dirt path. "Prepare for Mammon to nail us to the barge."

Samael skirted past Greer, tucking in his wings to fit through the door frame, and disappeared into the small building. She rocked on her feet for a minute, glancing between the group of orcs still grumbling over their crates and Egyn, who was busy munching on weeds growing from the base of the building.

Rain began to fall in thick droplets, wetting the dirt-covered path. Greer lurched forward and entered just as another gust of wind knocked at the sign hanging above the large, fogged window.

"—Don't need the barges, Samael. You've been able to fly across the channel for thousands of years," a man seated at a corner booth said.

Greer crept closer, sneakers shuffling against the stone flooring. The tall man, spindly based on how he hunched over the table, was tapping his long fingers on the wooden surface.

"I have Egyn this time," Samael said, his back turned to Greer as she approached. The man's black eyes slid past Samael, locking onto her. "And I also have—" Samael trailed off, glancing over his shoulder to see what had grabbed the man's attention.

"Ah," the man said. He slowly stood from his seat, black robes tumbling to the stone floor. If he had eyebrows, they would have risen. "You have Greer."

The wind whistled through the cracked glass panes of the window, the only thing breaking the silence between the three.

Samael was the first to speak. "Greer, meet Kharon. The Ferryman."

Kharon bowed his head, dipping his chin low to his chest. His skin was ashen and translucent, as though it were pulled too tightly over his skull. She shivered as she saw the maze of blue veins crisscrossing the crown of his head.

"I know who enters all of the waterways in this realm," Kharon began as he lifted his head. "You were lucky to have exited one. Not many can say the same."

Greer didn't reply, unsure of how to respond, and she felt a surge of relief when Kharon returned his empty gaze to Samael.

"My answer is final, Samael," Kharon went on, sinking into the corner seat again. His fingers steepled in front of him, elbows resting delicately on the table. "I will not allow a crossing in this weather. Additionally, I will not allow a crossing Azazel didn't approve."

Greer blinked at her father's name, and she let out a snagged breath when she realized what he meant.

"I don't need your approval, Kharon," Samael said, his voice dangerously low and quiet. His fingers flexed against the hilt of his dagger. "I can guide the barge across by myself."

"You know that I cannot stop you." Kharon lowered his stare to the bindings visible at Samael's biceps before lifting his gaze again. "The journey would severely diminish your strength, as you well understand. What lies in the waste is not something you want to face with limited power."

Samael's expression contorted into a menacing glare just as Greer stepped forward to place a hand on his forearm. She felt the muscles ripple and the skin pebbled under her touch.

"We don't have to cross here," Greer said soothingly, "we can find another way."

Samael turned on the balls of his feet and marched from the building without another word.

Greer went to follow when Kharon cleared his throat behind her.

"I would suggest," Kharon went on, his voice just as dangerously quiet as Samael's had been, "making yourself less conspicuous when traveling with a Primordial. There are powerful beings in Samsara who do not take your existence lightly."

"You're the first Primordial we've come across in weeks," Greer shot back, holding his stare unwaveringly. "If these beings knew I was here, they would have come."

Kharon remained still, his steepled fingers pressed tightly. "Your death will appear accidental, and it will not be witnessed. It's been foretold. You should be more careful."

Her jaw slackened ungracefully enough that Greer knew Celeste would have admonished her. "What did you say?"

"Tick tock, dearie. The clock runs out with your equal."

Greer scampered from the building in the next breath.

The rain now battered the shore, and by the time Greer found Samael through the sheets of downpour, she was dripping wet. The dark storm clouds from the bay had raced toward the channel, bathing the narrow waterway in charged, heavy air. Samael was pacing the furthest pier, now devoid of anyone waiting for a barge, and his gray feathers hung limply against his back. Greer watched as his hand still flexed against the hilt of the dagger.

Egyn brayed nervously as a crack of thunder split the space, pawing at a forming puddle with a front hoof.

Greer took a large step over a dirty runoff stream and crossed the dock toward Samael. Lightning spiked across the clouds, forking above the water. The rain plunking in droves across the wooden planks created slick spots she only missed by skating her sneakers across them.

Leaning against the forceful winds that whipped her sodden, weighted clothes around like a flag on a pole, Greer tapped Samael on the shoulder when she reached him. He looked down at her, wet locks of hair stuck to his jawline and cheeks. Another flash of lightning illuminated his cerulean eyes.

"We have to cross," he yelled over the storm. He paused to place himself between Greer and the howling winds, wrapping his wings around them in protection. It barely made a dent against the crack of thunder, but Greer could lift her head without the rain pelting her eyes. "We're sitting ducks if we wait here."

"Isn't there another way?" She called back. She wracked her brain to remember the map, more than likely stuck together with bleeding ink in the side pocket of her bag. "This shore parallels the other for miles."

Samael shook his head. "This is the only way to cross with Egyn." He heaved a sigh, unheard with the storm raging around them, and looked over Greer's head toward the barge rising and falling with the waves. "We have to leave."

Greer was peppered with rain droplets when Samael brushed past her again, and she whirled to watch as he launched himself over the side of the pier and into the nearest barge.

She blanched. "Now?" She asked incredulously as Samael lifted his fingers to his lips and whistled for Egyn.

The horse shook his head, mane matted into tangles, before clopping onto the pier. Samael threw open the side door to allow Egyn to step on when the next wave rose the barge to meet the dock. Despite his size, Egyn was agile on the slick deck.

Samael turned to Greer, propping his foot for balance on the short wall of the barge. "Do you trust me?" He held out his hand, his expression patient yet expectant.

Greer's lips parted in surprise as rain lashed against the side of her face. "You're insane!" She called back. "Can't we wait until the storm clears?"

"Do you trust me?" Samael repeated, hand still extended toward her. The flat barge dipped low with the waves before sharply ascending once more.

Greer thought she would be sick just watching it rock and roll on the channel. But that wasn't the question. She peered down the dock, tracking the scurrying orc group as they loaded their crates onto another barge three docks away. When she turned her attention back to Samael, scraping her hand over her braid out of nerves, she slowly nodded.

Samael stepped onto the wall of the barge, tightly grasping the rope to hold it steady against the storm. Greer wondered briefly how Egyn got into the deck so quickly, considering the gap between the dock and the barge. Her breathing shaky and quick, Greer clamped her hand onto Samael's outstretched one and allowed him to haul her aboard.

Greer stumbled on the lip of the wall, falling heavily into Samael. He stood firm against the deck, easily catching her around the waist. It might have even been romantic if it wasn't for the rocking boat churning Greer's stomach into chum.

She barely twisted to the side of the barge again before doubling over it and vomiting into the gap. Samael held her steady, hands against her waist and back as her gut clenched once more. Greer felt the tendrils of his power, soft and gentle before her stomach stopped rolling, and she was able to relax against him.

"You should go inside," Samael murmured in her ear, wiping the cold sweat from her brow. "Take Egyn with you. The journey across the channel is long. It'll take most of the day and into the evening."

Greer nodded, still queasy despite his power holding her together. "How are we getting across?"

Samael tipped his head toward the encasement built in the middle of the deck, revealing wooden walls with a single long oar bolted to the flat roof. "Someone has to steer." He winked, humor dancing in his eyes, and Greer nearly rolled hers before the barge rocked again.

Reaching over her, Samael loosened the knot securing the barge to the dock and wrenched the rope into place. It fell with a slap against the wooden planks. Greer straightened, knees wobbly and knocking as she struggled to steady her footing under her.

As Samael climbed to the cabin's roof, Greer took one final sweep of the Meridian of Indolence. Her gaze was planted at the base of the pier, and Kharon stood tall against the wind and rain. He was an ethereal sight, his black robes still and dry despite the growing storm. He lifted his wrist, tapping it twice with a pale, thin finger.

Greer blinked, and he was gone.

The barge swayed side-to-side, bounding back and forth as the wind continued to howl through the channel. Greer needed to figure out how long to stay in the cabin, listening to the rain pound against the wood and watching it leak through the seams in the planks. She sat at the old desk, littered with empty ink bottles and shed orc tusks, and tried to ignore the queasiness of her sore stomach.

Her heart skittered every time the creaking of Samael steering the oar or his heavy footfalls sounded above her. Greer turned her focus to Egyn, watching as he brayed nervously at the door and found he, too, was agitated every time Samael cranked on the oar, evident by the twitch of his tail. A small piece of Greer resented Egyn for his ability to remain steady against the storm. Still, it was overtaken by another roll of nausea that sent her dashing toward an abandoned bucket in the corner of the room.

A muzzle nudged her shoulder as she doubled over, and Egyn spent the rest of the time resting his heavy head against her. Greer had never been good with boats.

The storm eventually loosened its grip on the channel, and by sunset, Greer had emerged from the cabin. Pale and still coated in a cold sweat from her hours of seasickness, she placed her forearms on the deck railing. The wind had blown the storm clouds through the channel and into the bay, where they gathered, thick and tall, above the open water. The charged humidity had cleared, leaving behind a fresh, clean smell that wafted gently over the waves lapping at the side of the boat. The sun had begun to set, casting the barge in a sharply reflected golden glow.

"I see you made it out alive."

Greer turned to glance over her shoulder and watched as Samael approached her. He handed her a water pouch, and she took it gratefully.

"I see *you* made it out alive," Greer retorted, screwing the cap back on after a quick swig and handing it back. "If you're down here, who is steering the barge?"

"Still me," Samael chuckled, leaning his forearms on the railing beside hers. "It's easier to do when the water is calm."

Greer looked him over, lips pursed. He looked as pale as she did, his usually mischievous eyes dull and glossy. The markings on his arms were brighter than usual and tighter against his skin, pulling it taut as though they struggled to contain him.

She turned her attention toward the bay, seeing both meridians paralleling one another over the channel. "How much of your power have you used?"

Samael was still for a heartbeat before clearing his throat. "Let me worry about that."

Greer turned to square her shoulders at him, the breeze blowing the tendrils of her hair into her face. She tucked them back the best that she could. "What about what Kharon said? About the–"

Samael pushed himself off the railing. "Do you want to go on top of the cabin and steer the oar? You could probably see the Meridian of Greed better from up there."

The subject change was deliberate, and Greer allowed the passing without pushing. She shrugged, hesitating to look at the ladder bolted to the cabin's wall. She glanced back to see Samael smirking down at her, arms crossed over his chest.

"What are you afraid of?"

At the question, Greer's heart thunked uncomfortably in her chest. It hadn't been so long ago that Cian had asked the same thing. And she tried very hard not to think about Cian, but being reminded of him now, in this moment, was...painful.

But Greer felt something else rise within her— excitement. To see Samael's smirk. To see the sun on the water, warming her skin. The thought of the mounting challenge.

"Fine," Greer answered, and she pushed past Samael toward the ladder. "But if you think—"

She looked over her shoulder, and her brows rose when she saw the spot where Samael had been standing empty. Twisting on her heels, she slid her gaze along the barge's deck.

A shadow passed above her, wings on the wooden deck, temporarily blocking the sun. Greer craned her neck up, laughing when Samael banked left and right, his feathers rippling in the wind. She braced her hands against the ladder's rungs and climbed to the cabin's roof. The wood creaked beneath her feet as she moved toward the oar, grasping onto it for balance.

Samael circled above her again as she watched, admiring the freeing smile that curved on his mouth. The barge slowed its progression until it merely bobbed like a cork in the current. He stopped soaring just above the cabin, beating his wings to tread the air.

"Why isn't the barge moving?" Greer called up to him as she lifted a hand to shield her eyes against the brightness of the setting sun against the water.

Samael lowered himself to the flat roof. "The barges run on the currents directed by Kharon. Unless he doesn't give permission, the barges can run on the power of the Primordials."

Greer gripped the oar. It jerked against her hand as it trailed behind the barge. She put her weight against the plank. "It's heavier than I thought it would be." She glanced over to Samael. "Did you have to steer this the entire way through the storm?" With his nod, Greer went on. "So, you *are* insane."

Samael snorted as he moved to stand behind her. "Hold it here and here." Picking up her hands, he placed each one on the oar. "Let your power enter the oar through your fingertips. Tell it where to go." When she looked at him in alarm, Samael shook his head. "Relax. I'm here, nothing. Nothing will happen."

Greer blew a breath as she returned her attention to the oar, furrowing her brow in concentration. Her magic began to awaken deep within her, waves of power opening and stretching. Panic built as her heart quickened, and Samael placed one hand on the oar and the other in the crook of her neck.

"Calm," he said slowly, his breath tickling the top of her ear. A shiver went up Greer's spine. "Command it to come slowly; don't let it overtake you. You are in control."

Greer took another deep breath, forcing her muscles to relax and her heart to temper. Samael's thumb slowly caressed the top of her shoulder, reaching the base of her neck. A third breath. She let her power bubble up to the surface before plucking a single thread from the mass she could sense, and she sent it into the oar.

The barge rocked forward, jolting Samael and Greer into the wooden oar. She pulled back on her power, shifting and tugging on it until the barge began to smoothly cut through the waves. Samael released the oar but kept his hand on her shoulder.

"There you go," he murmured. "Easy."

They fell into a long minute of silence, and from the corner of her eye, Greer saw the bindings wrapped around his upper arms. When the wind picked up, puffing up the front of his shirt, she saw the bands wrapping around his chest, too.

Greer swallowed thickly, clearing her throat. "Are your markings the same as Arista's?"

"Principle is the same," Samael replied, lifting his hand to help guide the oar when the barge drifted to the right. "They are chains meant to bind me to my duty. They harness me to Samsara and Elysia, forcing me to sever mortal souls and deliver them where they need to go."

"Arista said your power was deeper than hers, so she only has one marking." Greer paused to side-eye the band around his left arm once more. "Why is it you have so many?"

The dunes were now visible in the distance, soft and waved from the wind. The leaves from the palm trees swayed.

"I made a bad decision that cost me my freedom," Samael said after a moment. He adjusted the oar again. "And it cost the life and freedom of my brothers."

Greer nodded slowly. "Those sisters in the woods...they mentioned your brothers. And about how the reason for their creation was stolen from them when your brothers were bound. Are those two things connected?"

"Azazel used the sisters' magic to bind me and give me a reason to remain in a body. He shifted their responsibility of collecting souls to me."

The oar pulled with the undertow, indicating the channel bed was lifting.

"You've been with me for weeks, though. How have you been collecting souls?"

"That is a complicated question that I can only give you a simple answer to. I can be everywhere and nowhere. Some of my power remains. It isn't something a Primordial can—" Samael stopped, clamping his lips shut as though he had said too much.

"What do you mean you—" Greer couldn't finish her question, and it was forgotten when the barge jerked again, running aground on a sandbar near shore. Much to her chagrin, Samael removed his hand from Greer's neck and unsheathed his sword from between his wings. "What are you doing with your sword?"

"The rivers dump into the bay, and if the souls don't make their way to the Meridian of Lust to continue upriver, they will be lost to Samsara." He paused as a splash sounded, and Greer looked to see Egyn wading through the sandbar toward shore. "The Meridian of Greed is filled to the brim with devils."

TWENTY-EIGHT

ODETTE

In the week following Odette's first training session with the humans, she realized no one, faerie or human, worked harder than Luisa. She soared in her ability to use the dagger, and Odette began to bring her sword to teach Luisa the fundamentals of fighting with it.

"She spends all of her alone time practicing move after move, even long after she's returned the dagger to you," Tomas whispered to Odette one night as they watched Luisa practice with Gael. She twisted, swinging the sword around to catch the dagger Gael held in his hand. She sent him a victorious grin as she forced him to relinquish the blade, the point of her sword pricked against his throat. "If she isn't here or with Kaique, she's in her room making sure she can master everything."

Odette wasn't sure whether to let her heart soar with happiness or let it crack in sorrow. Though Luisa shouldn't have to learn the new skill, or even be in the Court of Mist and Tide, it was clear that Luisa was getting better at defending herself every day. And Odette couldn't have been more proud of her.

Odette kept an eagle eye on Kaique when Luisa was around. Though he had not mentioned anything about Luisa's recovery following her attack, he created the impression that he knew precisely who had saved the human from certain death. He was so precise that, as they passed the courtyard near the kitchen during a morning walk he forced Odette to take with him, he had Aldonza backhanded by a soldier while she was picking mint from the garden.

While Odette had to bite her tongue and keep a blank face while looking down her nose at the female who crumpled to the tiled stone that lined the courtyard, she still managed to send a subtle tilt of her chin toward Aldonza, who peered at her from under Kaique's elbow. Aldonza's lips pressed into a tight line of understanding.

And, much to Odette's surprise, it was that night when the first set of soldiers approached the nightly group in the colosseum and requested a chance to assist in training the humans for escape. While Odette was wary of them at first, Karina assured her that none of those guards used her services and that they were the ones Luisa recruited. They could be trusted. Additionally, the group laughed when one of the guards admitted, with his hand scratching the back of his neck in discomfort, that he knew Tomas had been stealing weapons during dinner. He had even set daggers and knives out for the man to pick up, hiding them underneath the piles of dirty dishes.

The crowd of humans and fae was becoming too big for the subset of stone steps that spanned the colosseum. They now spread across the entire width of the colosseum and down toward the platform in the pit. Odette made the final call to have them work in mixed groups to stay as close to the hedges as possible. Tomas and Gael had begun to train with swords, while Luisa had continued to pour her efforts into training with the new soldiers that had joined the movement. Odette wanted Luisa to see different styles of swordsmanship, though she still made sure to challenge Luisa with new footsteps and unnatural grips to keep her on her toes.

And with every new fae member, with every new human that picked up a dagger or sword, Odette could see the hopeful gleam in the eyes of the humans. It pulled her into the past, forcing her to re-member the days when she was general and training new soldiers who had come of age in her father's kingdom. Her breath hitched in her chest when she realized she had missed leading in this capacity—and having a sword in her hand. It renewed her enjoyment of watching others discover new limits before soaring past those.

One night, a couple of weeks into their training sessions, Luisa was late. Everyone was already soaked from the pouring rain and their salty sweat, but many paused with heaving chests to watch Luisa approach Odette. Odette wiped her brow, blade in hand, as Luisa grasped her elbow and pulled her to the side, urgently whispering into her ear.

"And you're sure that's what Kaique said?" Odette asked quietly as she lowered herself to the edge of a stone bench off the side. From the corner of her eye, she could see a couple of guards glancing curiously over at them, pointed ears perked to hear the conversation better.

Luisa nodded as she sat down next to Odette. "He had just fin-ished— you know," she paused to clear her throat, sliding her gaze down to the droplets of water that darkened the front of her skirt. "There was a knock on the main door of the wing, and he left me in the bedroom to answer it. I snuck out to listen from the threshold. He never gets visitors that late. He and the guard were talking about sending a message to the Fae King about your location during the next shipment to the Court of Wind and Storm."

Odette swore under her breath. She knew it was coming, and she certainly wasn't surprised. She just thought she would have more time. "We're sitting ducks in this realm. Fuck, we still have weeks to go. That's enough time for Kaique to post an army at the rift to stop us from leaving." She stared at the bench in front of her in thought, narrowing her eyes at the puddles of water jumping with each raindrop that plunked against the stone.

"The ship leaves when the full moon peaks," Luisa went on when Odette stayed silent. "Fruit and herbs from this court are loaded on the boats at the dock. He sends his letters that way, hidden within the crates carried through the villages by the slaves. From what it sounded like, Kaique doesn't have any current ties to the Fae King, but is working with a member of his inner circle to gain access."

"The full moon peaks tomorrow," Odette said, gazing toward the moon, shadowed by the thick cloud coverage. "We don't have much time."

"We aren't too late," Luisa said, twisting on the bench to square her shoulders at Odette. "We can still head off the letter."

Odette nodded slowly, thinking it over. "I would have to leave after dinner." She paused to sweep her stare across the speckle of stars barely visible above them. "The docks are hours from here, and the ship will be scheduled to leave just before dawn."

Luisa lifted her feet, resting them on the stone bench below them to better set her forearms on her knees. "Is tracking the moon a faerie thing? Kaique does it, too. He'll watch it for hours."

"The stars and movement of the planets tell us quite a bit about our lives. About the past and the future. Nearly everything about the faeries and beyond center around the seasonal changes." Luisa parted her lips as though she were about to speak, but Odette pushed on. "Everything to the daemons runs on natural occurrences and manipulating even the smallest atoms around us. Our magic, the Mage's power, the wolf shifter ability. I can see the air as though it were a part of me. Change the tiniest molecules to what I want them to be. But the fae tracks the stars meticulously. The equinoxes, the solstices, and the full moons are like– they're like when the hatch to a cage is finally unlocked, and we can access what's inside."

Luisa's eyes darkened as she crossed one leg over the other, allowing her ankle to bob as it hung in the air. "Can't we just close the portals? Keep the fae away from humans forever?"

Odette sighed. "It's a little more nuanced than that, I'm afraid. The only person who can close the portals is the Mage, and she can only close them temporarily. Greer is—" She trailed off, biting the inside of her cheek. "She's different. It's complicated. I'm not so sure she can."

"You're hiding things from me," Luisa said, turning toward the training pit to watch Tomas and Gael hop the fence. Mud splashed onto their feet as they stepped into the puddles that littered the dirt flooring.

"Let's just focus on getting you out of here without being killed."

Luisa clucked her tongue against her front teeth. "What aren't you telling me? This— this Mage. This is the first time you've mentioned her. And wolf shifters?" She crossed her arms over her chest, shivering against the cool rain splotching her exposed skin. "I want to know, and I want to know now."

Odette appreciated the bluntness of this woman who had become something of a friend, though sometimes she felt as though Luisa was too curious for her own good.

"Greer is, well, she is part primordial," Odette replied after a moment, running a hand over her wet, red braid and pushing it over her shoulder. "Her father is the king of the underworld. He's gone by many names— Hades, Anubis, Pluto...Lucifer."

Luisa went quiet, her lips pressing into a thin line as her brows furrowed. "Lucifer? Like the devil?" She mumbled in Spanish before unfolding her arms from her chest and dropping them into her lap. "What have I been dragged into?"

Odette let her wings flutter behind her, working out the kinks in the leathery flesh that spanned the bands of muscle framing them. "Greer and I have a complex relationship. I assisted her a few months ago."

"My concern," Luisa began, her foot bobbing so quickly that her entire leg shook. "Is that there are angels in the world that know about this—" She paused to gesture around her. "And still do nothing about it." She tilted her head like a thought suddenly popped into it. "Is Greer the only part primordial?"

Odette shook her head in earnest this time. "I don't know. The Fae are too low in the hierarchy of beings that know the inner workings of the primordials. I don't know anyone besides my father who has met one. And I still don't know if he actually did or just said he did." She looked over to Luisa, who was biting the nail of her middle finger as she stared into the pit. "Why do you ask?"

Luisa's inhale was sharp. "Early in my stay here, I put on a Fae cloak and helped to bring crates aboard the ship before the full moon. I snuck onboard and hid in the cargo hold to escape, but I came across a set of letters. I didn't understand most of it, except they did refer to someone by the name of Leander, son of Michael, and how he, a man named Eligos, and the Fae King were working together to open the Fae realms. This...Leander was the leader. He cannot open them on his own and needs assistance from someone who can."

Odette snapped her head around to stare at Luisa. The rain pounded in sheets on them, thunder rolling in the distance as another storm began to crawl away from the sea. "Did you say Eligos?" A shot of shock rang through her, and without waiting for Luisa to respond, she went on. "We must get out of the Court of Mist and Tide. Greer needs to know who is behind the Fae King. She killed Eligos already, but if he was only the puppet and this Leander is the mastermind..."

Luisa and Odette exchanged fearful looks, a sickly feeling rising in the back of Odette's throat. Luisa's sentiments echoed in her mind...*what had she gotten them into?* This seemed to be escalating in ways even the stars couldn't predict what was coming next.

Odette waited with bated breath the following evening, pacing the parlor as she watched the sun finally set beyond the canopy of swaying trees. Luisa had volunteered to entertain Kaique to ensure Odette had the time to sneak from the palace grounds undetected. And it was when she finally clicked the lock on the main door out of the royal apartment and hoisted herself onto the windowsill that it became real.

She hopped toward the stone floor, spreading her wings on the summer wind. The brilliant iridescence was bright against the moonlight, shining like a beacon in the night sky. But, for once, Odette wished the deep navy blanket was hidden by the steamy clouds that rolled off the sea. She would have even taken the sheets of rain from the night before. A growing seed of fear was planted in Odette's stomach at the thought of Kaique or any of his goons studying the stars.

The grounds remained clear—it was still too early for the humans to begin their nightly routine of cleaning the gardens. She soared over the basalt stone wall, tucking her wings into her back to drop to the underbrush that lined the jungle. She shifted her gaze around the dark underside of the trees, trying to assess the best way through, when a crunch sounded on the trail behind her.

Swinging around and pulling a dagger sheathed at her hip in one motion, Odette locked eyes with a palace guard doing his rounds near the iron gate that enclosed the gardens into a prison.

They watched each other for a moment, and Odette took a menacing step forward. The guard reached into the pocket of his tunic and retrieved an item from inside. Odette tensed as he adjusted it between his fingers before flashing it toward her.

In the moonlight, Odette saw her father's coat of arms etched into a dull metal coin. It had been centuries since she had seen the badge, that is before Nerea had shown her the exact same thing. And Odette didn't believe in coincidences.

Her eyes darted back up to meet the guard, who flashed a small smile and a quick nod. He dropped the coin back into his pocket, dipping his gaze toward the dagger still clutched in Odette's hand. Lifting his hands in surrender, he backed away from her, boots crunching under the trail's gravel.

And Odette rocketed into the air once more.

The slaves had already begun to walk toward the docks, trudging along the muddy path, their arms loaded with crates filled to the brim with mango, bananas, dried garlic, and sugar canes. Odette wove in and out of the trees, careful not to rustle the leaves covering the thick branches of the canopy trees.

Insects buzzed, and birds swooped around her as they hunted the small rodents that navigated the jungle floor. Odette steered clear of the villages far below, watching keenly as the fae gathered to see the parade of humans carrying the cargo toward the docks. Some looked like they were on the precipice of assisting, but the soldiers guarding the humans pushed through, forcing the villagers to step back.

Odette swallowed past the knot forming in her throat as she realized how far the courts had fallen in Adair's hands. How ashamed she felt of herself for letting it. And how much work needed to be done for them to heal.

She banked away from the villages, following the sound of the waves crashing against the sandy beach. She honed in on it, perking her ears toward the noise and using it like a lighthouse in the stormy night. The trip was long for her wings, which hadn't gotten this amount of exercise in decades, but it was tremendously shorter than when she hiked to the palace on foot.

Nevertheless, she breathed a sigh of relief when the ship's mast rose above the canopy, rocking to and fro as the ship bobbed at the dock jutting into the sea. Odette landed on a branch at the jungle's edge, where the ferns broke into seagrass that dotted the sandy dunes. Her boots were slick on the smooth wood as she assessed the beach below, studying the humans crossing the ramp to board the ship.

Lower court members bustled on the deck, taking the crates from the humans and loading them into the hold below. Odette knew this ship would make a series of stops up the coast before finally docking in the Court of Wind and Storm, where it would reside until the next full moon.

There was a break in the shuffling, and the deck was clear enough that Odette made her move. Dropping from the tree, she let her wings open with a sharp *thwap* one final time as she soared on the wind toward the ship. The brine of the sea seeped into the cotton of her clothes, and the fresh scent of seaweed was heavy in the air. She balanced again as she landed, hiding on the main mast against the sails, flapping in the strong ocean winds.

"We take our leave in three hours," the captain called from the helm, his hand resting casually against a set of spokes making up the wheel. "Pack the cargo tightly, men."

Fae from all courts worked the circuit of ships that made their way up the coasts, and it would take nearly all of their magic to sail against the swirling, inconsistent currents. Fae with wings that shimmered in the moonlight, fae with deep brown skin who could manipulate the earth and the things that grew within it, fae with silky black hair who wore robes of fine linens and preferred weapons curved in comparison to the shortsword Odette carried.

The captain descended the stairs just as the ramp cleared, entering the door to his quarters beneath the helm. This was her chance. Odette stepped off the mast, landing on silent feet against the wooden deck. She crept onto the creaky staircase, keeping her footing on the swaying ship, and snuck into the cargo hold below deck.

Barrels of wine were stacked against the starboard side, tied together within the wooden cask hoops to keep them from rolling with each dip and rise while the ship was sailing. The crates were stored opposite, stockpiled like small pyramids against the bulkhead. Odette slunk through, ducking amidst the crates to hide from the new batch of humans coming aboard to load the cargo.

Odette went through each crate methodically and quietly, careful not to tip off the fae readying the ship above her. She searched crate after crate, sifting through grains, fruits, dried herbs, rolls of fine cloth, and more. She searched until her fingertips bled from pulling the lids from the crates, and her palms were crusted with sawdust and dirt.

But it wasn't until the final batch of crates that her fingers finally brushed alongside a set of thick parchment, nipping painfully at the sore underside of her nails. She clamped her fingers around the letters, pulling them from the lined rice crate and spilling the grains onto the floor in a deluge.

"Who's there?" a voice called from the staircase.

Odette's heart stopped in her chest, and she lurched forward to hide behind a stack of crates. The lid of the rice box barely returned to its place, and the grains were still scattered along the floor. The sailor made a shocked, choking sound, and Odette heard something squelch before a bouncing thud rattled each step.

Peering over the top of the stack of crates, Odette stood from her crouched position when she saw the head of a faerie rolling along the floor, smearing the rivers of blood in its wake. The headless body still lay on the staircase, red staining the bright blue silk robes.

"Come out, Odette," a voice called out in a hushed, throaty whisper. "It appears we have quite a bit to catch up on." The male dragged his blade along his dark green pants, shaking the locks of black hair from his eyes.

Odette let a tight smile pull at her mouth as she clutched the dagger she unsheathed at the sound of the sailor. "Hello, Renan. It sure seems like we do."

TWENTY-NINE

DELIA

Over the weeks, Kazzy had proven to be both an asset and an ally. Though Cian and Delia had not yet divulged their reason for tracking the Paladin Society, that hadn't deterred Kazzy. She never asked questions, spoke out of turn, and kept her distance from Cian's map of the basilica until she was permitted to approach it.

Delia's days had shifted during that time. While her mornings looked the same—stopping at a café for a pastry and coffee before taking a seat in the square—the afternoons had changed. Kazzy had carved out time to sit as close to the basilica as she could, subtly pointing out the carvings in the cobblestone, the colonnade, and the front doors themselves to Delia. Delia had then taken her cell phone and taken pictures of them, trying to discern the runes into something she could translate.

So far, Delia had no luck, but she kept the pictures nonetheless. She had a feeling she could use them in the future. For what, she hadn't a clue.

The more time Delia spent with Kazzy, the more she liked her. The wolf shifter was spontaneous and wild, willing to throw her plans in the air at the drop of a dime. Delia had a hard time releasing control, something she had kept close to her chest since the days of living in foster care, but she found that it was the slightest bit easier when she was releasing it to Kazzy.

Delia began looking forward to her daily time with Kazzy. The husky bark of a laugh Kazzy possessed was warm and inviting, and Kazzy seemed more than willing to surrender it even to the lamest joke Delia had to offer. They would sit on the ground nearest the fountain on the left side, sipping sodas and making up stories for random tourists in line for the basilica. A female's companionship was pleasant compared to spending the last few weeks with Cian.

Delia tried hard to forget what he had said—comparing Paige to Kazzy. She pushed it to the back of her mind with relative ease and locked her grief into a carefully built box that she buried in the confines of her heart. If she kept it deeply hidden and never thought about it, that box could gather dust, and Delia could move on.

In the evening, the three crowded the hotel room and combed each shred of documentation. Then, the plan began to form. But Delia couldn't help the sinking feeling in her gut that they were forgetting or overlooking something important.

The next afternoon, as Delia slinked back against the warmed stone of the fountain, she thought about the plan again, and, as she did the night before, she huffed when the same feeling that she was missing something consumed her. As she had Her gaze lifted, scanning the front of the basilica, all she could do was hope that all of this would be worth it.

Kazzy turned to look at her, resting a hand on Delia's forearm. "What are you thinking about?"

Delia didn't want to say how nervous she was for the upcoming heist, nor was she ready to delve into the intricacies of the grief she worked so hard to suppress, so instead, she glanced over at Kazzy and sent her a small smile. "What will you do for the full moon? Isn't it tonight?"

Kazzy took a sip from the water bottle they shared. "Sort of a myth," she answered with a grin, elongating her canines playfully before retracting them again. "I can control small things every day. My speed, my strength, my canines, and a bit of my claws." She paused to allow her fingers to sharpen, Delia watching on with fascination. Kazzy ran one long, thick nail playfully up Delia's forearm. "We *can* turn into wolves on the full moon, but it's our choice. At that time, we have complete control of our shifting."

"Why just at the full moon? Don't you want that power all the time?"

Kazzy allowed the clawed hand to return to normal fingernails. "There was a witch. We call her the Mage." Delia stilled but listened intently. "I wasn't alive when the last mage was around; she died a hundred-something years before I was born. But...my parents told me stories about her. What was her name...? Oh, Agnes! She was able to develop a potion that allowed us access to our powers at all times, and they told me it was incredible having that kind of control, full moon or not. But then Agnes was murdered by the Paladin Society as well, and all of that came to a stop."

Delia took hold of Kazzy's hand, turning it over so her palm was facing the sun. She ran her fingertips over the lines carving through the flesh, looking for any indication that the claws resided just under the skin. Nothing. It was soft and smooth. "Does it hurt to shift?" she finally asked.

Kazzy was watching Delia, her blonde hair ruffling with the autumn breeze. "No, not at all." She let her claws come out again, this time in Delia's hand. "It feels very natural. And turning into a wolf is...freeing. The most freedom you will ever feel in your life."

Delia swallowed, staring at her fingers moving over the lengthened claws. "If you scratched me, would I become a wolf too?"

Kazzy's smile dipped slightly, but enough for Delia to notice from the corner of her eye. "No. Being a wolf, a shifter, is genetic. Like the fae, like a siren. The only daemons who can turn others are vampyres and shtriga."

Delia slid her hands out of Kazzy's, dumping them into her lap. Kazzy withdrew her claws, and, at that moment, the air suddenly felt heavy and tense. Delia leaned forward to swipe the water bottle from the space between them and took a sip. Her swallow was difficult past the lump that had formed in her throat.

"You've heard my story," Kazzy said, breaking the silence. "Tell me more about you."

Delia cleared her throat, the water catching at the unexpected question. She hated sharing knowledge about herself—moving from foster home to foster home taught her to keep any information close. She glanced over to Kazzy, who had resumed looking at her with a curious and inviting gaze.

"Well, I grew up in Texas," Delia started, slowly tracing a finger around the condensation on the water bottle. "My mother married my step-father when I was eight. My younger brothers were one." She stopped to take a breath. "She died of breast cancer when I was eleven, and my step-father kicked us out of the house not too long after that. We entered the system, got split up, and that was it."

Delia stopped entirely now, the thick ball wedged in her throat seemingly growing in size. She quickly shook her head and cleared her throat again.

Kazzy's stare seemed to pierce through Delia's steel exterior into the tender, unhealed parts beneath. Delia squirmed under the intense scrutiny, turning her attention toward scanning the square. Delia felt a hand wrap around her arm; the touch was no longer gentle but a tight squeeze.

"And your brothers?" Kazzy inquired.

Delia shrugged her shoulders. "They would be twenty-one now, but I haven't been able to find them. I tried to adopt them from foster care when I graduated from high school, but I was told I was too young. I went away to Oregon and graduated with my undergrad four years later, then tried again. I found out that my brothers' adoption paperwork was finalized three days before in a closed case. I decided to go to law school after that to try and locate them, but nothing came out of it."

Kazzy said nothing as she pulled her gaze from Delia and looked toward the basilica, her eyes squinted against the sun. "It seems we both lost our pack, didn't we?" She pushed herself from her cross-legged position on the ground before holding a hand for Delia to grasp. "Cian will be expecting us soon. But...do you want to get dinner? Before we go back, I mean. I should eat before shifting."

Delia nodded as she reached upward and grasped Kazzy's hand. The wolf shifter pulled Delia to her feet before quickly letting go, shoving a hand into her jacket pocket. They made their way from the square, shoulders bumping as they wound through the late autumn crowd. Dusk had already begun, the setting sun casting long shadows as it lowered behind the terracotta buildings.

Kazzy clasped a hand around Delia's forearm and tugged her into a pizza restaurant around the corner from the hotel, grabbing seats on the terrace overlooking the hill. The lamps lining the street began to turn on one by one, their glowing yellow bulbs filling the shadowed alleys as the sunlight withdrew deeper toward the horizon. The scent of baking dough and crushed garlic wafted from the restaurant's interior, carrying on the phantom wind of every passing waiter making their way in and out.

The crisp breeze nipped as it curled into Delia's hair, and she pulled her jacket tighter in response, zipping the front for the first time all season. The waitress strolled over a moment later, lighting the candle in the middle of the table. The flame flickered as she twisted away.

Delia suddenly felt uncomfortable and anxious. It had only been months since Paige's death, and here she was, sitting at a restaurant in Rome with another woman. Though she had never brought up the death of her wife to Kazzy—and they never discussed whether tonight was a date or not— Delia couldn't help but feel as though she were betraying her long-time love.

And maybe she was? Or maybe Paige expected her to move on? But this quickly?

A hand wrapped around the back of one of the extra iron chairs, and the legs scraped loudly against the pavement as it was pulled out from under the table. Delia scowled as she looked up to see Cian collapsing into the seat. She couldn't help but feel the secondary relief wash over her.

"I'm sorry, sir, but we don't have any cash on us today," Delia said, her lip curling in protest as he took a deep sip of water from her glass.

"Ha. Funny," Cian responded. "I came with news. Saw you stop here from our window in the hotel room."

"You certainly use the term *our* pretty liberally for someone who has not contributed at all financially," Delia retorted with a glare, snatching the glass from his hand and refilling it from the bottle left on the table by the waitress.

Cian ignored her this time. "The runes in the pictures you took. The ones outside of the basilica? They looked familiar, but I could not figure out where I'd seen them before." He reached into the pocket of his jeans and pulled out a folded-up picture, tossing it onto the grated table. Kazzy reached forward to grab it, unfolding it before smoothing it out. "They're the same ones in the pictures from the zip drive."

Delia's head shot up. "You mean...*the* zip drive?"

Cian nodded his head slowly, keeping his stare intently on Delia. "*The* zip drive."

Kazzy glanced between the two in confusion as she passed the photo to Delia. "What does this mean for us then?"

"That means not only are the daemons incapable of breaching the church, but another *friend* of ours would also be. We are on the right track if Paladin is trying to keep the primordials out, too."

Kazzy snorted into her glass of water. "Primordials? You're joking. They're just bedtime stories."

Delia and Cian said nothing in response. It was getting to be more of a hassle than it was worth to keep Kazzy out of the loop. She glanced over to the wolf shifter, who was still chuckling under her breath.

"Do we need to keep up the charade?" Delia asked Cian. "I'm getting exhausted."

Cian leaned over the table. "Until we both agree otherwise. And I haven't decided yet." He swept his gaze over to Kazzy, who met it with hardened anticipation. "You said a few nights ago that more runes appear on the full moon in the square. I'm going to see them tonight."

"What are you expecting to find?" Kazzy retorted. "Humans can't see them, and that includes Delia. And if you stand there and stare at them, you'll certainly get made by Paladin in minutes."

Cian glowered at her. "While you're taking yourself for a walk and eating doggy biscuits, Delia and I will go up there together. I want to see them for myself."

Kazzy scoffed. "Suit yourself, then."

And it was only thirty minutes later that Delia made her way back up the hill and toward the basilica, this time with a stomach stuffed with pizza and only Cian in tow.

"We should tell her about Greer," Delia said as they crested over the apex. The crowd was thinner since the sun had set, making it easier to navigate the courtyard. "She's been with us for a while now and–" She halted in her steps as the beginnings of the moonlight began to peek from behind the wisps of clouds blowing across the navy sky.

Iridescent markings littered the square, each set in patterns that whirled and swirled through the cobblestone. Cian brushed past Delia. On the other hand, Delia kept her stare upward, where the basilica and colonnade had been outfitted with runes that twisted up each column and arced over the wooden front doors.

"Delia, I wish you could— Delia?"

She was no longer paying attention to the runes. Instead, Delia was focused solely on clamping down the scream that threatened to explode out of her.

There was a woman near the obelisk, a woman with a caved-in face. She stood—no, she was suspended—above the runes that covered the stone. The one eye that was still intact looked down on Delia in complete shock.

The woman glided toward Delia, her body coated in a shimmering haze that Delia could entirely see through. Then she realized the woman's face wasn't merely caved in but almost missing completely. The jawline and cheekbone on the right side had imploded as if someone had taken a large item and struck her with it. Where there was once an eyeball remained a dark, fleshed-out hole. The muscles of her cheeks hung in thick, bloody strips from the injury and the front of her pleated dress was coated in dark stains.

Delia glanced around, looking desperately at Cian and the remaining tourists still in the square. No one seemed to notice this woman's appearance, as she moved right through them as she made a bee-line for Delia. And Delia thought her heart would surely stop beating with every inch the woman came closer.

"You can see me," the woman said in a heavy accent, a tinge of hope in her tone.

Delia's mouth opened and then closed as she struggled to find words. God, she hoped it was a joke. It was just a terrible prank set by the Paladin Society for the full moon. The longer she stared, the quicker she realized it wasn't. The translucent woman was suspended mid-air, her slippered feet hovering inches above the stone.

"Oh, shit, no," Delia managed to say as she squeezed her eyes shut, taking giant steps away from the woman until the back of her knees hit the edge of the fountain. "Please go away. Please go away." Her stomach churned as fear pumped through her body.

"I need help," the woman continued, her hopeful tone shifting into a mournful plea. "I need to move on. I missed my chance. Please, help me."

"Please go away, please go away," Delia repeated like a mantra, her chest heaving with near sobs. Her eyes were still tightly shut, though she felt the temperature dip as the woman edged closer. And when she cracked her eyes open, Delia noticed foggy breaths, as if the weather had suddenly turned from a mild autumn to an icy winter.

"Delia?" Cian asked again, this time with an edge of horror. Delia's eyes flew the rest of the way open as she looked through the woman and locked her stare with his. A numb tingle shot up her spine when she realized the vampyre couldn't see the woman either.

"I've been stuck for centuries. I need your help. You're the first person in years that can see me. Please, I want to go home."

"Go away!" Delia let out a scream that startled the people across the square from her. "Please, please. I don't want to help. Please go away." Her voice was small and unsteady.

"I need you—"

But Delia was running, side-stepping the woman. Her sneakers slapped against the cobblestone as she stepped on each rune, not bothering to avoid them as she went.

"Please!" The woman called after Delia. "Please!"

Delia didn't stop until she was out of the bounds of the runes, and she spun on the balls of her feet to track the progress of the ghostly woman. She watched in shocked terror as the woman continued to approach, and when she came within inches of the first set of runes that encircled the square, the woman stopped just as abruptly as well.

The woman's eye darted downward before widening with dread. "Break the runes. Break the runes. Break the runes," she said in a hushed croak, the repetitive chant aimed toward Delia as the woman finally lifted her one-eyed gaze toward her.

In her desperation to catch Delia, the woman had accidentally come too close to a pattern of runes at the edge of a square. They lit brightly, illuminating the swirling pattern on the cobblestone. The slippered feet disappeared, then the hem of her dress, then her waist. The woman began to scream as she was sucked into the runes, a gut-wrenching, painful cry that echoed across the courtyard.

But no one, Cian included, was watching the woman disappear.

The apparition winked out in the next heartbeat, leaving the runes to glow brightly one final time before dimming to the iridescence that matched the rest of the square.

THIRTY

GREER

Greer watched Samael rearrange the weapons he hid on his belt. "What do you mean *filled to the brim with devils*?" She finally asked as he held his hand to help her out of the barge.

A crash and a roar filled the space between them as if on cue, stopping them from leaving the barge. Greer whirled to look at the beach. A crab, covered in gray armor and sporting pincers the size of a broadsword, dug itself out of the sand and scuttled toward the jungle thicket. The devil disappeared into the shadows of the palm trees. A second roar sounded, followed by a gut-wrenching rip and a squelch.

Wrinkling her nose, Greer glanced back at Samael.

"The Meridian of Greed speaks for itself," Samael grinned. "Are you swimming, or are you flying?"

Greer crossed her arms over her chest. "How much of your power did you use to get us across the channel?"

Samael's grin slid from his face. "Again, nothing you need to worry about."

"How much of it, Samael?" She pressed through gritted teeth. She already knew the answer and knew she wouldn't like it when he said it out loud.

Samael scratched at the back of his head. "Close to all of it."

"*All of–*" Greer tempered the panic rising in her gut. "Samael. You– we– how–" Another crash rocked the barge, and a snap of wood cracked, echoing over the beach. A bone-chilling screech followed on its heels, reverberating the floorboards under Greer's feet. "What was that?"

The grin had returned. "The devils know we're here. No point in waiting any longer on the barge. They'll swarm it before long."

"Can't we wait for reinforcements?" Greer asked, her fingers trembling with anxiety and adrenaline. "The orcs should be crossing soon. We could meet up with them and–"

"The orcs will go around the Meridian of Greed and port in Parab on the island's south end." The barge heaved again; this time, a muffled crunching tore through the wood still in the water. "They don't cut through."

"Why didn't we do that?" Greer's tone bordered on a shriek. An overwhelming sense of dread washed over her as the barge jolted for a third time. Something heavy hoisted itself aboard the underbelly of the barge, and it tilted enough for Greer to take a step to balance herself.

"We didn't have the time to sail around," Samael said, alarmingly calm despite the devils crawling into the barge. "Cutting through is the quickest way, despite the hurdle of the devils lurking about." He paused to quirk his head. "Swim or fly, Greer?"

Greer glanced over the side of the barge, chest tightening when she spotted a flash of fins and a gnashing of teeth at the surface. "Fine,

fine. Fly." Samael gestured her toward him with two fingers, and Greer unhappily lurched forward. "How far will we go?"

"I can get us past the jungle," Samael replied as Greer wrapped her arms around his neck. "I've instructed Egyn to go through it and where to meet us; nothing will touch him." He tucked his forearms under her knees and pulled her toward his chest. "The jungle isn't the problem, though. It's the desert beyond."

"Great," Greer grumbled, fumbling to lock her fingers around her wrist for stability. "Sounds lovely."

Samael rocketed into the air just as a devil broke through the barge's deck, teeth snapping at their ankles. His wings beating against the channel breeze had Greer's hair whipping around her face. She tightened her grip around his neck as her stomach clenched at the sight of the beach shrinking with every wing stroke higher into the sky.

Samael tipped them forward, soaring over the tops of the palm trees and the lush, green undergrowth. Despite her eyes blurring tearfully from the wind and hearing nothing save for the rush of white noise flowing past her ears, the scent of salt water mixed with the earthiness of wet vegetation was heavy in the air.

"The view is beautiful up here," Samael said, squeezing her with the hand wrapped around her waist. "You should look down."

Greer said nothing, afraid of the bile crawling up her throat if she opened her mouth, and kept her eyes fixed on the spot where his jawline curved toward his ear. Samael merely chuckled as he tipped them downward. Greer felt them circle for a few minutes before his feet hit the terrain, his boots sinking into the soft surface. She nearly threw herself out of his arms as soon as she could.

Stumbling on the sand, Samael caught Greer by the arm. She flailed in an attempt to keep steady and grabbed tightly onto his upper arm.

"Never again," she managed to squeak out, taking deep breaths to calm her frantically beating heart.

Samael laughed, low and throaty. "I think you'll change your mind."

Greer slid her gaze down the dune toward the thin band of jungle they had flown over. The channel was visible through the canopy of trees, and below in the bushy ferns, the leaves shook as devils rummaged through. She could hear the shrill cries from her position, each one as sad and mournful as the next. Behind her, deeper into the Meridian of Greed, the seagrass-dotted dunes swept into sandstone. Waves of heat rising from the dry river beds blurred the horizon in a hazy blue.

Samael began descending the dune, his boots sliding in the loose sand. Greer was pulled from her thoughts as she studied his gait, and by the slump of his shoulders and the limpness of his wings, she could tell that he was exhausted. Fear shot through her at the thought, but on top of that, a current of worry pierced through her as well. She had considered Samael to be an unstoppable force and, until now, didn't think there was a possibility that this journey would tire him out.

Greer followed him down the dune, sand dumping into her sneakers with every step.

The following week that they walked, the dunes soon turned into the dry sandstone she had briefly seen from above, the cracked shale of old river beds carving through the soil. Lizards sunned themselves on the rocks, sneaking in the last of the day's warmth as the sun began to sink below the horizon. The longer they walked, the more Greer realized they were venturing deeper into a vast canyon. Snake trails, sidewinding ripples in the shale, began to disappear due to the wind whistling through, and yellow grass, thick-stemmed and prickled, grew from the fissures in the rock wall.

Rock spires rose from the ground in the distance, oddly shaped and unstable.

Greer felt a pinch of discomfort in her stomach. She had been here before. She knew it. She felt it. She didn't know when or how, but she knew. For a brief moment, she thought the sun was getting to her. How could it have been possible for her to be here before? She knew that the freckles had appeared on her nose, and her cheeks were kissed a dull pink from the wind and relentless heat, so maybe that was it.

A crack sounded in the canyon where the rock wall gave way, pulling her from her thoughts. Shifting rocks and sand tumbled into the canyon where they stood, the dry dust coating Greer's tongue and throat. Egyn neighed at the noise, side-stepping the low-growing cactus spanning the desert floor. The urge to run seized her muscles, and Greer's thoughts were thrown back into the dreams she once had at the beginning of her power manifesting.

Whirling, Greer spun to look at Samael, who was watching her with a steady gaze.

"You. It was you." Her stare dropped to the dagger at his hip, the three emerald gemstones that had once been so familiar to her. Greer knew how it felt to have that dagger slip between her ribs. She swallowed thickly, heat pooling in her core as her mind flashed to the kisses they had shared in her dreams. His cerulean eyes darkened. "How–"

"We've been connected for far longer than you've been in Samsara," Samael said, his eyes sliding down to her lips. Greer thought it would have been an insane coincidence that he was pondering the same dream.

It was silent between them for a long minute. The wind blew, and mice scurried from rock to rock to avoid the hawks prowling overhead.

"You killed me," Greer whispered, barely audible against the howling devils in the distance. "Over and over again. In those dreams, you killed me."

"Yes." Samael's face was half-hidden in shadow as the sun continued to sink below the horizon, casting him in a golden glow that reflected off the red stone. "Among other things."

Greer's cheeks flushed at his words, her breath hitching as it grew faster. She remembered how it felt to run her hands up his abdomen and onto his chest, his fingers digging into the flesh of her hips. "Why?"

"Because we're destined to do terrible things to each other," he replied, scrubbing a hand down his jawline. He murmured a string of swear words under his breath, and before Greer knew it, he had crossed the dry river bed and hauled his lips to hers.

Greer's body responded before her mind caught up, her mouth opening for him as though they had done it a million times before. She supposed they had. Her hands fumbled with his linen shirt, scrunching it in her fingers as he deepened the kiss. Samael's teeth dragged at her lower lip, tongue lashing against hers, and she tasted him in wild and unending strokes.

He broke away, wrapping his hand in her hair as he trailed his mouth down her neck, his thumb brushing against Greer's lower lip. She nipped at it before tipping her head back to let him glide his nose up the sensitive column of her throat. His lips caught hers again as his fingers slipped under her shirt, tracing the outline of her spine. Samael pulled them closer together as she arched into his touch, and it was the moan that elicited from the back of her throat that he captured in his mouth.

Greer couldn't get enough. Of how he tasted. Of how he smelled. Of the way she fit in his arms. They were a tangle of teeth, tongues, and hands, and nothing could have ever felt this good or this right.

"When I tell you to run," Samael murmured into her ear, breaking away from her lips to drag his teeth along her earlobe. "You run. You don't look back. You don't wait for me. You take Egyn, and you go to Parab."

Greer's eyes flew open in time to see Samael reach over his shoulder, clasping the hilt of the sword sheathed at his back. In a flash of silver metal against the setting sun, Samael twisted just in time to bury his sword into the belly of a leaping devil. It shrieked as he withdrew the blade, and it fell to the shale in a heap of fur and blood.

Yanking the dagger from its leather cover with his free hand, Samael thrust it into Greer's palm and lifted her onto Egyn's back before shoving the horse toward the opposite end of the canyon. "*Run!*" he roared as he swiped the sword downward again, catching a second devil in the neck. The white-washed skull, pieces of dried flesh still clinging to the bone, was severed from the body, and it, too, dropped to the shale.

Greer's gaze darted over his shoulder, past his wings, to see a deluge of devils thundering up the canyon. Pincers, teeth, and claws bounded toward them in a hunt for fresh meat. The dried clay snapped beneath his hooves as Egyn took off, against Greer's better judgment, and the dagger vibrated against her palm in warning when she buried her fingers in his mane.

A sudden gust of power from Samael ascended, building and building, until it sucked the air out of the canyon. Greer's ears were ringing, her chest tight and heaving from the charged static rever-berating across the rock. The walls trembled around her as though an earthquake gripped the desert. Sand and rubble fell from the cliffs above her, painting Greer and Egyn in red dust that clung to her hair and skin.

Then, his power exploded.

In a rush like a wave, a violent wind flew down the canyon, pushing Greer off Egyn's back. Her shoulder and hip cracked painfully against the hard river bed when she fell, and that violent wind screamed past her ears. The evening stilled as gut-wrenching spasms convulsed through her head; the bones in her skull felt as though they were breaking. She clutched at her temples, fingernails gripping so tightly that they left half-moon-shaped crevices in her skin, rocking as agony came in the form of unrelenting snaps and shatters. She hadn't even realized she was crying out until the pain ceased, and the next breath she took sawed at her dry throat.

Greer was empty. Egyn was nuzzling the back of her neck in an apology of sorts. She hadn't noticed that either.

She quieted her heaving breath, listening intently for footsteps against the shale. Samael was...he was...he had to be... She hadn't paid much attention to what she felt down that invisible thread until it went silent, and it left a gaping crater in her soul that she hadn't known was filled in the first place. Not until it was gone.

Overwhelming shock pulled at Greer and, her spine curled forward as she clutched at her waist. She was at a loss for words, a loss for thoughts, and a strangled sob choked out of her when she realized what he had done, what he had done for her.

Thundering sounded in the canyon. Paw pads and bone pounding down the dry river bed, following her trail. There was nothing else for her to do except to either wait for the devils to reach her and tear her apart or fight back as long as she could. And she wouldn't allow Samael's sacrifice to be for nothing. She wouldn't face them lying down. Not this time.

There was a purr in Greer's hand, a quiet vibration that coiled up her arm. Wiping the sweat and dust from her brow, she sat up and glanced at the dagger still clutched in her palm. Markings were etched in the blade, similar to the ones that had once bound Samael, but something else lay beyond...

A shadow, a fog of a kind, danced within the dagger's metal. It called to a piece of Greer that she had been trying to suppress, tugging at the darkness of her primordial side. She could have sworn it was begging to be released, begging to destroy. To kill. She ran a finger down the flat edge of the blade, and it followed her movement, pressing tightly against her skin as though it could feel her.

The thundering was louder now, echoing over the canyon walls. The braying and shrieking of the devils came next, sharp wails and squeals and snorting of long snouts. Egyn paced behind her, his tail flicking with agitation as she stood to face the coming devils.

Greer did the only thing she could think of doing, and she didn't even know if it would work. If that darkness wanted to be released...then she would let it. She threw her hand over the dagger and allowed threads of her power to fall against the blade, wrapping tightly around the shadow. Then, she pulled.

The shadow broke free of the blade, exiting through the etchings that had once held it in place. It burst into the air, a threatening rush of gloom and danger. It swirled around her, blowing her hair and tugging at her clothes.

Where. Command. Where. It seemed to say, poking and prodding at her chest and arms. *Where. Tell me where. Where!*

Greer pointed toward the oncoming pack, and the shadow obeyed instantly. It grew into a looming cloud of blackness and dust, ratcheting larger and larger until it spanned the canyon's width. It billowed like a sandstorm, moving down the river bed like a curtain of death. Greer pushed herself up, dagger still in hand, and chased after the shadow.

Panicked squawks and pained screams sounded for a brief moment in time before being silenced. As the shadow moved, it left dozens of devils in its wake. Twitching bones and hairless carcasses dotted the land like stunted bushes. Devils scrambled up the cliffside, clawing desperately at the rock to get away before they, too, were taken. Still, their bodies cascaded down like tumbleweeds as they landed in the river bed, cracking noisily against the shale.

And there, at the end of the dying pack, lay Samael.

His body was broken and bloody. Large chunks of flesh had been torn from under the ripped linen of his shirt. Greer dropped to the ground next to him, brushing his hair off his brow and taking in the bruises blooming under his eyes. His sword was still clutched in his hand, black blood coating the metal and dripping onto the red dust in a macabre pool.

Greer swept her gaze over his body, swallowing thickly at the unexpected grief tugging at her heart. Her eyes stopped at the tear splitting the skin of his forearm, and she studied it for a heartbeat of time before her stomach twisted in her abdomen. She swore loudly, excitement rocketing through her belly.

The skin was knitting back together, slowly but surely. Samael was healing.

Parab. She needed to get him to Parab.

Greer shot to her feet once again and whirled around the canyon. Egyn was nowhere in sight, but she knew he couldn't have gone far if he was still alive. She hoped upon all hopes that he was.

Mimicking Samael the first day he had called Egyn to them, she lifted her fingers to her lips, whistling a sharp note that echoed across the silent canyon.

Then, she waited.

One minute, two minutes.

A pattering of hooves against the shale sounded, and Greer breathed in relief as the horse, silhouetted against the deep orange and navy sky, came cantering around the corner. He neighed as he approached them, lowering his head and nudging Samael's shoulder.

"Lay down, Egyn," Greer commanded as she let out a blast of power to wrangle the loose shadow back into her grasp. "We need to get him to Parab."

Egyn surrendered at once, dipping his knees until he rested against the river bed. His ears perked with interest as the shadow came to call, compacting into a palm-sized ball as it reached her. It played in her hand, weaving between her fingers.

Where? The shadow asked again, though this time it was less demanding, as though it had reached the peak of its power. *Where? Tell me where.*

"Under his arms, lift him onto Egyn." The words had escaped Greer, though she wasn't sure whether she needed to speak them.

Nonetheless, floating toward Samael, the shadow wrapped itself around the primordial's shoulders and tugged. Samael's upper body lifted from the ground, though he remained silent and unconscious, chin drooping toward his chest like he was a ragdoll. The shadow deposited Samael onto Egyn's saddle, and Greer pushed at his wings to help situate him further up. He slumped forward, head resting on Egyn's mane.

Samael was thick and heavy, his muscled body a deadweight against Egyn's back. Regardless, the horse quickly stood, the leather saddle creaking as it shifted. Greer circled the two quickly, making sure that Samael was, more than likely, going to stay put. Satisfied, she turned back to the shadow drifting near her shoulder.

"Tether yourself around him, hold him in place."

It floated off, wrapping around Samael's waist before sending hooked tendrils to the saddle, anchoring him to the horse's back. Blood leaked from Samael's nose, dripping onto the legs of his pants. Standing on her tiptoes, she untied the empty sheath from between his wings and knotted it into Egyn's leather reins.

She picked up Samael's sword, heaving it into the sheath. She opted to keep the dagger in her hand, a reminder that she was alone in all of this and the male at her side needed her now.

"To Parab, Egyn," Greer said, hauling herself onto Egyn's back and settling behind Samael. She took a deep breath and carefully wrapped her arms around his waist. She had no clue how long the trip would be or what else they would face; she just hoped that it would be quick.

At her urging, Egyn trundled forward, Samael swaying limply on his back as he moved.

Parab was not contained by any set of walls or gates like Veritas. The domed palace and flat-topped buildings appeared like a beacon on the horizon, growing up from the flat desert floor just before sunrise. The cast from the sun shone brightly off the golden tiles that lined each dome. As Greer drew closer, exhaustion setting in and threatening to take over, she saw the detailed stone archways that lined the narrow alleys, the bustling entrance to what she assumed was a marketplace, and the turquoise flooring that superseded the sandstone stairs. Though she had no idea where they were going, it seemed Egyn did. His hooves steadily clopped against the stone streets, calm and unhurried.

The horse led them deeper into the city, moving past stalls built into the stone buildings and covered in billowing linens to keep the sun from baking the bazaar. Despite the sea of people that brought the early morning to life, it was cooler in the market, and they easily parted as Egyn passed.

Unlike the wool clothes and oversized jackets of the city in the north, the citizens of Parab opted for robes and dresses of brightly colored silks and cotton, thinly made to combat the heat. The women and men sported head coverings, likely to keep the sun and sand from their hair, and they all wore elaborate jewelry— rings, bracelets, and necklaces made of fine gemstones and gold.

The day's heat was already warming the bazaar, and Greer wiped the sweat from her brow, smearing the red dust from her hair across her skin.

He hadn't woken yet. Not that Greer hadn't tried, though. She pulled at the nape of his hair, twisted the skin of his underarms, and even had the shadow poke him in the eye. Not a twitch or groan had come from him.

The only reason Greer had known Samael was still alive was his soft breathing, fluttering the locks of hair framing his face, and the kindling of the connection she shared with him. People murmured as they passed, pointing with disregard toward the half-dead Primordial atop the ashen-eyed horse.

Greer ignored them, focusing on the footpath instead.

Egyn turned up another narrow alley, clopping up steps that had them a level above the bazaar. The domed ceilings of the palace came into view once again, followed by the sandstone towers, the circular columns that held up open-air balconies, and a garden of palm trees and ferns surrounding manicured pools of water. The sweet scent of jasmine and water lilies replaced cooking meats near the marketplace, and the floral was calming and peaceful.

Greer gazed around, her lips parted in awe as she entered the palace grounds. This was how she imagined the ancient civilizations of Egypt, Greece, or Mesopotamia lived. And maybe they had if the Meridian of Greed had anything to do with it.

They wove through the pools, stopping at the base of a set of stone steps spanning the width of the garden. Six columns stood high above them, shielding the staircase in cool shade.

And, at the top of the steps, stood a man. No, not a man. Another Primordial. His power was palpable and cunning. The curl of it that encased Greer with curiosity made her squirm.

The Primordial was dressed in black armor, similar to her father's. Strapped leather sandals covered his feet in place of boots. His eyes, a deep shade of brown and lined with kohl, were almond-shaped and bright against the rising sun. His hair was raven-black and long, and he wore it down and adorned his locks with beads of turquoise and gold to match his meridian. The feathers of his wings were just a shade lighter than his hair.

The male held himself like a pharaoh and Greer couldn't help, but wonder if the ancient Egyptians had based Ra, God of the Sun, off of him.

Calling to them from the top of the steps, he spread his arms wide, and the upper arm cuff, shaped like a golden snake, seemingly slithered around his bicep. With a smile pulled onto his lips, he said, "Greer. Daughter of Azazel. You are welcome–"

His eyes slid to Egyn behind her, lifting to take in Samael, limp and unconscious in the saddle. He descended the stairs in a head-spinning second, casting the shadow off Samael with a simple flick of his wrist. At his command, the shadow descended into the dagger in Greer's hand, sinking below the etchings binding it to the blade.

Samael's position began to slip, eventually falling to the side. The male who came to his aid caught his large body with ease.

"Serket! Na'amah!" the man shouted, waiting for the two women to arrive.

The first female, Serket, appeared at the top of the staircase, wearing a dress of white silk with slits to allow for her wings. Serket approached Samael and the other male, her dark hair pulled in a long braid that draped her spine. As she lifted her hands to assist in bracing Samael, Greer noticed that her hand contained the same marking as Arista's, the dark rune along her thumb.

The second female, Na'amah, appeared a breath later, and, in her presence, Greer felt as though the air had been sucked from the garden. Na'amah was stunning. A dark curtain of hair hung past her shoulders, brushing against the dress of wine red that accentuated her tawny skin. Two long slits ran up from the hem, slicing along each thigh and ending high enough that Greer wondered how she was able to sit down without revealing herself to whoever sat opposite her. Her feet were bare, and her right ankle sported three black bracelets that jingled with each step she took.

The Primordial oozed sex, her hips swinging as she descended the staircase. Despite that, a sheathed dagger was tied to her waist, hung by a simple cord, and a sword strapped between her brown-feathered wings. Greer figured that Na'amah could run any man through faster than they could wipe the drool from their chin after setting eyes on her.

And, from the lethal edge to her gaze, Greer suspected that Na'amah knew it too.

"What happened, Mammon?" she asked as she approached the two bracing Samael. Her question came out as a purr, though Greer wasn't quite sure she meant it to. Na'amah gently brushed Serket to the side, placing one of Samael's arms over her shoulders.

"Ask Greer," the man, Mammon, replied.

Na'amah's gaze turned to Greer, taking her in for the first time. Watching as her eyes traveled from her dirty sneakers to the sun-kissed freckles spackling her nose, Greer stilled under the intense scrutiny of the Primordial. "The wastes?" Na'amah asked as she tilted her head toward the stairs. She didn't wait for Greer's response but went on. "Impressive."

Greer felt a spark of satisfaction nestle in her chest.

"Serket, take Greer to the guest chambers," Mammon said. His wings beat in tune with Na'amah's, and the two briskly flew Samael to the top of the staircase.

Mouth open in protest, Greer dashed after them, a sudden outburst of energy breaking through the exhaustion that weakened her knees. "Wait! I'm coming with you."

Na'amah turned to glance over her shoulder, looking Greer up and down once again. "Samael is very injured. There is nothing you can do to help him."

"I didn't ask you," Greer spat in response, following them into the square courtyard with six separate pools. Each was separated by a walkway and filled with fish that lazily swam in the warmth of the rising sun. A frog hopped off a lily pad, splashing quietly into the water as they strolled by.

Mammon let out a loud laugh. "You are your father's daughter, aren't you?"

Greer bristled but said nothing.

Mammon sighed. "Fine, yes, come. But don't expect he'll be awake by tonight or tomorrow morning. It will take the healers many days to get him where he needs to be." He paused, cocking his head to brush the locks from his brow with his shoulder. "How many devils were there? Dozens?"

A small smile pulled at Greer's lips. "A hundred or more, if I had to guess."

"And *you* took them all on with Samael's Venom?" Mammon's mouth downturned, not as a frown, but in pleasant surprise as his eyes slid to the dagger, the shadow within dancing against the etchings. "That is impressive, wouldn't you, Na'amah?"

"I've already complimented her on it, Mammon. Keep up, yes?"

Greer couldn't help but smile as Na'amah winked at her from behind the curtain of hair.

THIRTY-ONE

GREER

"You've been in here for three days."

Greer lifted her head from the edge of the mattress, glancing bleary-eyed toward the door. "I just don't want to miss him waking up." The admission would have once embarrassed her, but now she was too exhausted to care.

"Have you slept anywhere else?" Mammon asked as he pushed off the door frame he had been leaning on.

Shaking her head, Greer stretched her arms over her shoulders before rubbing the sleep crust in the corners of her eyes.

Mammon sighed. "Come with me. You need to eat." He snapped his fingers, the rings on his fingers glinting in the late afternoon light, and Serket bustled in, dressed in silks of sage. "You also need to bathe. Take care of yourself." He turned his kohl-lined eyes to look at the servant. "Bring her to my private gardens when she's finished."

Serket dipped low into a curtsey as Mammon swept from the room. "Come, Princess," she said, gesturing through the arched door frame.

"Greer. Just call me Greer." She looked over to Samael, hesitation keeping her rooted to the cushioned chair.

"He'll wake soon, Greer. The healers have been working around the clock. But Mammon's right. You should take care of yourself before she wakes."

Greer glanced toward the window, spotting the orange trees, bowing toward the sun, casting long shadows into the private guest courtyard. The trickle of water from the fountains could be heard through the rustling leaves. She cleared her throat as she stood, shaking the numbness from her feet and ankles from sitting for so long. She supposed it wouldn't hurt to bathe. She still hadn't since they arrived. She had told herself once Samael was okay, she would, and since he hadn't woken, she couldn't bring herself to.

Since she'd been there, Mammon had treated her with a kindness that Azazel lacked. He was warm and friendly, ensuring that Greer was supplied with a porcelain jug of cool water and a breakfast tray she barely touched. Sometimes, he sat next to her, quiet as the night, and other times, he would pass by the room and glance in to ensure she had everything she needed. More than once, Greer woke up to a thin sheet wrapped around her shoulders, and she knew from the remnants of power that he had placed it.

Greer followed Serket into the hallway, which acted as a main artery through the palace. The red clay walls marking the guest chambers stood staggeringly tall against the finely detailed stone archways. The ceiling consisted only of thick planks of orange wood that held loose cotton linens for shade. Ceramic pots lined the walls, where planted palm trees stretched toward the open air above. They gave a secondary source of shade, their large leaves waving in the breeze that cut through the hallway.

Even the floor under Greer's feet was extravagant. Bold blues and greens, arranged in intricate patterns, made up the path. With the beginning of each new courtyard, the floor transitioned to white marble. Wooden tables and cushioned chairs surrounded the pool of water, but the furniture stood empty that afternoon.

Serket peeled off the courtyard, entering a guest chamber through an iron gate. The landing room was small and cozy, with three arching columns holding up the mezzanine overlooking the space. A small table and blue cushioned chairs took up the middle, though a lounging couch had been placed beneath a dimly lit black lamp bolted to the ceiling of the balcony. They passed through just as quickly as they entered, taking the sandstone steps to the mezzanine and entering a second room, this time through a secured door.

Greer saw they had reached the bathroom, which was brightly lit and decorated in warm tones of dark wood and tiles the shade of orchid, calming and peaceful. Incense burned on a corner table, the soft scent of eucalyptus overtaking the jasmine and citrus wafting in from the courtyard. Glass jars of mud and sugar scrubs lined the wooden shelves on the walls. And, much to Greer's gratefulness, a round tub sat in the middle of the room.

Water was already filled to the brim, a soft steam curling from the surface, and five buckets of clean water sat at the foot of the tub. A set of white, fluffy towels was folded over the wooden bath rack next to the tub. A single plank of wood spanned the width, and a bar of soap and an iced beverage perched on top.

"You can undress behind the divider," Serket said, motioning toward the corner where a partition had been set up. "And come back here when you are done."

"I can bathe myself," Greer said, her eyes darting uncomfortably toward the tub.

"Of course, you can," Serket tutted in return, turning to hang a silk robe on a hook near the window, "but allow us to pamper you while you are here. You have journeyed all this way, yes? Parab is one of luxury and comfort. I doubt very much you found leisure in the Nakki Marsh."

Serket's eyes glittered with humor, and Greer had to give it to her...she was right. There wasn't any comfort or leisure found in the bog.

Her clothes were still crusted in mud and dust, and it took some time for Greer to peel each article from her body. Her skin underneath was red and raw, itching from the layers of muck that had built up over the last week and a half. After she had stripped down, clothes lying in a pile on the tiled floor, Greer stepped from behind the partition and walked toward the tub.

Serket's back was turned, busy picking a range of soaps and scrubs from the adjacent shelves, but Greer knew she also meant to give privacy. Stepping into the warm water, a soft groan of satisfaction rippled from the back of her throat. Sinking deep into the tub, Greer relaxed against the cool porcelain, watching as the dust and dirt-stained the water brown. She dipped underneath the surface, wetting her hair before pulling the tangled braid apart, matted with weeks' worth of oil.

"Close your eyes," Serket said as she knelt at the side of the tub, placing the jar of scrub she had selected from the shelf beside her on the floor. She reached down and scooped a handful of the scrub, rubbing both hands together to create a lather.

Greer obliged, resting her head against the edge of the tub. Serket started working at her hair, threading her fingers through the tangles. She massaged the scalp, loosening the dirt from the roots down to the shaft of Greer's hair. Serket poured a clean bucket of water onto

Greer's head, rinsing the scrub. She did two more rounds before Greer felt the lightness of clean hair, and it was then that Serket poured a small amount of sweetly scented oil on the top of Greer's head, letting it soak down the knots.

Serket was gentle as she picked through the tangles with a wide-tooth comb, and Greer leaned forward to tuck her arms around her legs.

"I can't remember the last time anyone washed my hair," Greer said softly, resting her chin on her knees. "At least, without me paying for it in a salon."

Serket chuckled under her breath. "Your mother never washed your hair for you?" The tugs against Greer's head were kneading and relaxing. "It's beautiful and thick, so many curls."

"My mother never did anything like this. She wasn't exactly someone that sought out physical contact." Greer cleared her throat. "I had a good friend in elementary school, and her mother taught us how to braid. For hours, she would take turns brushing our hair. One day, she taught us how to do our make-up, even though we were so young."

"What happened to her?"

Greer sighed. "Cancer. She died the summer before I turned ten. My friend's dad moved them across the country, and I never saw her again."

Serket was quiet as she worked on finishing the detangling before finally saying, "I'm sorry to hear that. Mortal existence is beautiful and fleeting." Her fingers massaged at Greer's scalp, rubbing the oil intensely into the roots of her hair. "We forget that when we live forever. It can be easy to pass the same flower when you know you'll have the chance to smell it tomorrow."

"Were you in the War of the Sixteen?" Greer asked, feeling Serket's fingers slow. "I've heard it mentioned. I don't know much about it."

"Yes and no. I did not wield a sword, but being the Primordial of Healing and Protection, I did much of that during the war."

Greer turned to look at Serket, taking in her brown skin and dark eyes. "Primordial of Healing and Protection? In Samsara?"

Serket's smile was small. "Is it so hard to believe?" She twisted Greer's newly untangled hair around her fingers, pinning it in a pile at the top of her head. "That there are primordials here that one would consider good?" She dipped a cloth into the water behind Greer's back and lathered the scrub onto it.

Greer felt the cloth swipe against her back, cleaning off the dirt and dust that was still caked there. "Did you choose to come here?" She spotted the dark marking on Serket's thumb when the cloth rubbed down her arm.

"I did. I was one of the few who had the choice." Serket dunked the cloth into the water again, wringing out the excess before tossing it away from the tub. "Many didn't, wanting to come to Samsara or Elysia. Some are still bitter about that. Others have found peace in where they are now."

Serket handed Greer a clean, damp cloth over her shoulder, a fresh gob of scrub on it, and turned to give Greer privacy for a moment as Greer stood to wash her chest, abdomen, and legs. She thought back to Arista—about how her handmaiden had expressed a desire to return home. How she never could. She sat back down, draping the cloth over the tub's rim.

"Do you regret your choice?"

Serket pushed herself up from her kneeling position and unfolded a thick towel from the rack. Greer stood as she grabbed it, wrapping it tightly around her chest. It had warmed in the sun and smelled lightly of resin.

"Not today," Serket replied. "Today, it led me to you." Greer knew that she meant it. "Come, let's get you dressed. Mammon is waiting."

Greer donned a strappy chiffon dress in dark emerald courtesy of Serket. The slits, though not as dramatic as the slits Na'amah preferred, climbed just above her knees. She was thankful for it once she began to cross the central courtyard, as the material was light and breezy enough to still be comfortable in the afternoon desert heat.

The private gardens of Mammon were tucked in the corner of the palace, only accessed by weaving through the narrow hallways and alleys that overlooked the bazaar. Greer was sure she wouldn't be able to find it again, let alone see her way back to the guestrooms when the entrance opened in front of her.

Greer first spotted the elaborately sculpted fountain, two wolves carved from white rock howling toward the sky. It had been set in the middle of a pool, one so big you could swim laps in it. Plants and flowers of all varieties lined the pool— stunning red, pink, and green colors swaying in the breeze and dipping their leaves into the cool water.

"Ah, she looks brilliant, my darling!" Mammon said as he approached. "She looks like she even belongs here." Greer opened her mouth to ask about Samael, but Mammon easily read her. "He still sleeps, nothing to worry over." Taking Serket's face into his hands, he kissed her heartily.

The gesture threw Greer for a loop, and Na'amah, lounging on a chaise in the shade of a eucalyptus tree, laughed at the expression on her face.

"Mammon and Serket are mates," Na'amah explained, swinging her legs over the side of the seat. Her wings *thwaped* powerfully as she shook them to settle the feathers into place. "Found one another after the war."

Greer turned to Serket, who was busy smiling at Mammon and plucking pollen from the fabric of his shirt. "Is that why you were allowed to choose?" Greer asked as Mammon took Serket's hand and led them both to the table under the shade of the tree.

"It's a powerful offense to keep mates from one another," Serket explained, settling her wings over the low backing of the chair. "Mammon and I would have torn the universe apart to be together."

"And they'll always let us know it," Na'amah muttered, gathering a small handful of olives from a tray near her chaise and dropping them into her mouth.

"I hope for you, dear sister, that your mate is found and you finally know what it means to love another," Mammon said, pulling out a chair and gesturing for Greer to sit down.

"Are you...related?" Greer asked delicately.

Serket laughed as she poured a cup of cold mint tea into a glass, placing it in front of Greer. "Not any more than you would be related to a neighbor. Mammon and Na'amah have a closer relationship than most primordials that lead a meridian."

Greer choked on the mint tea. "You're both princes?" she managed to sputter out. Mammon, she assumed, even though she hadn't been implicitly told. But Na'amah... "Or princess?"

"Primordial of Persuasion and Seduction," Serket said, pouring her glass of tea and taking a small sip. "She oversees the Meridian of Lust."

"And spends most of her days here," Mammon interjected, sending a wink Na'amah's way.

"You don't wear the armor," Greer replied apologetically. "I didn't think—"

"I wore the armor for thousands of years and led hundreds of legions into battle," Na'amah said. She leaned forward to remove her dagger from the looped belt and place it on the table. It had a similar curve to Samael's, though three gemstones of red jasper, each flecked with black beige, lined the hilt. "It has been a time of peace. Therefore, I prefer comfort."

Mammon followed Na'amah's lead by pulling out his dagger and placing it on the table. Three gemstones of teal amazonite, thick veins of white running through each stone, had replaced the red jasper.

"Not at the table," Serket clucked in admonishment. The two daggers disappeared in the next breath. "I understand that you've journeyed here from the capital city, so you must have gone through Wrath and Indolence. Did you meet either Abaddon or Balam?"

Greer shook her head. "If being attacked by spiders and nakki was their version of welcome, then the rest of their meridians leave much to be desired."

Na'amah snorted into her tea.

"Balam and Abaddon have always kept to themselves," Mammon said. "Abaddon, especially after losing his mate during the war." He paused to study Greer for a long moment. "Come with me. I have something to show you."

Greer followed Mammon out of the garden. The twists and turns of the narrow hallways and alleys were just as confusing as when they entered, but Greer found her bearings when they were deposited into the central courtyard that fronted the palace.

"My brother is many things," Mammon said, his leather sandals slapping against the stone steps as he descended toward the city. He was moving at such a brisk pace that Greer had to jog after him to keep up. "But a lover of history, he is not. Here in Parab, we celebrate those whose lives were cut short. We celebrate how they lived and died and their opportunity to return to the universe."

The beginning of the bazaar was marked by the sun-faded striped fabric that spanned the alleyway. A tannery stall, stuffed to the brim with bags and sandals, was filled with shoppers, one busy haggling with a shopkeeper wearing a money belt around his waist. A group of females, each wearing dresses of various thin fabrics, browsed at another stall selling pottery.

Mammon greeted every person they passed with a smile and a bow of his head. They greeted him the same way, some shaking his hand and others clapping him on the shoulder. It was clear to Greer how beloved their prince was.

Meat sizzled, and the fabric tarps above them snapped in the wind as they walked through the bazaar. Spices poured into baskets, baking bread, and stale smoke swirled together in a haze of scents, making Greer feel like her head was on a swivel. Small children ran past, holding wooden toys aloft, and one boy nearly knocked into one of the females from earlier. Greer watched as a woman pulled the boy into her stall, wagging her finger in a disciplinary fashion for not paying attention to others around him.

Mammon led Greer through the maze of souks, the noise of the bustling atmosphere dimming when they entered the squares. Rows and rows of wooden carts had been parked in the middle of the tiled area, each selling grilled chickens, freshly squeezed juices, and roasted nuts. Brown-skinned faeries and creatures with brightly colored scales coating their forearms were busy serving customers. The muffled sound of a flute crept over the top of the carts, and when Greer turned the corner to exit the square, she spotted a group of snake-eyed women performing a complex dance.

Outside the main thoroughfare, the city quickly divulged into a red-rocked jungle of multi-story homes and buildings. Laundry hung on wires that spanned the width of the road, and three males sat on stone benches, smoking pipes and chatting quietly. Its simplicity struck Greer. How they were here, in the underworld, and were living their afterlives as nothing more than...whoever and whatever they wanted to be.

A surge of bliss and contentment filled Greer's chest at the thought.

Finally, they approached a red-rock building at the end of the road. Dust kicked up around them from the wooden carts pulled by horses trundling down the path, coating the hem of Greer's dress in dry clay. The red-rock building was even taller than the palace. It was finished with a single arched door frame, elaborately carved and flanked by two marble columns. Inside the arch was a set of wooden doors, painted gold and rimmed with the same turquoise tiles that made up the palace floor.

Two guards, each sporting a large pair of cream-colored wings, stood on each side of the doorway. They turned in unison to open the set as Mammon and Greer approached.

The door led to the first chamber, dimly lit by three black candelabras containing a dozen pillar candles, each casting a soft, golden glow on the stone. Their footsteps echoed over the walls as they walked. The short hallway opened into the second chamber, vast and seemingly unending.

On the floor, tiles of orange, blue, green, and yellow were ensconced in various mandala patterns, extending halfway up the wall. Three marble columns stretching dozens of feet toward the high-vaulted ceilings were set in the middle of the room. Each column sported carvings of animals, warriors, and battle scenes, painted with brilliant colors that matched the flooring and walls.

"These are the Primordial Tombs," Mammon said, wrenching a lit torch from an iron bracket fastened to the first stone column. Greer followed suit, grabbing the one nearest the now empty bracket. "Each of these are brothers and sisters of mine who fought at my side when Azazel led the march against Elysia."

Mammon shone the light of his torch over the first tomb set into the floor. *Adoel, War of the Sixteen, Legion Seventy-Two led by Belial.* Greer swallowed thickly as she read each word, taking in their meaning.

"These tombs tell our story. Of the peace that rests here. Of the war that is to come." Mammon paused to look at Greer, who had swept her torch toward another tomb. "Of what was lost and what is still meant to be found."

"I'm not sure what my part is in all of this," Greer admitted as she read: *Rehael, War of the Sixteen, Legion Twenty-Eight led by Abaddon.*

Mammon left her question hanging between them and guided her through the tomb, stopping at the second column. "A prophecy tells of a person who will bring on the end of the universe as we know it."

Greer lifted her torch, sliding her gaze along the battle carvings led by a faceless being carrying a sword. They held an orb of light in their outstretched hand, three winged men carrying three different weapons trailing them. They were marching toward another winged man, this one clutching a scepter in one fist and a scythe in the second.

"That seems like a massive task for one person," Greer whispered.

Mammon nodded. "It is. But the death of one world will bring the creation of another." He circled the massive column, keeping his torch held high. "The universe and the realms within it are an ecosystem. A forest flourishes when the things that no longer serve it are destroyed. It creates opportunities for new life to evolve and to grow."

"But what dies for creation itself to continue?" Greer asked, glancing upward toward the carvings near the middle of the column. "Art? Beauty? Humans? Daemons? Or is it an understanding and way of thinking?"

Mammon pondered her for a moment, running a finger on his lower lip. "Do you believe death in the prophecy to be literal?"

"No." Greer turned to look at Mammon, locking her eyes with his. "I think it's a shift to a new beginning." She cleared her throat. "There are too many beautiful things in the universe. They don't all deserve destruction."

Paige came to the forefront, her smiling face floating in her mind's eye. And, for the first time since her death, Greer didn't collapse into a puddle of guilt and tears.

"What do they deserve?" Mammon questioned softly.

Greer shook her head. "I don't know. Maybe that's for the mystery person to uncover."

Footsteps sounded behind them, the gait unsteady and limping.

"Perhaps," Mammon said as Greer glanced over her shoulder, starting when she spotted Samael's faltering steps. "It may be too much for one person to uncover alone."

But Greer was no longer listening, and in the next breath, Mammon had disappeared in a crackle of power.

"You're awake," Greer said breathlessly as she approached Samael, the torch held tightly in her hand.

Samael still looked worse for wear. Deep bruises, shades of sickly green and yellow, spotted his chest and abdomen. His dark markings seemed brighter as they struggled to contain the power attempting to heal him. It was the first time Greer had seen him with his shirt removed, most likely due to the discomfort of having the fabric rub against his wounds, and it was the first time she realized that the markings banded his waist and hips as well.

"You came back for me," Samael said in response, his voice hoarse and cracked. "And I hear you took out all of the devils."

Greer shifted on her feet. "I had some help."

"My venom is a powerful tool. It was created to destroy, and you wielded it well." Samael lifted a hand to scratch the back of his head, and Greer averted her eyes from the layers of muscle that rippled with the movement. "Thank you for bringing me here."

Greer quieted for a long minute as she turned back to the column behind her. There was so much unsaid between them, so much she wanted to iron out. But, no matter how hard she tried, she couldn't find the words.

"This reminds me of home," Greer began instead, sweeping her torch to study the carvings. "I know it's selfish. Part of me wants to go because I finally had the chance to study ancient artifacts at a dig site in Greece, and I would love to make that dream become a reality." She heaved a sigh. "And a bigger part of me wants to tell Delia what I did, how I caused the death of her wife. The rest of me wants to visit Paige's grave and apologize for it. It's difficult being here when I know my life is just on the other side of the veil."

Samael cocked his head, his gaze gliding down her freshly washed hair, taking in the emerald dress and landing on her strapped sandals. "Mammon brought you out here, but are you up for one more visit?"

Samael held out his hand for her to take, and Greer lowered her gaze to stare at it. Something had softened within her, a piece of her heart that had once been hidden by darkness and grief. It was still there, but it had lightened. She slipped her hand into his, entwining their fingers, and let him slowly lead her from the tombs.

THIRTY-TWO

DELIA

"I just think there is something bigger," Delia said as she paced the hotel room floor, her bare feet sinking into the plush carpet. "You didn't see her— that woman. She got sucked into the runes. She just—"

"Are you sure that you're not sleep-deprived?" Cian interjected from his seat on the vinyl couch. The cushion squeaked as he adjusted, stretching the plastic material underneath him. "I didn't even know you could see the runes. You're not supposed to be able to."

"Are you accusing me of lying?" Delia shot back, halting in her progression to twist toward him with a glare.

"I'm just saying that—"

"We've been working together for weeks now," Kazzy said above the two. She leaned back to rest her head against the bed frame, a steaming cup of coffee she grabbed from the café at the base of the hill. "We're all tired. We've been going over everything non-stop. Now, we can keep going over the surveillance, but I can't imagine we'll find anything else." She risked a glance over to Delia, who had wrapped her arms across her chest. "I'm sorry, I have to agree with Cian. We have to revert our focus to Paladin."

Delia began to play with a loose string on the hem of her jacket. Her heart began to race at the thought of forgetting about the runes, and she turned her attention toward the polish on her toenails instead. "She wanted me to help her, and I did nothing." She slid her gaze over to Kazzy, scanning her sleep-tousled hair and the dark bags under the shifter's eyes from her night as a wolf.

Cian tapped his fingers against the cushioned armrest. "This can't be about Paige, Delia. There is nothing you could have done to save her."

Delia took in a sharp breath through her nose. "This has nothing to do with Paige."

"You told me that you saw her soul when she died," Cian remarked, his eyes darkening. "Are you sure you aren't projecting your guilt?"

"Kick rocks."

"Enough." Kazzy's voice was sharp as she bit over them once again. Raising her hand to rub her temple, she quickly added, "Please. Either tell me what's going on or go in the hallway to fight so I can nap in peace."

Cian and Delia deeply scowled at one another before Cian answered. "Paige was Delia's fiancée before she was killed a couple of months back by Eligos."

"I just said this has nothing to do with Paige," Delia repeated as she resumed pacing, though her footsteps now felt heavier and harder to peel from the floor. The unexpected grief that poured from the box she had stuffed away was threatening to pull her under. "And, besides, you didn't tell her the best part. *You* decided to try to sell the Mage out to Eligos. It's *your* fault Paige is dead."

Cian sent her a murderous stare. His mouth parted before snapping shut again, as though he were on the brink of revealing something and then thought better of it.

"The Mage is alive?" Kazzy asked, pulling herself up straight. "She— *the* Mage?"

"She was taken shortly after Paige's death. We think to Samsara," Delia went on, though her intense gaze never lifted from Cian. "That's why we're here. We want to see if the Paladin Society knows of any portals."

"To Samsara?" Kazzy chuckled, leaning back once more. "Samsara is just another story. There isn't really—"

"Fuck, Kazzy, not everything is make-believe. Greer is half-primordial," Cian bit out through gritted teeth. "She's the daughter of Azazel." He turned his glare toward Delia. "And we can't do anything we came here to do if you're off chasing hallucinations through Vatican City."

"They are not hallucinations!"

"I'm still trying to work through the news that we have a Mage again."

Delia glanced at Kazzy, seeing the coffee cup upturned and the dark liquid slowly staining the white comforter.

"We're getting information from the Paladin Society tomorrow, whether I have to throw you over those damned runes or not," Cian growled into the silence that spanned the three. "I'm done scouting out the basilica. We have a plan, and we'll be doing it tomorrow."

Still feeling like they were all missing something, Delia said nothing as she padded from the hotel room, letting the door slam closed behind her.

"You're going to be careful, right?" Kazzy asked, reaching out to squeeze Delia's arm. Delia heard the nerves in her voice, the tremble that shook her whisper. "I hate this. I wish I could go with you."

Delia looked over to Kazzy, the dimly lit chandelier above them illuminating her blonde hair like a halo. Despite her agitation at being ignored and insistence that the runes still meant something, Delia felt her anger ebb away at the concern shining through the wolf shifter's gaze.

"I'll be fine. And I promise to be careful." Delia heard Kazzy's breath hitch. "Where will you and Cian be?"

Kazzy sighed, gesturing over to the fountains. "I'll be over there. Cian will meet me when you are safely in the office." Her hand slid up to Delia's shoulder before she withdrew it just as quickly. "I'll be waiting the whole time, I promise."

Delia's watch vibrated on her wrist, the screen brightening as her alarm signified ten-thirty on the dot. She lifted her eyes, seeing the patrolling guard doing a round of surveillance leave the excavation office. He turned toward the black door, pulled it tightly shut, and locked it with a key hanging from his belt loop. Her eyes slid to Kazzy, who had seemed to pale in the silver winter moonlight.

Delia nodded only once before standing from her crouched position and beginning her walk around the colonnade. The tourists were few and far between this late at night. The sun was setting earlier and earlier in the late autumn months, and many of the visitors had already turned in hours before. The navy hue blanketed the sky over the city, just enough to show a spackling of stars. At the very least, the long shadows between the columns made staying hidden fairly easy.

Delia slipped past the final column, swinging around to the office door. She peered down at the gold handle and the decorative knob in the middle of the molding. She let out a breath before dropping to her knees in front of the door, taking out the silver pin Cian had provided her to practice with. She inserted the pin, wiggling it in the old lock. She placed her ear against the door's wood and listened for the click of the mechanism releasing.

One minute, two minutes, three minutes passed as Delia worked. She had practiced, but she wouldn't have called herself proficient. Her heart beat rapidly as the minutes ticked by, and she knew she was running out of time— some guards did not drag their feet on the night shift.

Just as Delia was on the verge of giving up, she heard the latch free, and the door gave way with a slight shove from her shoulder. She cracked the door just enough to slither through the gap, making room for the drawstring bag she had strapped onto her shoulders. She closed the door behind her and turned the inner bolt just in time to see four more guards rounding the corner to patrol the square.

Delia's stomach flipped, and she suddenly needed to run to the bathroom. That was close; way too close. The office was dark, only lit by the light from the half-moon streaming in through the window facing the square and the chandelier hanging from the colonnade's ceiling. Taking her first step was the most challenging part, and Delia hesitated to leave the shadowed doorway's confines.

That was, until a guard shone a flashlight into the window, missing Delia by inches. She held her breath as he peered in, sweeping the stream of light from one end to the other before moving on.

In the next moment, she was hurtling past the desks and into the hallway leading to the tombs of the popes beneath her. Her chest heaving and her hands trembling with nerves, she stopped to listen for footsteps.

Nothing. Silence.

It was too quiet, the kind of quiet that signified something was wrong, but the dead silence only increased the longer she walked. The stillness set off alarm bells inside of her. Delia shook her head and adjusted her bag straps before descending the hallway.

Delia pressed on, coming to the mouth of the necropolis and the dirt-covered staircase that descended into black nothingness. The heated humidity wafting through the shaft was enough to make her curls begin to frizz. With the lack of tourists in the small, crowded space, she thought the air would smell fresher. But the dank and dustiness of the space was just as overwhelming as it had been weeks before.

She grabbed her cell phone from her back pocket and turned on the flashlight. Her eyes squinted against the sudden light, and she took the first step onto the stone stairs. The settled earth packed in the crevices clouded around her feet.

The humidity grew the further she went, sweat building on her brow and the middle of her back, and the dust made her nose run like a faucet. She sniffed as softly as possible, but the sound echoed across the tunneled staircase.

It felt like ages that she descended the narrow passage, but as soon as her foot hit the tiled foundation of the necropolis. She swiveled her phone to look around. The darkness was complete and unending. Her vision was obstructed save for what little the light from her cellphone could reach. Against the dirt and stone of the excavated space, Delia was sure even her soft breath echoed in the chamber. There was a small attempt where she tried to limit her breathing to her nose, but the adrenaline made her chest feel stiff and heavy. She settled to let the dust coat her tongue.

Delia shoved her phone under her chin, bracing it tightly against her collarbone. She kept the light facing outward as she rifled through her jacket pocket to remove the smaller version of the map Cian had been rendering over the last few weeks. She unfolded it slowly, trying to keep the crinkling of the paper to a minimum.

The first tomb Cian had circled was coming up on her left-hand side. She power-walked to it, letting the drawstring bag fall from her shoulders, where it landed with a clang as the tire iron Cian had packed her bounced against the mosaic floor. Delia cringed, freezing to hear the inevitable footsteps thundering down the staircase.

When nothing came, Delia crouched down to run her fingers along the seams of the stone. The seal was old and crumbling, though the stone remained completely intact. She leaned over, inspecting the inscription before wrapping her finger around the stone containing the engravings. It didn't budge, and she didn't find any runes etched near the seam.

The next tomb was a columbarium near the tomb of St. Peter; the inscription at the foot of the grave set two feet above the foundation of the necropolis. Delia bent at the waist, touching the carving etched into the stone. They felt new, the lettering still sharp. With the first tomb, the inscription had been sanded down with time, even with the stone around it. From watching Greer inspect photographs of her work at the kitchen table, Delia knew that the inscriptions eventually rounded, forfeiting their sharp edges to age.

She let a breath loose as she tried to wrap her fingers around the stone before huffing in frustration. The stone was set too far back into the framing of the wall, so she bent over even further, twisting at the waist to tuck her head underneath it. Runes had been carved on the underside of the frame, where a seal would have held the stone to the tomb. However, only scrape marks were spotted across the top of the frame.

Delia pushed against the stone— it didn't budge, although she didn't expect it to. She straightened to standing, her back tight from the hunch, while she leaned over and began to inspect the area. She pulled at the statues surrounding the tombs, pushed on the tiles, and assessed every nook and cranny to find an old symbol or rune. Anything to make that stone slide open.

Delia dropped back, sighing deeply. Looking toward the drawstring bag, she saw the top edge of the tire iron lying haphazardly on the floor. Her shoulders sagged as she realized what she needed to do— even after she told Cian she didn't have to bring it. But every moment she was down in the necropolis was another moment of her coming closer to being discovered by the Swiss Guard.

Or, even worse, the Paladin Society.

Delia set her phone into the corner of the tomb and grabbed the tire iron, holding it like a baseball bat while she set her feet. She sent a silent prayer of apology to Greer, who would have been appalled at what she was about to do. Clenching her jaw, Delia swung as hard as she could at the stone. A noise resembling a blast ricocheted across the necropolis as the stone cracked on impact. She grimaced at the loudness of the sound. She knew it was essential to get through the stone, but the thought of getting caught was still unnerving.

The tombs around her shook with the sudden vibration, dirt, and dust spraying from the ceiling. Delia ducked, expecting the guards to come running at any second. As the cloud settled, there was...nothing. There was no noise from above and no noise indicating that anyone was rushing down the narrow staircase.

Still and unnerving silence.

Delia took a step forward to inspect the stone. A spot of impact dented the marker, fissures spider-webbing from the center of it. She pushed against it, the stone barely beginning to give under the pressure from her palm. She sighed, taking a step back and grasping the tire iron. She swung again, and again, and again, slamming the metal into the stone. The iron finally busted through, a small hole appearing amidst the cracks from the iron.

She dropped the tire iron to the floor, where it bounced against the mosaic tile, chipping the ancient, colored stone. Wiping the sweat from her brow, Delia removed her cell phone from the corner of the tomb. She knelt again to shine the light through the hole in the stone.

Where she would have expected a pile of bone dust, a slim, concrete staircase was in its place. A cool breeze wafted up the shaft, a scent of sterile newness so different from the old surroundings of where she stood. Grasping the framing above the tomb, Delia kicked at the crumbling stone. It gave way easily after being fractured by the tire iron, the stone jouncing down the steps before hitting the floor at the bottom. The skittering sound echoed back up the shaft.

Delia turned on the balls of her feet, grabbing the tire iron and the drawstring bag from the floor. She then wedged herself into the small opening, sharp stone scraping the back of her neck. The tightness of the stairwell forced her to keep her head ducked against the ceiling and, with every step she took, her heart beat could be felt into her fingertips and toes. The air cooled as she descended further into the chamber.

Delia lifted her head as she reached the base of the stairs, quickly scanning the room with an eagle eye.

The fluorescent lights were brightly set, beaming down on her with a mind-numbing hum that could still be heard over the fan rattling the vent above her. Electricity had been routed into the room from above, thick blue, red, and copper cords snaking through the ceiling.

Tall shelving units lined the walls in long rows, boxes stacked on each metal shelf. She slowly approached the closest one and made to lift the lid of the box seated at chest level, but the lock on the front contained a rune rather than a keyed hole. She dropped her gaze to the label stuck to the bottom of the box.

Volume 3, 1374

Delia glanced to the right shelf, then the left, and noted the final number increased when she moved to the right. It was a year. She walked along the shelves, turning into the row every so often to check the year on the front of the first box.

Delia took less than two minutes to find a box labeled with her and Greer's birth year, She stood in front of one labeled volume two. She lifted her hands, once again attempting to wriggle the lid from the box, when the rune illuminated for less than a second before a small window slid open. A needle appeared before her.

Delia felt her stomach constrict at the sight and stared at it for another second. Against her better judgment and led on by the curiosity coursing through her veins, she pricked her middle finger against the needle as quickly as she could.

The needle slid through the window, and a whirring sounded from the lid of the box as though it were analyzing her blood. It was silent for a long minute as Delia waited, and as soon as she was readying to walk away, a flap released from the lid.

Swallowing back her nerves, Delia rose onto her tiptoes to peer inside. A single manila folder lay stark against the gray interior. Her fingers brushed the cool metal, and an alarm began to blare as soon as her hand clamped around the folder.

Delia's heart leaped into her throat as she pulled the folder up and spun around, seeing the red light of the alarm flashing against the shelves. The alarm was ear-piercingly loud, echoing through the hollow chamber and pinging off the metal boxes. Her feet pounded against the concrete as she sprinted down the row.

The stairs.

Delia twirled back to the entrance, horror clawing at her stomach when she saw a thick, metal door had slammed shut when the alarm triggered. She was trapped. Bounding footsteps reverberated against the concrete, alternating with the screeching alarm. Shouts drew closer as Delia swept her gaze over the room, her desperate, darting stare roving for an exit. First, she spotted ten men filing into the room from a door behind the last shelf.

Then, it landed on a vent in the high ceiling above her.

Delia threw the manila folder and tire iron into her drawstring bag before tossing it back over her shoulders. Then, she began to climb the metal shelves below the vent.

They were cold against her fingers, and it took all of Delia's strength to pull herself up one at a time. She didn't stop, even though her lungs were burning under the effort and her calves were cramping with every push upward. Shouting beneath her rattled through to her bones. She made her way to the top, not paying attention to anything except how her body was screaming for her to stop climbing. Reaching the final shelf, she pulled herself up and rolled onto the top shelf, but she had to keep going.

Breath sawing her throat, Delia reached back and removed the tire iron from the drawstring bag, wedging it into the crevice where the vent met the concrete ceiling. The vent's metal groaned under the tire iron's pressure, and a heart-stopping number of seconds passed before the shield popped free. The sheet clattered, sliding off the top shelf and falling to the floor. From the shocked yell and the vibrating clang, Delia assumed the vent cover had hit someone attempting to climb after her.

Hoisting herself into the duct work, Delia crawled on her hands and knees toward the staircase entrance, following the thick electric cables that she could see through the vent covers she passed by. The duct turned upward, opening to a slim ladder that seemed to span unendingly above her.

Ignoring the roaring pain between her forearms and lower legs, Delia wrapped her hands around the metal rungs of the ladder and began to clamber up. She didn't know how long she climbed for, at least long enough for her palms to be red and raw. After some time, even the blaring alarm silenced, and all Delia was left with was her ragged breathing ricocheting off the thin duct sheets.

The ladder ended, and when Delia glanced down, she realized the bottom of the shaft had been lost to the darkness. She pressed her hand against the grate above her and pushed, soft lighting flooding her vision. She blinked, peeking over the edge of the flooring and skirting her gaze around the room. Her eyesight was directly in line with the feet of a marble figure, and when she lifted her gaze, she saw the monument of two women, a small angel, and a pope.

Delia flung the grate back, tenting the ancient, dirty rug that covered it, and wriggled herself free from the hole in the floor. She returned the grate and the rug to their rightful places at the monument's base when shouting echoed down the long hallway. She took off, the drawstring bag slapping against her back and her sneakers squeaking against the waxed floor. She didn't stop running, not as she wove her way past the chapels, sprinted past Michelangelo's Pieta, or busted through the basilica's front doors.

"Hey. Hey!" A Swiss Guard called after her before alerting the others with a wave of his hand.

Delia pushed her legs to move faster, the bag banging against every part of her body.

"Come on!" Delia heard Kazzy scream from the other side of the fountain. "Come on, Delia! Run!"

The guards were gaining on her. Twenty feet, ten feet, eight feet. She heaved a look over her shoulder in time to see one man swiping his meaty fingers toward her in an attempt to grasp one of the drawstring straps. She lunged forward, past the runes in the stone, where Cian finally reached her.

Delia felt Cian throw his arms around her waist before Delia flew through the air. It wasn't until she regained her sense of balance that she realized Cian had tossed her over his shoulder, easier than if she were a sack of potatoes. With preternatural speed, Kazzy led the way through the square, and the Swiss Guards left behind began to lag, their hands over their heads in disbelief.

THIRTY-THREE

DELIA

Delia had been back from St. Peter's Basilica for two hours. The drawstring bag sat untouched on the bed, each too nervous to open it. Delia stood guard near the drawn curtains, peeking through the gap toward Vatican City. There seemed to be no commotion coming from the top of the hill, though she had a distinct feeling that they were being hunted by the men and women moving swiftly past the hotel.

Kazzy finally stood from her seat next to Cian on the vinyl couch, quickly crossing the room. Delia watched as she reached down to grasp the drawstrings, hesitating momentarily with her fingers hovering above the bag before sighing and yanking the opening apart. The manila folder was bent at the bottom corners, courtesy of Delia's desperation to shove it in hastily.

"Care to share with the class?" Cian asked as they watched Kazzy scan the folder's contents. He had been incredibly cranky since returning to the hotel room, so Delia figured that every passing second they didn't find something useful was a waste of time for him.

Kazzy's brow furrowed as she held the paper out for Cian to take. "It's just an address. No name or anything else."

Delia kept her focus on Cian. His eyes widened with shock as he absentmindedly pinched his lower lip between his pointer finger and thumb. Finally, his gaze lifted and locked with Delia's. "It's your address."

Delia's mouth fell open, and she drew her head back. "My address?" She reached forward to take the folder from Cian's hands, swallowing back her nerves as she scanned the contents.

And there it was...the address to her apartment.

Her eyes slid up to Cian, a sinking cold settling in the pit of her stomach, but he had already pulled his cell phone from his pocket. Time seemed to slow as he punched a number into the dial pad on the screen.

"What are you doing? It's five in the morning," Kazzy said, sinking onto the edge of the mattress.

But Cian had already placed the phone on speaker. And the voice who answered gave Delia a shiver of disgust.

"Brother," the male voice said, a satisfied purr to his tone. "We have been getting into trouble, haven't we?"

"Jonas," Cian spat through gritted teeth, his lip curling into a sneer. "I'm surprised you answered your phone."

"Nothing much you can do to me when I'm halfway across the world with your potion," Jonas said, letting out a deep and gratifying sigh. "Though, I don't think I'll be taking it soon. I'm so enjoying the perks of stepping into Eligos's shoes." There was a throaty female moan in the background. "Such fun toys to play with."

A burning nausea crawled up Delia's throat, strong enough that a bitter tang coated her mouth. She managed to swallow it back.

"And I thought the plans went to the wayside when Greer killed Eligos," Cian went on.

Jonas's chuckle was muffled as though there were something in his mouth, and the throaty female let out a second moan of pleasure. "If you thought Eligos was the mastermind, you are not as bright as I once thought." There was a sharp intake of breath, a far cry from the moan a few seconds before. "Eligos was the puppet."

"Doesn't that make you the puppet now?" Delia asked, unable to keep the question to herself. Cian's eyes darted up, a warning flashing in their green depths.

An abrupt scream penetrated the space, followed by a snapping crack and a thud, as though something significant had fallen to the floor.

"That's too bad," Jonas said, his voice tight. Delia thought it sounded like he was struggling to temper his anger. "I was quite enjoying her."

Kazzy's open expression blanched, cringing away from the phone, her face a mask of repulsion.

"Where did the Paladin Society get Greer's address?" Cian asked, pushing through the sound of the woman's death. From his accusatory tone, Delia had the feeling he already knew.

"You're on the wrong side of the war, brother," Jonas pressed on, by-passing the question entirely. "With Eligos gone and out of the way, Leander has been able to revamp his plans. His pairing with the Paladin Society is nothing short of genius."

"Who is Leander?" Kazzy piped in, chewing on her lip in concentration.

Jonas went quiet for a long moment before responding. "Greer could only get us so far, Cian. Could only get *you* so far. The plans the Paladin Society has to close the portal to Samsara and to ensure that we have everything we need in this world....power, glory, dominance–"

"What are you on about?" Cian interjected as he ran a hand through his hair.

"There's only so much the Paladin Society can do for Leander," Jonas replied quietly, with a sinister edge. "The souls they harvest at their headquarters can fuel him for a short time." Kazzy and Cian snapped their stares over to Delia. "But when Leander gets a hold of Greer's magic and opens the tombs... it will be a whole new world for us. The rise of the daemons."

"Tombs? What tombs?" Delia asked, a hand covering her throat. The smell of freshly brewed coffee began to waft in from the hallway, a disjointed contrast to the conversation before her.

"Azazel is the key," Jonas said, almost reverently. "With the tombs opened and the bound free, we can work to restore the balance taken from us and given to the humans." His voice rose, becoming angrier with every word spoken. "The Paladin Society wants Samsara to be cut off, wants us to be–"

"They're lying to you," Delia snapped. "And if you truly believe that, then it's clear some type of sick, divine intervention kept you from being wiped off the planet centuries ago."

Jonas went quiet as Cian closed his eyes, his chin dipping to his chest.

"A word to the wise, Delia Savas," Jonas finally said, his voice no more than a dangerous whisper. "The next time you search for the largest, most well-reaching society that has ever been, I urge you not to use your full name to register for a tour. Especially if you go charging into the headquarters without disguise and use your blood to open a file. It won't be long before the Paladin Society sniffs out your connection to the Mage. Greer can't stay hidden forever."

With that, the line disconnected.

Cian threw his phone so hard that it cracked against the wall, denting the material under the wallpaper. The phone slid to the floor, lying still against the baseboards. Delia saw the shattered glass front, the screen spiderwebbed and flickering.

"Calm down, Cian," Kazzy warned, her fingernails sharpening to claws.

Cian was struggling to contain his anger, and Delia felt frozen to the bed as she watched his fangs punch through his gums, hearing the rage-filled snarl that sunk into her flesh.

"We have to go find them," Cian finally said, his desperate gaze flicking between Kazzy and Delia. "We need to track down the upper leaders of the Paladin Society tonight. We have to kill them before this plan goes into action."

Delia went rigid, pressing her lips into a fine line. "We have no information about them. We don't know the names of the leaders, we don't know where to find them—"

"We do know where to find them," Cian interrupted. "You just broke into their headquarters. They are all in there. This is our chance. We need to go back."

Delia went quiet, but Kazzy spoke up. "How do you expect us to get in there?" she asked, twirling her blonde ponytail around her fingers. "You and I don't have access to the basilica, and we can't send Delia alone. She'll be killed on sight."

Cian was pacing the hotel room floor, a finger tracing his lower lip. "Then we wait outside of the runes. We wait for them to come to us."

"And, what, murder them in cold blood in the middle of the square?" Delia asked incredulously, the sudden flare of adrenaline forcing her to stand. Her hands were at her sides, splayed out in disagreement. "We still don't know who they are. We could kill an innocent person by accident. It's too risky. We need to go back home and—"

"And what?" Cian shouted, rounding on Delia. "Sit in your not-so-safe apartment making plans like we did with Greer for the last few months?" He paused to scoff. "That's what got us into trouble the first time. We need to act now."

Delia bristled but ignored the digging insult. "We need more information. We don't know what this Leander is willing to do, and from the sounds of it, Greer is hidden away...for now. If we figure out how to end the Paladin Society, truly end them, then we can cut Jonas off at the source."

Cian snarled. "If you hadn't made such a fucking mess going in there, we could have sent you back to get more material."

Kazzy took a few steps forward, readying to place herself between Cian and Delia, but Delia didn't back down. "We all knew the possibilities of what could happen when I went in. We were prepared for it," she said slowly in an attempt to reason with him. "Greer would not want us killing people on her behalf."

"Screw what Greer wants," Cian growled. "She doesn't know what she wants."

Delia took a deep breath to calm herself, though her blood roiled with rage. "We need a plan to take down the Paladin Society and make sure we don't lead them straight to Greer. This is bigger than we thought it was going to be. We can't react off the cuff."

Cian punched the desk, the wood splintering under his fist. "We need to take down Paladin now while they are still looking for us. They are distracted, which makes them vulnerable. And we need to get them before they have a chance to get to Greer—"

"You are not her knight in shining armor," Delia flung at him, her voice rising as her patience waned. "She does not need you to step in and save her. She needs information, the same information we need. And we need others to help us with this. We're in over our heads."

"Greer took months to act." Cian took a step forward, but Delia continued to hold her ground. "And I'm not going to stand around and wait for you to pick through everything."

"You don't know Greer as well as you think," Delia gritted through clenched teeth. Her hands had balled into fists, fingernails biting against the palms of her hands.

Cian let out a humorless laugh. "I think I know Greer pretty well at this point. Even more than you claim to. Remember, she came to me instead of you for help."

That reminder broke Delia, shattered her into a thousand pieces. She had been the person Greer went to for the last ten years. She had been the one that Greer laughed with, cried with, and celebrated with. And it hurt more than anything to be reminded that her best friend had gone to this animal instead of her.

"If you know her as much as you think you do," Delia started, a tremble shaking her voice. "Then you would know she will never love you, not after what you did to her. Not in a million fucking years." She paused to take another breath, the adrenaline tightening her chest. "So you can go after the Paladin Society. Hell, you could even kill the leader of it all yourself. But she is never going to want you back."

The vampyre's eyes darkened with anger. "If you think that, you should know the truth, too. Your beloved best friend is the reason your wife is dead. Greer is the one who summoned Eligos. Greer is the one who didn't do the spell to contain him correctly. Greer is the one who brought Eligos to your doorstep."

Kazzy's lips parted in disbelief, her stare fixing on Delia.

"You're lying," Delia said softly, shaking her head.

"No, I'm not." Cian's voice was dangerously calm. "Why do you think she told you that she fucked up? It wasn't because Eligos happened to cross her path. Your kidnapping, your wife's death...I made my choice, but Greer made hers too."

Delia stepped back as though Cian had physically smacked her. She wrestled with her mind, pulling back the memories of Greer sobbing over Paige's body. Her apologies and how she kept repeating how sorry she was. It didn't make any sense to Delia at the time, but it made sense now. Her heart broke open, the fractures in her chest welling with sadness and grief as she stared hopelessly between Kazzy and Cian, lost and tragically helpless.

"Delia," Cian started softly, the anger ebbing away from his voice. He reached out to touch her, but his arm was ripped away.

Kazzy's tight grasp was clamped around his forearm, her claws snagging against the sleeves of his jacket. The fabric split, three thin lines cutting into it. "You've done enough."

Cian shook his head and pressed his lips together. Turning on the heels of his feet, he stalked across the hotel room and threw open the door. He was over the threshold in the next beat and didn't bother to slow the door as it slammed shut behind him. Delia grimaced with the sound.

"Del—are you okay?"

Delia wrapped her arms around her chest. She had shuttered her wailing grief into a whisper, boxing it up and stuffing it to the depths of her soul, throwing herself deeper into Paladin as a distraction. And now it was free—screaming and thrashing and biting. And loud, it was oh so loud. The hole she had managed to patch had been ripped back open, tearing pieces of flesh with it.

It was raw, and Delia was ruined.

Her eyes snapped over to Kazzy, who had lifted her head toward the curtained window with the intense stare of a predator on the hunt. With an involuntary pull, Delia imagined her as a giant, gray wolf, her snout working in the air, pointed ears flicking against the early morning sounds of the city. Something had gotten the wolf's attention, and Delia felt it wasn't good.

Kazzy crossed the room in a series of light-footed steps, stopping at the window to peek through the slit in the curtains. Delia watched as the soft glow of the navy and orange sky clashed against her blonde locks. Kazzy's eyes ran along the cobblestone street, the streetlamps glaring against the water puddles of the late-autumn rain.

"Oh, shit."

Suddenly, Kazzy yanked the curtains shut, holding them tightly closed with her fingers. Her knuckles turned white under the pressure. Her eyes darted up to meet Delia's, and urgency coursed through Delia like a poison.

"It's Cian."

Delia was next to Kazzy in the next breath, prying the curtain apart once more. She spotted Cian pacing in front of the hotel, his chin dipped toward the rain-slicked stones of the walkway. Small puffs of air rolled from his lips like a misty fog.

He hadn't seen the three guards who locked in on him, one gesturing faintly toward him and another taking a pair of black stone cuffs from the pocket of his blue pants. While the uniform was similar to that of the Swiss Guard, from Delia's vantage point above them, she noticed slim, silver bands circling the upper arms of their sleeves. Each was etched with thin sigils similar to those found at the basilica.

Delia lifted her fist to pound on the glass, but Kazzy quickly pinned her arms to her sides. "We cannot let them know we are up here,"

Kazzy whispered, her breath skittering against Delia's neck. "There is too much at stake."

Delia watched as the guard clamped a cuff around the wrist of an unsuspecting Cian, clearly still lost in his thoughts. His strength seemingly ebbed from him enough that the third guard was able to inject him in the arm with a clear liquid retrieved from the inside of his jacket. Cian collapsed to the ground, weakly lifting his hand in a poor attempt to push them away.

"How did they know he was a daemon?" Delia asked, her vision clouding with the lightheadedness that overtook her. "How did they know who to take?"

"He was recognized," Kazzy answered, and Delia felt a shiver go up Kazzy's arms. "They saw him at the basilica."

The guards grasped Cian under the shoulders and lifted him to his feet. His head circled limply as his chin grazed his chest. In the next breath, they moved, Cian's feet dragging against the stone behind him. He was carted into the shadows of the surrounding hotels. Then he was gone.

THIRTY-FOUR

Odette

The ship dipped and swayed as Renan and Odette stared at one another, daggers still in hand. The head continued to roll along the wooden floor of the cargo hold, grotesquely bumping into crates and barrels as it went. Blood dripped steadily from the severed neck, puddling under the planks of the stairs. Small rivers ran from it with each crashing wave that hit the ship's hull, as though the puddle were a sea of its own.

"You have something I am very interested in obtaining," Renan went on, carefully stepping over the body as he descended the stairs. "I need those letters."

The bustle of the fae readying the ship still sounded above them, footsteps echoing through the cargo hold. From the sound of wood scraping against wood, it seemed like the ramp bridging the vessel to the dock had been pulled.

Odette tightened her grip on the parchment, feeling the sharp edges pinch against the inside of her palm. "I think we should have a discussion first because these and what they contain are very important to me."

The bulkheads creaked as the ship dipped again, the ropes straining against the weight of the barrels. Shouts reverberated through the hold as the magic thrummed around Odette, gaining momentum to power the crew forward.

"We're running out of time," Renan said through gritted teeth. He held out his hand, palm facing upward. "I need those letters. Luisa, she–" The ship pushed away from the dock, and Odette could feel the water churning beneath her feet. "Adair cannot get his hands on those. Please."

Odette wasn't sure what it was— perhaps the pleading look in his eye or the desperation hovering over his face like a mask. She remembered the first night she met Luisa, seeing Renan whisper something in her ear. How he seemed to watch Luisa with the apt attention of an older brother. She ripped the letter down the middle, handing him half. "Now we have no choice but to trust one another."

Renan took a deep breath as the crew above them loosed the sails. The ship bound forward, rocking Odette back as it took to the sea. "We have to go now," Renan said, holding his hand for Odette to grab onto. "You take to the sky, I'll take to the sea. We'll meet in the jungle just beyond the beach." Odette hesitated enough that he pressed on. "Like you said, we have no choice but to trust one another now."

Odette lurched forward and stepped over the pool of blood, shouldering past Renan before clambering up the rickety, wooden stairs. She peered out from the cargo hold door, locks of hair whipping in the wind created by the lower fae from her court. Hoisting herself onto the deck, Odette sidled to the port side of the ship, where a handful of Court of Cedar and Sand fae were busy hauling the massive braided ropes back into the ship.

Before she could think, Odette leaped from the side of the ship, and to avoid being spotted too soon, she didn't allow her wings to catch until she was nearly at the surface of the waves. She banked to the stern, the leathery flesh flapping against the phantom jungle wind. She didn't bother to see if Renan had followed.

As instructed, she headed toward the jungle just off the beach. She soared upward to the canopy, landing deftly on the thick branches. She crouched against the trunk and rested a hand to brace herself, twisting toward the sea to scan the beach for any signs of Renan.

And it wasn't until she caught sight of him amongst the foaming waves crashing against the sand that she finally breathed a sigh of relief. She watched him for a long minute, his figure silhouetted against the bright moonlight to ensure he hadn't been followed. When she saw him look toward the skies for her, she hopped from the tree and glided toward him, landing on soft feet at the top of the small dune he had been scaling.

Renan stopped in his tracks, foot sliding against the loose sand, as he looked up at her. The dagger was still clutched in his hand, though the sea had washed any blood from the blade, and Odette was pleased to notice he had used his water magic to protect the other half of the letter from getting wet.

"Explain," Odette said shortly, adjusting the hilt of her dagger in her hand. "Quickly."

Renan shook his head, flecks of water shooting out from the locks plastered to the side of his head. "You first."

Odette launched herself toward him, digging the point of her blade into the column of his throat. "I am stronger, faster, and much older, Renan," she said softly, a threat of violence cresting her tone. "If you don't wish to have your head parted from your body, as the unfortunate man from just minutes ago did, I would rethink your choice of words."

Blood trickled down Renan's neck, eyes flashing with anger, but he began nonetheless. "I heard Kaique speaking to another guard member, asking him to send a message to Adair. I'm sure it's the same message Luisa heard and gave to you." Water dripped from his hairline, following the curve of his nose. "I followed him last night and watched him tuck the letter into a rice crate. I knew it was essential that Adair did not receive that message—"

"Why?" Odette interrupted sharply, still keeping the pressure of her blade upon his neck.

"Kaique killed my husband when he took over, and I've been forced to head the guards ever since. If Adair raided these lands looking for you, the humans would never have a chance to escape. Luisa, she would never—" He paused to let the dagger drop from his hand, which landed in a thud against the sand. "She's been a good friend since she's been here. I don't want to see another person I love murdered in cold blood or otherwise by the Fae King's armies."

Odette's heart clenched as though someone were tightly squeezing it.

"I've protected her as much as I could since she's been with Kaique, though there isn't much I could do without giving away my position." Sensing there was no need to keep the threat up, Odette released the blade and took a step back from him as he kept talking. "She's the one who approached me two years ago about starting this network to help the humans and half-fae escape. She would— she kept Kaique entertained during the solstices and equinoxes so he wouldn't be tempted to leave while I smuggled them from the courts."

Odette ran a hand over her brow, wiping away the salty sea breeze that caught in her hair. "Did you say helping half-fae escape?"

Renan nodded. "There are human slaves in two of the four courts. Here, as well as Storm and Wind. The other two courts have helped us form an underground passage of sorts, smuggling children out of the realm before they are found. I have a contact on the outside, a half-fae by the name of Nerea–"

"Nerea?" Odette said, her eyes darting upward to catch his stare once more. "What does Nerea have to do with this?"

"How do you know Nerea?" Renan asked, his gaze narrowing in suspicion. "I was under the assumption that she knew of no one from the courts."

A look of angered disgust crossed Odette's face, though she managed to temper the yell that threatened to burst from her. "Nerea hid me when I escaped from Adair over two hundred years ago." Renan's eyes widened in shock. "And she certainly never told me she had contact with the courts. Wait, so that means...if she has had contact with you this entire time, that would mean she already knew...How long has she known of her father's death?"

Renan swallowed. "I can't be sure. I was tasked with cleaning Kaique's father's quarters after his death, and that's when I came across Nerea and her father's correspondence. Quenti saved them in a bundle that he stored in a secret compartment of his desk. I was able to work out everything for myself after reading them. Following Luisa's idea two years ago, I reached out to her, and about a year ago, she began to meet me at the rift every season change. We've been able to smuggle twelve half-fae children and twenty humans since then."

Odette was sure she would snap Nerea's neck the next time she saw the woman. She slipped her fingers into the side of the envelope and retrieved the half letter. Unfolding it, she scanned the note, taking in the words she knew were already in there, but made her stomach sink nonetheless.

"You can take this," she said to Renan, holding it out for him. "I don't need the entire letter to understand what it says. The humans are planning a coup. Some of the lower court is involved due to information given to Kaique through a guard involved in the training." Odette took a moment to sheath her dagger. "Additionally, he is holding me in the Court of Mist and Tide until Adair can gather the army to come and secure me."

Renan lifted each side, comparing them together. "Do you know who your traitor is?" he asked, folding each half of the letter before handing one back to Odette.

"No," she replied with a shake of her head. "But if you know who the guard who met with Kaique is, I would be happy to take care of them for both of us."

Renan shifted on his feet, his heels sliding further down the dune. "I'm sure I can find out. How would we explain his disappearance without giving our side away?"

Odette slid her gaze toward the sea, where the moon reflected like a brilliant orb from the lapping waves. The ship had turned north, heading up the coast to make its first stop. At some point, if it hadn't happened already, the crew would discover the body of the sailor in the cargo hold. And someone would be sent overboard for it.

"We can have another ally send word that he went to a village to visit family, though it may only be a temporary fix if his body washes up on shore or is stumbled upon in the jungle." Odette tapped her fingernails against the leather sheath strapped to her waist. "We need more weapons, and we need to distribute them to the humans as stealthy as possible so they can be ready when the solstice arrives."

Renan nodded his head, taking a tentative step forward. "I know the guards involved in the network. They assist me in smuggling the humans and half-fae out when the rift is open. Some are participating in your meetings. Others work to distract the guards loyal to Kaique." He paused to look at Odette, their eyes locking together. "I can shuffle the guard duties so the guards involved with us can distribute weapons, and the humans can safely store them in their barracks." He swept a hand through his hair, pushing the locks behind his ears. "I just wish we had more time to contact the other courts. They have been ostracized since refusing to name Adair as their king."

There was a long pause as Odette weighed her thoughts. It was foolish of her to come here without realizing how much the courts had changed in the two hundred years she had been gone. It was equally as foolish for Nerea to send her here under the guise of a lie, no matter how badly Nerea wanted Odette to see how far her kingdom had fallen. On the other hand, having Renan would be highly advantageous to her efforts. She decided, once and for all, the risk was worth the reward. "Is there a way to get a message to someone outside the fae realm?"

"Outside the fae realm?" Renan reiterated, taking in a deep breath through his nostrils. "Not to the human realm. At least, not before the rift opens."

Odette bit the inside of her lip. "What if that person wasn't in the human realm? What if it was a primordial and they were in Samsara?"

Renan's brow pulled together. "Samsara? Who would you want to send a message to in Samsara?" He shook his head. "Even if that were possible and the primordials weren't just stories our parents tell us as children—"

"It's not a guarantee to work—" Odette interrupted. Suddenly, they heard footsteps of people approaching and hurried to tuck into the shadows of the underbrush. They paused, wondering if they had been caught, but saw guards none the wiser heading toward the docks. Being pressed for time, Odette hoped the waves against the beach were loud enough to drown their conversation. "And I'm not sure she is there, but I worked with the Mage a few months ago in the human realm. She disappeared suddenly—into thin air."

"The Mage," Renan repeated softly, his eyes hungrily studying Odette's face. "She– she's alive? After Agnes, I thought...who else knows about her? Kaique, he never..." He looked at Odette as if she made the sun rise every morning and set every night. "This changes everything."

Odette leaned a shoulder against the trunk of a canopy tree, the tips of her wings twitching in irritation. "This changes nothing until we figure out how to send a message to Samsara." She ran her finger along the pommel of her blade. "The primordials are real, Renan. Greer— the Mage— is half. I've known for some time. Other than you and Luisa, only a few know of her existence."

"What is she waiting for then?" Renan asked. "She must know about these slaves. Agnes knew. She forbade Adair from allowing slavery, or she would withhold her magic from the fae." He traced his lower lip with his finger. "How can she keep the humans like this?"

"She doesn't know," Odette said, flicking a bug from the front of her tunic. "She only found out about her powers weeks before she was taken. Agnes and I had a complicated relationship, but...Greer is a good person. She'll do what's right."

Renan blew out a breath. "Kaique's father forbade it, you know. After Agnes died, Adair allowed it once again. Quenti thought it was in bad form." He chuckled, the rumble deep in his chest. "If only he could see it now. It wasn't until Kaique became the Lord of Mist and Tide that the humans were dragged here."

Odette watched Renan flex his forearms as he toyed with the end of his tunic, feeling the sea breeze as a cool mist on her cheeks. "You've gotten humans out of this court before," she finally said. He lifted his gaze toward her. "How do you think we should do it this time?"

"I've only been able to pass through handfuls of humans at a time. To get all of the humans out of the palace, through the villages, and to the rift before it closes...it won't be easy. That doesn't even count the lower court members who want to come. And we have to anticipate the fight with either Kaique or Adair as well."

Odette went silent, listening to the seagrass swaying and the monkeys calling as they began to wake for the day. "You don't think everyone will make it out." It wasn't a question.

"I don't think everyone will make it out alive. Our best thought is how can we get as many people out as possible."

Odette took in a deep breath and let it out slowly. The sky was beginning to lighten where the horizon touched the sea. The inky black had begun to shift into a deep purple streaked upward toward the white clouds reflecting off the water. "I think the better question is: how do we change the Court of Mist and Tide so that those left behind aren't subjected to Kaique until we can return?"

Renan tilted his head. "What are you thinking?" When she hesitated in her answer, he went on. "You plan on killing him?"

Odette grasped the hilt of her dagger, unsheathing it once more. She watched as the blinking stars and the last remnants of the full moon glinted off the blade. "Tradition dictates that whoever kills the seated Lord becomes the new one. If I kill Kaique and become Lady of Mist and Tide, I can personally see to it that the humans and fae will live comfortably until they can leave. At least, if they choose to."

The corner of Renan's mouth curved as his lips split into a half-smile. "There has never been a Lady of any court in the history of the fae, even now."

She lifted her eyes from the blade. "You males have fucked things up for far too long now. I believe it's time to change the guard if you will."

His half-smile turned into a wide grin as he placed his hand on his chest and bent his head toward her. "Then tell me what you need me to do, my Lady."

THIRTY-FIVE

GREER

Samael led Greer past the tombs and to the outskirts of town, where tall reeds bent under the weight of small twittering birds. The walk was long and slow, and they spent most of it in silence, but the rushing of water over stone perked Greer's attention.

It was peaceful. Red and beige sandstone, wind-shaped and smooth, lined the river. The hollow shafts of grass growing on the bank dipped under the hem of Greer's dress, scraping at her calves. Samael parted the reeds to let her through, and Greer stepped onto the bank, her sandals sinking into the wet sand.

Samael bent down to place his fingertips into the water, and Greer released a soft gasp as glowing orbs rose to the surface. Each was haloed in a refracted rainbow, the dazzling white light so bright that Greer needed to shield her eyes.

"The Meridian of Greed is where the souls come to reflect on the meaning of their life," Samael said, gesturing Greer forward. She hiked up her dress before kneeling next to him. "This river is one of peace, happiness, and discovery. It signifies that they are halfway through their journey. Many souls don't make it through the channel, as the in-between of Indolence and Greed produces the most devils. But if they can make it here–"

Samael paused as a basket floating atop the surface bobbed in the eddies and scraped over the stones. Greer tilted her head to get a closer look at it, seeing the inside was filled to the brim with beaded and copper jewelry, clay pottery, and the jagged tip of a spear carved from granite.

"Items for their journey," Samael pressed on, answering the un-spoken question that Greer had begun to pose. "Many people here believe that supplying the souls in preparation for the latter half of their journey will give them a better chance to climb out of the final river whole."

"Why?" Greer asked, dipping her fingers into the river. The water was cool, and when a soul brushed against her skin, she felt a swelling of emotion in her chest. "Why make humans do all of this work?"

"Azazel believed, as did most of the Primordials that lead the Fallen, that humans were meant to learn to be good. But they needed to be given more time. Souls I select for Elysia go to that realm, but those I select to come here are placed in the first river in the Meridian of Envy to reckon with their lives. Some rivers will be easier than others. Most won't make it through all seven."

"If they refuse to reckon or climb from the river and come out as a devil," Greer began, retracting her hand from the water and wiping the droplets on the fabric of her dress. "And they die again. Do they have the chance to retry the reckoning?"

Samael shook his head, lips pressed into a tight line.

"Where do they go then? When they die for the second time?"

Samael stood from his kneel. "They become the sand, the flowers, the dust on the streets. They cease to exist, becoming nothing and returning to everything. No conscience, no sentient life. Making up each particle of the universe."

Greer shivered, straightening her legs to a stand and allowing her dress to fall back into place. She was quiet for a moment, listening to the water crash over the rocks and the splashing of souls as they breached the surface like shark fins. She allowed the scent of fresh wildflowers and wet sand to take over, briefly wondering who those wildflowers and wet sand used to be. She closed her eyes to enjoy the simplicity of that minute.

When warm lips brushed against her own, calloused fingers gently holding her chin, Greer cracked her eyes open. Samael was there, the sun brazen and strong just over his shoulder. It illuminated the tips of his wings in a golden bath, peeking between the breaks in the feathers.

She didn't know where he ended, and she started, but Greer allowed herself to fall into him. His breath hitched in his throat when she finally pulled away, turning back to watch an insect buzz across the tops of the reeds.

"What about Elysia?" Greer asked. "What happens when the souls go there?"

Samael lowered his hand from her chin, letting it rest in the crook of her neck. "Under the ruse of paradise, Michael began to harvest souls." He ran a hand over his hair. "Mortal souls are pure energy and, despite him being one of the most powerful beings in the universe, he refused to give any of his power to his children—"

"There are more of me?" Excitement and hope ballooned within her. "Why didn't Azazel tell me?"

Samael blew out a breath. "Are there more of you? Yes and no." He paused to scrub his hand over the beard that had grown in the three days he had been unconscious. "Michael had two children. Darya was first, and her mother was Michael's mate. She was presumed killed in battle during the War of the Sixteen. Darya was Michael's pride and joy. He transferred ten percent of his power to her at birth and was never the same after her death."

"And the second?" Greer pressed.

"The second is Leander. Michael wanted an heir, and he—" Samael's brow furrowed. "Well, let's just say he wanted an heir. Leander was born nearly a thousand years ago to a Greek woman, and his wings ripped her apart during childbirth."

Greer cringed, crossing her arms over her chest. "And where is Leander, then?"

"It's been a long time since I've paid Leander attention." His tone was clipped, signaling the end of his interest in Michael's son.

Greer chewed on the inside of her lip. "What happened to Paige?" The words were out before she realized she had spoken them. She had been wondering for a long time but was too scared to ask. She wasn't sure, now that the question had been posed, that she really wanted to know.

Gesturing toward the river, Samael answered, "In the river. I sensed you— Azazel and I sensed you when you broke through the obsidian in your bones. When we finally located you and found your friend, I had already marked her dying soul for Elysia. But—"

Greer stared expectantly at him, waiting for him to continue.

He did with a sigh. "Azazel couldn't bear the thought of his daughter losing her best friend to Michael, so we stole her."

"You stole— Samael, if she's in the river, then that means she could end up like one of those...those things." Greer blanched at the thought, gaping in disbelief.

"It means she has a chance to live," Samael reminded her gently. "She would have had no chance if she went to Elysia. Her soul would have been consumed." He paused to study her before adding. "Your friend was a good person. Fate had it marked on her soul. She will make her way through the rivers. Have faith in her."

Greer swallowed thickly, wiping away the tears that pricked the corners of her eyes. "Did Holly make it through the rivers?"

A frog plunked into the river, breaking the new silence between them.

Samael sighed again, rubbing his brow with the tips of his fingers. "Holly was gone before I got there to bring her soul here. Azazel has been looking for her for twenty-six years. We assume that Elysia took her, but that means..."

"That means she's gone." Greer was quiet for a moment, watching the golden-hued horizon as the sun tipped over the top of the palm trees. "And that'll happen to me if Michael finds me?" When Samael didn't respond, she went on, "Mammon talked about a prophecy written in the tombs. Of someone ending the world as we know it. What do you think about that?" She carefully studied his expressions, assessing for any change.

But Samael just shrugged, a frown pulling on his mouth. "I think it's nothing more than rumors for bored, immortal beings to focus on."

Greer couldn't help the disappointment that flooded her.

Done with the topic, Samael grabbed her hand and said, "The Meridian of Greed has some of the best food in Samsara. Why don't we head back? I'm sure Mammon will go all out tonight since I told Na'amah we would move on soon."

Greer agreed, but uncertainty stirred in her gut. After hearing about both the prophecy and Leander, and more specifically, Samael's resistant efforts when she brought them up, she had more questions than answers. If she had planned on spending more time in Samsara, she figured she would have put more energy into finding out, but she had to keep her focus on the task at hand, which was going home.

Regardless, Greer tucked the topics into the back of her mind and followed Samael back through the reeds. With his limp, it would take them enough time to get back to the palace, and she had a feeling he was right about one thing...she was sure Mammon would know how to throw a party.

Greer was right.

The party had started by the time they entered the palace grounds, Samael hobbling as his strength waned with every final step. The garden had been transformed into a desert oasis of lithe acrobats, twisting and contorting on the stone pillars that had appeared in the fountained pool. Fragrant wreaths of sweetly scented flowers crowded the overflowing table of meat pies and fruit while a thrumming beat of drums and lutes echoed in the background. Painted faces turned to stare, taking in their arrival with peaked interest.

Serket parted the sea of people in brightly colored dresses and robes of chiffon, silk, and satin as she approached them. "Finally, you arrive." Eyes heavily lined with kohl and golden beads tied into locks of her hair, Serket swept Greer away from Samael before Greer could object.

Greer glanced over her shoulder toward Samael, but he had already been absorbed by the crowd collapsing into place.

"You must dress. That one is far too filthy for such an occasion." Serket's voice was barely audible over the low-hummed chatter and clinking of silver goblets filled with ale. "I have just the one."

"What occasion?" Greer asked as Serket snaked their arms together, though Greer already had a clue.

Laughter skittered across the surface of the pool, and despite the setting sun, lit torches illuminated the garden in orange.

"The princess's return to Samsara, of course. It's been long awaited by our people."

Greer's heart sank as she took in Serket's playful gaze. "Serket, I'm—"

A roar of excitement interrupted her, and Greer turned toward what had drawn the crowd's attention. Mammon had risen from the dais, where perched atop was a sandstone throne lined with thick strands of braided gold and amazonite gemstones, matching the hilt of his dagger. His smile was wide and genuine, dimples forming in the corners of his young face.

Mammon held up a hand, and silence fell.

"My sisters and brothers," he started, sweeping his gaze over the party. "Souls of the fae, of the wolf shifters. We're all gathered here to celebrate the return of the heir. To celebrate her–"

A piercing scream echoed across the pool, and Greer snapped her head toward the source of the noise. The cry for help had ended abruptly, leaving only ripples in the water and a wet stain darkening the stone perimeter. *Is that blood?* Greer wondered in horror. A nervous quiet settled over the crowd. Onlookers peered into the water, brows furrowed, and necks craned.

Greer's eyes widened, and she watched, seemingly in slow motion, as a scaled-back breached the pool's surface. And, when she sent a look of confusion toward Serket, Greer was alarmed to see that the primordial's terrified stare was fixed on the water.

Before Greer could take her next breath, the head of a crocodile launched out of the pool, jaws open and sharp teeth gleaming, and locked its bite around a male partygoer. The male let out a strangled cry, thick rivulets of blood draining onto the sandstone before he was pulled under the water. He did not resurface.

Panic surged through the crowd as people attempted to scamper from the poolside, stomping on freshly manicured flowers and greenery lining the paths. Screams erupted as three more creatures slunk from the water, golden-fur claws slapping against the stone. Greer was frozen in place, jolting back and forth as she was shoved out of the way of fleeing patrons. She tried to discern what was in front of her.

The head of the creature nearest her was a crocodile, or at the very least, as close to a crocodile as it could be. A seemingly wicked smile formed, showing off rows of curved teeth lining the jaw's top and bottom. Black eyes, the torches' reflection glittering in their depths, anchored onto the jostling citizens. The front legs were that of a lion, retractable claws swiping and thrashing at those who had collapsed, injured, on the garden floor. However, the back half of the creature was the barrel-shaped and smooth-skinned backside of a hippopotamus.

"Guards!" Mammon cried out, whirling toward his throne and grasping a bronze-tipped javelin, the metal blades constructed in the shape of a diamond. Aiming, he launched the javelin like a missile over the pool's surface. It spiraled as it arced through the air before piercing one of the creatures through the middle of its eye, pinning it to the garden bed.

A dozen primordial guards, each clad in fighting leathers and sporting sickle-shaped swords, appeared out of the shadows of the palace. They parted the frenzied crowd, stepping over the injured and dead to bring down their weapons on the creatures with devastating effect.

Serket was tugging at Greer's arm, hand wrapped around the wrist, to pull her back into the confines of the palace. But Greer's horrified stare was glued to the other side of the pool, where a sobbing child had been separated from her parents in the chaos.

And a fourth creature had lumbered from the water, ambling toward her.

Greer ripped away from Serket and hiked up the skirt of her dress as she bounded down the stairs. Serket's shouts were lost as soon as Greer entered the fray. Blood pooled in the cracks of the sandstone, and smoke spiraled from the downed torch that had engulfed the dry foliage in flame. Three soldiers had taken on one of the creatures, each dancing around the sharp teeth and claws. Despite its size and stature, the creature easily evaded each cut of the swords.

A series of screeches filled the air above her head, and when Greer glanced up, she ducked in time to avoid a giant, swooping bird. She hit the garden floor, knees cracking painfully against the stone, as she covered the back of her head with her hands. Talons scraped against her arms, deeply shredding her skin, before banking toward the water and aiming for the performers still stuck on the stone pillars.

Peering up, Greer caught sight of the red-feathered bird with wings made of orange flames, embers flowing behind it like a jetstream as it crossed the dark sky. She watched as Samael rocketed into the air, catching the bird by the neck with his bare hands and snapping its bones with a twist of his wrist. He let the bird go, and it crashed into the pool's water, waves cresting and lapping against the stone pillars.

Ignoring her knees, still numb and knocking from her fall, Greer pushed herself to stand and lurched toward the child, still sobbing in the corner of the garden. She leaped over a small bush, sandals sliding against the graveled soil, before scooping the child into her arms and darting toward the palace once more.

The child threw her arms around Greer's neck, her sharp screams piercing the short space between them. A second bird swooped toward them, banking through the swirling smoke, and Greer shot out a hand, letting a desperate and unsteady jet of energy fly from her. The power hit the bird square in the chest, falling into a spined cactus and impaling on the long barbs encompassing the plant's flesh.

"Greer! *Greer*!"

Serket was calling for her, bent over a guard who was bleeding profusely from a cut in his belly. As Greer ran for Serket, the child still wrapped in her arms, she had to swallow back the bile that rose in her throat.

The guard didn't just have a cut. His abdomen had been torn open. His intestines splayed onto the stone beneath him, and a stream of blood was spurting from a lacerated artery, forming a puddle in his crushed groin. Serket was busy stuffing the loose intestines into the open cavity, using her power to heal the femur bone jutting from his leg. The guard's skin was pale and ashen, drained from the fluid he had lost in the attack.

"We have to get him to the palace," Serket said as Greer arrived, covering the crying child's face to hide her from the sight. The front of her silk dress was stained red, her hands and arms streaked with blood. "Please."

Not having any other choice, Greer whispered to the child to close her eyes, shifted her onto her hip, and bent down to snake her free arm around the guard's shoulder. He let out a groan of pain as they began to drag him toward the steps that led to the palace, a long streak of blood following them. She had just enough time to wonder how they would tug him up the stairs when Samael dropped in front of them. He said nothing as he bent down and hauled the guard into his arms.

"Go up the stairs. Now," Samael grunted, straining under the weight of the guard.

"Samael, your power," Greer started, but she was ushered forward by Serket, who had planted a firm hand on her lower back.

The screams had quieted as the guards finished off the last of the crocodile creatures, and before Greer entered through the set of main doors still ajar at the top of the steps, she saw Mammon bank across the dark blanket of sky. A sickle-shaped sword was clutched in his hand, blood dripping from the blade and landing in splatters on the stone below.

"What were those?" Greer asked, her voice strong despite the deeply shaken nerves that pulled at her soul. "What the fuck were those?"

"Ammits and bennus," Mammon answered as he landed between Greer and Serket, having entered over the walls of the open-air courtyard they had taken shelter in. "They are creatures native to this land. Not devils." He added the last statement to clarify as Greer opened her mouth.

A woman pacing the courtyard and wringing her hands let out a cry of relief, her arms held out for the child as she approached. The child began to cry again as she wriggled from Greer's arms, lumbering into her mother's grip with red-rimmed eyes and chest-deep hiccups.

"Thank you," the woman murmured, squeezing Greer's forearm with gratitude and dipping her head respectfully. "Thank you, my daughter, thank you."

"The better question," Samael said through gritted teeth, placing the guard on the tiled floor as Serket rearranged his intestines once again. "Is what they were doing outside of your control?"

Greer glanced between Samael and Mammon, sensing the rising tension between the two primordials.

"The end begins with an uprising," Mammon responded, and Greer recognized it as the beginning of the prophecy etched into the columns of the tomb. "On the wings of those who had been sleeping."

Samael's jaw clenched tightly. "Or maybe your power over this land and its inhabitants is waning, Mammon."

Mammon's eyes darkened as he growled, "Careful, Samael. You are bound. It is you with waning power."

"Enough from you. Both of you," Serket cut in, her eyes darting between the two males staring menacingly at one another.

"The prophecy has come to life, Samael," Mammon said quietly, ignoring Serket's warning. "It is within your best interest to learn what comes from it."

Greer didn't miss Mammon's subtle glance in her direction.

"The prophecy is nothing save for the musings of three women stuck in the woods for the rest of their immortal lives."

Greer felt her heart jolt in her chest, tugging forward like someone had grasped it and pulled. The flush crept up her neck as she studied Samael, and his unwavering stare was still set on Mammon. So he had known what she was talking about when they were at the bank of the river. Betrayal twisted, small and powerful, in her gut.

"What we need to focus on now," Serket began again, wiping the blood from her hands and onto the front of her dress, "is burying the dead." She paused to turn toward Mammon. "The men and women of this city are going to demand answers. It's been thousands of years since we've seen such destruction."

Mammon slid his eyes toward Serket, and they softened as soon as they connected with her own. "You're right, my love. Our focus should be on those we have lost tonight." He placed a hand on the back of her head, pulling her in to kiss her fiercely on her temple. "We'll plan a celebration of life. Of their return to the universe."

"Greer and I will be leaving tomorrow," Samael interjected. "We must continue onto the Meridian of Pride for Greer's return to Gaian."

Serket's head snapped toward Samael. "Gaian?" she asked, her brow knitting together in confusion. "What would bring you to return to Gaian?"

"It's my home, Serket," Greer answered quietly. "I don't belong here."

Serket's confusion crumpled into devastation as she returned her attention to Samael. "But, the bond. Your—"

"Serket," Samael warned, a stamping of finalization to his tone. "Enough. It is her choice to leave, and I am respecting it."

Serket clamped her lips with a soft shake of her head before weaving through the crowd of injured to find the most critical lined at the courtyard wall. Greer narrowed her eyes at Samael, who passed her by without a second glance.

Greer was in her bedchambers, sitting on the cushioned windowsill overlooking the guest courtyard, listening to the water trickle down the fountain's stone. Darkness had overtaken the city, and for the first time since her arrival nearly a week ago, not a single candle was lit in the palace or the bazaar below. The city had already begun its period of mourning, the bed of stars and the soft glow of moonlight providing the only means of illumination. The air still smelled like smoldering wood, overtaking the usual jasmine that wafted from the garden.

But at least, Greer figured, the tang of blood on the breeze had finally lessened.

Two guards had died, as had twenty partygoers, and their bodies had been transported to the tombs to be prepared for burial. The rustling of servants scrubbing the blood from the stone and scooping remnants of the fight into the garbage was the only thing breaking through the otherwise silent palace.

Greer remembered the earlier conversation, noting that the Sisters of Fate hadn't entered her mind in quite some time. Between crossing the wastes and Samael's near-death experience, they had been shoved away. But with Samael naming them following the attack on the garden that evening, Greer had removed the eye from the safe storage of her canvas bag, now holding it in her hand.

They studied one another as she sat on the windowsill, holding it between her fingers as her wrist rested on her bent knee. Greer wondered for a brief moment what the eye would tell her if it knew how to speak when, suddenly, a sharp snap outside of her window sent a zap of surprised power into the eye.

The pupil widened, color overtaken by black, and Greer thought she had been plunged headfirst into a tub of ice water. The feeling started at the crown of her head before oozing down her back, and her vision clouded before whitening entirely in a flash of bright light.

Greer squinted and blinked, struggling to clear the spots that flashed in her periphery when she realized that she was no longer seated on the cushioned windowsill. Fog rolled around her, blurring the people into silhouettes and the voices into garbled murmurs.

"One, two, three, four...see, mommy, see!" A small voice called out. "Mommy, mommy!"

Greer blinked again, and as if she were in a rubber band, the scene snapped into focus. She looked around and saw she was standing in a ramshackle motel room, the maroon carpet frayed and worn. Small, circular patches had been burnt into the corners as if someone had put out a cigarette in that very spot. The wallpaper was peeling near the ceiling, where brown water stains soaked through the drywall.

A small kitchenette was on one side, and a mattress on the other. Greer swallowed thickly as she spotted a woman— or the corpse of a woman— spread atop the floral, faded comforter. Her eyes were wide and unseeing, an uncapped needle lying next to her upturned forearm.

"They never knew that the woman who raised me was my step-mom," a familiar voice said, and Greer felt her heart leap into her throat.

She spun on her heels, her eyes landing on the white-blonde child seated cross-legged on the floor. No more than four years of age, she was counting puzzle pieces over and over again. Greer's eyes slid to the woman seated and leaning against the far wall, her forearms resting on her knees. Paige. She was whole and unharmed, still sporting the ponytail that Greer was accustomed to her wearing.

"I never told anyone I sat in this room with her until housekeeping came two days later. I didn't even tell Delia." Paige paused to scoff, scratching the back of her head. "I should have told her. I don't know why I didn't. She would have understood."

"P—Paige?" Greer managed to stutter out. "Is that...are you real?"

Paige's gaze darted upward, her lips parting in disbelief. Her younger version continued playing on the floor like nothing was hap-pening around her. "Greer? What are you— why are you— are you dead?" She stood, stepping over the puzzle pieces littering the floor.

Greer shook her head. "No, I was brought here. To Samsara, I mean, by my father. But then the eye...I don't...where are we?"

"I don't know. After I died, I was brought to the edge of a river. I got in, and I started reliving these memories." Paige flickered, a static running through her like a bad connection.

Greer's stare widened. "Paige? Paige!"

"*Gre-er*! *Gre—*"

The scene began to fog again, Paige's body shimmering into smoke and darkness.

"Paige!" Greer sobbed, attempting to run toward her best friend. She reached out, swiping her hand toward Paige's arm. Mist unfurled instead. "Paige, I'll find you! I swear, I'll find you. Don't leave the river, Paige! Don't leave the—"

Greer's vision blackened as she was yanked back, as though someone had hooked something sharp at her belly button. Glaring eyes, emerald green and angry, appeared before her. In the next breath, Greer was tossed back into the bedroom, scraping her arms on the sandstone as she slid across the tile.

THIRTY-SIX

GREER

"You saved that little girl."

Greer glanced to her left, warily watching Samael cross the ferry deck toward her. "I didn't have a choice." She returned her attention to the horizon, squinting against the evening sun's reflections off the current lapping against the ferry.

"Yes, you did."

Samael had made good on his promise to leave the Meridian of Greed by the following day, much to Serket's displeasure, and they retrieved Egyn from the stables, where he had been pampered for the past week. Greer was ushered out of her bedroom early, having only fallen asleep an hour or so before, and was still bleary-eyed as she was loaded onto the ferry shortly after that.

Orcs bustled back and forth, taking advantage of the good weather by scrubbing the deck and rearranging the cargo from the belly of the ferry. One orc, Greer assumed the captain, steered the single oar from atop the captain's quarters. His beady, black eyes constantly swept across the channel.

"Something is on your mind." Samael didn't pose it as a question, but Greer shook her head anyway.

"Nothing. It was just a long night."

In truth, Greer had spent most of the night trying to crack the eye's code. She tried summoning her power, wringing her mind for any Mage magic she could remember, and even resolved to throw it against the door. It bounced like a rubber ball back to her, and the iris narrowed into a glare. She finally gave up when the rising sun stained the skyline a deep maroon, and she crawled under the covers, collapsing in exhaustion.

Samael looked as though he had half a mind to argue but thought better of it. The wind pulled hair from his bun, whipping it around his face and jawline. "The port to the Meridian of Pride will be busier than most," he started, absent-mindedly tracing the wood grain pattern with his fingertips. "The Obsidian Mines keep it busy for most of the year."

Greer's brows rose. "I'm surprised they mine obsidian here." She glanced at him, taking in his clenched jaw and tense shoulders. "Isn't it your kryptonite or something?"

Samael snorted. "Or something." He sighed. "Obsidian is still used for several things. In jails to keep lowly daemons at bay, supplying shackles and chains to the fae realm, blades against devils. Placing a Primordial in obsidian is considered an offense of the highest regard. I doubt you would find much use for them anyways."

"What makes you say that?"

Samael clicked his tongue. "It takes centuries for a primordial to master their power through obsidian. Most never do. Orcs are truly the only creatures it doesn't affect. That's why they mine and trade it."

It was Greer's turn to snort. "So I'm not powerful enough, is what you're saying?"

Samael didn't answer.

The ferry had begun to slow, the captain laying heavily against the ore to drop speed. The approach toward the docks, a miniature city in itself, was swift, and Greer was happy that the orcs' expertise had the ferry tied to the pier in record time. As the boarding ramp was situated and locked into place, Greer grabbed Egyn's reins to lead him from the ferry, but not before giving his freshly braided mane a stroke.

The horse didn't seem to mind, though his ashen eyes darted to watch each passing orc unload the crates stacked nearest the hatch door leading to the hull. Greer's legs were jelly as she hit solid land, the crushed volcanic stone crunching beneath her sandals.

Greer had opted for another chiffon dress for the journey, this one the color of sea glass, and she was immediately glad for it. The Meridian of Pride was a hot grassland with rolling hills and low-growing bushes. The grass had long since dried in the sun's heat, the brown stalks swishing with each wind pass.

Samael pushed past her, walking on the winding dirt path that led through the row of rickety, wooden establishments. Two busy trade centers, an alehouse that smelled of freshly baked bread, and a warehouse that stored stacks of crates shoved haphazardly through the door.

Greer's stomach rumbled as an orc pushed open the alehouse door, sending a stream of the scent of beef stew toward her. She barely had time to gulp a cup of mint tea, let alone pick at the plate of food they had dropped in front of her at breakfast. It was the first time she had felt hungry all day, considering the moment she stepped on the ferry her stomach had painfully clenched.

But Samael, much to Greer's chagrin, had already bypassed the alehouse and was headed deeper into the prairie.

Greer shuffled after him, grumbling under her breath.

By the time they had apexed the first hill, looking beyond the winding path flanked by stunted, shrubby trees, Greer could see a cluster of buildings in the background. They followed the dirt road through the fields, and a train of a dozen carts containing thick chunks of rock nestled inside passed by. Headed toward the docks, the carts slowly trundled down the gravel road, swaying back and forth with the shifting weight.

Brilliantly shaded tufts of purple heather grew amidst the grass, and bumblebees wove through the feathery plumes that rustled under the phantom wind of their movement. Greer found herself running the palm of her hand over the grass, letting it tickle her skin. It made her forget she was hungry, at least for that moment.

The castle was less than an hour's walk from the docks, and Greer found it instantly unpleasant. Large, black gates made of thick iron stood erect against the walls that enclosed the courtyard. Stone turrets spiraled toward the sky, similar to Azazel's palace, but Greer found these imposing rather than stunning. And, despite the shining sun and the cloudless sky, she thought the dramatic shadows cast by the towers were uncomfortably depressing.

Samael and Greer passed through the gate, watched closely by two gargoyles on each side holding their bows taut and arrows pointed at them. The four guards stood still as stone, and it wasn't until Greer drew closer that she realized they were guards dressed in heavy armor and not gargoyles.

The courtyard was square and symmetrically built, the walkways bracketed on either side by vast bushes of red roses. Expertly trimmed, each rose bush was in the beginning stages of blooming. Greer was confident that it might have been beautiful at one time or another. But she couldn't quite bring herself to think it was now.

"Meridian of Pride, ironically enough, is the smallest meridian," Samael muttered as he led Egyn through the garden and tethered him at the post furthest away from the rose bushes.

"What's with the walls?" Greer whispered back. She didn't know why she was whispering—the courtyard was empty—but it seemed like a place where eavesdroppers would lurk.

Samael scrubbed a hand over his jawline. "Ramiel prefers to keep a tight leash on his meridian. The Obsidian Mines, the ports, the realm portals are all vital to his claim on the land."

Greer snapped her gaze up to Samael. "Portals? As in...more than one?"

"There are three here. Gaian included," Samael responded with a nod. "Let's not get ahead of ourselves here, though. Without explicit instructions from Azazel, Ramiel can do as he pleases with the gates. Even if that means denying us access."

Greer felt her blood run cold. "He would do that?"

"Ramiel is..."

Whatever Samael thought he was, Greer didn't find out. From the shadows of one of the rose bushes stepped a man.

He bore black wings, the darkest Greer had seen, and they matched his oily, black hair. It hung lank and limp to his shoulders, framing his jutting cheekbones and pale skin. His nose was upturned as though he had the misfortune of eating a rotten piece of fruit, and the expression made Greer feel just as equally unpleasant toward him as she did toward his palace.

"Samael," the man said, his voice slick. His eyes slid down Greer, and his nose would have upturned even further if it were possible. "What a pleasant surprise."

Greer's brow shot up to her hairline when Samael bowed, low and deep, to the man in front of them.

"Prince Ramiel," Samael crooned, his voice equally crafty. "I thank you for seeing us on short notice."

But Ramiel was no longer paying Samael any attention. He had turned those glimmering, soulless eyes toward Greer, staring at her expectantly. Greer suppressed the urge to sneer, though barely, and dropped into a bow rivaling Samael's.

Ramiel smirked. "Your father hasn't taught you much as manners go."

Samael growled on Greer's behalf, but Greer understood the connotation. She didn't belong, and Ramiel would make sure of that.

Ramiel heaved a dramatic sigh and turned on the toes of his boots, motioning at them over his shoulder. "Come. I'm sure your journey was long. We shall see what I have available for lodgings on this short notice." He leaned to his right and plucked a rose from the bush, lifting it to his nose to sniff it. "They're wonderful flowers, aren't they?"

He turned back toward them and extended his arm in Greer's direction, handing it to her. She reluctantly took it, making sure not to prick her fingers on the thorns she was sure he left on purpose.

"Yes, quite lovely." Greer's answer was clipped and short, garnering a blank stare before Ramiel's smirk grew.

Much to Greer's displeasure, Ramiel immediately separated her from Samael. A pair of sword-carrying guards had led away Samael while Greer was swept into the darkly morose hallways by Ramiel. He walked with his fingers linked behind his back, and beneath the black robes he bore, Greer had spotted the familiar dagger strapped to his waist.

"I had the chefs whip us up something for dinner," Ramiel finally said as he tugged open a set of absurdly tall double doors. "I'm quite sure it'll be to your liking."

"And Samael?"

"He'll find his accommodations."

Greer wanted no part of the game Ramiel was desperate to play; she would have much rather strangled the primordial with his belt, but she entered the chamber nonetheless.

The dining room was small, containing a black table with four chairs on each side. It had already been set for dinner—a carafe of red wine and two long-stemmed glasses perched delicately on the gray table runner. Light streamed in from three windows, gothic-styled with red stained glass that reminded Greer of blood puddles, but even then, the room was still too dark. The iron chandelier wasn't lit despite the complete set of column candles.

"Sit."

Ramiel's hand was wrapped around the back of the chair, the gesture not lost on her. Feet on auto-pilot, Greer lurched forward to approach the dining room table. When she had settled, Ramiel grabbed the folded cloth napkin from her plate, snapped it once, and then laid it in her lap.

Greer suppressed the urge to bolt from the seat, but she knew he still heard the exasperated sigh that slipped from her nose. Mostly because he had leaned over her to pour a half glass of wine, close enough that his robes brushed against her arm, and she could smell the rotten stench of his breath.

"I'm curious," Ramiel started, now circling the table to pour his glass before taking a seat across from her, "What brings you to the Meridian of Pride." He gestured with two fingers toward a side door, where a figure bustled into the room. "My daemons certainly wouldn't be the draw. Most of them choose to reside in other meridians."

The servant, a shorter male with hooded eyes and a down-turned mouth, spooned salad onto Greer's plate. She glanced at it, studying the chopped greens, fresh tomatoes, and grated cheese. Her mouth began to water, but she kept her hands clasped tightly in her lap.

"Who are your daemons?" Greer asked, lifting her gaze toward Ramiel.

He fixed her with a surprised stare, brows knitting slightly, as he leaned forward to grasp his wine glass. "The fae, of course. Hasn't anyone told you where they all come from?" He clicked his tongue, a condescending *tsk* echoing through the glass next to his lips. "Mammon created the shifters, though I'm sure you gathered that from the abhorrent wolf fountains scattered around his palace."

"Yes," Greer lied stiffly, and Ramiel's eyes glimmered maliciously in return.

"You must be very powerful to have gotten through the Meridian of Greed, especially with all those devils— oh yes, I know all about that. Hard to miss the gossip, though I do try."

Ramiel picked up his fork and gestured toward Greer's plate as the servant lit the candelabra between them. The glow from the flickering flames gave the dining room a romantic hue that Greer didn't appreciate in the least bit.

"I would like to think so." She picked up the fork and crunched it into the chopped greens. "I like to think I've prepared well." Another lie, but one that Ramiel couldn't contest.

"Indeed." Ramiel studied Greer, his pointer finger tapping the side of the wine glass in thought. He sucked in a breath. "Let's get down to why you're here, shall we?" He leaned forward, placing his forearms on the edge of the table. "You want to know more about the daemons."

He knew why she was there. He must have. She didn't give a shit about the daemons. He was toying with her. And he was enjoying it.

Greer sent him a grim, toothless smile. "It must take someone highly astute to read intentions so...easily."

Ramiel's smirk tightened. "Careful, princess." The word rolled around on his tongue as if it were something dirty, his tone degrading and mocking. "I might not be so forthcoming with the information you want."

A second servant pushed the door open, sweeping in with dishes balanced in both hands, each covered by a silver dome. He waited as the first servant removed the salad plate and placed one dish in front of Ramiel, pulling the dome off to reveal a steaming plate of beef, potatoes, and carrots. He wrapped around the table next, removing Greer's salad plate and replacing it with the dinner dish.

Greer's stomach growled again. She ignored it.

"What information are you willing to part with?" Greer followed his lead, waiting until he had placed the first slice of beef into his mouth to pick up the dinner fork lined neatly against the plate.

Ramiel finished chewing before answering. "What are you willing to bargain for?"

She softly cut into a piece of beef, sliding it into her mouth. The flavor explosion nearly had her falling mouth-first into the plate, but she resisted. "Next to nothing. I'm not so sure you have anything worth trading." Greer was becoming irritated with the banter, and she was becoming just as quick to show it.

Agitation flashed over Ramiel's features as he placed another bite of beef between his lips. "You are not as clever as you think, half-breed. You lack the knowledge of how the Paladin Society sewed distension into the ranks of the daemons. You know next to nothing about the realm from which you hail."

Greer's eyes snapped up to meet Ramiel's, heart sinking when she saw his sniveling smirk widen again. "Sewed distension? They used to live in harmony, then?"

Ramiel was quiet, putting down his fork to steeple his fingers together. "Not for thousands and thousands of years." He parted his hands to take another sip of wine. "Are you willing to trade access to Gaian since that's what you seek? Are you willing to stay in this realm until you get your pathetically earned power under enough control to open a portal to gain information?"

Greer clenched her teeth together. "No, I'm not." She set her fork down with a clatter that echoed off the stone walls. "And I feel you don't want me to trade my access to Gaian."

Ramiel stood, eyes glared in rage and warning. "You don't know what you speak of." He leaned forward to place each hand flat against the table, staring at her like a fly caught in his spider web. "You think you're going to waltz into this realm and—"

Greer lifted her chin, keeping her eyes bored into his. "I may not know about my power or what it means to be here, Ramiel." She spat his name back in the same condescending tone he had used to call her princess. "But, what I do know from the little we've interacted is you will be afraid of me."

Ramiel went seethingly silent. The smirk wiped clean from his mouth. "You don't even know where to start." His voice had begun to rise, his knuckles whitening as his fists clenched. "Our daemons have marketed themselves as different beings through time. Werewolves as shifters, chupacabras, and wendigos of the indigenous people in the Americas. Vampyres as aswang of the Philippines and asanbosam of the western countries of Africa. Demons as djinn in Islamic lore. The fae were alux to the Mayans and elves to the Celts. I could keep going, but I won't waste my breath."

In the amount of time he had given his speech, Ramiel was now standing behind Greer. She kept facing forward, refusing to give in to his desperation for eye contact.

"Why tell me that then?" she finally asked, leaning to grab her glass of wine. Greer took a casual sip, seeing Ramiel's fist wrapped around the back of her chair from her periphery. "Why not let me return to Gaian so you'll never see me again?"

Ramiel yanked her chair back, sending her body jerking forward. She let go of the wine in surprise, and the glass shattered against the rug over the stone floor, staining the gray fibers with red. He circled to her front and leaned down to place a hand on each armrest, trapping her.

"Because I would rather see your corpse rotting in a tomb than let you leave here with as much power as you have now."

Greer didn't know what came over her, but a white-hot flash of anger vibrated through her. And before her next heartbeat, she had reeled back her elbow and punched him square in the jaw.

THIRTY-SEVEN

ODETTE

There was a secret they all shared. A secret that was getting Odette through her days with Kaique and her nights training the humans. A secret that kept her working tirelessly to guarantee every person, human or fae, had access to swords and daggers for when the solstice opened the rift.

Instead of meeting at the colosseum in the evening, the soldiers had decided to teach the humans in the barracks where the slaves lived. It kept them out of sight of prying guards, who seemed to be out in plentiful numbers now that one of their own had mysteriously vanished while visiting family. This also allowed the humans to keep weapons on hand for when it was time to make a run for it.

Odette was feeling time weigh her down like an anchor in the sea. And, with each passing day, it was hard not to grow anxious that the walls were slowly closing in on her. On the other hand, Kaique seemed to have caved in on himself. He had become paranoid, snapping his gaze repeatedly at Odette with a sense of delusional anticipation. At the very least, his narrowed focus was solely set on Odette, and he hadn't seemed to realize his guard had also been involved.

However, a few mornings after stealing the letters from the ship, Odette sipped a steaming cup of coffee as she overlooked the gardens. Tomas was busy clipping the ferns to a scientific precision while some of the fae who worked in the kitchens were busy using their magic to manipulate the water in the fountain pools. Water-made dolphins jumped upward through the stream while visions of angel fish and neon tetras seemed to glide just under the surface.

The sun's soft rays crept over the tops of the jungle trees, casting shadows over the pools of water set into the basalt stone. A shout of anger echoed through the halls, drawing Odette's attention toward the apartment door. Brow furrowed, she had just set the now empty mug onto the windowsill when the door burst open, and a frazzled Yara crossed the threshold.

"Please, come quick," Yara said through panting breaths, her face a deep red. "It's Luisa. She— she's at the colosseum with Kaique."

Odette launched forward, grabbing the sheathed sword from the table in the middle of the room. "What happened?" she asked as they exited the apartment.

Servants were bustling up and down the hall, a chaotic tension flowing like an underground river. Yara's legs struggled to keep up with Odette's long ones, and she broke into a jog as they rounded the corner that led to the stairs.

"I'm not sure," Yara replied breathlessly. "There was screaming coming from his quarters nearly an hour ago. I only gathered that she had been snooping and found a set of letters. She tried to sneak them from his room and was caught." She wrung her hands as they descended the stairs into the courtyard. "You have to hurry, please."

"Go get Renan," Odette ordered, strapping the sword to her waist. She launched herself into the sky, flapping her wings once, twice, three times before barreling toward the east gardens and where the colosseum was now built.

The stone benches were filled with both human slaves pulled off their jobs to witness what Kaique had in store for Luisa and lower court servants shepherded in by the soldiers still in Kaique's guard. Caio and his band of higher court fae were already seated on the platform overlooking the pit, their forearms resting on the long table used for dinner. And there, on the pit, Luisa had been chained to a wooden post.

She had been forced onto her knees, blood dripping from her lower lip. Her right hand was strapped to the square stone in front of her as Kaique, a sharpened sword in his hand, paced in front of her.

"Luisa, you have been caught attempting to smuggle stolen correspondence from the Lord of Mist and Tide," Kaique began, his robes billowing in the jungle wind as he turned to face her. "The punishment for your crimes will be the removal of your hand, cut at the wrist, and cauterized to prevent your imminent death." Behind him, a second guard emerged onto the platform, carrying a white-hot iron stake.

Odette rocketed forward just as Kaique raised the dagger above his head. She hit the platform on her hip with precision, sliding on the wood as she unsheathed her sword, her blade clashing with his just in time to save Luisa's hand. The sting of metal on metal vibrated up Odette's arm, shaking her bones and rattling her joints in their sockets.

But Luisa was whole and unharmed, save for what Kaique had already done to her.

"I would think otherwise if I were you," Odette seethed through gritted teeth. She launched herself up, kicking her leg to catch the guard behind the knee. He fell from the platform, an iron stake landing on his chest as he hit the ground. Odette heard the cry of surprise followed by the sizzle of heat on flesh. In the next instant, her hand was threaded into Kaique's hair, exposing the column of his throat to the sky.

"Caio!" Kaique managed to rasp out as Odette shoved the tip of her sword into his neck. "Caio! I demand you seize her."

Caio sat back in his seat, crossing his arms over his chest, a wide smirk dancing on his face. While Odette knew that Caio had no interest in saving her or the humans, she also knew he was the type to eye the court's throne for himself. Her gaze slid over Caio's shoulder in time to see Renan creep onto the platform and slit the throat of the male seated at the end of the table. The seven males leaped back as more guards flooded the platform, the clash of blade against blade echoing across the stone of the colosseum.

The fight at the top of the platform distracted Odette long enough that Kaique swung his body around, slamming a closed fist into the side of Odette's head. Her sword cut a thin line across Kaique's neck as she jerked back in surprise, droplets of blood pebbling on his neck. He twisted away from her, stripping his robe from his body and tossing it to the floor of the pit, where it fluttered to the dirt-covered ground.

"I know of your plan to leave this place, Odette Milne," Kaique said as he pulled a dagger from inside his tunic. "I can't allow you to do that. The Fae King will be very upset if he comes to this court and you have vanished."

He lunged forward, slashing his dagger in her direction. She dodged the move quickly, sending Kaique stumbling over a lifted wood plank. The commotion on both platforms attracted a crowd to the bottom of the pit. Guards still loyal to Kaique struggled to push through the crowd of humans and lower court fae, who had gathered around the staircase to prevent them from storming the stage.

Odette stepped to the side, dancing gracefully around Kaique as she swung the sword and caught him in the arm with the blade's edge. He hissed in anger, clapping his hand over the wound, sacrificing his hold on his dagger in the process.

Odette circled him, a predator after prey.

"Kaique," Odette said in a charged voice, loud enough for even the slaves still on the stone benches to hear. "You have been accused of the murder of your father, the rape and assault of multiple women, and holding the lower members of this court hostage to further your standing in the eyes of the false king."

Kaique lurched to grab his dagger off the ground, and she kicked it away from him, where it balanced on the edge of the platform. "You were always a terrible sparring partner," Odette said. The crowd rippled with laughter as she saw a vein bulge in his forehead, his face changing from a shade of purple to a flaming puce, almost camouflaging the blood that still trickled from his neck.

Kaique yelled furiously as he extended his leg in an unsuspecting kick that caught Odette in the gut. She staggered back, her wings spreading to help her catch her balance once again. Kaique took the moment of weakness to strike, grasping the dagger from the teetering edge and whipping around to slice a tear in the leathery skin of her wings. With her ability to fly drastically hindered, at least for a few hours until the split healed, she would have to rely solely on the skills she had been taught since she was a faeling in the training grounds with her father.

"I will not return to Adair," Odette simmered. "Because I am not his to claim." She charged forward, tucking her injured wing tightly to her body so it didn't slow her down.

They began a twirling, slicing, and slashing dance as they fought to what Odette knew would be death. Clutching the hilt of her dagger, she thrust her knuckles forward and made contact with the side of Kaique's jaw. His head snapped toward his left shoulder, and he spit out the blood that filled his mouth. He pounced, catching Odette in the chest and forcing her to the platform floor. The sword slid from her hand. They wrestled as Kaique settled a bent knee onto her chest and wrapped his hands around her throat.

From the corner of her eye, Odette caught Renan ripping the strap from Luisa's arm and assisting her to her feet. Luisa bound toward Odette, but Renan held her back. Odette knew that he understood what the fight between her and Kaique meant. Whoever won would be the uncontested successor to the throne.

Everyone would have to wait and see whether that was her or Kaique.

Odette's fingernails scraped against the back of Kaique's hands as he tightened his fingers, closing her throat. Her breath went ragged. And though Odette's vision had begun to blacken, she saw that Luisa had fallen to her knees, tears streaming down her cheeks.

"Take back your power!" Luisa cried out through guttering cries. "Take it back!"

This fight meant everything to her, Odette knew. It meant everything to the humans who had been forced into slavery and meant everything to the lower court members of the fae who had been unable to leave the palace for the last ten years. Many of them had lost family to Kaique's cruelty.

If Kaique won, Odette would be forced into the palace's dungeon until Adair showed up to claim custody of her. She would be locked in her old cell, where the Fae King would resume his defiling assaults on her. She could not, would not, let that happen again.

Luisa's words thrummed through Odette, forcing her vision back into focus as she repeated them like a war chant. *Take back your power, take back your power, take back your power.* Kaique's lips were pressed into a tight line, his hips seated against hers as he straddled her. The vein in his forehead pulsed with each squeeze of his fingers against her throat.

Odette let out one final breath, the last one she had in her chest, and hooked her knee around his calf and twisted. He was propelled off of her, and she spun to her feet, grabbing the sword that had fallen mere inches from the tips of her fingers. The blade's edge cut her palm as she flipped it around to grasp the handle.

She waited on the edge of the platform, humans and fae gathered beneath her until Kaique sprung forward, his arm extended toward her. She had finally caught onto his fighting style, and once she realized his favorite moves, she locked onto that predator versus prey drive that pumped through every daemon.

Odette lifted her sword and swung it down as she stepped to the side, her blade catching Kaique at mid-forearm and cleaving his wrist from his body. His hand and his dagger flopped to the ground with a sickening thud. He let out an ear-piercing scream as he dropped to his knees, clutching the stump of his arm to his chest.

Blood spurted from the nub, his other hand coated in layers of the sticky, red substance as it leaked between his fingers. Odette planted the tip of her sword under his chin, forcing his head upward to look at her. He resisted at first, but the point dug into the underflesh of his head. His eyes, already red-rimmed and swollen from his tears, locked with hers.

Odette crouched down in front of him, the crowd beneath them so silent that a pin could be heard falling onto the dirt floor of the colosseum. "The throne is mine," she said quietly, and she watched with satisfaction as his jaw clenched tightly, grinding his teeth together. "You are to leave these lands through the rift at the solstice and are barred from returning." She stood from her position, sheathing her sword into her belt.

"Fae law states that you must kill me," Kaique spat at her, still cradling his leaking stump. "Do not leave me like this. It is the highest disgrace."

Odette studied him for a long minute. "You don't deserve to be killed," she finally stated. "You deserve to return to whatever hole you crawled out of, a pariah to the fae realms for the rest of your long, miserable life."

Renan stepped forward and grasped Kaique under the arm. The crowd at the base of the stairs parted, allowing Renan a pathway as he dragged Kaique toward the pit floor and threw him to the ground. Dirt, blood, and gravel stained his royal tunic as he scrambled and dashed toward the gate where the Serpent of Fire had once appeared. A pair of guards opened one side, not giving him the respect to open both. Kaique disappeared into the darkness of the tunnel, not once looking back.

Odette spun to check on Luisa, surprised to see Renan, the soldiers, and the lower court members with their heads bowed and hands placed over their hearts. Renan stepped forward, a smile parting his lips.

"What now, my Lady?" he asked quietly, and the murmuring of the congregation immediately ceased.

"Prepare the humans for departure. They will be returning home. Slavery is abolished in the Court of Mist and Tide." A trill of excitement threaded the crowd as humans hugged one another, bursting into tears. "Any member of the lower court will be allowed to leave the palace if they so wish. Everyone willing to fight for me will be welcome. We will be marching on the Fae King by the following equinox."

Odette's profession rocked through the crowd, and they split once again as she descended the steps. The guards followed her through the maze of hedges and into the fountain courtyard. She said nothing as she crossed the basalt stone pathway and opened the marble hall's double doors. She continued to say nothing as the blast of fresh air made the flames in the sconces dance, casting long shadows on the walls.

She stopped at the bottom of the steps, looking up at the dais and toward the green-cushioned throne. The hall had an energy shift; it already felt lighter and brighter. The throne looked inviting without Kaique seated there, but Odette turned her back on it.

The dais belonged to Nerea, the true heir to the throne, and the Court of Mist and Tide. With them, it would stay.

The pack of guards surrounded her, awaiting her instruction. Odette surveyed the crowd, noticing quite a few guards were missing. She assumed they had followed Kaique from the grounds.

"We need to form a plan to get the humans from the realm," Odette started, looking each guard in the eye. Renan had sidled up to her right-hand side. "I assume that Kaique will flee when the rift is large enough, giving us time to move everyone else out." She took a deep breath as she turned to Ranan. "And we need to know exactly what was in those letters from Luisa."

One guard stepped forward from the back of the crowd. "Were— were you serious that we can..." He trailed off, looking around at its brothers. A few gave him nods of encouragement. "That we can go home if we want to. I— I have a daughter in one of the villages nearest the rift and—"

"Yes, you can," Odette said, locking her eyes with the guard. "You have no further obligation to guard the palace or follow me against the Fae King. If you prefer to remain in the Court of Mist and Tide with your daughter, I respect your decision. My only ask is that you lead a small group of humans to the back on your way home."

Tears pricked in his eyes, but the male swiped them away before anyone other than Odette could notice. He sent her a grateful smile, nodding his head vigorously. "Yes, yes, of course. Of course."

"Whether you leave or choose to remain here, the same request stands for all. More humans are in this palace than fae, and we'll need all the help to lead them out." Luisa entered at the back of the hall, rubbing the bruised strap-line on her forearm. Odette nodded at her, signaling they would meet in private. "If you want to join us against the Fae King, please consult my Captain of Intelligence, Renan. He will be able to make a list of fae willing to come and account for the weapons we require."

Renan wrenched his head to look at Odette, but she was already moving to the door beside the dais. He shook off the guards, who had hounded him as he followed Odette from the hall. Luisa curved past the crowd, threading herself over the threshold and into the courtyard that lined the kitchens.

"Captain of Intelligence?" Renan asked with a raised brow as they crossed the courtyard and entered the hallway of the guest apartments. Luisa slowed her jog to a brisk walk as she caught up.

"If you choose to accept it, of course," Odette responded as they ascended the stairs. "You have no obligation to assist me if you have family." From the corner of her eye, Odette saw Luisa bristle.

"It would be my honor to be your Captain of Intelligence, my Lady," Renan said, placing a hand over his chest.

Odette waved at him, dismissing the formalities. "Stop doing that. Calling me Odette will work just fine." They entered the foyer of her apartment, and from the open window, music and celebration wafted into the room. She noticed the empty mug still planted on the sill. So much had happened since that cup of coffee.

Luisa, it seemed, could no longer hold back. She stepped toward Odette, anger flashing over her features. "He is your Captain of Intelligence," she said, knocking her head toward Renan in a gesture. "What about me? I did all of this. I found the letters. I worked for years, and now..." She tightened her lips together that familiar and intense gaze rattling Odette's soul.

"Luisa, you're free," Odette replied, furrowing her brow. "You can go home. You can go back to Colombia."

Luisa scoffed, crossing her arms over her chest. "I don't have anything to return to. My family is dead. My job is gone. I haven't been part of that community in years. I—" She stopped, trailing off before shifting her weight from one foot to another. "I have nowhere else to go. I thought I would join the humans going home, but now...there are bigger things at play."

Odette walked forward. "This is going to be dangerous. Very dangerous, especially for a human."

"An entire group of humans is planning on following you into battle," Luisa retorted. "Or was all of that training for nothing?"

"A group of humans?" Odette lifted her hand to her throat in shock.

"Yes," Luisa said simply. "We have something to fight for, too. For the other humans in the other realms, what would happen if Adair left the courts and took over the human realm."

Odette cleared her throat. "I wanted to give you a spot in my court, but I didn't want to assume you would want to stay with the fae." She paused as Luisa straightened her back. "Regardless, I remain with my decision to name Renan my Captain of Intelligence." Luisa seemed to deflate under those words. "Because I need someone to be my right hand, the general to my armies, and the voice of reason in my ear. The future is unknown and likely tumultuous. I need someone to tell me the truth."

Luisa lit up in a way Odette had never seen before, the light reaching her eyes and setting her bronzed skin to glow like the rising sun. "I swear," she said breathily. "I swear I will follow wherever you lead."

Odette smiled. "How about we walk side-by-side and figure it out together? Starting with everything you learned in those letters." By the look on her face, Odette thought Luisa liked that even better.

"You understand your mission?" Renan asked the male, kneeling in the river and the rushing water cresting around his waist. "You understand what you must do?"

"Yes," the male said, lifting his chin toward the canopy trees above him. "Find the Mage named Greer. Give her the message contained in the letters."

"Do you think this will work?" Luisa murmured at Odette.

Odette swallowed thickly, watching the two men from the muddy bank. "It has to. We don't have another choice."

"What is the message?" Renan said as he made his way to the male's back. "What do we need you to say?"

"Leander is with the Fae King. He wants to open the tombs that set the Ananke free. They are readying an attack on Odette."

"Your body will be returned to the jungle, brother," Renan said as he lifted his dagger and placed the blade at the male's throat. "Nothing will be wasted, and nothing will be in vain. We thank you for your sacrifice."

With a quick flick of his wrist, Renan slit the man's throat, the blood running down his bare chest and dyeing the river water a deep shade of red.

"May your newly healed wings take you to the Primordials," Odette said, reciting the fallen soldier's grace from the Court of Wind and Storm. "And may they welcome you and make you whole."

THIRTY-EIGHT

GREER

"You know how to make a first impression."

Greer's head snapped up, and her eyes locked with Samael's through the slats between the metal bars of the dungeon Ramiel had thrown her in. She didn't know how long she had sat on the stone floor, power sluicing from her due to the obsidian laced in the walls. Her fingers were numb from the drafty cold blowing through the narrow corridors.

"Did he tell you what happened?" Greer paused to rub her broken knuckle, the bruise already a deep blue as it struggled to heal against the obsidian around her. "He probably lied anyways, what an ass."

Samael chuckled, the sound skittering through Greer's bones. "He'll never admit you clocked him. Good hit, though."

Greer bit her lip to suppress the grin threatening to split her face. She pushed herself from the stone floor to approach, noticing that Samael had leaned a shoulder against the stone frame encasing the door. "How did you know where I was?"

"The moment you entered this room, your power ceased to be detected. It wasn't hard to deduce where he had thrown you." The side of Samael's mouth quirked. "Though, it took convincing the servants to figure out what happened."

Greer crossed her arms over her chest. The light from the single-lit torch flickered over half of his face, casting the other half in shadow. "Are you going to let me out?"

"About that." He paused to sweep his gaze over the dungeon. "Ramiel won't let you out."

Greer's lips parted in surprise. "What do you mean *won't let me out*? Does he expect to leave me down here?"

Samael shrugged. "A little food, a little water. You would make the right pet." She snarled in response, and Samael lifted his hands in surrender, flashing a set of iron keys wrapped around a finger. "I had to call for reinforcements."

Greer's back stiffened. "Reinforcements?"

"Reinforcements," a second male voice sounded from behind Samael.

Greer's stomach upturned when she watched Samael step aside to allow Azazel forward. Her father studied her with intrigue as he approached, though not with the biting disdain and anger she had expected.

"You've gotten yourself in quite the situation." Azazel held his hand, and Samael dropped the keys into his palm. "It took me coming here to...convince...Ramiel to let you go."

The iron jangled together as Azazel stuck the key in the lock, which clicked with a twist of his wrist. The door swung open, squeaking on rusted hinges, and Greer spotted Ramiel in the background. His vengeful stare was fixed on her, and Greer managed to keep from waving at him by threading her fingers together.

"And it was still no easy feat."

Her eyes slid to her father's as she exited the cell. "You're still talking?"

Azazel's brows rose as he studied her. "I would watch my words if I were you. I could have let you rot here."

"Duly noted."

"You should have paid a far higher price for disrespecting me in my meridian," Ramiel snapped, and Greer was glad to see his hand instinctively reach for his jawline.

"You know, I never quite got the full story," Azazel said, hanging the keys on a hook outside the cell.

"It matters not, Azazel," Ramiel retorted, dropping his hand. "When will we end this charade of yours to keep her in the dark?" He stepped forward, though Greer would have slunk into the shadows with Azazel's glare. "We have played our parts well. I want her gone."

"Ramiel—" Samael growled, but Greer had already spun toward Azazel.

"What is he talking about?" Out of the cell, Greer felt her power bristle in her fingertips, awakening under her stressful commands.

"Keep it under control, you petulant child," Ramiel sneered. "Do you honestly believe your father didn't know where you were the entire time?"

"Ramiel—"

"You forget, princess, that primordials can tap into the whereabouts of one another, so long as there is no obsidian interfering. Your father knew where you were every minute, every second you were gone." Ramiel's laugh was cold and cruel. "You were never in danger. You were never going to leave here." He paused to gesture toward Samael, who glared at Ramiel as if he might shred him into ribbons on the spot. "Which can only mean your guide was under his employ the entire time."

Silence fell between them, sliced only by the water dripping from between the cracks in the ceiling. Greer sucked a tooth before letting an unladylike snort escape.

The snort turned into a chuckle, which turned into a string of giggles...which culminated in Greer clutching the wall next to her, sending rats scuttling across the floor as her belly-clenching laughs had her doubled over.

She was so stupid. So. fucking. Stupid. Of course, he knew where she was. He wouldn't have let her out of sight—the heir to Samsara.

Greer pushed past Samael, and his hand locked around her upper arm. "Greer, I—"

She wrenched it from his grasp in the next breath, glancing casually over her shoulder. "Go fuck yourself," she said with a shake of her head.

Greer realized that this betrayal didn't hurt as badly. She awaited the deluge of pain and anger to flood her as it had with Cian. But she realized that she had half-expected it all along. She turned away from Samael, but not before noticing the crumpling anguish that twisted behind his eyes.

Greer ignored it.

"Take me back," she told Azazel, their matching gray eyes locking together.

With a wave of his hand, a portal ripped open, tearing time and space into a glimmering void of haloed light. Greer walked through it without a second look behind her.

She reappeared in the familiar bedroom she had been running from for the past six weeks. Everything remained the same, down to the empty decanter that had replaced the one she shattered by tossing it over the railing. The deep purple felt more like a prison now than when she left.

Greer was unsurprised and unhappy to see Azazel appear in the portal before it winked out, leaving them in the dark. Candles, the flames dancing in the breeze that entered through the crack under the door, were lit without a second thought. Greer felt a surge of anger at how easy that power came for him.

"I hate this room," Greer finally spat after a long minute, dropping into a seat near the small table that held the empty decanter. "It's so...dark."

Azazel raised his brows. "This was your mother's favorite color. I thought it would make you feel closer to her."

Greer's eyes darted up to him before sweeping around the room. "How was I supposed to know that?"

He frowned, studying her. "You can change it whenever you like. It's your room."

She clucked her tongue against the roof of her mouth. "We both know I can't do that. I'm more likely to set the place on fire." She considered it wasn't half bad a thought.

"May I sit?"

Greer tossed a hand toward the chair before crossing her arms back over her chest, her knuckles now healed after being removed from the obsidian cell. Rain had begun to patter against the circular window overlooking the city and lake. From the chair, she could see small figurines bustling along the cobblestone streets that comprised the square's lower half.

"I feel as though I should explain myself." Azazel's tone was unsure and wavering, as though he had never been in this situation before.

Greer turned her stern gaze toward him, cocking her head. "A few months late for that, do you think?"

His jaw clenched, the muscles tightening beneath his skin. "I'm trying to do the right thing, Greer. There is much you don't understand. Leander, he—" Azazel paused to sigh sharply through his nose, nostrils flaring.

"Samael mentioned that name. He's Michael's son."

Azazel nodded, running a hand through his blonde waves. He shifted in the seat, wings flicking with agitation. "Leander was the second son of Michael after his daughter was—"

"I know this already. Michael forced a woman to have Leander. This has nothing to do with me."

His fingers tapped against the surface of the desk. "This has everything to do with you. To do with your power. Leander, he...he wasn't born with any natural magic. Michael gifted him wings and the ability to siphon power from others."

Greer glanced over to Azazel, remaining silent.

He sighed again, rubbing two fingers against a temple. "Leander was made aware of your existence the moment you were conceived. The moment I gifted you my power—"

"I heard it was quite a lot."

"A third is more than quite a lot. A third is unheard of." He paused to glance at the decanter, and it immediately filled with amber alcohol. He picked up two glasses, poured a three-finger amount into each, and slid one toward Greer. "Leander has been slowly siphoning power from daemons in Gaian for as long as he has been alive. It's the closest thing to my power he can get to. Until—"

"Until me." Greer picked up her glass and took a biting swig. "What does he want with it?"

"There are theories. Closing the realms. Reuniting the Primordials. We've been removed from Elysia for such a long time, it's hard to say." Azazel took a sip of his drink. "Putting you and your mother in Gaian was the most difficult decision I ever had to make."

Greer looked over at him, assessing his hunched shoulders, the shadow behind his eyes, the thin line of his lips. And, for the first time, she saw it for what it was...sorrow and pain. She swallowed, glancing back toward her glass. "Why did you leave me there? Why didn't you— Holly could have stayed here. Stayed safe."

Azazel shook his head. "There are rules put in place that even I can't break. A mortal living in Samsara while alive is one of them." He cleared his throat. "Holly had to leave the moment she gave birth, and you needed her more than you needed me. I laced you both with obsidian. Holly had visited Montana as a child with her mother and thought it remote enough to live while you grew. I never— we never—"

Anger tore through Greer, and she struggled to temper her rage. "Why didn't you come back for me after Holly was killed?"

"I looked for you, searched everywhere—"

"Why didn't you search harder?" And there it was. The anger and sadness sliced through her, leaving shreds and ribbons in its wake. "I was raised by a woman who hated me. I hated who I was. Hated what I was." Greer swiped a tear from her cheek. "And it's complicated because she died to protect me. But not before trying to keep me in the dark first."

"People hate others they don't understand, can't comprehend."

Greer turned a scathing look toward Azazel. "That isn't why I hate you. You left me there. Left me to fend for myself and not to know who I was—"

"I told you that—"

"If you wanted to find me, we both know you could have." There was a heated beat of tension between the two before Greer went on. "Even Samael said he could sense me long before I was here. You could have asked him."

Azazel stiffened and blinked. "What did you say?"

"Samael. He could sense me. You could have asked him."

He shot up from the seat, the amber alcohol dumping on the plum carpet. Greer jolted, stunned at the sudden movement.

"I have to go," Azazel murmured, crossing the room in a dizzyingly short time. He wrenched the door open.

"Am I under lockdown again, then?" Greer called after him, annoyance cutting through with her words.

He paused, hand enclosed around the doorknob. "No. We both know you don't have enough control to hide from me. You never did."

Greer snarled at his exposed wings before throwing her own glass after him, and it shattered against the door's wooden frame.

"I know what you think of me," Azazel said from the other side of the threshold. "But your mother was the love of my life. And I'll never stop searching for her. I hope to know you one day as she would have wanted us to."

The library was still Greer's haven, and she sought it out when it cleared for the night. Fat raindrops plunged against the dome, echoing over the sandstone floor and narrow stacks. A small ball of hovering fire lit the space around her as she nestled against a case, book propped in her lap as she read.

A *thwap* of wings sounded as a pair of boots hit the floor. Samael had donned his fighting leathers again, a sight Greer hadn't seen since before they entered the Meridian of Greed. She was almost sad to see the casual attire go.

Greer didn't bother acknowledging him, opting to turn the page of her book instead. Samael cleared his throat, but she just continued reading.

"I know you're ignoring me," Samael said, crossing his arms over his chest. The leather creaked with his movement, the dark markings glowing against the ball of flame.

"I'm aware."

He was quiet for another moment. "I hope you know, the last few weeks—"

"Meant nothing to you. I'm also aware of that." Her eyes crossed to the next page, but her finger began tapping against the binding. An irritating flare of heartache burst in her chest. "The only thing I want to know is why."

"Why?" Samael repeated.

Greer stuck a finger in the crevice of the book to keep her place before flipping the cover shut. "Why? Why bring me to the Meridian of Pride, risking your life? You were involved in this bullshit."

Samael shifted uncomfortably on his feet. It was clear that he had never experienced a series of pointed stares. "In my defense, I truly didn't think you would last more than two days. I thought you would beg me to return you to the palace."

Greer's expectant look curled into a scowl as she returned to her book, opening it briefly before shutting it again. "You knew, though. You knew that he was watching where I was, and you just—" She paused to push herself from the ground, firmly keeping the book in her hand. "I want to know why. You kissed me, we—" She trailed off, stepping back from him.

A sigh escaped Samael's lips as he shook his head. "The kiss had nothing to do with this. Azazel, your father—" He ran a hand over his jaw, scratching at the stubble of his beard. "We made a deal that he would find a way to free me if I could convince you to learn how to control your powers."

Greer chuckled under her breath. "And did he? Find a way to free you?"

Samael's hesitant nod was all the answer she needed.

A short breath of disbelief shot from her nose. "I truly thought we had bonded, Samael, and all this time you were...working an angle?"

Samael stepped toward her, but Greer raised a hand to stop him. "Greer, I never— we *did* bond. I thought you wouldn't make it two days, but watching you heal, seeing how your mind works, realizing that you saved me—"

"You lied to me. You knew he did not intend to let me go back home." Greer took another step back, shaking her head. "Just— just leave me alone, Samael. I don't want anything to do with this realm, my father, or you." She watched unfeelingly as his face crumpled with hurt. "And if I have to sit here for eternity, then so be it."

"We wanted nothing more than to keep you safe. Leander, he—"

"You made that choice for me, Samael!" Greer's voice had risen, ringing shrilly through the library. "After you told me that it would always be mine. You took that from me and handed it to my father. You used me to get out of this shitty bargain you found yourself in."

Samael reached for her, but she ducked the advance. Instead, she spun on her toes and marched away, leaving him standing amidst the stacks, silent and alone.

Azazel had told her that she couldn't control her power and there would always be someone looking after her because of it. And, for the first time since she had arrived in Samsara, she knew what she had to do.

As Greer passed the last bookshelf before exiting the library, she pulled three books from the final shelf labeled *Mystic Powers and Ancient Rites of Samsara* before climbing the stairs toward her bedroom. She needed to learn control, and there was only one way she could do it.

THIRTY-NINE

DELIA

"It's been almost two weeks," Kazzy said quietly, peering through the new hotel room window curtains, one they had moved to under a fake name following Cian's capture. "And we haven't seen a single hair from his head. We have to face this, Delia. He isn't coming back."

Delia slammed her laptop shut, pressing the tips of her fingers into her temple for a long minute before glancing over to Kazzy. Through the slit in the curtains, Delia could see the rain following in thick drops from the November sky. "And what do I do then? Tell Greer that I lost a third of the vampyre trio to the Paladin Society?" She shook her head, letting out an exasperated sigh through her nose. "No, she would lose it."

Kazzy turned from the window to square her shoulders to Delia. "I would think Greer would be happy. Considering he was the one to sell her out in the first place." She parted her lips as though she were on the verge of going on before snapping her lips shut again.

But Delia caught the hesitation. "What were you going to say?"

Kazzy swallowed nervously, twisting her ponytail around two fingers, and Delia watched the column of the wolf's throat work for the few moments of silence that stretched between them.

"Both Cian and Greer were the reasons for your wife's murder," Kazzy finally went on, her tone soft and slow. "Maybe it's time for you to move on from both of them as well."

Delia felt her stomach lurch from the unexpected mention of Paige and Greer's hand in her death. She shot a warning glare over to Kazzy. "I'm not losing Greer. She— she made a mistake—"

"A mistake that she was advised against by multiple people—"

"Whose side are you on here?" Delia retorted, anger seeping into her trembling voice. "Because I thought you wanted the Mage around again. And to do that, we have to find Cian because Cian is one of the only ones that I know who can figure all of this bullshit out."

Kazzy sighed, sinking onto the vinyl couch. "I just...there are over nine hundred churches in Rome alone. We've barely been able to check twenty of them. We could be here for years looking for Cian if we keep at it." She surveyed Delia with that intense wolf stare that made Delia squirm. "And you're wasting your life chasing a ghost. Or a friend who didn't bother to look at the fine print before invoking potent magic..."

"We're going to find Cian," Delia repeated, ignoring Kazzy's final attempt to persuade her to leave Rome. "Because I'm not losing Greer."

There was a knot that had begun to form in Delia's gut. A knot that grew bigger by the day, twisting her stomach into fits of panic and sorrow. Because Kazzy was right, by all accounts, Delia should let Greer go to the wayside. And, at this point, she still might have to. She didn't know. Greer had been her best friend for a decade and had seen her through the ups and downs of school, dating, and trying to find her brothers.

And, when she sat down to think about it, Delia didn't know if Greer could ever explain herself to the point that Delia would forgive her anyway. The thoughts swirled in her head, the decision that hung over her— it was enough to tighten that knot and make her sick to her stomach.

But Delia couldn't talk to Greer if she was still in Samsara. And she couldn't get to Samsara without Cian. So, Cian was, for once, the priority.

Kazzy put down Delia's notebook, letting the paper slap against the plastic cushion. "Let's start back from the top, then. Paladin wouldn't have taken him to St. Peter's because of the runes. Dismantling them for one vampyre is too risky. Should we keep looking at the grid we made of the city? Or should we branch out?" She paused to bite her lower lip. "I just wish we had more eyes on these places."

An idea rooted in Delia's mind made her shoot out of the office chair, leaving it spinning in her wake. "You're a fucking genius," Delia said, marching toward the bed and slinging her jacket on. "A. Fucking. Genius."

"I know," Kazzy said with a smile. "But remind me why I'm one this time?"

"Eyes, Kaz. We need more eyes," Delia replied, grabbing her crossbody bag and planting it over her shoulder. "We need people who can check the churches. Even those with runes."

Kazzy's eyes narrowed. "What are you thinking?"

But Delia was already over the threshold, the back of her coat whipping as the door slammed shut behind her. She ran through the lobby, passing the blonde girl who always sat on the couches facing the basilica and onto the walkway. She ran over the wet cobblestones, passing the storefronts decorated with Christmas lights and the pine trees erected on the more prominent corners of the main streets. Her breath showed in the evening air like puffs of steam, but she didn't stop.

Delia powered up the hill toward Vatican City, a place she hadn't visited since her narrow escape. Now, it was necessary. She stood on her tip-toes as she entered the square, trying her best to see over the heads of the tourists.

There. There was one.

Delia hadn't paid much attention to the visitors when she first began studying the basilica. She figured many of them were only there for the day. It wasn't until the ghostly woman had accosted her during the previous full moon that she began to watch Vatican City and the surrounding area more closely. At that point, Delia realized there were a decent number of people in the square who weren't necessarily visiting.

Delia made a beeline toward a woman standing under the colonnade, a darkened bruise coloring her face like a shadow. The woman stilled as Delia approached, watching her warily.

"I thought you would have gone," the woman said in a thick accent, tilting her head. A thin line of flesh opened at her neck with the movement, revealing an expertly slit throat that Delia hadn't noticed from afar. Her stomach flipped in response. "We had been talking about the woman foolish enough to break into the basilica. It was the most exciting thing that's happened here in decades."

Delia suppressed the shudder that threatened the base of her spine. "I need your help," Delia hissed under her breath, pretending to glance down at her phone to make it seem like she wasn't talking to herself.

The woman's eyes narrowed further, and from her periphery, Delia saw the wary gaze shift to suspicion. "I'm not interested," the woman said, turning to glide away.

Delia's hand lashed toward the woman out of instinct, startling them both when her finger enclosed the thin wrist. The two froze, staring down at the connection. The woman's essence felt cool, an icy solid that seemed to melt under Delia's touch. The part under her grasp turned wispy the longer she held, and Delia couldn't help but unlatch her hand and wipe her palm on her leggings.

"H—how?" the woman asked, her head wobbling dangerously on her shoulders as her jaw slackened. "How did you do that?"

"A few months ago, I witnessed the death of my wife. I saw her move on. Ever since then, I've been seeing spirits. I don't know why."

The woman was still rubbing her wrist, but her brow was deeply furrowed as she listened intently. "Why me? Why do you need my help? Hundreds of others in the city have not yet passed on."

"You're the first one I could find," Delia answered honestly. "Some of you are easier to spot than others. But I have a proposition for all the spirits willing to help."

The woman snapped her gaze upward, her gloomy eyes connected with Delia's. She was silently hesitant, but the curiosity shining through her features urged Delia to continue.

"I have a friend— an acquaintance, Cian. He's a vampyre. The Paladin Society stole him." The woman's eyes flashed at the mention of the society, but Delia pressed forward. "I need to find him, and I need to find him fast."

The woman seemed to shift, the front of her nightdress ruffling with the movement. "Where do you expect him to be?"

"We have documents from the Paladin Society that show the use of various churches in Rome, so we think he has to be in one of those, but we don't know which one."

The woman shimmered under the red glow from the Christmas tree decorated near the middle of the square. The sun had officially sunk below the horizon, dipping the sky into bleak darkness. Tourists jostled around Delia, vying for the best picture of the nativity scene and the lights of the basilica against the dark of the night.

"What is your proposition?"

Rainy mist started once again and Delia flipped the hood of her jacket over her head. "Why are you still here? Why didn't you move on?"

The question must have surprised the woman as her furrowed brow loosened and her lips thinned into a tight line. She contemplated Delia for a moment before replying. "I refused to move on when I was given the chance by the angel who came to collect me, thinking I would get a second chance at life. Instead, my soul adhered to the object used to kill me."

Delia nodded her head slowly, her mind racing. "Does that happen to everyone who refuses to move on? Their soul joins with the object used to kill them?"

"Yes, unless their death was natural. In which case, they are doomed to stay with their body, wherever they may rest."

"And if the object is destroyed? Or the body?"

"My soul is forced to move on."

Silence gapped between the two women as Delia rubbed her lower lip. It wasn't until a visitor bumped her shoulder that she was pulled from her thoughts.

"If you and the others you can find help me," Delia started slowly. "I will find your objects and destroy them. To help you all move on if you want to."

The woman's thin lips parted, her chest rising in a fake breath. "You— you would do that?" She toyed with the lace front of her night dress.

"Yes," Delia replied breathlessly. "Please, tell them that. I will help everyone who helps me."

The woman straightened, dropping her fidgeting hand back to her side. "I will assist you, but I can't promise how many others may also want to join in. Where can we locate you if we find him?" Delia rattled off the name of the hotel and the street it was on. The woman nodded. "I will send someone to you. Our souls cannot travel far from the objects we are connected to, but many of us intersect one another." She gazed wistfully over her shoulder, looking at the basilica standing tall against the night.

"What happened to you?" Delia asked quietly, watching the woman's expression change from bitter to hopeful to bitter again. "What are you attached to?"

The woman looked back at Delia, eyes sweeping over her face. "I was married to a man who was a surgeon but also had a terrible temper when he drank. I had gone to sleep and accidentally let the fire dwindle. He came home to a cold house. He beat me in our bed before taking one of his instruments to cut my throat." She gestured up to her neck unnecessarily, Delia thought. "I died from my injuries in our home, and I was buried in a family tomb on the outskirts of Rome. I was doomed to walk the earth where my home once was until excavators found the surgical instrument and donated it to the museum attached to the basilica. I was moved with it."

"If I entered the museum, could you lead me to it? You know exactly where it is?"

The woman nodded, spinning in the air to face the church. "I will find souls to help. And we will come to you when we have found your friend."

It was another two days before they heard anything, and Delia spent most of that time wringing her hands while pacing the hotel room. "Do you think I made the right choice?" she asked Kazzy for what seemed like the hundredth time. "We don't even know if this will work, and we haven't looked at any other churches since."

"Either it works or it doesn't," Kazzy said in a soothing voice. She had lounged on the bed, flicking through channels on the television. "If it doesn't, we'll resume looking ourselves."

"And it would have been a huge waste of ti—" Delia cut herself off with a piercing scream, her heart jolting out of her chest.

"What?" Kazzy asked, leaping off the mattress and readying herself into a fighting stance.

A ghost had appeared. A teenage girl that Delia had known from the lobby of their hotel, though she didn't realize the girl was dead until now. However, seeing the girl up close and taking in the faded bruises that encircled her neck was obvious.

The girl flicked her long hair over her shoulder and scowled at Delia in the only way a teenage girl could. "I thought you knew someone was coming."

Delia bent over, placing one hand on her knee and the other on her chest, her breaths hard and uneven. It took a moment for the sound of her beating pulse to drop from her ears and for the tips of her fingers to stop throbbing. But when she finally straightened up, she looked at the girl equally annoyed.

"Most people announce when they enter a room," Delia shot back, planting her hands on her hips. "Instead of just popping up out of nowhere."

Kazzy's stance relaxed. "Is there a ghost in here?" She squinted, looking around the room as though she could see if she tried hard enough.

"Yes," Delia responded through gritted teeth.

The teenager rolled her eyes.

"For the record," the girl said, her hair swishing back and forth with the exaggerated head movements. "I don't think you'll help us, but I was told to come here and tell you where your friend is."

Delia's eyebrows rose high on her forehead as she waited. "And?" she prompted when the girl stayed silent, exasperated.

The girl smacked her lips, getting on Delia's already fried nerves. "Baths of Caracalla. Underground. In one of the aqueduct passageways that connect the cisterns."

Delia repeated it to Kazzy, who immediately grabbed her cell phone and began an internet search.

The girl cleared her throat, and Delia turned her attention back to the ghost. "I want to move on. I've been stuck in this godforsaken hotel for three years. Get me out of here."

Delia was having a hard time feeling sorry for the girl. "What are you even attached to?"

"Aren't you supposed to know that?" the girl shot back in that snotty inflection that made Delia want to wring her throat.

"That's not really how it works," Delia managed to say as sweetly as possible.

The ghost heaved a sigh. "Ugh. Fine. Come with me." She spun around and glided toward the door. A shudder went up Delia's neck as she watched the girl disappear. She popped her head back through the door a second later. "Are you coming? I would prefer not to wait all day."

Delia was thrown out of shock by pure irritation as she lurched forward to yank the door open. The girl was waiting in the hallway when Delia stepped over the threshold and glided away as soon as Delia appeared.

"Elevator down to the first floor," the girl said shortly, sinking through the carpet as she spoke. "I'll meet you there."

Delia followed her directions, against her own will, punching the elevator button and waiting for the telltale ding. The doors slid open, and she stepped into the car, the marble bright and shining from the lights centered in the ceiling. She hit the button for the first floor, and the car jerked into motion, descending to the lobby with a slow tug of the cables.

The hotel lobby was busy. A handful of couples were waiting in line to check in at the front desk. Other visitors were coming in from the street, the early winter air blasting through the automatic glass doors. Delia crossed her arms over her chest and shivered—the short-sleeve shirt she wore was not nearly enough.

"Um, over here."

Delia's head snapped to the left, spotting the teenage girl standing in front of a door to the side of the crackling fireplace near the opposite side of the lobby. Delia went through the crowd, keeping a side-eye on the employees to ensure they didn't stop her. They seemed busy enough, frantically typing on their computers to search for bookings.

She hurried over to the girl and shouldered the door open, trying to create as little of a gap as possible, where it emptied into a long hallway.

The floor shifted from the striking marble of the lobby to worn-down carpet. The hallway had no windows, only flickering fluorescent lights that hummed against the off-white, chipped paint that coated the walls. It was clear to Delia that this hallway was meant for storage, the strong scents of bleach and chemical citrus wafting from underneath one of the doors she passed. The whir and slap of wet linens in the washing machine, combined with the clacking of metal zippers against the drum of the dryer, filled the silence.

The girl took a sharp left, floating through the solid wall without looking back. Delia followed, turning the cold doorknob and entering the room. It wasn't much bigger than the closet in her bedroom back home. Long shelves lined the walls, each clad with piles of folded linens, pillows still within their plastic sheathing, and recently cleaned towels that retained a slight detergent smell despite the mustiness of the room.

Stopping below the shelf in the far corner, the girl pointed toward a stack of used pillows. "That. That is what I'm stuck with." She kept her gaze averted away from the shelves above her.

Delia cocked an eyebrow, her stare pinning the third pillow from the top. "That's it? Where did the bruises on your neck come from then?"

As a fleeting memory dashed over her young face, a phantom shiver seemed to work its way up the girl's spine. In the next breath, she hitched a scowl on her features, lip curling into a tight sneer. "It's not like I got to choose how I died."

Delia returned the scowl but reached upward to grab the pillow nonetheless. The rest tumbled to the floor. "Is there a specific way I need to destroy this?"

"A fire? I don't know. Aren't you some kind of psychic?"

Delia pointed the pillow at the girl. "Lose the attitude, child, or I toss this pillow into the ocean and let you sit at the bottom for the rest of your miserable existence." The ghost clamped her mouth shut, jaw tightening against the barb she had inevitably drawn up for herself. "Good. Now, what's your name?"

"Sophie," the girl answered through tight lips, her eyes flashing in contempt.

"How old are you, Sophie?"

Sophie's eyes darted up to meet Delia's, her face hardening. "I was seventeen when I was killed. Guess that still makes me seventeen."

Delia wanted to feel bad, but the struggle to dig any empathy from the depths of her gut was weighing her down. "Until we find my acquaintance and until we know that you aren't blowing smoke up my ass to get what you want—" She waved the pillow again, and Sophie visibly flinched. "Then I'm keeping this in my hotel room."

"I've never been happier," Sophie spat.

At that moment, it was apparent to Delia that she needed to find Cian and destroy the pillow...and fast. Before she murdered the teenage girl for the second time.

FORTY

DELIA

The Baths of Caracalla were nearly a fifty-minute metro ride followed by a ten-minute walk from the nearest station. Delia watched as Kazzy fervently checked her cell phone screen, limbs shaking with jittering nerves with each passing minute. It was less than an hour until Kazzy could shift, and while Kazzy had explained in great detail how she did it, it was still making Delia nervous.

The two women left the train station, beginning the walk toward the baths. The weather was mild, though the sharp wind and the misty rain quickly coated Delia's pants. She shivered, hugging her arms to her chest in a poor attempt to conserve heat. Kazzy, on the other hand, was seemingly comfortable in her loose shirt despite the rain clinging to the hair pulled into a ponytail near the top of her head.

Delia saw the archaeology site from afar, the terracotta stone walls erected high above the grass field. Two towers stood tall, bracketing the gravel walkway that led to the interior of the ancient structure. Bright lights blanched against the stone, new meeting old. It was quiet, save for the new sounds of rain pattering the crumbled rock path and the wind rustling what remained of the dead leaves still holding against the season change.

They picked up their pace, keeping to the shadows cast by the bright ground lights. The complex was easy enough to enter, merely by stepping over the thick rope that spanned two black metal poles, and Delia felt the grass crunch beneath her feet, now dead with the winter cold.

Dust fluttered from the delicate wall as Delia's shoulder scraped against the stone to stay undetected. Her heart pounded in her throat, in her ears, and down to her toes as they navigated the grounds. There weren't enough places to hide if a guard came around the corner.

She swept her gaze across the complex. Delia took in three translucent, cloud-colored bodies that glided around the lawn. She stepped out of the shadows long enough to signal toward the spirit closest to them— a man dressed in long robes and bare feet that barely tickled the ground beneath them. He looked at Delia and glanced around the grounds before looking back at her again. She nodded toward him, waving him over with a quick flick of her wrist.

His gaze was wary as he came closer, and though his tone was hushed, Delia could tell he was speaking in a different language.

"We're looking for a man being kept in the tunnels underground," Delia attempted to communicate with him. "Brown hair. Tall. Kind of an asshole."

Kazzy snorted behind her, and Delia smirked before turning her attention back to the ghostly man. He ran a wispy hand over his face, brow knitting together in confusion. He sent her another string of unknown words.

Delia paused to clear her throat, glancing back to Kazzy for assistance. She remembered that Kazzy was not able to see the apparition in front of them. Delia squared her shoulders toward the ghost one last time. Baring her teeth and hissing, she lifted both hands and used her forefingers to mimic fangs protruding from her gum line.

"Are you— are you playing charades right now?" Kazzy asked with bewilderment etched into her features.

"We can't understand one another," Delia mumbled, dropping her hands to her sides in exasperation. It seemed that the man knew what she meant, though. His eyebrows rose, and his eyes widened as he emphatically nodded his head. He gestured with a sweeping arm for them to follow. "Come on, he wants us to follow him."

The man seemed to simmer in the dim lighting as he led them deeper into the complex, weaving through the bath system and to the other side of the grounds. They stopped at the top of a staircase leading down into a tunnel system lit with those same dim lights.

Kazzy grabbed Delia's arm, pulling her back. "He's here. I can smell him." She pointed to the moon, lit up against the darkness that had swept over the complex. "I'll be able to track the time better up here. I'll shift and follow your scent down to where he is. Wait for me before going on."

Delia nodded before gesturing for the ghost to lead her onward, who began his gliding descent down the slick stone stairs. She sucked in a deep breath and blew it out before grasping the cool railing. With every step, the air stiffened with underground humidity. It came startlingly quickly, opposite the crisp winter air steps above.

Delia walked slowly, careful not to kick a loose stone down the stairs. The man reached the bottom of the shaft, turning toward the left. Delia followed, her foot planting on the foundation of the tunnels.

Brick formed the rounded walls, creating large passageways that spanned in either direction of where she stood. Large spotlights, brilliant in the darkness, were fixed to the stone above her head. It took Delia a moment to adjust her eyesight.

Her footsteps echoed against the stone, the sharp ricochet the only sound in the silence of the tunnels. She hurried down the passageway after the ghost, who hadn't seemed to notice she had lagged. He wove through the maze, taking a right, a left, and two more rights. They passed large cisterns that once held thousands of gallons of water and ovens to heat the baths above. Now, all that remained were the muddy puddles covered in a thin film that seemed to dance on the surface.

Deeper into the underground, the tunnel opened to a large room flanked by columns erected from the walls. Black fences, hip height and positioned into a square to give tourists a look into the excavated regions below, pebbled the cavern. Though cracked and crumbled in more than one spot, Delia could still make out the ancient patterns of the stone beneath her feet. Stadium-style seating connected the columns on the long sides of the hall, presumably for people from long ago to sit. And, much like the entrance, the chamber's ceiling was vaulted and rounded.

"Mithras," the man said, pointing toward another door at the end of the long chamber.

Delia gestured for him to go further, but he put up his hands and shook his head. He would not lead her any longer. She nodded thanks at him, sending a small smile his way. He bowed at her before disappearing through the stone wall to their left.

Delia took another deep breath, planting one trembling foot before the other as she crossed the long hall. She approached the darkened doorway on the other end, sticking her head over the threshold and into the next room. The lighting, dimmer still in the antechamber, reflected off the wet stone and tile. She ducked against the shadows of the threshold, peering around the corner.

And there, in the middle of the room, Cian was strapped to a large wood plank.

His head hung, his chin dragging against his chest, and blood dripping from the corners of his mouth. Three figures stood in a semi-circle around him, each cloaked in long, brown robes and white masks that completely obscured their faces.

"We can continue this, vampyre," a low voice growled, his hand spearing out to clamp around Cian's cheeks. He yanked Cian's chin up as the second figure turned to a table filled with bowls and glass syringes, picked up a syringe, and dipped the needle inside the bowl, drawing the flange back until it filled to the brim with an unknown liquid.

Cian's eyes fluttered open, and Delia watched as his pupils pulsed in an attempt to focus his vision. His mouth opened, giving a half-hearted snap of his fangs toward the first figure, who retracted his hand under the brown robe.

"Give him more," he said as he stepped away from Cian.

The second man turned toward Cian, syringe in hand, and placed two fingers on Cian's cheek to push his head to the side. Cian groaned as the needle sunk into the flesh of his neck. The plunger was pushed down until the liquid had been completely injected into his system. Cian groaned with pain and a shudder before throwing up onto the stone floor. The sick splashed onto the hems of the men's robes.

The third figure shifted enough that a shaft of light from the nearest flickering bulb on the floor and what Cian had just vomited up. A shot of shock traveled up Delia's spine when she realized the sick wasn't sick at all...but blood. Cian looked so weak, blood dripping from his lips and onto his front. His dirty and torn shirt was already stained deep red with it.

"We can continue with the obsidian injections, vampyre," the third man said in a throaty voice that prickled a sense of familiarity in Delia's gut. "Or you can tell us where to find what we're looking for."

Cian groaned again but managed to mumble "fuck you" before vomiting another pool of blood.

"You cannot keep much longer," the second man, still closest to the table, interjected. Delia could tell from the conversation that he had refilled the syringe with more liquid, and the ground obsidian had dissolved in water. As if meant to confirm her thoughts, he said, "The obsidian is weakening you, forcing the blood of your victims from your body. You will begin turning into a husk of yourself by tonight if you do not feed." His voice was younger and fuller, and his accent was just as familiar, but it was still hard to place.

"Then get it over with already," Cian groaned in that quiet, strangled voice.

"If you do not tell us, we will put you back in your cage and go after your companions," the first man threatened, grasping Cian's cheeks and forcing his head up again.

Cian's smile was slow, teeth covered with streaks of blood. He gave a low chuckle. "If you knew where my companions were, you would have found them already."

Delia felt her heart soar in her chest. Despite the torture, the obsidian water, and the weeks spent in a cage...he had not given them up.

A low pattering sounded in the tunnels, different from the echoing footsteps of their chamber, turning the three men's attention toward the doorway. Delia threw herself backward, hiding in the shadow on the other side of the wall. The pattering became louder and louder as it neared. Delia's lips drew back into a smile...Kazzy.

The wolf skittered around the corner, the leathery pads of her paws sliding against the slick stone and broken tiles. Her canine form was massive— nearly twice the size of a wild wolf— and there were subtle differences in her form. Her snout was longer, and her ears more rounded. Her fur was solid white, long, and sleek.

She was breathtakingly beautiful.

"Shifter!" The first man yelled as he spotted her crossing the long hall, sprinting toward the antechamber with thundering steps.

Kazzy stopped at the threshold of the door. Her thick fangs bared as she growled at the three men holding Cian captive. She crept through the frame, and Delia watched the tips of her ears flick as she turned her eyes on each one. The second man shuddered as she stalked forward.

Delia peered around the corner again, watching Kazzy lift her snout into the air. Her nostrils worked, sniffing quickly before turning her attention toward the wooden table on the right side of the room. She strolled toward it, taking her time as the men carefully watched her through the slits in their masks.

Kazzy rounded the table and paused, regarding the men once more. She reeled her back legs into the air in a flash and kicked the table over, sending the bowls clattering to the floor. The second man dropped the syringe he held, his eyes widening with shock. The glass smashed as it hit the stone.

"P—papa?" the second man stuttered out as he jolted out of the way of the overturned table, his chest heaving from ragged breath.

"Hold your ground, son," the third voice sounded. He extended an arm in protection. "The wolf isn't here for us. It is a mortal enemy of the vampyre. It must have smelled him."

Delia's heart sank to her toes as she finally placed the voices. Lorenzo and his father...the two men who had given her the tours of St. Peter's Basilica and the necropolis. Her stomach tightened uncomfortably, remembering fingers scraping against her ankle as she tried to escape. She wondered if it was one of them.

Kazzy's growling was growing louder with every passing second, her bared fangs dripping with drool. The men had abandoned their attention away from Cian, now focused solely on the wolf shepherding them away from the vampyre. She took one step, then another, before stopping with a preternatural stillness that made Delia hold her breath as though breathing alone would break Kazzy from her concentration. The green eyes of the wolf darted back and forth, studying the three men.

Lorenzo's hands were trembling under the sleeve of the robe.

Kazzy waited for another heartbeat before launching herself forward, planting her front paws on one of the men. The man stumbled back, the hood falling from his head, and Delia recognized him as Lorenzo's father. He let out a strangled yell as he fell to the floor, head cracking against the stone. His yell shifted into a gurgle as Kazzy clamped her teeth around the exposed column of his throat. Delia felt bile bittering her tongue as Kazzy twisted her head, ripping the flesh from his neck.

Blood spurted, coating the white of her snout in red, before running in rivulets from the wound. It pooled in the hollow of his collarbones before snaking over his shoulder, soaking the fabric of his robes.

"Papa!" Lorenzo screamed.

Delia watched Lorenzo's knees wobble dangerously, threatening to buckle from under him. She swung her gaze back to the man bleeding on the floor and watched as the light in his eyes dimmed before darkening completely. The first man, still unnamed and unknown to her, lurched forward and grasped Lorenzo under his arm, hauling him toward the back of the antechamber, accidentally knocking Lorenzo's mask off.

Kazzy was too quick for the two. She shoved her large body between the men, peeling them apart from one another. Lorenzo tripped over the body of his dead father. The first man quickly removed a dagger from under his cloak, the metal glinting harshly under the lighting, and slashed at Kazzy with renewed force. The tip dug into her flank, deep enough to draw blood but shallow enough that it didn't seem to cause any damage.

Kazzy whipped around, her jaws snapping angrily at the man. He slashed the blade again, more frantically this time, and Delia saw the mistake just as Kazzy's calculating eyes fell on the extended arm. She lunged forward, sinking her teeth into the man's wrist. He let out a screech of pain, ear-piercing and echoing. The dagger fell from his hand when his fingers reflexively opened under the pressure of the wolf's teeth.

Delia hurled herself into the room, her wet sneakers slipping on the slickened stone. She lost her balance only once, catching herself with a hand in the warm, sticky liquid that coated the ground. She didn't think about it any further as she powered forward, sliding to a messy stop at the foot of the large, wooden slab Cian was strapped to.

She reached up, fumbling with the leather bindings that held his wrists and ankles. They were gritty with ground stone, and when she pulled her hand away, she recognized the black crumbles as obsidian.

Clever, Delia thought as she unlocked the wrist restraints.

"*You!*" A shout emanated through the chamber, reverberating over Kazzy's broad shoulder. Delia whipped her head to the side, her eyes locking onto Lorenzo. Face shrunken with fury, his once clouded vision began to clear with recognition.

"Lorenzo, we need to go," the first man managed to seethe through a tightened jaw. He had somehow extracted himself from Kazzy's jaws...though Delia had a feeling the wolf had allowed him to. "Get behind the runes."

It appeared that Lorenzo was struggling with how to proceed. His eyes continuously slid from his father's dead body before going back to Delia.

"*Lorenzo!*"

The tour guide's head snapped back to the cloaked man, finally breaking the intense stare he had pinned Delia in place with. Lorenzo reached for his colleague, clamping a hand around the bloody, penetrating wound. The man dragged him toward the door at the back of the room, behind a set of etched runes Delia noticed for the first time.

Kazzy continued snapping at their heels, her flank and paws coated in blood.

Lorenzo stopped past the runes, his hands bracing on the door frame. "You will never be far enough," he hissed at Delia, eyes flashing dangerously over the scene between them. "I will find you, and I will kill you for what you did to my father."

Delia's eyes narrowed in a challenge, but he was tugged around the corner before she could respond. He disappeared into the darkness, the hem of his robes whipping behind him as he went. Delia turned back to Cian, crouching to unstrap the ankle restraints. He slid off the angled slab, groaning as he crumpled to the floor.

"I had them, you know," Cian grumbled, shifting with a stiff moan to lay on his back. "I was just about to break these locks and kill them all when you showed up."

"Vengeance was going to be swift, I'm sure," Delia retorted. She grasped his hand and placed a steady arm behind his upper back, helping him to sit up. "You smell like a dirty aquarium."

Cian glanced at her, shaking his head and rubbing his eyes with his dirt-crusted palms. "You came for me. Why?"

"I couldn't let you die here. It would be so embarrassing for you."

Cian snorted, slowly extending his hand to pat her awkwardly on the arm. He sent her a small smile, and, at that moment, Delia knew that saying he was sorry or even saying thank you would still be difficult for him. And, at the end of it all, she realized she didn't need to hear him say it. She wrenched forward, throwing her arms around his neck and pulling him into a tight hug. His arms circled her waist for a moment before turning his nose toward her neck, inhaling deeply.

"Why did you have to make it weird?" she asked with a scowl, pushing him away.

Cian shrugged a weak shoulder. "I haven't fed in three weeks. Turns out, you might be my type after all." His attention shifted to the giant wolf still stalking at the edge of the runes in the background. "And you."

Kazzy stopped, tilting her massive head as if in question.

"Why didn't you kill them? You let them go?"

Kazzy stepped forward, shoving her snout toward the dead man before pretending to retch.

"You don't like the taste? Baby."

Kazzy let out a playful growl.

Cian groaned again as he tried to get to his feet, but he collapsed to the stone in the next breath. "I'm not sure how I will get out of here." His limbs shook feebly as he lifted a hand to run through the oily locks of his hair. "Damn obsidian stone is going to take hours to clear."

Kazzy didn't hesitate. She stepped forward, paw pad settling into a large crack in the stone, and carefully clenched the back of his shirt with her teeth. Cian's arms and legs went limp as he allowed Kazzy to pull him out of the chamber, the pools of blood smearing beneath his body as he passed over them.

He pointed a finger at Delia, who was struggling to contain her laughter. "One word of this to Greer, and I will end your life."

FORTY-ONE

GREER

Books were piled on every surface of the bedroom. Stacks on the windowsill, turned upside down on the bed to mark her place, on the small table that housed the still-full decanter. Greer hadn't touched the amber alcohol since her initial meeting with Azazel nearly a week ago. She had too much on the line. ,

She started with smaller pieces of her power. Turning the black-based lamps into a wicker one and transitioning the color of the end tables from dark wood to white. When she accidentally set her bedframe on fire, and Arista barged into the room after seeing the smoke unfurling from under the door, Greer swallowed her pride and asked for help.

And Arista was more than willing to oblige.

It was when the two women worked late into the night, Greer's tongue stuck between her teeth in concentration, that she finally began to make the most progress. She focused on manipulating the air around her. She learned how to pull on the magnetic forces from the ground beneath her. Her wide-sweeping arcs of magic slowly narrowed into accurate streams. She could pinpoint her power into a weapon more practical than the daggers or swords Samael and Odette had been pushing her to learn.

And, more importantly, she stopped setting everything on fire.

At least as often as she had been.

Nearly ten days after returning to Veritas, Greer was sitting on the floor of her newly decorated bedroom, legs outstretched in front of her and a leather-bound book— titled *History of Ancient Magic and Rites of Samsara*— lying open on her thighs. The early afternoon sun streamed in through the circular window, and, these days, the room didn't feel so dark and gloomy. Arista was sitting at the table, her cream-colored wings draped over the low back of the wicker chair as she flicked through her book. A pile was still stacked next to her elbow.

"I just don't know, Greer," Arista said, sighing as she flicked the book shut in frustration. She set her elbows on the table and placed her chin in her hand. "I don't know how else to get you back to Gaian without going through the portal in the Meridian of Pride. Unfortunately, your power just isn't ready to create them yet. Who knows where you will end up? " She paused to push the first book aside, taking another off the top of the pile and placing it delicately in front of her. "And I think we both know that Ramiel will have you thrown in the dungeon if a hair on your head ever crosses his border."

Greer snorted, carefully turning a page of the thick parchment paper. "Even if I'm the princess?"

"Even if you're the princess. Azazel was crowned king because he led the legions into battle. But he leaves most of the meridians to run themselves. Until you were arrested, I can't remember the last time he had to step in."

Greer looked down to read what was on the new page, but a phrase quickly caught her eye, etched into the parchment page in black ink. She had to read it twice before she comprehended it. Her heart ratcheted in her chest, and her breath caught in her throat. She hadn't responded to what Arista said.

"Greer?" Arista said after she realized the same thing.

Launching herself from the floor, Greer's footsteps were hurried as she scurried to the side of the table, pointing at the passage in the book. "Look. Right here. *The Meridian of Indolence, though originally set aside for daemons, has become a refuge for unique creatures and beings. Most notably, the dead witches of the Mage line created by Azazel, King of Samsara, have set up a small village there and are frequently called upon to act as arbitrators for disputes between daemons. They can access the Gaian realm through a special system gifted to their line.*" Greer glanced up, looking expectantly at Arista, who had begun to reread the paragraph.

"The Meridian of Indolence," Arista finally said, brow furrowing in thought. "That is southwest of here, a two to three-day walk at the most." She cleared her throat, eyes darting up to look at Greer. "Less time if you have a ride."

Greer bit her lip, stepping away from the table to pace back and forth.

"You have to go," Arista said, grasping the book as she stood. "The Abandoned Pastures. That is where you'll find the Mages. You have to go."

Greer stopped and deeply inhaled, taking in the Dragon's Blood incense stick that burned in the bathroom. She watched the swirling smoke visible from her stance on the other side of the threshold. "How would I get there, and with what ride?" she finally asked, glancing back toward Arista. "I'm being tracked like a rabbit in the winter."

Arista shifted on her feet, her eyes narrowing on the white fringe chandelier hanging from the ceiling. "I have an idea. Could you be ready tonight?"

"Tonight? What are you—"

But Arista was already sweeping out of her room, the feathers of her wings disappearing around the door frame.

Greer packed the smallest bag, one that could be hidden beneath a jacket. She was ready when the sun was setting behind the mountains in the distance, the deep orange and gold piercing the darkening clouds that nestled against the range. It had begun to snow now, thick flakes drifting toward the valley floor. It was better than the freezing rain of the months before, but Greer knew it would still be an uncomfortable journey.

There was a knock on the door, and before Greer could respond, Arista entered and quietly shut it behind her. The lock clicked into place.

"Okay. Ready?"

Arista had donned a dress of thick wool, a fur-lined cloak with slits for her wings tied around her neck. Greer glanced down at her layered leggings and sneakers, briefly noting that she would probably freeze before the days were up.

"What's the plan?" Greer asked.

"We're going down to the square for a drink," Arista replied. "And we'll go from there."

Greer stared at Arista, swallowing thickly against the nerves that knotted in the back of her throat. "That's the plan? To go for a drink?"

Arista scoffed. "Well, that's not the *whole* plan." She lowered her voice, sweeping her gaze back toward the door as though expecting someone to be there. "But I'm certainly not going to be telling you here." She tapped her ear before gesturing around the room. "You never know who is listening."

Greer snapped her lips shut as Arista approached the door, but a second question bubbled up. She had been pondering it since the night she lit her bed on fire, but she had been too afraid to voice it until now. "Why are you helping me?"

Arista paused, her glove-laden hand hovering over the door knob. "I was once revered by humanity." The words were soft and sorrowful, a mourning to the past she was remembering. "I want out of Samsara. I want to feel useful again. And I think you'll be the one to help me do that." She chuckled, shaking her head. "Funny enough, it was because you treated me so horribly when you first arrived."

A knife twisted in Greer's gut. "I am sorry, Arista. For what it's worth."

Arista waved her off. "I would have never come to this conclusion if you had been nice to me." She turned the knob and tugged the door open. "Come, we're running out of time."

Greer followed Arista through the hallway that overlooked the library and down the spiral stairs that emptied into the marble chamber that opened to the terrace. Their footsteps were quiet yet hurried, but a male voice echoing toward them had Greer's hand flying to her chest in surprise.

"Arista, Greer. Where are you off to?"

Azazel approached, flanked on his right by Samael. Greer fixed her eyes on her father, ignoring Samael's studying gaze locked onto her face.

"Her Highness is set on going to the square, your Grace," Arista said with ease as she bent into a low curtsy. Greer forced her face into an expression of disinterest. "I warned her that you would forbid it unless she were accompanied. I will go with her."

Greer said nothing, merely nodding in agreement. She was afraid that if she had opened her mouth, she might have emptied her stomach on the marble tile.

"A second trip to the square today, Arista? That's quite unusual for you." Azazel's brows rose. "Have Samael come. It's dark, and there are...creatures lurking about now."

Samael moved forward, the leather creaking as it rubbed together, but Arista expertly put up her hand to stop him. "Her Highness has called it a *girl's night,* your Grace," she said with a small, apologetic smile. "She has described it as a rite of passage for females to acquire glasses of mead together as a form of bonding. If Samael is there, I very much doubt the validity. Am I correct in thinking that, your Highness?" Arista swept her gaze over to Greer, expression open and eager.

"Yes, yes, that's correct," Greer squeaked, nodding vigorously.

Arista's turned her stare back to Azazel. "There isn't much to worry about, your Grace. We'll be in the square."

"I could think of a few things," Samael growled, eyes narrowing on Greer. She continued to ignore him, lifting her nose in response instead.

Azazel pondered them for a long moment, Greer's breath like a ball of lard in her chest. "Yes, Arista. Lovely idea. I hope you both have a great night." His assessing stare swept over Greer before a final nod of approval dipped his chin.

Arista curtsied once more before turning on the balls of her feet and marching from the chamber. Greer didn't give Samael or her father a final look as she shuffled after Arista, her heart still ratcheting against her rib cage.

And it wasn't until they were halfway down the switchbacks that Arista finally exhaled, the mist swirling in the cold air in front of her mouth. "I didn't think that was going to work," she said, glancing over her shoulder.

Greer followed suit, half-expecting Samael to soar into the space above them, but only the blanket of cloud coverage and the stars peeking above the mountaintops were visible. "That doesn't make me feel better, Arista." She side-stepped a large rock jutting up from the packed dirt of the trail. "Your lie was smooth, by the way."

Arista's brows knitted together. "What lie?"

"About getting a drink."

"Oh, that." Arista's giggle erupted through the cold. "We *are* going to get a drink. I'm a terrible liar."

Greer's head swung toward Arista. "What do you mean we *are* going to get a drink? I thought we were running out of time?"

"We are running out of time," Arista said, picking up her pace, gravel crunching beneath the soles of her boots. "But it's going to be important that we were in a tavern when you knock me unconscious and take the obsidian that I've hidden in the bathroom there."

"*What*?" The question came out more of a shriek than Greer liked, the shrillness of her voice startling Arista into tripping over her feet.

"What do you mean, *what*?" Arista interjected as they turned the corner and descended toward the square. A group of vampyres passed on their left, their eyes raking up and down Greer and Arista in interest. "I couldn't bring it with me. Azazel and Samael would have sensed it in an instant."

"So the plan is for us to enjoy a drink, have me knock you out in the bathroom, steal the obsidian, and run for my life toward the Meridian of Indolence?"

"Don't be silly," Arista replied, navigating between the people crowding the square. "The plan is for us to enjoy a drink so we are both spotted in the tavern together, have you knock me out in the bathroom, steal the obsidian to prevent anyone from sensing and tracking you, and *then* run for your life toward Egyn in the fields beyond the lake. I doubt you'll have more than three minutes before this place is overrun with guards looking for you. You'll want to be quick if you don't want to be spotted trying to leave the square."

"This is a terrible plan, Arista. I'm not prepared for this in the least bit." Greer reached forward to tug open the tavern door Arista had led them to, the smell of ale and stew wafting on the music-filled air.

"Can you think of another plan?" Arista shot back as they squeezed through the crowd of laughing Fae males, each sipping out of tankards.

Greer grumbled under her breath as they sidled up to the bar, awaiting the bartender to make his way down to see them.

The clinking of silverware against plates and the low-murmuring of conversations filling the space were the two things that Greer could focus on as Arista ordered them two small glasses of mead. The band in the corner, two fiddle players and a female with a flute played a lively tune, and the crowd bounced and swayed to the beat. Greer felt her anxiety building with every passing second, and she, subsequently, took a large gulp of mead as soon as Arista handed it her way.

"Stumbling drunk out of the square will not give you the time you need."

Greer nearly choked as she turned toward Arista, an incredulous look on her face. "Since when did you get so mean?" Greer asked, wiping her chin with the back of her hand.

"I thought I would get a barb or two in before you leave," Arista retorted with a grin, taking a small sip of her mead.

Greer rolled her eyes. "Is that any way to talk to a princess?"

Arista snorted, the most unladylike noise Greer had ever heard her make. "Some princess you are." She dropped a pair of coins on the bar, and the bartender immediately scooped them up before being deposited in the till. "Make your way slowly toward the restroom."

Greer pushed through the crowd, Arista tight on her heels, and pivoted to avoid a barmaid toting a wooden slab laden with tankards and a freshly baked loaf of bread. The hallway leading to the restroom cleared of patrons, and she breathed a sigh of relief when she pulled the door open to reveal a pair of empty stalls.

Arista set her glass of mead onto the sink before reaching down to rifle under the exposed plumbing and pull out a neatly wrapped package tied with a thick, beige thread. She tossed it into the sink, where it tinkered against the porcelain before resting near the drain.

"Okay," she said, turning to look at Greer. "As soon as you knock me unconscious, grab the obsidian and slip through the window. Your power will ebb away, and they'll be alerted of its absence when you touch the stones, so do not delay. Go straight through the square and skirt the lake. You'll find Egyn there. One of the obsidian stones is for him. Make sure you tether it around his mane, or else Samael will be able to find him." Arista cleared her throat, shaking her long hair out over her shoulders. "Okay, hit me."

With a sigh of disbelief, Greer raised her hands to chest height. Her fingers slowly curled into fists before she let them drop to her side. "Are you sure this is going to work? And what about you, won't they know you supplied the obsidian? If I get caught—"

"You'll never get out of the palace again," Arista finished for her, hurriedly gesturing toward Greer. "And...don't worry about me. As you once said, powerful people don't pay much attention to those who are plain. This restroom won't stay clear for long, so let's get on with it."

"Thank you, Arista," Greer replied as she lifted her hands again, and she meant it. She felt the familiar thrum of power pulse from her chest, ricocheting down her arms and blasting from the palms of her hands. The phantom wind hit Arista in the gut, and the primordial crumpled to the ground with a sickening thud.

Greer stepped over Arista's body and threw open the window to the restroom, briefly sticking her head out to glance down the alley. The coast was clear. She twisted on her feet to snatch the obsidian stones from the sink, pocketing them inside her jacket before clambering out of the open window. The twisting and tugging took a few seconds longer than she wanted to get the bag on her back through. By the time she navigated the window, she felt that wall brick inside her, concealing her power within.

Time was ticking now.

Stepping out of the alley, Greer fastened the hood of her jacket over her head and made a beeline for the shores of the lake. The square was bustling with vendors and tavern patrons, each paying her no mind as she slipped in and out of the crowds of chatting daemons. Her breath swirled in front of her; each step felt as though it had been taken in slow motion as she turned to glance toward the palace...

...Just in time to see a blast of power reverberate from the terrace that overlooked the city, the trees on the mountainside swaying in the remnants of it. Gasps and cries of surprise from the people around her as Greer's heart pounded in her ears. She shoved against succubus, who sent her a snarling look just as the tendrils of her father's magic reached the square. And, even though she knew that he wouldn't be able to sense her, she took off running toward the shore of the lake.

There was a limited amount of time now, and Greer knew Azazel would be searching for her.

The water had frozen even more in the last eight weeks, the surface still as glass. The ice was thick, with deep cracks carving a path leading toward the lake's deepest parts. But Greer didn't stop running. Not to marvel at the moon reflecting off of the mirrored water. Not to make sure that her feet had traction against the slick rocks. Not even to try and stretch out the stitch that had formed just under her ribs on her right side.

Just as Arista said, she spotted Egyn outside of town, braying and pawing at the ground in frustration at being tied up as long as he had been. He neighed as he spotted her, tossing his head excitedly as she approached. She glanced over her shoulder for the second time. Her chest burned as she pulled the cool air into her lungs to catch her breath. But seeing the guards soaring down from the palace and toward the city had her moving even quicker.

With fumbling fingers, Greer pulled the small package from inside her jacket. She tugged at the cord, releasing the knot with surprising dexterity despite the frigid temperature, and clumsily threaded a lock of Egyn's mane through the hole in one of the stones. When satisfied that it wouldn't come loose, Greer heaved herself into the saddle.

"Meridian of Indolence, Egyn," Greer said through clacking teeth, leaning down to pat the horse on the side of the neck. "The Abandoned Pastures."

And like a bullet out of a gun, Egyn took off into the night, the palace growing fainter in the distance.

FORTY-TWO

GREER

G reer rode through the night, not allowing the exhaustion to take her, and was sure she had reached the Meridian of Indolence by the time the sun rose above the meadow. Greer had expected a terrain similar to that of the Meridian of Wrath, vast amounts of dead forest and grassy knolls, but the Meridian of Indolence was calm...peaceful even.

The meadows were seeded with long grass, and bees flitted between the yellow and red wildflowers that dotted the landscape. In the cold morning, Greer could see the dew clinging to the spider webs built between the tall reeds flanking the shallow creeks. Winter hadn't quite touched the meridian as it had in the mountains, though she was readying to march across the land.

Water gurgled over the river rocks, and the sway of grasses blowing in the wind were the only sounds, save for the muffled footsteps of animals rustling the dry leaves. The smell of warm earth and clean air hugged the breeze rolling down from the distant mountains. Greer swallowed, wondering for a brief moment how much time she had.

Egyn had been cantering for most of the night, stopping only for a quick drink of water, so she brought him to a stop, dismounting him and watching as he made his way to a patch of grass. His tail lashed against the flies rising from the long grass, attempting to land on his exposed back legs.

Greer glanced around, her eyes sliding across the horizon before her heart stuttered in her throat. There, at the bank of the creek, stood a woman. Greer almost shouted in surprise, hand flying to her chest. But the woman was watching her closely, head tilted in curiosity. Greer lowered her hand, staring back at the woman warily.

The woman was dressed in a cotton skirt, the fabric ruffling in the wind, and the corset was tied tightly up her front. The shift she wore underneath was off-shoulder and sported rumpled, white sleeves that exposed her upper arms to the elements. She didn't seem to mind, despite the biting cold that had begun to move across the valley. Her dark hair was tied into a bun and covered with a white handkerchief knotted at the base of her neck.

And as Greer studied her, noting the shape of the woman's eyes and the slender features so similar to hers, she took a step toward her.

"Who are you?" Greer called out. Egyn nickered at her voice echoing across the meadow, but he didn't lift his head to investigate.

"I'm Agnes," the woman responded with a smile. She gestured toward the creek bed in front of her. "And you, my dear, look just like my Beatrice. Shall we walk?"

Despite her heavy footsteps, Greer lurched forward, stomping through the long grass until she was within feet of Agnes. It was silent between the two for a long minute, Greer struggling with what to ask or where to begin. This woman, her ancestor, the last Mage. Agnes held herself with such composure and a sense of confident leadership that Greer couldn't help but shrink in her shadow.

The bed of the creek was soft, though not entirely muddy. It gave way underfoot, making the ground uneven. Golden shafts pierced through the clouds drifting across the sky, illuminating the meadow in a bath of morning light.

"You have traveled far for someone who doesn't want to speak," Agnes finally said, clasping her hands delicately in front of her. The movement drew attention to Greer's own hands, which were swinging carelessly at her sides. She immediately crossed them over her chest.

"How did you do it?" Greer blurted out. "Being the Mage. Figuring all of this out."

"I had help. My mother, for one. Some vampyres, some werewolves, for two. Many members of the fae." Agnes's smile was small and filled with ease as she turned to peek at Greer from under her lashes. "I was the Mage for centuries, Greer. Please do not compare yourself to me. You will do amazing things in your journey. I'm sure of it."

Greer let out a breath, shaking her head. "That's the primordial power, not me. Raw energy can only get you so far." She paused, clearing her throat. "I've been compared to you a fair few times already. I just...I want to get back home. How can I tap into the power that allows me to do that?"

Agnes was quiet for a moment, contemplating the question. "I accepted the Mage powers when I was nearly your age. Twenty-six. My daughter was young, and I gave her to my mother to raise, knowing I could never see her again." She stared into the distance, toward the mountains jutting up to the open, blue sky. "There wasn't much I knew either. I learned as I went, I found what approach worked for each creature, each member of the council—"

"But you didn't—" Greer interrupted, halting in place. "You didn't help Odette reclaim her throne. Why?"

A quiet sigh escaped from Agnes, and a shadow of sorrow passed through her eyes. "My biggest regret was allowing Adair to take the fae throne. I knew what he had done to Odette. I knew what his plan was. I even talked to your father after my death, wondering if there was more I should have done or could have done. I've made many mistakes, Greer."

Greer cocked her head slightly, brow quirking. "You talk to Azazel?"

"Yes." Agnes began to walk again. "He is quite proud to be your father. When you first went into hiding with Holly, your mother, he came to me. He was concerned that he had sensed Mage magic and your primordial powers. It was my idea to insert obsidian into your body." Her smile trembled before falling entirely. "He came to me to see if there was a way to retract it from afar after we learned of your mother's death. He wanted to find you. There wasn't a way. I told him we must wait for you to break through."

Greer went quiet, rolling the new information around in her mind. A chirping cricket sliced through the silence between them when Greer decided to press on, unsure of how much time she had left. "And the daemons?" she asked. "Ramiel mentioned they were once united as one against the Paladin Society. Is there a chance to reunite them again?"

"Reuniting them would be...difficult," Agnes began slowly, fixing the fabric covering her hair as the wind adjusted the knot behind her head. "But not impossible. After the Library of Alexandria's fall, any documents written by previous Mages were lost to the Paladin Society. The daemon factions split soon after." She chuckled at the shocked look on Greer's face. "The Mage line took great care of the ancient documents in the library. Julius Caesar was a member of the Paladin Society, of course, so I suppose they still have the scrolls and documents stolen during the fire. To your question, you would require a new council. It will help with Eligos gone. I tried to limit my interactions with him."

Greer's eyes swept over to Agnes, studying her thin lips and long nose. "Eligos had you killed, didn't he?"

Agnes nodded. "I knew he was coming. My soul was tired, and I knew it was my time to be called home."

"Cian took your death very hard, I think," Greer pressed. "He still thinks about you."

"Cian is quite the character, is he not?" Agnes chuckled again. "I'm not surprised he's the one who found you. I would have bet many pieces of silver it would have been him."

Greer cleared her throat, tucking a stray lock of hair behind her ear. "Cian sold me out to Eligos. He tried to trade me for a potion that could cure anything. His vampyrism, to be specific."

"I also wish I could say that surprises me. Cian was always prodding me to find ways to be human. A potion to walk in the sun, a potion to stop requiring him to feed on human blood, a potion to cure him. He would have traded me if the right deal came along."

"Did...did you love him?" Greer asked the question slowly and quietly, wondering if it was a notch too invasive.

Agnes pulled her lips into a slight smirk. "I was very fond of Cian. I loved another very much and was lucky to have spent many centuries with him before I died."

"Is he still alive?"

Agnes nodded. "I suppose he would be. The death of a primordial is not easily forgotten. I'm sure your father would have told me."

Greer stumbled over an exposed rock. "You...you were with a primordial?"

Agnes glanced behind her, a look of concern crossing her face as she watched something unseen near the horizon. "The mages began to expect you when your power winked out, and I was sent to greet you here. I have two important things to tell you." She reached forward and grasped Greer's hands with her own. "First, I was found by a newly dead fae who sought out the mages but was looking for you. He wanted to send you a message from Odette. Michael's son, Leander, is trying to find a way to open the tombs. He is readying to march on Odette in the Court of Mist and Tide as we speak. You must not let him do so."

Greer's brows knitted together. "I—I'm sorry. The tombs, what tombs?" Her mind automatically flashed to the tour she had taken with Mammon and the story of the prophecy he had told her.

"Secondly, you are the daughter of the Mages. You come from an ancient and powerful line of women. Everything we have done was for you to succeed now."

Greer noticed that Agnes's hand had become translucent, and her skin was cold against Greer's. "Why are you telling me all of this?"

"Balance your primordial power with your inherited magic. Be the Mage. Be the strong woman I know you to be. If you do that, you can tap into anything these realms need from you. Anything."

Greer blinked, and Agnes was gone.

Greer's eyes were locked on the spot where Agnes had stood for a series of heartbeats before she sucked in a breath, unaware that her lungs had been beating in protest against her chest. She spun on the creek's bank, trudging through the river rocks and reeds back toward Egyn, who was still happily munching on the long grass of the meadow. Insects flew around her as she split the grass with her hands, finally reaching him as the sun began to tip above the mountains, bathing the meadow in mid-morning winter light.

Reaching upward to grasp Egyn's saddle, Greer paused before hoisting herself onto his back. Her eye caught the obsidian still looped in his mane, and deciding to take a calculated risk, Greer untied the stone and tossed it into the creek. It sank beneath the surface, disappearing beneath the murky, shallow water. She watched as the ripples widened and expanded before disappearing entirely.

Then, she waited.

The sun marched across the sky, and the clouds shadowed the meadow in dark patches. Greer picked at the wildflowers and made mini bouquets, which she tied to Egyn's saddle. She tossed rocks into the creek in a poor attempt to teach herself to skip them over the surface. Then, when the sun had reached midday, and the rays warmed her like a heated blanket, she lay in the grass and took a much-needed nap.

When she awoke, Greer was startled to find Samael seated in the grass next to her, absentmindedly peeling shafts of grass apart. Wiping the sleep from her eyes, she sat up and looked at him.

"It took you long enough," Greer said with a groan, stretching her arms above her head.

Samael scowled. "It took me hours to fly here." He paused to toss the grass shaft into the water, watching momentarily as it followed the current down the creek bed. "You're lucky I convinced him to come here by myself. He was ready to fillet you over an open fire. I can only assume that's what you wanted after *you stole my horse and put obsidian on him.*"

Greer didn't bother to look sheepish. "I came to find Agnes. I wanted to know how the mages tap into the realms."

"Smart. Azazel will not be pleased to hear you figured that out."

She ignored him, deciding to press on. "Agnes said something to me when she was here. Adair and Leander were marching on one of the fae courts to try and open some tombs."

Samael stilled, his shoulders stiffening and his fingers pausing from pulling a second strand of grass from the bank. He glanced side-long over to her. "I'm not sure what that has to do with you."

Greer's eyes narrowed on him. "You know what she is talking about, don't you? What are the tombs?"

Samael's lips pressed into a thin line, but he remained silent.

"Samael—" Greer trailed off, sweeping her stare over the markings that encircled his upper arms. She looked at them closely for the first time, leaning toward him intensely to study the patterns, the swirls, and the dips of the dark etchings. They were different from the one Arista bore. And she realized she had seen them before—on the columns in the Meridian of Greed. Greer snapped her eyes up to meet his. "You aren't a Primordial, are you?"

Samael was watching her. "No."

"What are you?"

He stared off toward the mountains in the distance, quiet for a long moment, before answering. "An Ananke, a being that even the primordials must yield to—a creator of realms and worlds. My brothers and I...there are eight of us in total. I made a deal to end the fighting during the War of the Sixteen. A deal that required binding us in the forms we had taken during the war. My brothers...three of them are locked in tombs in Gaian. The fourth has been imprisoned in Elysia. The fifth is bound in the Aeglecian realm. Two more are nowhere to be found."

Greer let out a sigh, searching his face. "Death," she said quietly, recalling the stories on the tombs and the secrets he had revealed to the phouka. "You're Death."

An Ananke of Time and Death and Pestilence...there was Time, and there was Death, Greer Myers, and, in the beginning, they were together as one. The Sisters of Fate's words rang through her.

"Yes."

She swallowed, peeling her gaze away from his. "If the tombs are opened," she began slowly, the breeze ruffling her curls over her shoulder. "What happens?"

Samael blew out a long breath just as the sun peered from behind a cloud, haloing his cerulean eyes in gold. "Opening the tombs is the first step to merging Samsara and Elysia again."

Greer shook her head, brows knitting in confusion. "Isn't that a good thing? Reuniting all of the Primordials?"

"The Gaian realm was created following the treaty signed after the War of the Sixteen, giving both Elysia and Samsara power. To reunite the two, the Gaian realm would need to be destroyed."

Greer's lips parted, her face cooling as the blood drained from her cheeks. "Samael, you have to go over to the fae courts and stop Leander. He can't be allowed to do this—"

"My hands are tied, Greer," he replied bitingly. "I can't fight Leander. My bindings prohibit it."

"Take me over there then."

Samael's head snapped to the side as he looked at her, startled. "I can't take you over there. Your power is not controlled enough. You'll be no match against—"

"Why don't you let me worry about my power, Samael," Greer replied in the same biting tone.

He sighed, shaking his head in frustration. Greer watched the muscles in his jaw tighten as he clenched his teeth together. "Azazel has forbidden me from taking you to Gaian."

"We aren't *going* to Gaian," Greer retorted, a smirk curling the corner of her lip. "He said you couldn't take me to Gaian. He didn't say you couldn't take me to the Fae realm."

Samael side-eyed her, scrubbing a hand over the stubble of his beard. "If you die, your father will never forgive me."

Greer pushed herself off the ground, swiping the dirt and grass from her pants. "If I die, I come back here anyways, and that's what he wanted all along." She extended a hand down toward him, an expectant stare on her face. "I want to do this, Samael. Like you've always said— it's my choice."

"Fuck," he grumbled under his breath, taking her outstretched hand. "Fine."

Greer braced against the soft meadow floor as he pulled himself up, and in the next heartbeat, a portal had ripped open the space behind them. She shed the jacket she still wore, letting the obsidian stone within fall to the ground. Power began to build within her, its beginnings tapping on the wall that had been erected.

"And Egyn?" Greer asked, tilting her head toward the horse still happily eating through the meadow.

"Will find his way home," Samael said. "Let's go."

FORTY-THREE

ODETTE

The palace had emptied, and most fae did not want to stay behind in a home that had become a prison. The few who decided to stay were assigned to dismantle the basalt wall surrounding the grounds and destroy the colosseum. They accepted willingly, relieved that they could remain in the only home they had ever known.

Most of them had been stolen from the villages at young ages or had been born at the palace, but Kaique killed their families in the coup. Those fae decorated the gardens for the solstice and made platters of roasted meats, fruits, and nuts for the humans to return to the beach to await the week until the rift opened again.

It was a celebration of the arrival of the summer season, the abolishment of slavery, and the opportunity for everyone to be reunited with their family—loved ones they hadn't seen in nearly ten long years.

The gates had already been propped open by Renan's order, and Odette allowed Luisa and Renan to lead the way into the jungle early in the afternoon. Odette was stuffed from the day of eating and partying, wishing she could curl up in bed and take a nap instead. But with the large number of humans needing transportation and the small amount of time they had to do it, she knew they needed to get a move on.

Many lower court members who returned to the villages brought groups of humans with them, three or four at the most. It was easier to guide in small groups if Kaique was waiting in the jungle's shadows. So far, no problems had arisen from the former Lord of Mist and Tide. Odette only hoped that it would continue.

The air felt sticky against her skin, the humidity of the summer thickening as the sun set beyond the canopy. The group trampled through the jungle as Renan led them through the pathways that had turned to mud in the late spring rain. They slid against the slick muck, a few older humans struggling to navigate it as easily as the fae did. Even Odette had decided to fly over the crowd instead of trampling alongside everyone else.

The rivers were engorged with rain, and the afternoon showers were enough to dump buckets of water on the jungle. Odette took a deep breath as she flew, inhaling the sweet scent of new growth and wet earth.

They walked and walked and walked for hours. Every village they passed was still celebrating, both from the upcoming solstice and the return of their loved ones. Adult villagers cheered and danced around the humans as they marched by while the children picked flowers to hand to the women. Though the walk was long, Odette could see each former slave stand a little taller as they made their way through the villages.

The moon was half-risen above the canopy before the group reached the beach and its rolling waves. The sea was calm that night, lapping gently at the sand and wooden dock that jutted from the shore. Even the grass was at peace, swaying in the breeze and tickling their calves as they broke through the jungle's edge.

Two women burst into tears as they reached the top of the dune, quickly comforted by a fae soldier and an accompanying human male. The beach, to them, was where it all started, and Odette was sure that emotions were high as their time in the Court of Mist and Tide was ending.

Odette touched back down to the ground, heading straight for the sea. She kneeled on the wet sand, water soaking into the knees of her cotton pants, as she reached into a coming wave and splashed a palmful of salted water onto her sweaty face. She swiped it into her hair, slicking the red strays against her scalp.

Groups of humans that had made their way to the beach in the days prior crossed the warm sand to greet them, tired smiles plastered on their wind-swept and sun-kissed faces. Near the docks, fae soldiers had set up tables of roasted meats and fruits that had been gifted to them by the villagers during their journey through the jungle. Many newcomers made a quick beeline toward the table, hunger pulsating behind their eyes.

Renan clapped his hands together, rubbing them quickly as he approached Odette's side. "We'll need a few soldiers to help the humans leave the rift when it opens. One to separate the water and create stairs out of the shaft, a second to clear the water from the pools, and the third to create stairs down the falls."

Odette nodded her head, knee still planted firmly in the sand. "Getting the humans out first is going to be key. It is more important that they leave before the rift closes than for the soldiers to." She glanced at the crowd of former slaves gathered at the dock's base. "We'll have to instruct them on how to leave. Remind them not to stray in the vastness between realms. I cannot promise where they will land if they do."

"And what of the humans who want to join us in fighting against the Fae King?"

Odette caught sight of Tomas and Anaise, arms threaded around one another in comfort as they sat with their bare feet touching the water.

"I want to ensure Kaique leaves the realm before we make any decisions," Odette replied, sliding her gaze back to Renan. "We can take one of the merchant ships on its return, use that to sail to the other courts, and plead our case."

Renan bobbed his head back and forth in thought. "We can consider it. Although, many of the sailors are those who support Adair and his campaign."

Odette sighed, rising to a stand. "We have some time to think about it, fortunately. Getting the humans out will be the priority at this point." She put her hands on her waist, sweeping an intense stare across the dark horizon. "Do you think this has been too easy? There's been no shadow of Kaique or his followers in the last few days."

Renan nodded in agreement. "Yes, it has been too easy." It was quiet, save for the pummeling river water in the distance and the humming of insects in the darkness. "I don't believe we're getting lucky. I believe you should have killed him when you had the chance."

Odette wholly ignored his quip. "No, I don't believe we're getting lucky either. Something feels wrong."

The shore was teeming with life, lower court fae, and soldiers bustling up and down the beach. Small bonfires littered the sand, made from piles of wood and ferns pulled from the jungle floor. The stars still twinkled above, mirroring against the glass-like sea.

It happened in an instant. One moment, Odette was surveying their surroundings, trying to find the source of the discomfort that twisted her stomach in knots. The next, she was sent tumbling to the sandy ground, a hole ripped in her wing from an arrow that split through it. She heard Renan yell as she was plunged into an oncoming wave, the cool, salty water sending a shock through her body.

Torches had been lit high in the canopy trees, illuminating the silent shadows behind the branches and leaves in a glowing, orange haze. Kaique was crouched amongst them, looking down at the frantic crowd with a malicious grin. Lined on either side were faeries, bows nocked with arrows pointed down at the humans and soldiers. A male to the immediate right of Kaique was reaching toward the quiver belted between his wings, adjusting a new arrow onto his bow.

The humans began to scream as lower court members and soldiers drew their swords, readying themselves for the coming fight.

"Go! Go!" Tomas began to yell, his feet still bare and pants rolled to his knees as he waved his hand toward the crowd, pushing them further onto the wooden dock and out of the range of the arrows. His face had drained to a ghostly pale under the moonlight.

Odette furiously looked over her shoulder, scanning the newly healed wing that was now shredded once again and thanking the primordials that the arrow didn't hit anything that would have caused pain. She pushed herself from the waves and lifted her eyes, noticing the emblems sewn into the leather fighting gear of the faeries that flanked Kaique.

The Court of Wind and Storm.

"How did he find..." Odette began to shout toward Renan, but she ducked another arrow that flew in her direction. It landed with a sharp *plunk* into the rolling waves behind her.

"Did you think," Kaique called over the heads of the crowd, straightening to stand on the branch. "That I would leave the Court of Mist and Tide without secondary protection? Did you truly believe the Fae King would allow you, Odette, to enter a Fae court without him knowing?" He tipped his head back to laugh. "These soldiers have been sitting in wait for weeks, waiting for my command to enter my land."

Renan drew his sword, brushing Odette's arm with his own as he readied his blade. Kaique stepped off the edge of the branch, using his magic to manipulate the droplets of water that collected on the greenery into small airborne pools. He walked on the surface of them as though they were made of stone, descending downward with his arms held wide. "All it took was me exiting my palace and finding the captain of their unit. We've been waiting for days for you to arrive here. It's truly too bad you took as long as you did. If it weren't for the wait, the second-in-command wouldn't have been able to send word to the Fae King informing him of your plans. I'm sure he'll be very pleased to see you again."

"Don't you get tired of listening to yourself talk?" Odette spat at him. Court of Storm and Wind soldiers leaped from the branches, landing skillfully on the dunes below.

The former Lord sent her a tight, humorless smile. "Arrest her," he said simply.

The scene exploded like the tension under a boiling surface had become too great. Lower court faeries and former slaves barreled over the beach, their swords raised in battle as they became a raging, protective force to the ones huddled at the end of the dock. The first set of archers spread their wings and pushed into the air, keeping their bows nocked and pointed at the defense. They loosed their arrows after a single call from the unit leader, sending them soaring toward the oncoming line.

Renan forced his hand back as though grabbing an item he left behind before slamming it forward once again. Under his command, a wall of seawater shot forward, building in depth between the Court of Mist and Tide and the archers. The arrows bounded off the wall, plunging into the vertical depths and sinking to the sand below. This time, the second row of archers rose at a different angle and sent their arrows flying. Renan uprooted another wall to protect his guards, and the arrows bounced away.

The lower court guards burst through the wall of water, leaping into the air. They used the water from Renan's wall just as Kaique had, creating stepping stones that they used to surge up, up, up toward the hovering Court of Wind and Storm soldiers. They slashed their swords, cutting through wings and sending the faeries crashing to the dunes below. The soldiers that were able to maneuver around in time to avoid the blades sent gusts of wind ripping through the air in an attempt to force the Court of Mist and Tide guards from the water stones. A few were successful, the guards plummeting from their pedestals and landing with sickening crunches on the dunes below.

It took no time for the sand to be stained red from faeries struck by arrows or bleeding from their wings. Tomas, Gael, and Luisa had leaped into the battle with a ferocity that sent a wave of pride through Odette, their swords clashing against the blades drawn by the downed Court of Wind and Storm soldiers.

Odette drew her sword and ran head first into the attack, her feet squelching against the wet sand and slick stones lining the beach. She blocked a blow sent down by a blonde-haired soldier and pivoted on her feet, slicing her sword in an underhand swing that severed the tendons at the back of the man's knees. He let out a guttural scream as he fell, his hand clamping tightly against the back of his leg. That scream was cut to a gurgle as Odette's sword punched through his throat.

"Get her! Get her!" Kaique was roaring as he backed toward the jungle, and Odette easily cut down another faerie.

She snapped her head to the side when she heard a familiar voice cry. A gut-wrenching, horrified gasp escaped her lips as she saw Tomas, his body impaled on the edge of a blade. It was ripped from his gut in the next moment, blood dribbling from the corners of his lips, and he fell to his knees with a thud that was swallowed by the ongoing battle around them. Luisa howled with rage and agony, her sword shredding the air as she made her way toward the man who had become a father figure to her.

Odette rushed over, feet gliding over the wet sand, and caught Tomas before his chest hit the ground. He was shaking as she turned him onto his back, the blood that coated the front of his tunic staining her fingers. His hands fumbled frantically as he grabbed Odette's shoulders, and she cradled him to keep him calm. His eyes widened, his breath ragged, and then he went still.

Luisa's wail punctured the night as she collapsed to her knees next to them, shredding straight through Odette like a hot knife.

One male was at fault for this, and one had gathered the troops to capture Odette and garner favor from Adair. Odette stood, carefully setting Tomas's body onto the beach, and spotted Kaique crouching next to a canopy tree near the jungle's edge. His cowardice yanked a feral anger from her that she could no longer contain. Her sword still drawn, her tunic now covered in Tomas's blood, she called over to Renan to watch her back.

"No," Odette heard a voice call out from behind her. She looked over her shoulder to see Luisa, her dark hair hanging lank and wet over her shoulders, droplets of blood coating her face like freckles. She clambered toward the nearest dune, her sword hanging from her fist. "He's mine."

Odette looked between the two, the clashes of blades and the squelching of blood raging around her, and took in Luisa's wild gaze and Kaique's cowering figure.

"He's all yours." Odette knew that there was a chance Kaique would kill Luisa, even with his missing hand. She also knew that Luisa deserved the opportunity for revenge, to take back her power, her control, and her life. "Take it all back, Luisa." The words rang between them, a mantra that had become their secret code.

Kaique's chuckle rumbled over the dunes. "You think you can take me, Luisa?" He stood from his crouched position, lip curling in a sneer. "I should rip you apart right here."

Luisa stopped a few feet from him, breath tearing in and out of her from climbing the dune. "You aren't doing anything to me anymore." She lunged forward, catching Kaique off guard. He didn't expect an attack from her. He fell to the side and grimaced as his stumped arm caught his fall. She lunged again, this time slicing his cheek with the tip of her sword.

Kaique yelled angrily, throwing out his hand and forming the water droplets around him into a whip. It cracked against Luisa's face, the skin instantly purpling and swelling into a welt. He smirked as he sent another lash of water, and Luisa rolled to the side to avoid it. Kaique swirled his hands, and the water instantly tightened around Luisa like a restraint, pinning her hands at her sides.

Renan, who had been eyeing the interaction despite his duel, broke the water apart with a swipe of his hands. Luisa fell to the sand, her palms skidding against the seagrass. She managed to hold onto the sword by the tips of her fingers and shot up, darting toward Kaique like a cannon blast. He easily circumvented her movement, twirling in a motion that had his robes billowing around him.

"Odette!" Luisa yelled in frustration, snapping her head around to find the Lady of Mist and Tide. "I need you."

Kaique's face opened in fear as Odette locked her gaze on him, the preternatural fixation settling onto him. His eyes darted around, looking for any Court of Storm and Wind soldier to guard him, but the closest ones were either lying face down in the sand or were still tucked into their battles. Odette's smile was villainous before she took a deep breath and charged forward.

Luisa and Odette moved as one against Kaique, their swords clashing against his now-drawn dagger. They danced around him. When one was attempting a distraction, the other was lurching forward. Renan blocked any of Kaique's attempts to tug on his magic, immediately striking down the manipulated water with his magic. Kaique abandoned his powers soon after, leaning on his ability to fight instead.

And Odette knew that was a big mistake on his part.

She jumped, using the thick trunk of a canopy tree to ricochet herself back toward Kaique, landing behind him with expert precision. She wrapped her arm around his neck, jamming it into the crook of her elbow. His fingernails desperately scratched at her forearm as she squeezed. The tips of his ears turned a deep shade of puce.

"Now," Odette said breathily, nodding her head toward Luisa. "Now he is all yours."

Luisa said nothing to Kaique, only staring him in the eye as she stalked toward him, every bit the predator Odette knew she could be. And that gaze never left Kaique as Luisa plunged the sword into his heart. His eyes bulged from the sockets as he peered down at the blade penetrating his chest. He let out a throaty gasp when Luisa wrenched her sword out of him, the blade making a horrid sound of metal scraping against bone.

"That's for my family," Luisa said before jabbing the sword into his gut. He groaned, blood dribbling from the corners of his mouth in a nearly identical pattern to Tomas's. He jerked forward as she withdrew the sword with another yank. "And that's for Tomas." She thrust the sword one final time into the crotch of his leather armor. "And that one is for me." She ripped the blade upward, connecting the genital wound with the abdominal one, cleaving him nearly in half. His intestines spilled onto the sand at their feet, rolling out of him like long, thick worms.

Odette loosened her grip on his neck, and he tumbled forward just as the sun broke over the horizon. Dead.

Relief washed over Odette as she stepped back, breathing in the salty sea air as though she had never smelled anything so sweet. Luisa collapsed against the dune, tossing her sword onto Kaique's dismantled body. A chuckle bubbled up Odette's throat as she saw the strange scene before her, finally taking in the empty and unseeing eyes of the male who had given her nothing but trouble for nearly eight hundred years.

Luisa slid her stare over to Odette. "It's done now, isn't it?"

Odette had opened her mouth to reply but didn't even have the chance to get the words out when Renan was shouting from across the beach.

"Incoming! Odette! Incoming!"

Odette whirled around, blood draining from her cheeks when she saw what Renan had spotted soaring over the open sea.

"It's Adair and his army!" Odette shouted back, recognizing the signature-colored leather armor that he bore. She readjusted the sword in her hand as Luisa bolted upward, collecting her blade from Kaique's chest. "Hold your ground!"

But as she looked around, assessing the broken and exhausted guards who had barely defeated Kaique, she swallowed back the fear. There were too few left, and the ones that remained could barely hold up their weapons. They were all going to die, and there was nothing she could do about it.

When Odette had that flicker of a thought, she felt a sinking feeling in her stomach that turned her bile into a burning poison. She saw a flash of golden light tearing a hole into the space above the beach.

And it was when two figures emerged through that makeshift rift, Odette felt the swooping sense that hope brought when all was undoubtedly lost.

FORTY-FOUR

GREER

"G*reer?*"

Greer's head snapped up, sweeping over the crowd before landing on Odette's familiar face. The faerie's chest was heaving as she struggled to pull in breath, the fabric of her clothes ripped and covered in blood. The sword she bore hung limply at her side, the tip digging into the beach.

"You— did you get our message?" Odette called out, her tone skeptical and disbelieving.

The crowd split as Greer approached, dirty and sweat-coated faces turned toward her, their eyes wide as they tracked her and then Samael. He stiffly trailed behind her, sword at his back and dagger at his hip.

The crowd had begun murmuring, whispers in a language foreign to her ears. Greer wished she had time to take in the jungle-lined beach and the imposing canopy trees towering over it, but that would have to wait.

"Yes, I got your message. Do you know someone named Leander?" Greer asked.

The woman beside Odette, her long hair disheveled and tangled, sent distrustful glances to Greer and Samael. She shuffled closer to Odette, hand tightening on the hilt of her sword. From the corner of her eye, Greer saw Samael set his hand on the pommel of his dagger. He might be unable to match Leander while he was bound, but Greer suspected he would run anyone else through without a second thought.

"Leander?" Odette repeated, wiping the back of her hand across her brow. She managed only to smear the dirt and blood together. "If he's with Adair, he's in-bound now." She pointed over Greer's shoulder.

Greer spun, a horrified expression clouding her face. She thought she had more time to prepare. There, in the bay, an army was streaming toward the shore at break-neck speed. Flapping leather wings beat against the open breeze, their bodies covered in leather armor with gleaming swords strapped to their waists. They banked in groups, soaring over the cresting waves as they approached, hundreds of legions making to surround the army commanded by Odette.

But Greer could easily pick Leander out of the lineup. He had brilliantly blonde hair and white, feathered wings to match. With every passing second that he flew closer, his square jaw and wide nose became clearer.

"This might not make sense right now," Greer said quickly, turning back toward Odette. "But he's trying to find a way to break the treaty that would merge two realms. And, if that happens, the human realm will cease to exist."

Odette swore loudly as the woman beside her darted her wide, brown eyes between the two. "How much time do we have?"

"I don't know," Greer responded earnestly, shaking her head. "I'm not sure how he plans to release the bound ones." She swallowed, glancing over her shoulder again.

Wind began to whip around them, sand painfully lashing at their cheeks. The fae members of the Court of Mist and Tide had begun their initial assault, creating large spheres of water that they thrust in the direction of the armies to knock them from the air.

"Hold your ground," Odette cried out as a thrum of anticipation reverberated through the readying army. She looked toward Greer, chin bobbing toward the man and woman at her side. "Greer, meet Luisa, my general. And Renan, my Captain of Intelligence." She paused to swallow. "If we're going to die together, we may as well know everyone's names."

Greer sent Luisa a small smile, but she was sure it looked like a grimace. Luisa didn't try but dipped her chin toward her chest in acknowledgment. The next moment, Luisa was barking orders at the melding of fae and humans that flanked her right side.

"Take this."

Samael pressed something into the palm of Greer's hand. She glanced down, surprised to see the emerald-lined dagger. It purred a welcome, the venom within swirling under the etchings that held it in place. Swallowing thickly, Greer lifted her gaze back up to Samael, who had unsheathed the sword from his back.

"I can't help you with Leander," he reminded her, twisting the blade in his hand, "but I can clear the path." His eyes dropped to her lips, and for a moment, Greer thought he would kiss her. He cleared his throat. "Don't let Leander touch you. If he comes into contact, he can drain your power."

She nodded in reply as another gust of wind whipped at her hair, tugging it from the braid she had tangled together. Samael looked her over once more before rocketing into the air, beating his wings to send him up. He shot forward, sword clutched in his hand and sent a wave of power toward one of the Court of Storm and Wind battalions. Their wings froze in place, and with shrieks of panic, they tumbled from the air and fell into the bay in a series of splashes. They did not surface again.

The battle clashed on Greer's left, sword on sword, fae against fae. Shouts of pain and zinging of metal spliced through the air as the beach stained red. Thunder clapped against the dark storm clouds that had gathered over the bay, rain angrily pelting the battle that had begun to rage on the shore.

Boots landed on a piece of driftwood in front of Greer with a snap. Leander sauntered toward her, flanked on his left by a fae male, each footstep sinking into the sand as he walked. And, despite what others had told her, Greer found herself a little unimpressed.

Leander's hair was a white-blonde and cut short, a distinction between himself and the other primordials that Greer had met. His features, though, were undoubtedly human now that she could see him up close. Leander's square jawline wasn't contoured or sharp, and his eyes were a little too far apart. He was average height, lacked overall muscle definition, and would have best been described as lanky. His wings, not as brilliantly white as Greer had initially thought, were noticeably smaller than the other primordials.

"Cousin," Leander said with a maliciously playful grin, his arms spread wide as he assessed her. "It's nice to finally make your acquaintance." He paused to reach over his shoulder, unsheathing a sword from his back. "I've heard so much about you."

Greer held back her flinch at the sight of him twirling the sword in his hand. She reached up to scrap a soaking lock of hair from her forehead, droplets of water dripping down her face.

Leander watched her gleefully as the second male at his side moved forward, his leathered wings tucked in tightly to his back. "How could I have forgotten my manners?" Leander said off-handedly, gesturing toward the male. "I'm sure you've heard of Adair, the Fae King. Adair, meet your Mage."

The fae male had auburn hair, similar to Odette's, cut in a stark line just above his shoulders. His hazel eyes were sharp and unforgiving, the black pupils like pinpoints against the bright flashes of lightning that forked across the sky. He, too, was dressed in leather armor, though his was a deep shade of red that clashed heavily with his hair and pale skin.

"We came to pick up something of ours that you may have," Leander began again. "Odette. Where is she?"

Greer's lips parted as she started to reply, but Odette's entrance cut her off, and the fae male at Luisa's side, Renan. The rain was coming down in punishing sheets, gale-force winds whipping the bay into a frenzy.

"You made that easy," Leander said, clapping his hands together. The sound was barely audible over the storm. "Odette, if you just come with us, we'll happily be on our way."

Odette remained silent, her lips forming into a thin line. With her sword still clutched tightly in her fist, she watched Adair with a predator's gaze, her own amber eyes flashing with low-humming rage.

Leander used the tense stand-off to lunge toward Greer with an outstretched hand, but Renan was quicker in pulling Greer backward. Greer gasped in surprise as Odette stepped forward to slice her sword across Leander's path.

"Do not touch her," Odette growled, eyes narrowing on Leander.

The male straightened, adjusting his leather armor back into place. Greer noticed the armor had the same coloring and style as Adair's, and she wondered if Michael knew Leander was there. Samael appeared above them, wings beating against the wind to keep him in place.

"Someone made you aware of my talents," Leander casually went on, as if the act of his lunging had never happened. He looked down at his sword, absentmindedly studying it underneath the heavy black clouds in the sky. A strong wind whipped the jungle canopy behind them, leaves plucking off their branches and twirling toward the sandy beach. "I was hoping you would have remained ignorant. I'm afraid it makes things a little more difficult for me."

Greer shot a lick of power at Leander, a sharp thread that lashed across his face. It lacerated his cheek, leaving a deep gouge mark in its wake. Leander lifted a hand and gingerly touched the welt, blood pebbling from the wound.

"It's been a long time since someone was able to get the upper hand on me," he said softly, any amusement disappearing from his eyes.

In a flash that seemed even quicker than the lightning that lit up the space between them, he swung his sword toward Renan, who answered with his blade. They connected in a sharp clash of metal on metal, the edges whining against each other.

In the sudden chaos, Adair had grabbed Odette. She responded with a swipe, cutting one of the Fae King's fingers off with a curt flick of her wrist. The cry of pain and anger was treated like a summoning for the Court of Wind and Storm soldiers, who were near enough to hear it.

The legions attempted to barrel toward their king, his bleeding hand cradled against his chest but were met abruptly by a new throng of Mist and Tide guards funneling out of the surrounding jungle, swords were drawn.

The beach exploded in a flurry of duels.

Odette and Adair had begun their dance toward death, swords meeting with sounds that rivaled the clapping thunder. Odette reached down to grab a handful of wet sand, throwing it into Adair's eyes as a diversion.

Renan had taken on Leander, who was just as skilled with his sword as any other primordial. The driftwood they stepped across sagged dangerously under their weight as they fought to see who would retain the high ground.

Luisa had appeared, sprinting into the fray to replace one of the Mist and Tide guards who had been cut down. She rolled to the side to avoid a striking blow, the fae's sword buried in the sand. She used her momentum to swing her sword upward, landing a slicing strike to the side of his neck. The fae male dropped to his knees as blood spurted from the wound.

Greer caught movement from the corner of her eye and spotted a jeering legion, slowly removing his sword from the sheath at his back. He lunged, and Greer scurried backward, managing to keep her feet balanced. He sent a lethal blow toward the side of her head and his sword wedged into a piece of driftwood near the edge of the jungle. He tugged on the hilt, seemingly underestimating her as he took his eyes off Greer for less than a second.

Greer took the offense, her dagger powering through the air. The male jarred, trying to escape her blade, but it was too late. The dagger split his forearm open, ripping the flesh down to the bone. He let out a guttural scream as the wound smoked, black coloring his veins as the venom sped toward his heart.

He was dead half of a breath later.

"Fool," Adair spat, kicking the male as he stepped over the body, still sparring with Odette.

Renan and Leander had clambered off the driftwood and fallen trees, still side-stepping, jumping, and blocking one another as they danced through the wet sand. While Greer had been fighting, Leander had picked up a second sword— more than likely from the dead Court of Wind and Storm legion lying face-up in the rolling waves, his eyes staring unseeingly toward the darkened sky.

Sweeping her gaze over the roiling crowd, Greer felt sick—male fighting male. Female fighting female. Fae fighting fae. Fae fighting humans. Each dealing blow after death blow to their counterpart.

The factions of daemons were fractured far deeper than she knew, and Greer realized Ramiel was right. She was naïve to think she, a twenty-seven-year-old woman, could step in against creatures far older and stronger than she might ever be. Raw power be damned.

Leander and Adair had brought far more soldiers than Odette. They were still fighting as though their lives depended on it...and she guessed it did.

The tang of blood melded with the briny air of the sea. The cracks of thunder almost covered the sounds of painful, dying cries. She just wanted it to be over— she needed it to be over.

Heart shattering, Greer lifted the dagger to eye level. It vibrated in her hand, purring the familiar call she had felt for the first time only weeks ago. *Let me out. Let me play. Tell me where.* The lump in her throat grew until it was difficult for her to swallow, and she released the venom into the rain.

"Find the fae against us," Greer whispered to the shadow.

Devastation followed on her command. It dipped and swerved through the crowd of fae, the Court of Wind and Storm legions dropping like stones to the wet beach, their eyes still open and their mouths gaped. They never knew what killed them, no single blow or festering wound. Death was quick and cunning, silently taking them in the night.

The Court of Mist and Tide soldiers were left stumped and stunned, their swords hanging limp by their sides as they stared at the fallen bodies around them. They were dead, every one of them that the venom had touched. Greer watched as the shadow moved deeper into the foray, unseen by anyone else.

Leander desperately screamed to see his army drop within seconds, a rough, fiery cry that echoed through the wet, dark trees and into the surrounding jungle. He kicked out at Renan, his half-primordial strength cracking the male's ribs and sending him flying into a downed tree. His head propelled backward, smacking against a buried rock. Renan crumpled to the ground, blood trickling from the wound in his head, unmoving.

Greer hurried toward him as Luisa hopped in to take over the duel with Leander. As Greer ran, she called out his name, landing next to him only seconds later, wetness from the sand seeping through the knees of her pants. His wounds had already begun to knit back together painfully slowly.

No longer amused or entertained, Leander realized he was losing, and he shifted his fighting style to reflect it.

Renan was still knocked out cold, but his breathing had begun to deepen, and the bleeding had ceased. Greer stood, her gaze sliding toward the clashing swords of Odette and Adair, each soaked to the bone, water rolling down their leather armor.

Greer looked past the destruction surrounding the beach— the downed trees, the shattered driftwood, the bodies lying haphazardly on the sand— and saw two fae males with their hands wrapped around each of Luisa's arms, Leander suddenly out of sight. She was struggling to pull away as they dragged her toward a tethered ship, her heels digging into the wooden planks of the dock.

Luisa's terrified screams were high-pitched and gut-wrenching as she placed a foot on the hull, and Greer heard a bone snap as one of the guards attempted to push her onto the deck. Greer took off running, calling the venom back to her. When she reached the ship, Greer shoved the dagger into the side of the first unsuspecting soldier, and he dropped to the dock, clutching the wound with both hands. Blood bubbled between his fingers, and from where she had stuck the blade, she knew it would be fatal.

The venom came after her, silent as the night, and overtook the second soldier. He collapsed to the deck of the boat with a sickening thud. Dead. The first guard's eyes went wide at the sight, and they swept across the ship to see what had dealt the final blow to his partner. He never saw the shadow descend on him, taking his life just the same.

Luisa was sobbing, clutching her lower leg between her hands as sheer panic rumbled out of her. Greer ran over, hesitating to lay her hands on Luisa. The break was bad. Her bone ruptured through the skin, pointing toward the storm-filled sky like a grotesque compass.

"Luisa, I need to set it before we can help it," Greer said over the woman's wracking sobs, gazing into the sky for any sign of Samael. From Luisa's reaction, Greer had a feeling that the panic was less about the broken bone and more about being dragged off by two males.

Greer braced the leg north of the fracture, and Luisa twisted to vomit on the dock. Greer didn't stop as she grasped the woman's foot and pulled with all her strength. The bone slid under the skin, the grating sound sickening as bone rubbed against bone. Greer did her best to send a comforting wave of power through Luisa, but it was useless. The pain was too great.

Luisa shuddered and slumped to the side, her hair splaying into the pile of sick that coated the wooden planks. Greer crouched, moving quickly to continue setting the bone. It was probably in Luisa's best interest to be knocked out during this anyway.

Just as she began to pull against Luisa's foot again, Greer felt a hand clamp onto her shoulder. Her power began to wane, weakness jolting through her like a zap. She spun around, grasping the dagger from the dock and whipping it toward her assailant with as much force as she could muster. She caught Leander's arm, who hissed in pain as he slapped a hand over the new wound.

Greer smirked in triumphant relief before her body seized with the realization—she had never returned the venom to the blade. Her eyes swept across the beach, frantically searching for the shadow of death before seeing it against the hull of the boat. Leander had used the slightest bit of her power to pin the venom away from him.

A second thought jolted in her belly...Leander could see the venom.

Moving again, Greer spliced the dagger through the air as she let out a frustrated yell at her stupidity. Leander easily side-stepped it and clamped an open hand around her forearm. He took in a deep breath, and she felt her power pull from her as though he were sucking it through a straw. She fell to her knees, struggling to free her arm from his grasp.

With each breath Leander took, more of Greer's primordial power drained away.

"It's not fair, you know," Leander said through gritted teeth, blood still dripping from the wound in his arm. "How much power you got from your father. They liken our fathers to twins, you know, and I got nothing from mine. Not a fucking drop." He paused as Greer slashed at him with the dagger, but the motion was weak and half-hearted. He easily kicked the blade from her hand, sending it skittering across the dock. "I'm sure you know by now that primordials can decide how much power to give their offspring, and you got a third of his. A fucking third."

"*Greer*!" Odette was yelling out as she continued to fight with the Fae King, watching helplessly from across the beach. Greer could see them dancing across the sand from the corner of her eye. "*Greer*!"

Greer's vision was blackening, speckled dots forming in the corners of her eyes. *Stay awake, stay awake, fight back*, Greer pleaded with herself. She managed to clear enough mental fog to see Odette send a blow to the Fae King, knocking him in the forehead with the hilt of his sword.

Adair stumbled into the waves beating at the sandy shore, lightning silhouetting his figure. He breathed, wiping the blood and dirt from his sweaty brow. And as Odette came for him one last time, he spread his leathered wings and took off into the stormy sky.

"*Coward*!" Greer heard Odette scream. "*You coward*!" But he had already cleared the trees by the time Odette navigated the heavy winds and lashing rain, the leathery flesh flapping near the hole in her wing.

Leander released Greer's arm, tossing her to the dock like a flour sack. She fell, sprawling onto the wooden planks with a thud. The storm quieted, or her mind tuned out the wind roaring over the bay. He bent down next to her, scraping a lock of sticky, wet hair from her forehead. She felt sick to have him touch her. Greer lifted her arm to push him away, but it flopped back to the dock.

Leander smiled, brimming with the power he had taken from her. "You and I would have been a formidable pair in another life." Samael dropped to the dock, sending a menacing stare to Leander, who widened his smile in return. "And I'm sure I'll see *you* soon, Death."

Casting a hand to the side, Leander ripped open a rift near the end of the dock. And without another word, he crossed through the portal and was gone.

FORTY-FIVE

ODETTE

The post-battle haze was always the worst part in Odette's eyes. Seeing the aftermath sprawled across the beach, the unseeing gazes of the humans who were no longer with them, and the blood-stained sand of her people was harder than she remembered it being. There were wars, and there was...this—the heartbreaking ending to what Kaique and Adair had collectively done to the faeries.

And Odette knew it wasn't over yet. With Adair fleeing the beach just as Leander stole Greer's power, she knew her claim to the fae throne was dicey at best. It would take her besting Adair just as he had done to her father to win back the courts.

That was if the courts weren't too far gone to accept reuniting again.

Odette swallowed as she slowly crossed the dock to Greer's seated position. The winged male she had brought with her crouched in protection behind her. As she approached, he swept his terrifyingly intense gaze over to Odette, daring the faerie to say anything that would upset Greer further.

Odette cleared her throat anyway. "I want to talk to her alone." Her voice felt shaky and unnatural, but she fought to hold it steady against a power that weakened her knees.

The male parted his lips to refuse, but Greer ducked away from his touch. "There are souls to collect, aren't there, Samael?" the mage said, her tone sour as she gestured toward the bodies Renan and the surviving humans had begun to pile onto the ship bobbing at the other end of the dock. "Why don't you run along and have fun."

The male scowled at her but pushed himself to stand regardless. "I'll be at the dunes," he replied, though Greer said nothing as he launched himself into the air, Odette's hair ruffling on the phantom wind behind him.

"Is he— is he a primordial?" Odette asked, lowering herself to a seat on the edge of the dock. The storm clouds had blown away, no longer fed by the Court of Storm and Wind, leaving the sun to shine brightly against the calm waters below them. Odette watched for a moment as the waves lapped gently against the wooden posts of the dock before turning to study Greer's profile, still glaring at her lap.

Odette sighed, leaning back onto her hands. "You know, I should probably thank you for coming to help us. You've already done more for the fae than your ancestors did. Perhaps even all of them combined." Greer stayed silent still, so Odette pressed on. "Did he take all of your magic? Leander?"

Greer shook her head, closing her eyes as though enjoying the salty breeze against her cheeks. "No, he didn't. He can't take the permanent ability from me. He can only steal from others, not create anything himself. He empties the well of power others have, ingesting their souls if they're dead. Then, when he uses it, he drains it from his stores. I can't—" She trailed off to take a deep breath. "My soul just feels fileted and raw. My magic is refilling, though I don't know how long it takes to regenerate entirely."

"It's usually a few days for me," Odette responded, squinting as a cloud passed over the sun, dulling it from view. "When I use all of my power and can no longer manipulate the molecules around me, I know I did too much."

Greer turned to look at her, brows pulled high on her forehead. "Is that what it is? Manipulation?"

Odette smirked. "What did you learn while you were gone?"

"That I'm a failure," Greer responded, her voice shaky as tears gathered at the corners of her eyes. "That I'm not meant for this." She blew out a long breath. "I'm sure I'll be dragged back to Samsara soon, and I'll never be let back out."

The two women were silent for a long minute. The only sound breaking the space between them was the sound of bodies being lugged onto the ship.

"You'll never be let out?" Odette asked, her brows knitting together in question.

Greer's low chuckle was devoid of any humor. "My father will be sure to see it through. I've caused enough trouble in Samsara for the lifetime of an immortal."

It wasn't right, Odette thought, forcing the mage into a realm that was meant to be her prison. She wanted to rage with Greer, to tell her to fight back, but that wasn't what either of them needed.

"When you return," Odette started slowly instead. "Will you find someone for me?"

Odette saw Greer picking at her cuticles from the corner of her eye. "Who?" Greer still managed to ask.

"A fae male named Eoghann," Odette replied softly. "I want him to know that I came back after all these centuries, after all this time. I made it back."

Greer nodded slowly. "Where will you go next? Make sure the cushion on the throne isn't too worn down?"

Odette snorted as she leaned forward to wrap her hands around the rugged edges of the dock. "Adair is still out there, and I'm sure he's reeling. I can't truly claim the throne until he is gone. He's my responsibility now."

"And Leander?" Greer asked, wiping the tears away from her dirt-crusted cheeks. "What about him?"

Odette glanced at her in surprise, taking note of the flush that began to darken the tips of her ears. "Don't you think he's your responsibility now? He stole your magic, he—" Just as Odette had taken a breath to finish her thought, a tremor rocked the ground underneath them.

The waves rippled like a giant energy source suddenly rocketed underneath the surface. Greer and Odette turned to stare at one another, frozen to their seats. On the ship at the other end of the dock, Gael and Yasmin had halted as they descended the ramp.

Greer grasped Odette's leg as a second tremor tore through the land again, so violently that the dock rattled and the monkeys chittered in the swaying trees. Odette twisted around, raking her gaze toward the ship, where Gael and Yasmin curled around a side of the ramp, clutching onto it as though they would soon tip into the sea.

And it was possible they would— the ship bobbed dangerously in the disturbed water, bounding up and down in the newly formed waves.

"Samael?" Greer called out as a third tremor ripped through. "What is—?"

The male landed with a thud on the dock's planks, his commanding presence demanding Odette's attention. She couldn't help but notice the look of dread that plagued his features.

A fourth tremor rippled through, and the ramp was yanked away from the dock this time. Shouts of shock echoed across the beach as Gael and Yasmin plummeted into the sea. Odette lurched backward as she skittered to standing, making to launch herself into the air in an attempt to scoop them from the water, her injured wing be damned.

Just in time, too.

A fifth and final tremor, stronger and longer lasting than the previous four, tore through the dock. Tall waves crested over the planks in menacing crashes as Samael scooped Greer into his arms and took off into the sunlit sky. The dock cracked under the pressure, sending Odette stumbling as she attempted to run toward shore. Another wave peaked, knocking her off the planks and plunging her into the rolling sea below.

The water was shockingly cold despite being heated by the sun. Odette thrashed under the onslaught of waves, the crashing foam above and the swirling currents below making it nearly impossible to tell which way she needed to swim. With sudden force, a hand wrapped around her upper arm, yanking her to the left and dragging her back into the humidity.

Odette broke to the surface with a gulping gasp, her heart stuttering when she realized the hand wrapped around her was Samael's. He deposited her on the sandy beach just as the tremor stopped, much like the aftershock of an earthquake would, and the crowds of faeries and humans awaiting the next tremor went silent. It never came.

"He did it," Samael said, a hint of awe undercutting his voice. "He opened the tombs."

Odette turned to look at Greer, but something else caught her eye instead. Horror coated Odette's face, parting her lips and widening her eyes as she watched the black sigils tattooed onto Samael's arms fade before disappearing completely. She didn't know what it meant but knew it couldn't have been good.

There was an involuntary curve at Odette's spine, one that sent her to the ground, head bent low in the presence of the male. His power pulsated from him, growing in intensity with every breath. Odette managed to peer from under her lashes with surprising difficulty, as though her gaze didn't deem her worthy of looking upon him. With a narrowly moving sweep of her stare, she could see the remaining Court of Mist and Tide faeries and the humans in similar kneels of deference. Her magic recognized his as part of her own— a being deserving of submission and adoration.

However, Odette was mostly shocked by Greer's lack of reaction. She stood tall next to him as though her power made him an equal.

Samael was looking at his hands when Odette could tear her gaze away from Greer, twisting them around as though he hadn't bothered to study them in a long time. There was a crack like thunder, and a hole split open before them— not a rift like Odette was used to seeing during the change of the seasons, but a gaping hole ripped through space and time. She could peek through it as though it were merely a doorway, her eyes landing on the familiar sight of the rainforest and the thundering waterfalls that led to the Court of Mist and Tide.

The human realm. He had given them a way home.

FORTY-SIX

GREER

"No, Samael, home is *right there*," Greer said as she stepped toward the portal he opened for the humans. Former slaves, those kidnapped from Gaian. It was the first thing she would ban. "Your bindings are gone. I can just *go* now. You don't need to listen to Azazel anymore."

A thrum of power, agitated and angry, pulsed through the air as Samael followed her step, reaching out to grasp her arm. "You aren't going back to Gaian. Not now, not like this."

Greer tried to pull away as Samael tore open a second portal, but her strength waned. The feeling of betrayal she thought would sink low in her belly never came, and she realized...this was just like Samael. Stoic, predictable, and still loyal to her father. Even if there were an option for him to go against Azazel, he would never take it.

"If you bring me back," she started, glancing over her shoulder to see the humans clambering through the portal back home. "I'll never be able to leave."

Home.

Greer's chest tightened at the thought of the Oregon mountains, which would be snow-capped in the distance now. She would welcome the endless cold rain if it meant cozying with Delia and a steaming cup of tea. From the corner of her eye, Greer spotted Odette assisting an elderly woman onto the banks of a muddy river, the pounding waterfall still visible in the distance. She looked like she wanted to intervene for Greer's sake but thought better.

"Not now," Samael only repeated as he dragged her toward the portal. "Not like this."

The rushing of a phantom wind between worlds had become all too familiar to Greer as Samael led her from the fae realm. But instead of emerging on the terrace of Azazel's palace, as she thought they would have, they entered a long chamber hall lit by dozens of torches bracketing the black stone walls.

The chamber was different from what Greer had seen in her time through Samsara, fitting no meridian's aesthetic. No ceiling encapsulated the hall, and the evening sky was visible from every angle. Stars had begun to wink in the twilight, reflecting against the glossy, black floor. Pillars rose from the ground, jagged and thick.

It was quiet, peaceful even. It made the hair on the back of her neck stand on end.

Greer turned toward the opposite side of the hall, sweeping her gaze along the long dais at the top of a small set of stairs. It was similar to the hall used to hold court, but this one felt more rugged...more powerful. The dais held eight thrones of the same jagged, black stone as the cavernous hall. Each throne was equal to the next, though she noticed that a different colored gem was embedded at the pinnacle of the seat backing. The gemstones of the primordials and their daggers.

The breeze that arced over the chamber's top was cool and sweet, smelling of lilacs or lilies.

Greer's mouth dried when a set of echoing footsteps approached her from behind, and she glanced over her shoulder to see Azazel step from a stone bridge that led...she didn't know where it led. A rolling smoke covered the sight of the bridge's other side, and it still swirled from his exit. She took in his brilliant, white wings as he passed her, wings that had no place in the dark hall. She straightened fully as Azazel took his seat on the throne in the middle.

"Arista is quite fine, though I'm sure she will think twice before assisting in your escape again," Azazel started before looking toward Samael, his smirk growing when his eyes dropped to the places where the markings had once been. "Welcome back, my friend. I trust that your powers have returned in full form?"

Samael stepped forward, and Greer felt his power flex as though he were stretching the threads and testing the boundaries after thousands of years of containment. The bond that connected them was bright and taut, easy to reach for now. She could feel his strength, the darkness that stirred in the shallows of him, and the plethora of relief he felt at his newfound freedom.

Even though he knew it signaled the beginning of the end for Gaian.

Defeat flooded Greer, her shoulders drooping as she shook her head. That damn bond was going to only strengthen with her father now that his bindings were broken. He was going to leave Samsara; she knew he would, and he would keep her here. There was no other way around it. She had failed, and now she needed to lie in the bed she made for herself.

"I'm leaving here," Samael responded, eyes boring into Azazel's. "Greer is coming with me."

Greer's head snapped upward, lips parting in surprise. "I am?" The incredulous tone of her voice was questioning, disbelieving. Did she have it all wrong?

"My brothers have been locked away for millennia. The Gaian realm has changed, and Leander is out to track them down." Samael stopped, shifting on his feet to turn back toward Greer. "We could use each other now. I could help you find your friends and support you in telling them the truth if you want to. Your powers and your magic could assist in finding my kin. My brothers will have hidden themselves well." His cerulean eyes bore into her gray ones, and Greer felt her stomach clench at the intensity behind them. "But I will give you the choice, as I have promised you in the past, and I will not take that away from you. If you decide you do not wish to join me, I will bring you back home. Your real home, as you say."

Azazel's gaze narrowed on Samael, but Greer and Samael ignored him. Her breath hitched in her throat, mind racing.

Home, home. She could go home.

And whatever was written on her face told Samael everything she was about to say. Greer's lips pressed into a thin line, tears pricking the corners of her eyes. "I'm sorry," she started, chest constricting as she saw pain flash across his features before clearing just as quickly. "Being here is...I haven't changed my mind. I want to go home. I want to live a human life."

Azazel's leather boots were loud against the stone floor as he descended the stairs toward them. His fingers curled around the hilt of his dagger before straightening, and for a brief moment, Greer thought he would reach for her. To comfort her? As an attempt to keep her in Samsara? She didn't know. His smile was too quick before faltering, a different kind of pain reflected in his eyes.

"You will not be able to live a human life, Greer," Azazel said slowly as though choosing his words carefully. "You are immortal now. You will not die a natural death. You will not age like those around you. You will watch your friends grow older and weaker, and witness Samael come to claim them in the end." He took a deep breath and, for the first time, Greer saw through the iron walls that trapped him. "I promised you could return if you could control your magic, but you should understand that you no longer belong there."

The heaviness in Greer's stomach made her abdomen clench, and she bit the inside of her cheek to keep the tears from falling onto her cheeks. She looked up toward the sky, counting each star that peered through the blanket of clouds covering the night. Even the moonlight was strangled.

"I want to live as much of a human life as I can," Greer finally said, ignoring the sour taste of dread at the thought of leaving Samael, returning to Oregon, and facing Delia for the first time in months. Of leaving Paige alone in the rivers that cut through each meridian. She had been working toward this, had crossed realms to do it, yet a pinch of regret bloomed within her. "And I want the obsidian put back in my body."

Not expecting Greer to add that last part, Samael's shoulders stiffened, sending a ripple through the feathers of his wings. Greer watched the corner of his jaw work as he clenched his teeth, a telltale sign that he was suppressing the need to share his thoughts. Greer felt a deep wash of sadness and grief surge down their bond, sudden and overpowering.

Azazel was studying her, his head cocked. For a long minute, Greer felt the lighthearted, floating sensation of hopefulness and a sense of calm overtake the anticipatory anxiety from Samael that gripped her.

"No," Azazel finally said, shaking his head, bringing all that hope to a screeching halt. "No, I will not replace the obsidian in your body."

With her bubble popping and the calm she felt previously replaced with resentment, Greer's mouth twisted as she scowled at her father. "It's my choice," she said through gritted teeth, enunciating each word for emphasis. "Having the obsidian back–"

"Samael may give you a choice to go back home," Azazel cut in, a stern expression narrowing his eyes as he slid his gaze toward Samael, "and I can no longer oppose him." He returned his attention to Greer. "But I will not cut you off from your power when Leander is searching for the other Ananke."

"If I had the obsidian, I wouldn't be found—" she began to argue, but Azazel's voice rose in volume and intensity as he interrupted her again.

"That is what your mother and I thought when I sent you both back to Gaian after your birth!"

Time slowed as Greer and Azazel looked at one another. She felt equal parts hollow and heavy, pulling and pushing, fighting to gain control. Finally, she took a small step forward as Samael melted backward into the darkened shadows of the hall, giving the two their space. "What happened to Holly, to my mother...it wasn't your fault."

Azazel's stare turned iron-hot and filled with fire, a look that Greer somehow knew all too well. "You don't know what you're talking about. You don't know the exhaustion it takes to go on after losing the one you love. The knowledge I hold of fighting to keep someone safe who vehemently does not want it..." He trailed off, snapping his mouth shut as though realizing he said too much.

"I know that blaming yourself for her death has done nothing except eat you from the inside for nearly twenty-seven years."

He blew out a long, angry breath. "I promised to protect both her and you. I vowed it before the stars in the universe, before her. I broke that promise in her life and now in her death."

Understanding pierced through Greer. Understanding of a father fighting to shield his child, fighting to make up for lost time, fighting to rebuild the promise that he had made to the love of his life, and doing all of this with no guidance on how to interact with an adult daughter he had no relationship with. Before she realized that her feet were moving forward, Greer closed the gap between them and wrapped her arms around his waist.

Azazel froze, and Greer thought he would pull away, withdrawing from his need to be alone. She knew that feeling well, too; it was something, she realized, she had inherited from him. Instead, his shoulders slumped forward as he enclosed his arms around her, and Greer felt a single tear drip onto her cheek, one that she could no longer hold back.

"But you have to realize the answer isn't keeping me here against my will," Greer murmured into the leather armor, fighting past her trembling chin to keep her voice steady.

"I know," Azazel replied, his tone distant and dull.

He stepped away from her, and Greer took a moment to wipe the wetness away from her cheeks. A necklace appeared in his palm, a single black stone intersecting the delicate silver chain. Gesturing for her to turn, Azazel reached forward to clasp the stone around her neck. Greer swept the loose hairs away from the chain, and as the stone lay against her skin, she felt her power dull before disappearing almost entirely. The connection with Samael, one that had become a quiet friend to her, went with it. She swore she heard a breathy, sorrowful exhale sound from behind her.

"I had this made for your mother, something I would have given to her when you were older, and the obsidian could have been removed from your bones. I'll give it to you now...for your protection," Azazel said, "and your privacy." He paused to swallow, and Greer knew he was struggling with what to say, but he continued. "It may not stop daemons from finding you, and it may not completely stop your power from manifesting, but its removal will allow you to access your magic if you need it."

"Thank you," Greer replied— and she meant it. She touched the cool stone gently with her fingertips, probing the uneven edges.

"When you're ready to come back," Azazel went on, slowly nodding, "you will be welcomed home. Samael—" He paused to turn toward the male, still firmly within the shadows of the closest pillar. "Good luck."

While Greer didn't say anything in return, she had a distinct feeling that Azazel recognized this wasn't a final goodbye. Neither of them said another word as Azazel opened his wings and flew out of the chamber, disappearing into the night sky.

FORTY-SEVEN

Samael

Samael stood on the balcony overlooking the library, his forearms resting on the railing and the familiar decanter of amber alcohol swinging precariously between his fingers. This spot used to be his favorite. When overwhelmed, he would look up at the stars through the glass dome and remember the freeing feeling of being unbound from the constraints of a physical form. He would watch the clouds march across the sky and wonder where his brothers had hidden. He would take solace in knowing he had no one to blame for his bindings except himself.

But now, Samael was free. Yet, he still gazed over the dark, empty library and expected to hear the rustling of book pages as Greer flipped through them, thinking she was alone. He hoped he would hear them.

But when nothing pierced the silence, he hated his once cherished shelter.

He hadn't thought it would hurt this much when he brought Greer back to the Gaian realm. Not nearly as much as when she donned the necklace, severing their bond in the blink of an eye. And when she walked away without a second glance, Samael begged the earth to swallow him whole. Since then, he couldn't help but reminisce about how her laugh made his stomach swoop uncomfortably, the taste of her lips against his, and how she should have been with him.

However, nothing in this universe was a done deal, and he knew better than to think it was.

"I'm surprised you're still here," a voice behind him said, cutting through the quiet and echoing over the stone floors and narrow library stacks.

Samael glanced over his shoulder, spotting Arista half-hidden in the shadows. "I'm leaving tonight," he responded, returning his attention to the empty chamber. "I just needed the day to re-center."

Arista timidly approached before resting her hands gently on the stone railing. "I'm just as surprised that Greer left."

Samael pressed his lips into a thin line at the sound of her name spoken aloud. "I'm not. She was always clear of her intentions to leave." He just thought he had time to change her mind.

Arista seemed to understand the words unsaid. She lifted a hand to tuck a loose lock of hair behind an ear. "I should rephrase. I'm surprised that you let her go."

Samael stilled, the decanter clinking dangerously loud against the stone. "Why would that surprise you?"

"You are not the only one who could sense the bond between you both. Being the Primordial of Fertility and Beauty certainly has some positive aspects."

The feeling of her gaze against his cheek pierced through him, but Samael kept his stare fixed on the moonlit shadows passing over the stone floor below him. He had felt Greer the moment she punched through the obsidian for the first time and how she poisoned that animal who attacked her.

Samael remembered the deepness he felt when that bond between them blew wide open, a connection that crossed barriers and could undoubtedly move mountains—then, spilled in her fear when the man's hand had begun to blacken beneath her power, followed by her confusion before she lost consciousness. He had been summoned to her and, on his arrival, had recalled seeing a bystander call for the authorities.

He took in the scene before him, saw the man writhing in pain on the ground, and a sudden flood of wrath poured through him as though an unstoppable dam had broken. It was a wrath that he had never felt before that moment. That man should have lived, would have lived if Samael hadn't fought against every inch of the bindings to cleave the man's soul from his body and throw him into the first river of Samsara purely out of anger. He needed days to recover after that.

Samael's entire world had shifted that first day he could sense her, but the obsidian had sealed just as quickly. Desperate, he reached out to Greer, and the only way he knew how was through dreams. He would send her visions, scenes, and emotions through that bond, hoping she would find him.

Samael realized that, as half-human, Greer might not be able to sense him the way he sensed her.

So he waited, searched for her, and waited some more. Then, the day finally came when her power broke through entirely, and he tracked that bond until he was at her side. It was the first time he felt whole in thousands of years.

But Greer was coated in blood and sobbing, grieving the loss of a friend to whom Samael had a duty to return to the universe.

So he waited again, watching as she fell into a pit of despair so deep that he wasn't sure she would ever emerge. Then, he realized he despised her human emotions and her inability to turn them off. He was unable to count how many times he wanted to chuck her off the side of a cliff or into the murky waters of the bog. He wanted to shake her back to life and experience the fiery woman he knew was trapped.

Despite all of that, he watched as she read that damn book night after night. Studied her as her mouth quirked at the funny passages and her brow furrowed in concentration at the serious ones.

The first time Greer glanced at him, not out of hatred but out of curiosity, Samael's heart thunked out of place. And he knew he was in a load of trouble when she began to feel comfortable enough to open herself up to him, to voice her fears and dreams. He began to learn what made Greer tick, and before he knew it, she smiled at him in earnest for the first time, and he fell straight past that mating bond and right into her.

Samael knew he would never recover from his continually fracturing heartbreak at her departure. But, instead of voicing all of this to Arista, he merely muttered, "It was always her choice."

Arista was contemplatively quiet for a few beats, her fingers running over the rugged stone. "You're the only Ananke I've ever met," she said slowly. "But I'm aware of them all. You're the first one I've ever heard of having a mate."

Samael yanked the cork from the decanter, lifted the bottle to his lips, and took a deep swig. "We are in quite uncharted territory, aren't we?"

Arista's lips parted in shock. "It is true then. You and Greer, you're—"

"She has made her choice, Arista, and that choice does not include me." Samael knew of plenty of primordials who had declined the mating bond, Ramiel included. And he briefly wondered how Ramiel got up in the morning, even centuries later.

"Do you still feel her?" She asked, pressing on despite the finality Samael tried to impose in his tone. "The bond, I mean."

Samael took a second swig. "No, she has the obsidian necklace from her father." He paused to clear his throat. "The first time she touched me, she may as well have re-centered the universe. She certainly re-centered mine."

Arista reached over to grab the decanter and took her swig. "I wish I knew a love like that."

Samael snorted as he threaded his fingers together, letting his hands hang limp over the railing. "No, you don't."

Silence filled the space between them once again, one that was so throbbingly loud that Samael thought it echoed in his ears.

"Where will you go?" Arista asked, handing the decanter back to Samael.

"Of my brothers that I know the location of, three of them were entombed in the Gaian realm," Samael said with a sigh, rubbing his temple in thought. "Leander has released them, and he hunts them now. A fourth has continued to be held hostage in Elysia under Michael's command. The fifth remains in the Aeglecian realm, bound by a djinn he cannot release himself from. The remaining two have been hiding since the War of the Sixteen ended." He paused to slide his gaze toward Arista. "Do you want to come with me?"

"Me?" She responded in astonishment. "C-come to the Gaian realm? Why?"

Samael shrugged. "I need someone who can help track my brothers, and I've...overheard you a few times voice your want to leave Samsara. Greer said no, so—"

"I'm a second choice, then," Arista interjected dryly.

"No, not that." Samael adjusted his wings, letting them shift against his back. "That's not how I meant it. I could use the extra hands."

Arista blew out a breath. "I've never been to the Gaian realm before. And you're leaving tonight?"

Samael finished off the decanter. "In the next hour."

"Where do we start?"

The decanter clinked against the railing as Samael let it balance. It swayed on the narrow stone. "Maher is the most dangerous of them all. Leander getting ahold of his power would be fatal to many humans. He's my priority, and he'll make it difficult for me to track him down."

Arista nodded slowly. "Where do you think he'll be?"

"Where the most conflict is, I'm sure, being the Ananke of War and Conquest."

The decanter finally tipped to the side and plunged to the library floor, shattering against the tiled sandstone. Samael hoped that it wasn't a premonition of what was to come.

FORTY-EIGHT

DELIA

"**N**o, just stay put. I want to do this on my own."

Delia clasped the pillow tightly in her fist as Kazzy looked on, brows furrowed and lips tightly clamped as though she were swallowing back a retort.

But Cian understood. He nodded his head, back resting against the cushions of the couch. "Tell her thank you for us—" He trailed off to clear his throat. "For me."

Delia turned to look at Sophie, who was staring at Cian like the sun rose and sank with him. She stifled an eye roll, though just barely. "She said to kick rocks."

Sophie's heated glare tore away from Cian to snap onto Delia. "I did not say that. Delia, tell him I did not say that!"

Delia tucked the pillow further under her arm, sighing in defeat. "You're moving on in five minutes anyway. Do you really want him to know that he's your prince charming? Keep what's left of your dignity."

Cian's curling smirk was the only response, but that seemed good enough for Sophie. The resounding hum she made from the back of her throat said it all.

The walk to the alley behind the hotel was longer than Delia had anticipated, and she found an uncomfortable pinch twisting in her stomach with every step she took.

"How did you die?" Delia asked as she knuckled the elevator button. The car clanked against the shaft as it ascended to her floor, the warm, stale air of the tunnel pushing out of the seam between the doors.

Sophie looked over at Delia with surprise. Since returning to the hotel room the night before and promising the pillow's destruction as soon as they could obtain a set of matches and firestarter, Sophie had softened her stance just enough for her to be tolerable. And Delia found herself reminded, once again, of the little brothers she had left behind.

"I was on a week-long trip with my school for my upper sixth year." Sophie began to fumble with the edge of her shirt, just as ghostly translucent as she was. "I–I wanted to do something more exciting than a tour, and I wandered away from the group while we were at the Trevi Fountain but ended up getting lost. I found myself in an alley, where I was taken by a man back to this hotel. He told me he would kill me if I made any noise, and I was scared. I followed him up to his room, but...I remember his hands around my neck and then that pillow over my face...until—" She trailed off, heaving in a breath as they exited the elevator into the lobby of the hotel. "The next thing I knew, I was looking down at my body and being asked to move on by a man with big, gray wings."

A shiver stole Delia's spine, though she wasn't sure whether it was from the story or from the sudden chill that swept over the main road as they crossed through the set of automatic doors. She navigated around a group of tourists bundled in winter coats and long scarves, heading for the alleyway beside the hotel.

"Why didn't you move on?"

Delia saw Sophie shrug from the corner of her eye. "I thought I could just return home. I wanted my mom and was warned that I wouldn't be able to leave, but I didn't listen." Sophie heaved a sigh as they turned the corner, a dim, flickering streetlamp casting an orange glow over the contents of the alley. "I don't think the cops ever found out what happened to me. My parents have to live wondering where I went or if I'm okay. I wanted the chance to give them closure…"

Pausing in front of a garbage bin, piles of overstuffed bags surrounding the container, Delia turned to look at Sophie. And it was the first time in so many days that she really looked at her. Young and pretty. Her brow set in a permanent scowl, one that Delia had come to learn was merely a defense. Her eyes, perhaps once a darker color, were now hauntingly and heartbreakingly sad.

Something tugged at Delia's chest. "Do you want me to pass along a message to your parents for you?"

Startled, Sophie stared at her. "You—you would do that?"

"Yes," Delia responded. "Whatever you like."

"Tell them…tell them that I love them, that I miss them, and that I'm okay now. And that…tell them that I buried my stuffed teddy with Mr. BeefCakes when I was ten. So they'll know your message was from me."

"Done." She turned away from the girl to flip the lid of the garbage container, pulling out extra bags to make room to stuff the pillow inside

"Do you think it'll hurt?" Sophie asked in a soft voice, one that made Delia pause.

Delia swallowed thickly, looking over her shoulder at the young girl. "No, I don't. I think you'll find peace." Her words must have sunk into Sophie because the furrowed brow eased just enough to notice. "Are you ready?"

Sophie's chest rose in a phantom breath, her head quickly nodding. Delia looked down at the pillow, which settled neatly within the garbage bin, and coated it in lighter fluid. She struck a match, pausing for long enough to glance back at Sophie, and threw the flame into the bin. Fire whooshed upward, the flame searingly hot, as it licked at the fabric. The corner of the pillow had already begun to curl into a dark brown.

"I should have known you would find someone to help you move on," a low voice said over the crackling fire. Delia jolted, her heart pounding against the inside of her chest. "You were a thorn in my side the moment you died."

Delia spotted a tall man through the flames and the haze from the smoke. Muscular with long brown hair tied in a bun at the back of his head. A sword tethered between a set of gray wings...wings. Her breath sawed at her dry throat at the sight.

"I'm ready now," Sophie stated, stepping from behind the bin and marching to the man, arms swinging at her sides. "How do we do this?"

The man chuckled, holding out his hand.

"Wait!" Delia cried out, extending an arm to clasp onto Sophie's wrist. The two peered at her, Sophie with annoyance and the man with curiosity. "You'll— you'll care for her, right?"

The man's smile was soft. "She'll be safe where she's going."

With a swipe of his hand, Sophie's form shifted into the little ball of light similar to Paige's all those months ago. She rose into the air, faster and faster, until she cleared the edge of the building above them.

In the next blink of Delia's eye, Sophie was gone, joining the winking stars that pebbled the night sky. He turned back to Delia, head cocked as he studied her.

"I remember you," he said quietly. "You're a friend of Greer's."

Delia felt a jostle of shock run up the back of her neck. "How—how did you?" She paused, assessing the man just as he had done to her. "Wait...were you...you were there that night. The night my— the night she—" Delia swallowed, though it felt like a rock had lodged in her throat. "How can I see you now?"

The man's wings shifted as though uncomfortable with her gaze. "For a few reasons. When I collect a soul and a living person is touching them, some of my power can get transferred over, but just enough to glimpse over the veil. That is why you could see Sophie and, my guess is, others. I have recently been released from my binding to Samsara, so it may be easier to see me now."

Delia straightened at the mention of the underworld, her ears perking with the word. "Samsara. Is Greer with you?" She peered beyond the man's shoulders, half-expecting her best friend to be hidden beyond the garbage bins.

The man stilled, the tips of his wings flicking. "No, she returned to Oregon yesterday. She is no longer with her father."

Delia dropped the box of matches after hearing Greer's safe return home. She and Cian had spent months researching ways to bring her back, and despite now knowing the part Greer played in Paige's death, she still had questions. *Was she okay? How did she get home? What happened to her?*

But as the man turned to leave, the gemstones in the hilt of his sword glinting in the dimming flame, Delia voiced only one thing. "Wait," she called out again, her voice croaking from the cold. He paused, gazing down at her. "Sophie said she chose to stay. If she chose to stay, then Paige could still be in Oregon."

The man's stare shifted into one of remorseful understanding. He slowly closed the distance between them, Delia rooting herself in place. She had to lift her chin to keep the eye contact they shared. "Paige will not be in Oregon."

Delia let out a huffed, impatient breath. "She could have come back. After you sent her away, she could have returned. Maybe it just took time for me to see her. If I go back now—"

"She will not be in Oregon," the man interjected firmly, though not unkindly. "Because she chose to move on. She knew it wasn't her place to remain here."

Delia felt that rock, once lodged in the back of her throat, slide to her lungs. They burned with the effort it took to breathe, the cool air mixed with the last of the smoke, turning her voice raspy. "She— she would have stayed if she knew. She wouldn't have— she couldn't have—"

The man looked down at her with an expression overflowing with pity, one that Delia couldn't stand to look at any longer. She shifted her stare downward, watching the dying flames consume the last of the pillow, melting the plastic of the garbage bag beneath. The acrid smell was a shock to her senses.

Delia had spent all of her time throwing herself into this investigation. She had traveled halfway across the world to forget herself, to forget her pain, and to forget Paige. She had shoved away any morsel of grief, burying it so deeply within herself that she thought it would never resurface.

And her hope had been kindled at the thought of seeing Paige again, even if it was in ghost form. It had consumed her in the fleeting moments the man had come to collect Sophie, and she had allowed it to consume her completely. Just like that, it had been snuffed out nearly as quickly. All that was left was the hollow, ash-filled box, opened wide like Pandora's once had been.

Delia's grief swallowed her whole. A choking sob bubbled up her constricted throat, and she felt the burning of tears pricking the corners of her eyes. The man's arms shot out to catch her just as her knees gave way, and he held her up, not allowing her to crumple to the garbage-riddled floor of the alley.

Instead, he held her close, tucking her tightly against his chest. And Delia, for the first time in months, allowed herself to curl her fingers in his shirt, allowed the guttural scream to be pulled from her, and, finally, allowed herself the space to feel the unending deluge of grief that she had been hiding from.

FORTY-NINE

GREER

The winter wind had swept through Oregon, clearing away any remaining breaths of autumn. Frost covered the grass, clinging to it like an old friend who had been away for too long. It had been a peaceful return from Samsara, and though Greer hadn't yet seen Delia, her first stop had been to Paige's grave.

Greer had scraped the remnants of the dead leaves from her headstone and had placed an evergreen wreath there, carefully leaning it against the marble marker. Winter had always been Paige's favorite time of year. She had loved the joy of the holidays, the warmth of freshly brewed coffee in her favorite mug, and the child-like delight she posed when Greer and Delia plugged in the Christmas tree for the first time.

Greer felt her heart squeeze tightly in her chest as she fingered the obsidian necklace around her neck. There was a perfect spot in the corner of her living room for a holiday tree, a place that Paige had picked out when she helped Greer move to the rental house on the outskirts of town. Paige had proudly announced it, her hands on her hips and lips pulled into a wide smile.

If Greer closed her eyes, she could still see Paige standing there.

The lock on the door jangled, yanking Greer from her thoughts. A wave of anxiety crested through her, and she wondered if Leander had found her already. She hesitated for a moment, her mouth tugged into a frown before she slowly pushed herself from the accent chair in the corner of the room and tip-toed toward the front door. The knob wiggled again, followed by a sharp curse and a muffled stomp of one's feet against the wooden porch.

And, when Greer spotted the familiar curly hair dancing in the cold wind above the framing of the window, she wrapped her hand around the knob and pulled the door open.

Heat rose up her throat. Greer was speechless as she saw Delia standing on the welcome mat, her cheeks and nose tinged pink. Greer threw herself forward, not caring that the whipping wind was blisteringly cold against her bare toes, and wrapped her arms around Delia's neck. She was aware of Delia's stiffened position as Greer sucked in a deep breath, taking in the simple scent of her best friend's vanilla shampoo.

Greer heard Delia sniff and felt the drip of something wet against her bare shoulder before finally pulling away. She drank in Delia's red-rimmed eyes, the salty tears that stained her cheeks, and the rugged breaths Delia took to calm herself down.

Those breaths, Greer knew, were something Paige had taught her.

"Where did you go?" Greer asked, stepping back to allow Delia to cross the threshold into the warmth of the house. "I– I've been home a week now, and I've gone to the apartment every day."

Delia pursed her lips into a thin line, slowly shaking her head.

Greer felt herself still, stomach bottoming as though she had fallen off of a cliff. "What's wrong?"

Delia said nothing for a long moment, merely taking the time to study Greer with intense scrutiny. "What happened to Paige?"

Greer gaped at her best friend, the lump in her throat tripling in size. She subtly shifted, lifting one foot at a time to try and warm her feet. She felt a distance between her and Delia, something she hadn't expected before she had the chance to talk with her. She gestured inside once again. "Come inside, please, Dels. I'll make you some coffee. I bought the kind you like, that Snickerdoodle one. We can talk and—"

"I don't want to come in," Delia stated. She took a deep breath, nostrils flaring, before blowing it out. Her breath clouded before her, thick against the winter air. "I want to know what happened to Paige."

Greer trembled, feeling the weight of her decisions crashing down on her once again. What did Delia know? Delia hadn't posed her demand for the truth as a question but as a statement. Greer had been gone for months. That was plenty of time for...her thoughts shifted to Cian, Isaac, Jonas, or any of the daemons Delia could have interacted with after she was taken. Her swallow was audible, even above the wind, but she wasn't a coward, and Delia deserved to know. "What did you hear?"

"It doesn't matter what I've heard. I want to hear the truth, and I want to hear it from you."

Greer could feel Delia's wrath coming off of her in waves. She slunk down, withering under the formidable stare of her best friend. "I—I summoned Eligos, and he—" She paused to take a breath, wiping the tears away from her face. She didn't deserve to cry, not now. Not in front of Delia. "It's my fault. I didn't bind him correctly. I was in over my head, and I didn't listen to Cian or Odette." She shot a hand forward, gripping Delia's as though she could bridge the growing gap between them if only she squeezed a little tighter. "Delia, I take full blame for what happened that night. I want to return to the past and never take that stupid grimoire from Cian. I wish none of this had ever happened. I should have listened to your warnings about the vampyres. And Paige...she's—"

Smack.

Greer stumbled back, her shoulder colliding with the sconce that swung in the wind, as she clutched her throbbing cheek in shock. Delia lowered her hand back to her side, and her jaw clenched so tightly that the muscle near her ear was ticking.

"Dead, Greer. She's dead," Delia finished Greer's sentence for her.

Guilt and shame swam through Greer, and she desperately wanted to crumple under Delia's intense scrutiny but didn't allow herself to. It was Delia who had lost someone, Delia who could relate closer to Greer's father than she ever could. And it was Delia who deserved to throw any vitriol and rage that she could muster toward her.

Nothing pierced the silence between the two, save for the creaking branches from the tree in the front yard. Cold shuddered through Greer, her skin pebbling against it, but she didn't dare move an inch.

And then Delia was lunging forward, crackling sobs escaping her lips, as she wrapped her arms around Greer's shoulders. As they cried, the two crashed against the metal threshold of the door, tucked against the frame.

And cried.

And cried.

Greer didn't know how long they were on the ground. Her feet prickled uncomfortably beneath her, the home's heat no longer warming the backs of her arms and shoulders. Snow had begun to fall in large clumps, quiet and peaceful against the clouded, gray sky. And Delia was still quivering, tears still falling from her swollen eyes.

"I wish I could take Paige's place," Greer finally said, and she meant it. She would have traded places with Paige in the blink of an eye.

"You can't though. Paige is gone, and we're still here," Delia responded, gently pulling away to wipe her nose on the sleeve of her jacket. "I don't know where you and I go from here, GG."

Greer felt her heart seize, the frozen landscape before her entering her chest and hardening what was once open and warm. "I know, Dels. I—saying sorry will always be shallow and insufficient compared to how I actually feel," She blew out a breath, letting the unspoken words linger between them. "I just want to take it all back. I wish I never got involved with this."

Delia made a noise of agreement at the back of her throat. "I need some time," she said, pushing back further. Greer closed her eyes, letting the grief settle onto her shoulders like a weight. "I need to work through this. I need to think. I...I don't know if we can ever be the same."

Greer nodded her head. She had half-expected it. She had known the possibility was always there. Losing Paige was hard, and knowing she was stuck in that damn river made Greer see red. But losing Delia, who had been a sister to her for a decade now...someone may as well have cut out her heart.

"I reached out to Henry, my old boss at the university, and pleaded my case for my sudden disappearance. He's going to give me a second chance, and he's allowing me to join the team currently in Greece; I guess they need more hands on deck. I'll be headed out of town soon and gone for a while. Close to a year and a half, I believe?" She paused to glance down at her fingers curled into her lap. "Hopefully, that'll give you the space to think."

Delia pushed herself up to stand, brushing the dirt and thawing ice from the hip of her pants. "I can't make any promises, but I'll reach out if and when I'm ready."

Greer sniffed. "That's all I can hope for, Dels."

Delia regarded her for another moment, and Greer was sure she would say something else. Instead, Delia blew out a final breath before spinning on the heels of her shoes and clopping down the stairs of the porch.

Greer watched her go, still curled in the door's framing, silent tears pouring from her eyes. She deserved this, and Delia deserved better.

Greer knew she would spend the rest of eternity hating herself for what she did to Paige and Delia. She could only hope Delia didn't take that long to forgive her. One day, it would be her turn to enter the river, and Greer couldn't stand the thought that she would have lost Delia before death even came for her.

Greer leaned back to reach into her pocket, pulling out the eye of the sisters' that she had kept hidden for the past week. She stared down at it as it stared back up at her. And she briefly wondered how much she could take before it crushed her under the weight. Before she spent the rest of her miserably immortal life regretting the choices she made.

EPILOGUE

AMARA RAHIM

"Following the devastation of the nearly dozen major earthquakes…"

Click.

"The destruction from the tsunami that hit the coast of Japan following a bizarre set of earthquakes…"

Click.

"…The town is picking up the pieces after three volcanoes erupted simultaneously…"

Click.

Amara Rahim turned off the television and dropped the remote control on the cushion of the white leather couch, taking a final drag of her cigarette. Leaning forward, she pushed the remnants into the glass ashtray on the coffee table and blew out the smoke in a long exhale. It was a terrible habit. She would probably think about quitting tomorrow.

She sighed as she collapsed backward, listening to the sounds of honking cars and bustling pedestrians entering through the third-story window of her walk-up apartment. The window was ajar, and the cool February breeze coming off the Mediterranean coast was too enticing. Smells of roasting meats and baked pies followed on the wind. Her stomach rumbled.

Later, Amara told herself. *She would eat later.*

She was expecting a visitor in the next few minutes.

Amara stood from the couch, stretching her arms overhead as she let out a groan, long and low. Her sleek, black hair hung loosely down her back, shifting against the denim button-up she had tucked into her short, flowing skirt. If anyone had looked in on her, they would have seen a run-of-the-mill twenty-something Beirut native with a run-of-the-mill fashion sense living in a run-of-the-mill apartment.

However, Amara Rahim was anything but.

A soft tap on the door reverberated over the tiled floor. Two knocks, pause, three knocks, pause, one final knock. She waltzed over to the door and, after peeking through the keyhole, cracked it open. In the hallway stood two men dressed in suits, their eyes hidden by thin sunglasses.

She fought against rolling her eyes as she opened the door further and stepped to the side, allowing the two men to enter. She caught the scent of strong aftershave coming from the younger, and he eyed her bare legs hungrily as he stalked past. Sighing through her nose, she closed the door and locked it behind them.

"Nice place," the older man stated, taking off his sunglasses and tucking them into the inner pocket of his suit coat. "We sure do pay you well, it seems."

Amara held her ground, arms crossed over her chest. "I'm good at what I do."

"We taught you just as well."

Amara clamped her lips shut, unwilling to engage in the dichotomy. She was good at what she did because she had to be, not because she was taught to be. If she had continued to work the way she was taught, the way he's saying they taught her, she would have been killed years ago.

The older man stepped deeper into the apartment, his dress shoes clicking against the white marble flooring. Amara watched as he swept his gaze over the open kitchen with black countertops, the white couches in the living room, and the bedroom hidden behind two sliding black doors that held fogged, opaque windows.

Modern and minimalistic. Nothing personal. Nothing intimate. Just the way she liked it.

"My colleague and I have a job for you," he finally said, turning back to look at her with his hands folded at his front. "This one comes straight from Vatican City itself."

Amara made no move to respond, her gaze flicking between the two as she waited. Evidently, this news— whatever it was supposed to be— was meant to cause a reaction. She quirked an eyebrow and said, "And? What is it?"

"You would think someone of your standing would be thankful to have a job from Vatican City," the younger man said as he stepped forward. His jaw clenched tightly as he stared into her hazel eyes.

Amara stared back, lips pressed into a thin line. "You assume I haven't had many orders from the Vatican." She turned, walked into the living room, and grabbed the pack of cigarettes from the coffee table. Shaking the box, she let one slide into her palm. She placed the tip between her lips and thumbed at the lighter before taking a long drag. "You are my fourth meeting this week from the Vatican alone. What I haven't heard is why I should accept your offer over the others."

The younger man bared his teeth, stepping toward her. "Because my father was killed. That's why."

Amara tossed the lighter onto the table, where it clattered against the glass, and took another inhale of the cigarette. She crossed an arm over her chest, hooking the hand into her elbow. "Fathers are killed every day," she stated, flicking the ash from the end. "Doesn't mean I should hear you out."

"We traveled for hours—" the younger man said, his voice shifting into a near whine that made Amara want to rip her ears from her head.

A third drag. She waited.

"You are the best assassin the Paladin Society has to offer," the older man interjected, trying another tactic opposite to what he implied only a moment ago. He held out his hand to silence his colleague as Amara could tell he was on the verge of saying something else. "Trained from childhood, eight high-ranking kills under your belt by age sixteen. Your reputation precedes you."

A fourth drag and a sigh. "Flattery will get you nowhere."

The younger man huffed in frustration. "We are legacies in the Paladin Society, and you will do what we—"

The curved blade Amara hid in the waistband of her skirt was at his throat before he could finish his sentence. She felt him swallow as she pressed the metal further into the bobbing lump of his Adam's apple. She took one more drag from the cigarette, reached forward, and put the end out on the front of his suit coat. It sizzled, the bitter smell of burning fabric smoking as a hole burnt through to his white dress shirt. She tucked the butt of the cigarette into his breast pocket, tapping it lightly.

He paled, his swallow becoming a frightened gulp as she dragged the blade from his throat, leaving a thin, red line. Not a lick of blood and the mark itself would probably disappear during the time he was still in the apartment, but it sent the message she wanted it to send.

The older man stepped in, a tight smile curling his lips. "I feel we may have gotten off on the wrong foot. My colleague and I are here to request a hit on someone we believe you will find very interesting."

Amara stepped back, the bottoms of her feet cold against the marble. She waited again, flipping the curved blade in her hand as she did so.

"Two months ago, the father of my colleague was killed by a wolf shifter during a routine session with a vampyre." Amara's brow tightened, eyes narrowed as she assessed him, but he pressed on. "One of the people rescuing the vampyre was a human named Delia Savas. She mistakenly gave her full name during a tour booking at the Vatican. Young, American."

"I'm losing interest."

"Delia was followed home after she left Vatican City and we found her visiting a woman, Greer Myers. According to credit reports pulled on her name, Greer had suddenly gone off the grid for nearly two and a half months following the curious death of Delia's fiancée, so we decided to look into her further. We've learned that she was involved in another curious death of a man who had attacked her in an alley, a man who was seemingly poisoned despite only touching Greer. Additionally, we were able to pull GPS reports on her Jeep. We found that she visited an old Paladin member named James Whittley, whose own daughter disappeared with the known daughter of Azazel, curiously with the same name. We've since tracked her to an archeology dig site in Greece."

Amara tilted her head, frowning slightly. "You want me to kill the friend of this Greer?"

The older man shook his head. "Delia is an inconvenience, yes, but there is no indication that the two are in contact any longer. We want the other one, Greer. Daughter of Azazel and, who we believe to be the last living member of the Mage line. We've been seeking her for decades now. Bring us her head, and we'll reward you beyond your wildest dreams."

Amara stared up at him for another moment. "My dreams are quite wild. What kind of reward did you have in mind?" The two men exchanged looks, and to Amara, it was evident that they had thought she would bite just on the prospect of killing this woman. "Allow me to clear your confusion. This Greer is Azazel's daughter. Yes? You wish for me to kill the daughter of a primordial without any monetary repercussions? I will need to go into hiding for life and abandon my name and my work. And for what? To say I killed the last living member of the Mage line? That won't pay my bills."

Amara unfolded her arms from her chest, planted her hands on the dining room table, and clicked her red nails against the glass. Waiting.

"That's what I told them when they asked me." The voice was a soft caress, hungry and filled with need.

Amara swiveled around to face the door, eyes narrowing as though she would be able to see who was on the other side. "Who did you bring with you?"

"Jonas has similar alignments to us," the older man answered, though his face had paled considerably. "He was assisting Eligos before his death and is now assisting Leander, son of Michael."

Amara darted her eyes between the two before again landing on the door. "Since when has the Paladin Society partnered with the likes of Eligos?" Her stomach pinched an uncomfortable churn she hadn't felt in nearly ten years. "Speak quickly."

"The tombs have been opened," the younger man said, eyes gleaming excitedly. "The Ananke have been released. At this time, we have only accounted for one— Samael, Death. A motion has begun to close the realms and exile the daemons. It requires the death of the Mage." He paused to glance over at his companion, who was tight-lipped. "We'll pay you one million dollars."

"One of the jobs I was offered this week was one point five million dollars for the death of a siren stalking the shores of Cuba." Amara leaned forward, pressing her hands deeper onto the table. "I won't entertain anything under five. If you find my price too high, I am happy to point you toward my colleagues. They aren't as good, and there's a chance they might get the job done, but there are no promises."

The older man clenched his jaw again, and Amara was pleased to see the whites of his knuckles as his fingers flexed into a fist. "Twenty thousand dollars now as a deposit," he countered as he reached into the inner pocket of his jacket and pulled out a bundle of bills. He dropped the stacks onto the table between them. "Additional three million when the job is done." A wicked smile appeared on his mouth. "You accept this job and succeed, and we will also petition the Paladin Society to grant you freedom."

Amara stilled, halting the progression of her thumb running along the edge of the bills, flicking through them as she counted. She glanced up at the two men. "Who says I want my freedom?"

The older man chuckled, shifting his weight as he scrutinized her. "The Paladin Society has eyes and ears all over the world. Cicero is a personal friend of mine. I know your attempts to buy your way out of his employ."

Amara hated the pleased look that was deeply etched into his features. And she especially hated being pinned into a corner. "If I go into this dig site in Greece and attempt to kill her out of the gate, she'll sniff me out in a second." She resumed flicking through the bills, ignoring the twisting in her chest. "This requires secrecy and, more importantly, time." She glanced up at the two men, both eagerly awaiting her reply. "Why don't we take a seat at the table, gentlemen? Let's talk about the details I have in mind."

Human Main Characters

1. Greer: The Mage

2. Delia: Greer's best friend, alive

3. Paige: Delia's fiancée, deceased

4. Luisa: General to Odette's Army

5. Erin: Anthropologist

Faerie Main Characters

1. Odette: Heir to the throne, Court of Storm and Wind

2. Nerea (Nuh-ray-uh): Half-Fae, Court of Mist and Tide

3. Renan (Ruh-na): Captain of Intelligence, Court of Mist and Tide

4. Kaique (Kai-ik): Lord of the Court of Mist and Tide, deceased

Vampyre Main Characters

1. Cian (Key-in): Greer's former fling

2. Isaac: Unknown at this time

3. Jonas: Working with Paladin

4. Darragh (Dah-ra): First created

Wolf Shifter Main Characters

1. Kazzy: Cian/Delia's partner-in-crime

2. Gawin: First created

Primordial Main Characters

1. Azazel, King of Samsara: Greer's father, Primordial of the Underworld

2. Arista: Primordial of Beauty and Fertility

3. Mammon, Prince of Greed: Primordial of Greed and Wealth, Creator of the wolf shifters

4. Na'amah, Prince of Lust: Primordial of Persuasion and Seduction, Creator of the succubus

5. Serket: Primordial of Healing and Protection, bonded to Mammon

6. Ramiel, Prince of Pride: Primordial of Pride and Arrogance, Creator of the fae

7. Leander: Half-primordial, son of Michael

Ananke

1. Samael: Death

Acknowledgements

Wow! This book was an absolute labor of love. Exploring the depths of grief and joy and sadness and all the things was so healing for me. One of the best parts of releasing the second book in this series is being able to dive back into the world of Greer and her friends, and taking a microscope to their journey. I've had the honor of learning so much from fellow indie authors in the past year and, truly, this story would have been much harder to write without their time and guidance.

I want to first start my thanking my husband, Joe, for stepping in and closing my laptop for me when my mental health was out of whack. To my family for continuing to push me on! None of this would have been possible if it weren't for your unfailing love, support, and words of wisdom. You've carried me to the tallest mountains and sailed with me through the depths of the seas. I love you, I love you, I love you.

Thank you to my amazing editor, Mozelle Jordan, for continuing to challenge me. Your mentorship and feedback has been out of this world. Thank you to my just as amazing cover artist, Rebecca Frank, for reading my mind and exploring the depths of this series with me in ways that I didn't know were possible.

Finally, thank you to my readers. Being an indie author is incredibly isolating and difficult, but you have also managed to make this journey fun and exciting for me. I am grateful for your support in ways that you couldn't begin to comprehend!

About the Author

Author and full-time respiratory therapist, Sadie Hewitt grew up in Ann Arbor, Michigan and is a diehard Michigan Wolverines fan. She doesn't claim a home anymore, rather chooses to travel the country with her football-fanatic husband and two feral, yet lovable, dogs. She loves to write in urban paranormal fantasy and fantasy romance, mostly about powerful women, morally gray men, found families, and a sprinkle (or pour) of magic and spice.

When she's not thinking of ways to completely crush her readers, you can find Sadie scaling mountains around the world, catching up on her own TBR, and checking out the local coffee shops.

To be the first to know about Sadie's latest releases and upcoming projects, visit www.SadieHewitt.com

BE SURE TO CHECK OUT...

THE AUDIENT AND THE PHANTOM NIGHT!

Inspired by The Legend of the Flying Dutchman and the world of Beauty and the Beast, sail the seas in this action-packed fantasy filled with searing romance, outlawed magic, and sea-faring danger.

Fenna Terrigan never expected to leave her seaside village. She was too quiet, too gentle, and far too kind to take on life outside of the bookshop she works at. But when her brother shows up on her doorstep begging for aid with a pirate lord hot on his tail, Fenna will do anything to protect him.

Devlin Cato is the captain of a cursed ship and can step foot on land for one day every seven years. Once again, he's found himself using it to chase a deserter across the continent. his hunt is short-lived when Fenna agrees to take on her brother's twenty-five-year debt in exchange for leaving her smoldering city to heal.

As Fenna spends more time aboard the phantom night with the ship's mysterious and seductive captain, she soon finds herself caught between loyalty to her brother and her fiery passion for Devlin Cato. But the path to ending the curse isn't as easy as it seems when Fenna's dark secret is discovered. a secret that threatens the very foundation of the continent's stability and one that anyone would be willing to kill for.

www.ingramcontent.com/pod-product-compliance
Lightning Source LLC
Chambersburg PA
CBHW031231310726
48971CB00004B/958